Thomas L. Nichols, Valentine Nicholson

Esperanza

My Journey Thither and What I Found there

.

Thomas L. Nichols, Valentine Nicholson

Esperanza
My Journey Thither and What I Found there

ISBN/EAN: 9783337127824

Printed in Europe, USA, Canada, Australia, Japan

Cover: Foto ©Andreas Hilbeck / pixelio.de

More available books at **www.hansebooks.com**

MY JOURNEY THITHER

AND

WHAT I FOUND THERE.

"And better than this home of love,
We seek a surer rest above,
Where sheltering wings around us cast,
Shall hide us from the stormy blast.

CINCINNATI:
PUBLISHED BY VALENTINE NICHOLSON.
1860.

This being the first edition of a new book, persons desiring to procure copies and failing to find the same in book-stores conveniently near, are informed that a single copy will be forwarded by mail to any address in the United States, *postage free*, on receipt of one dollar by the publisher.

Booksellers supplied on terms of liberal discount.

Address **VALENTINE NICHOLSON,**

CINCINNATI, OHIO

INTRODUCTION

Iᴛ is just that the reader who takes up a new book, should find on its pages a concise statement of what the volume contains.

Those who introduce either strange persons, or new books to others, assume a degree of responsibility not always well considered.

A friend, confiding in you, and trusting your discretion, may accept the person, or the book you introduce, as worthy the same confidence reposed in you.

"Esperanza" signifies "Land of Hope;" "My journey thither, and what I found there," can only be fully understood by reading all the chapters of the book.

A glance over the contents will give a general idea of what the book treats upon. Every chapter has its own peculiar attractions, and each one its lesson of instruction.

The book is in the form of a series of letters, purporting to have been written by a young gentleman of the city of New York, who starts on a journey to the "Far West;" his object is to seek for a pleasant location for the future home of himself and "Clara," his affianced.

The first several letters bear date from various points on the line of the journey, the others are most of them written at Esperanza during the visit which he enjoyed there.

The descriptive history of his journey begins at the depot of the New York and Erie Rail Road.

The young gentleman enters the cars and finds them crowded. A lady passenger motions him to a seat beside her. In this early part of the acquaintance they find themselves both traveling west, and agree to bear each other company. He accepts an invitation to visit her home and her friends.

They make the journey by way of Niagara, Buffalo, Cleveland, Columbus, Cincinnati, stopping for a day or two at some of these points. Various interesting incidents occur, yet the pleasure of reading the book must not be marred by naming them here. From Cincinnati they travel by steamboat down the Ohio river to the Mississippi, down that river a long distance, then up one of its tributaries to Esperanza, the beautiful home of Miss Elmore.

After twenty chapters of this book had been stereotyped, the opinions and faith of the author were in some respects so changed, that he engaged in a different field of labor.

The stereotype plates, together with manuscript for additional chapters to complete the volume, were then placed in the hands of the writer of this notice, with privilege to revise, change or abridge the manuscript, and publish or dispose of all at discretion.

The picture of the "School of Life," at Esperanza, is painted skillfully and in beautiful colors.

Human life, in purity, peace and love, is compared and placed in contrast with life in lust, discord and jealousy.

The thoughts of the writer are stated with remarkable clearness, and oftentimes in language very beautiful.

There is manifested a candor and an earnestness of purpose, proving the author to be one willing "to do, and to dare," for whatever he believed to be the cause of truth. On one subject treated upon, there are opinions advanced, which, to my mind, appear erroneous. I frankly acknowlege the permitting of those sentiments to go before the world, is to me a two-fold cause of regret; first and most, because of the deceptive and poisonous nature of all error, and its tendency to propagate itself wherever the seeds are sown; and also, because the mind of the author has changed since writing the same.

The only alternative was to suppress many vital truths, or permit a few errors to appear in connection with them. Remembering the expression of Jefferson, "Error of opinion may be tolerated, when reason is left free to combat it;" believing also, that truth has nothing to fear from the expression of mistaken opinions, or from the "freedom of thought, freedom of speech, or freedom of the press:" after meditating deliberately, my decision was to "let the tares grow with the wheat until harvest."

That to which I have alluded as being objectionable, will be found on the pages where the writer was treating upon the question of love, and the true relation which the sexes should bear to each other.

Members of the society who are living in such great harmony and happiness at "Esperanza," are some of them represented as having intimate relations of love, and sharing the responsibility of offspring with more than one of the opposite sex. It is my own religious opinion, that upon a correct solution of this one great question, rests the entire subject of redemption and salvation from sin, sorrow and all human suffering. Original salvation must square the account made by "original sin," before the millenial day can dawn on the earth. I believe it, in accordance with the divine law, that no man or woman can ever find entire peace or tranquil rest of spirit, until the affections rest upon one love. with a positive assurance and faith that this one, in a conjugal sense, is entirely and exclusively their own, whose loving sympathy satisfies all the deep askings of the soul, hushing into silence all inclination of the spirit to wander abroad for other conjugal connection; every one thus truly mated with their own, will feel pained at the thought of having their partner in offspring mingle the finer spheres of life and love in sexual union with any other; and that no other unions, except such as are thus wholly one with each other, are worthy of the sacred name of marriage, or can give the right to parties of becoming partners in offspring.

Christ and the apostles, by example and by precept, bore testimony against the popular opinions and customs of both the church and the world on the subject of marriage; may there not be a deeper meaning and other reasons in, and for their course, than even professing Christians have ever thought or believed.

"I have many things to say unto you, but ye can not bear them now."..... "Suffer little children to come unto me, and forbid them not, for of such is the kingdom of heaven." If little children throughout the entire earth were only permitted to come unto Christ through the divine law of chaste and loving generation, then the noise and confusion of so much disputing on the subject of *re*generation might very soon pass away, and especially so, if the little Christians could have the example of all around and near them, living to the line of the Christian prayer: "Thy kingdom come, Thy will be done on earth, as it is in heaven."

And now, having given the preceding caution respecting what I deem the principle error in this volume, believing as I do that the truths contained will greatly overbalance whatever of error there may be on the pages, hoping also that whatever influence the book may have upon the minds of those who read it, will be to encourage the growth of virtue, purity and peace in the soul, so that eventually large multitudes of men and women may be able to speak truthfully of themselves, and say,

> "Gently I took that which ungently came,
> And without scorn forgave:—Do thou the same.

I submit the book, cheerfully accepting my own portion of responsibility.

VALENTINE NICHOLSON.

ESPERANZA;

My Journey Thither, and What I Found There.

FROM NEW YORK TO NIAGARA.

MY FRIEND—It is late, and my mind and heart are full. The roar of the great cataract is in my ear; the vibrations of the solid rock-ribbed earth jar the windows of my little bed-room, and even shake, with a slight tremor, the table on which I write.

I feel the soft pressure of your hand, I see the fond glances of your tearful eye, I feel your breath warm upon my cheek, and taste the sweetness of your parting kiss. All is vividly present to me at this moment; and then the roar of Niagara murmurs so deeply that we are hundreds of miles apart! Your dear picture, which has rested on my heart all day, now lies before me, and smiles upon me as I look at it with dim eyes. The light falls life-like, through those brown silken curls, on that white forehead and delicate cheek; the arched brows are full of truth and hope, and the full, loving lips seem ready to open and call me by some dear name. I smile and sigh at once. I press the dear image to my lips and heart; and I write you the adventures of my first day's journey toward the Land of Promise in the Far West.

After the happy heart throbs, and the sweetly sad adieus of our moonlit parting hour, I slept sound, awoke with the dawn, and prepared to leave the great city, so many years my home, and ever dear to me as yours, to seek out the home of our future. The sun rose over Brooklyn, and glittered on the bay. I said good bye to old Ocean through the narrows, and looked round proudly on that

7

magnificent scene, connected with so many happy associations; for there was Castle Garden, where we had listened to music together; and Staten Island, and Weewhawken, the scene of merry Pic Nics.

But the ferry-boats don't wait for sentiment, and I was soon at the New York and Erie Railroad Depot, and saw the iron bars, which, placed end to end, were to bring me over mountain and valley; and which they have very satisfactorily accomplished.

The train was filling rapidly—nearly all the seats were taken, when I discovered one vacant half of a seat—a lady occupying the other half. The presumption was, that her husband, or other male protector would soon come and claim it; but as this was not certain, I went wishfully toward the vacant seat. I think it was a real attraction that drew me. She did not wait for me to ask if the seat was engaged, and then make a cold ungracious answer, as I have seen done so often; but looking up with a calm bright look, that seemed to scan me thoroughly, she smiled a welcome, and with an indescribable air of self-possessed dignity, motioned me to the seat beside her, which I took. It was the only one, but had there been many, I should have wished to take it. Darling, it is a confession I am beginning, but do not be alarmed. Summon your love and your trust in me, and be sure that I can not be unworthy of either.

I must describe her. She may be thirty years old; a little above the medium height, with a well rounded figure and graceful attitudes and movements. Her eyes are hazel, with long, shining, black lashes, her brows well formed, her nose purely cut and slightly aquiline, her mouth moderately large, and beautiful; teeth white and even, complexion a pearly brunette, with an abundance of wavy, curling, glossy, pretty hair. Her hands and feet are not so small as yours, but delicately shapen. She wears a simple straw hat, and a traveling dress of a severe, but still elegant simplicity. Her gloves, and boots, and the few ornaments she wears are in the best style. But above all, her manner, so gentle, so kind, yet so full of dignity and repose, gives you a feeling of confidence and rest, when you come into her presence. I feel sure that you would see her as I do, and with the same feeling.

As I took the kindly proffered seat at her side, I expressed my thanks, and the hope that we should have a pleasant journey.

"The thanks belong to you, perhaps;" she answered, with a quiet smile. "A woman traveling alone, should be thankful for protection; and, besides, said she, looking drolly at some rough looking men, who were searching for vacant seats, "I might have had much less agreeable company."

This might have been a compliment, but it was not, in its manner, or its meaning, but the expression of a sincere thankfulness that some of the coarse, brutified men who passed us could not claim a seat in such disagreeable proximity.

"Do you travel far on this route?" I asked, as the train started.

"I go to Niagara," she said, "on my way beyond the Mississippi. I visited the Falls ten years ago, and go a little out of my route, and stop a day to renew my acquaintance."

Was it Providence, or Fate, my Clara? I will believe in good angels, and benevolent destinies. Have I not started in this trust, hoping to be beneficently guided to the home of our happy future?

"And you?" she asked, with a smile at the abstraction into which I had fallen.

"I—it is my own journey. I am also going far west, in search of a home. I also go by Niagara, to see it for the first time."

" Ah, well—then we may get acquainted," she replied graciously. It is the word, Clara; for whatever she may be, her manner is queenly. She has in every word, and at all times, the repose of either an unconscious innocence, like that of a little child, or of a conscious goodness, at peace with herself and with every one about her. I have not in the fifteen hours past, detected one movement of affectation or coquetry. I would as soon think of flattering a sunbeam. If I admired her, it was because she compelled my admiration; and if I expressed it, it troubled her no more than Niagara is troubled with the enthusiasm of its wonderers.

I fear that I pain you with these details. I do not wish to be unjust to you, my love, but you can not, at once, understand this woman, nor the kind of feeling I had for her, from the first moment I sat beside her. And you must be patient with me and let me

describe her as fully as possible, for I will conceal nothing from
you. Whatever can come into my heart and life you have the right
to know. I love you supremely—I love you only. The feeling I
have for this pure and beautiful being is admiration, and if I can
define it—a kind of devotion, such as one might feel for a superior
being, but not the fond and personal love which lives in my inmost
heart for you. It is written—though it might have been better,
had I continued my narrative without these declarations. But I
will now give you, as clearly as I can, the progress of our acquaintance.

"Do you reside in New York?" I asked, as the cars paused a
moment at Paterson !"

"No!"

Never was one little monosyllable so expressively spoken, not even
by Rachel. There was a radient happiness in the "no;" not a
scorn or unappreciation of our great commercial city, but her whole
face lighted, and her tone seemed filled with the love of some other,
and happier home. You will think this a strange interpretation;
but do we not know how much may sometimes be told by a single
word, or glance, or sigh ?

"No," she answered; "it is my first visit to New York for
several years. I wished to look at its familiar streets once more,
to visit a few friends, who are still bound in it, and see what
progress the world is making."

I went on to speak with enthusiasm of our improvements—
Taylor's, the Academy of Music, the Crystal Palace, etc., but I
stopped, when I saw the smile half pitying, half ironical, with
which she listened to my rhapsody.

"Your Taylor's Saloon," said she, " is a barbaric gewgaw, as
unpleasant to a refined taste, as a Chinese band is to a musical ear.
Your Academy of Music seems ready to crush you with its heavi-
ness and profusion of ornament. Your Crystal Palace is a pretty
show building of itself, but out of all harmony with its uses; and
with its plows and statuary, steam pumps and pictures, is as grotesque and discordant an exhibition as can well be conceived; yet
it is a very fair epitome of civilization, and a failure, like that."

" But did you find nothing in New York to admire ? " I asked, with a shade of bitterness at this wholesale desecration of our idols.

" Yes ;" she calmly replied, " there are things which discordant institutions can not utterly spoil, and others, which are signs of progress. I found human hearts, not yet crushed or withered. I saw a few beautiful women and children ; some pictures, with promise in them—and ships, and steamers. I have heard good music well rendered. In making my purchases, I found some sensible, honorable merchants, and manufacturers evincing much skill. For the rest, I found, as always, a vast aggregation of miserable humanity, fretting, struggling, and wearing itself out in wretched conditions, with no eye to pity and no arm to save. I do do not wish to see it again, or to think of it."

" Well, I, too, hope soon to leave it all," I said ; " I am going to find some growing little village in the far west, where I can build a little cottage in a little garden, marry a little wife, keep a little store, and be happy. We shall have no opera, but my Clara will play and sing to me ; and we shall take the papers, and magazines, and be very happy."

I wondered at myself, for this frankness, but it seemed as natural to me to open my heart to her, as to breathe. She turned toward me, and seemed to look through me, into my inmost self, with a calm sad look. I felt the spell of her presence, as if her being took hold of mine. At length she said, in low tones, but clear and penetrating—" My friend, this is not your destiny."

" Why not ? "

" Because I perceive that you are worthy of a higher and better one ; that you are not only capable of a truer life than the one you have—both hopefully and scornfully pictured, but that you have the wish for, if not the idea of, a life which will better satisfy your nature."

" If you can tell so much, will you not predict my future ? " I asked.

" Your future is before you," she said, with a certain impressiveness, I can not describe. " It will be fulfilled from day to day. This *now*, is the future of your yesterday. Were you not brought to me; and will not this meeting influence all your future life? Should I speak to you in this way, if I were not assured of it?"

Every sentence she uttered, plunged me into deeper depths of unknown feeling, and newly awakened, or forgotten thought. It was abruptly, almost rudely, but very earnestly, that I asked— "who are you?"

The light of a beautiful smile swept over her face, and dimpled in her cheeks.

"I am a human sister of yours," she said, "if you please to own me. I am some years older than you, and a good deal wiser. For the rest, I am what you see, and feel me to be."

"I am well satisfied with all I see and feel," I said.

"That is not quite true. With what you see, perhaps; not with what you feel. Your attraction to me conflicts with your idea of duty to another. You distrust yourself, and still more, the little wife, that is to live in the little cottage, in the little garden, and so on, like the house that Jack built."

"Distrust her!"

"Oh, only her estimation of your present occupation and emotions."

It *was* my thought: but, Clara, dear! how could she know it? It is true, that you often have intuitions, which tell you of my feelings, before they are spoken; but that is because our hearts are one:—how should this woman be able to penetrate my most secret life, and read in it things which I have tried to conceal from myself. For it is true, that this life, even that which I go to seek, and hope to enjoy with you, does not satisfy me. Yet it seems the best that is possible to us, here upon the earth.

"But I have not satisfied your curiosity," she continued, after a pause of a few minutes, during which she seemed to be considering as to what she had best tell me. "You see that I am a woman and a sister; my age, and external appearance are open to your observation. You can judge of my mind and culture, by my conversation. There is no reason to complain, I think, of distance or reserve, in my behavior. If the form and features, looks and tones, are the expressions of the Spiritual or inner life, it is for you, according to your opportunities, to get acquainted with me. Why should you not know me, as well as I know you?"

"I don't know why; but you seem to belong to some world I am not acquainted with. I met you in the cars, as I might any other lady traveler. It is not strange, in this country, for a lady to travel alone, any distance. You have been to New York, visiting and making purchases, and there is nothing unprecedented in that, still I feel that I do not know you. There is a mystery somehow or somewhere, which I can not yet unravel."

"All in due time, my friend, if you prove worthy;" she replied gaily, "but, in the mean time, would'nt you like to know some little particulars; whether I am married or single; whether I am called Susan or Kate; or Brown or Smith?"

"No," said I, heroically. "Those are all external, accidental, or conventional matters, and of slight importance. Your being married or otherwise can be nothing to me, and what is in a name?"

"It is convenient, sometimes—you have one, I hope."

Here I had been as good as asking a lady her name, and had not yet given her my own. I apologized for this stupidity, took a card from my pocket, and gave it to her. She looked at it musingly and said—

"Frank is a good name, and Wilson a common one; was your father a clergyman?" I nodded assent. "Your mother was a Harding; excuse my questionings; curiosity is a woman's weakness, you know."

I answered affirmatively, with an increasing excitement of my own.

"Then we are almost relations," said she; "for I knew your mother, and loved her before you did. She was my teacher, before her marriage. I have often wished to see her, before she went away; and now she is very pleasant to me."

O Clara! was it the Spirit of that sainted mother, who guided me to that woman, who seems to me so good, and pure, and wise? But you shall judge, for I shall write all I can of her. She would love you, and you would feel toward her as I do. I asked her no question further, but left her to tell me what she would; but she said no more for a time, looking out upon the savage scenery of the mountains through which we were passing. I had the unopened morning papers, but had no desire to read. The presence in which I sat, even with the various spheres around me, and amid the roar of the train, and the flying scenery, seemed to raise me up to a new plan of feeling and thought. I sat in this presence, which seemed to surround me, in a life-sphere, with which my own mingled, like the harmony of musical chords. I find it difficult to express this sense of the pure, rich life of this woman, which seemed to the inner sense like the prevading aroma of apple blossoms, and gifted with a penetrating power like magnetism.

Seeming to read, or rather to feel, my thoughts, she turned to me and said : " I am very glad that I have met you; and that you are so well developed, and so little injured, as I find you. You have your mother's looks, and her heart. She was a pure, good woman, bound up in her creed, which fettered her reason, but could not destroy her affectionate nature. Are you free from the bondage of her theology ? "

" I reverence the memory of my mother," I said, " and I try to believe and do as the world wishes me to."

" But not with entire success, I imagine," she said kindly. " What your mother wished, when she was here, and what she wishes now, may be quite different. She sees now that many of her former ideas were erroneous, and seeks to impress your mind with her present views of truth and goodness. Do you not find your deepest life revolting against the creeds and forms in which you were educated ? "

" It is true—but I fear, sometimes, that it is wrong to yield to such feelings ? "

" Do you find that they incline you to wrong doing ? "

" Rather the reverse."

" Do your beliefs and your loves seem to you to be matters of volition ? "

" I can not see that they are."

" Is it not best, then, to leave them in freedom; giving the soul liberty to expand, and grow, and advance in its true life ? "

I could not answer, for I was full of thought. This may not

come to you as it did to me, so much was in the tone, the manner, the pure articulation, and musical modulations; so much more in the expression of her face, and the magnetism of her presence. I pondered what she said, and the far reaching meanings of which her few words were but a faint shadowing.

"If belief is spontaneous and involuntary," I said at length, "if love is a free attraction of the Spirit, not to be controlled by others, nor even by ourselves, what becomes of all our sects, creeds, and social laws?"

She only smiled at this question.

"Marriage, for example, is a solemn promise, or contract to love one and one only, until death shall part them."

"No longer?" she said very quietly, "What then?"

"This world is as far as our laws can compel obedience, or punish the violation of a contract," I replied—but my mind darkened with the doubt, whether such contracts can bind, or such penalties ensure the love of any being. And I found employment for all my reflective powers; in which I was not disturbed; for she sat in perfect composure, inviting no conversation, and, as I imagined, silently aiding me in the solution of these problems.

The train stopped for dinner, and I rose and asked my companion if she would dine with me.

"Excuse me," she said, in an entirely different, and playful mood. "I am not fortunate in Railroad dinners; and prefer to cater for myself. Will you not join me? I have enough for both."

I could not resist the temptation. She opened a basket, filled with delicious peaches, plums, and a kind of cake, which seemed made expressly to eat with them. When we had eaten, she poured from a small traveling flask, into a goblet that packed with it, a glass of a bright, pure, delicate wine, and drank it; and then, pouring out another, gave it to me. There was no affectation of offering it to me first. She took it simply as her right, and to set me the example. Was it not beautiful? I had drank good wines, but never such as this—and as I tasted the last drops, enquiringly, she answered, and said:

"I saw the grapes ripen, and helped to pick them. I assisted in making the wine, and know that it is pure and good. It has the aroma of our home; the love of my loved ones.

I wished to ask of that home, and those loved ones, but I could not—for if you think I have any familiarity with her, I have not yet succeeded in describing her. True, her presence is repose; her sphere is full of kindness; she seems to know my thoughts; her own are often spoken without a word. But a familiarity, or the indulgence of an impertinent curiosity, or paying a trifling compliment to her, I can not imagine. I think she might pass around the world, and never see a man who would not treat her with reverence.

It is very late, my Clara, and the day's ride, even with so much to interest me, was long and wearisome. New thoughts and feelings also helped to exhaust me; though the influence that inspired them seemed to sustain me. I must finish my letter.

We left the New York and Erie Road, as you will see by the map I gave you, at Elmira, and came to Canandaigua, and thence, over a flat, dull country, to Niagara. Over the last portion of the route the road was uneven, the cars noisy, and my companion rested and perhaps slept. As we approached our journey's end, she pointed me to the broad river Niagara, Grand Island, and Navy Island, and the distant lights in the Canadian villages.

"What hotel," I asked, "do you propose to stop at?"

"It is indifferent—we will try the International."

"Shall I see to your baggage?" I asked, hoping now to ascertain what I had not wished to inquire.

"Yes, if you will take the trouble," and she gave me a check for her trunk. "You will want my name to enter on the register. Just now, I do not happen to have any at my disposal. Perhaps you will lend me yours."

Forgive me, dear Clara, for what I am about to confess to you. I have asked her forgiveness, with tears, and she has pardoned me. I said, hastily, and most mistakingly:

"Shall I write Mr. Frank Wilson and————" The word was not spoken, but she knew what it would have been, and quick as lightning, yet very gently and sadly, said—

"Sister!"

"The word recalled me to myself. I silently handed her into the omnibus, at the station, secured our baggage, and when we came to the great hotel, I waited my turn, and wrote on the register "Frank Wilson and Sister." Two adjoining rooms were given us, and we went to supper. She ate sparingly; but conversed cheerfully about the morrow, and challenged me to a trip to Canada, below the Falls, before breakfast. With a pleasant good-night, she left me in the parlor, and went to her room; and I to mine. O Clara! I would have given so much, rather than to have thought that unspoken thought. I was wretched as I deserved to be. Your picture looked at me reproachfully. I had forfeited her esteem. I took out my paper, but could not write.

As I sat in this mood, listening to the solemn roar of the near cataract, there came a knock to my door. My heart bounded to meet it. I opened; it was she; but how radiantly, how divinely beautiful. Fresh from a bath, her traveling dress exchanged for an exquisite white wrapper, she came to me with a bright smile, and in a voice of music said:—

"Brother : have you not something to say to me?"

"Yes, one word;" I said, with the tears gushing from my eyes, and sinking on my knee before her—"Forgive!"

She bent down, silently, and gently kissed my forehead. Peace came into my heart. She gave me her hand, and I rose and pressed it to my lips.

"Good night, my brother!" she said softly, and, like an angel, vanished.

Good night, my Clara!
2

A DAY AT NIAGARA.

DARLING! I have seen Niagara! Henceforth this wonder of nature is to live in my memory, associated with thoughts and feelings which will mold all our future. How much I wished that you were with me! Yet, I have the fear, that, though it might have been a happier day for me, it would have been less full of the destiny, that this future has in store for us.

I slept sweetly, with your image on my heart, lulled by a murmur that seemed to come from the center of the earth, mingling in deep throbbings with the roar of the nearer rapids. I was waked by a light, playful tapping on the door, which might have connected the two rooms, and I sprang up, and opened my blinds to the sunshine, and the mist-cloud, tinged with rainbows.

In a few moments I was in the great reception-room, on the first floor, where my beautiful companion welcomed me with a cheerful "good morning." When I apologized for being late, she said, "You write long letters. I went to sleep by the scratching of your pen. I hope you have given me a favorable introduction."

We sallied out of the hotel, and I took a new look at her, with rested eyes, and by the morning light. She seemed younger and fairer than yesterday; for her silver gray walking dress was the perfection of a morning costume for such a jaunt as ours; and it was only when she spoke, in her more serious moods, that it seemed that she must be as old as I judged her yesterday.

"Shall I be your guide?" she asked, "for every rock and tree seems familiar to me, and it is a great pleasure to introduce one to strange scenes"

18

" Yes—I am strange to you; but I ought not to be. It is you who are really strange; and I seem so to you only because I am natural You see so little of what is genuine in men and women, that a simple honesty and natural freedom surprise you.

" Now, lend me your eyes, as well as your ears; follow me down this stairway, and do not look up until I tell you."

I did as she directed. I went down the hundred and fifty feet of precipice, by a very convenient, but provokingly artificial covered stair case, with the roar growing every moment more tumultuous. I followed my guide, with downcast eyes, seeing only the broken masses of limestone, agitated waters beating among them, and a pair of delicate feet and ancles, picking their way daintily over them. The roar grew louder and nearer; the ground trembled; the spray came in gusts in my face, when, gaining the surface of a flat rock, my fair guide laid her hand on my arm, and said, reverently, " look up."

A torrent of bright water seemed pouring out of heaven. Those who are disappointed with the first view of Niagara do not get such a view as this. I stood in an ecstasy of astonishment and delight. My eye swept along the American fall, near whose extremity I stood, past the walls of Iris Island, into the great Horseshoe, where the mass of the mighty river pours down, and whence come those deep pulsating thunders, to the Table Rock of the Canadian shore.

I shall not attempt to describe the indescribable majesty, and terror, and beauty of that scene. The waters, which pour over the rim of the cataract, a deep blue, almost green, fell in the morning's sunlight, in vast columns of glittering diamonds, and then rose again in clouds of mist on which were painted arching rainbows.

Retracing our steps, we were soon seated in a row boat, and embarked upon the boiling cauldron, into which this world of waters pours its everlasting flood. The morning breeze from Ontario blew gently up the great gorge, that the cataract has opened, which is spanned by the beautiful Suspension Bridge; and this upward breeze saved us from the misty showers, while an extra fee to the boatman induced him to skirt along the eddy of the American shore and Goat Island, so as to cross the great gulf as near as possible to the principal fall. I had the best view, and the fullest enjoyment of the scene. Its terrors were lost to me, in its glorious majesty and beauty; and, the feeling of sublimity, with which I was impressed, mingled harmoniously with my sentiments toward the strange, but beautiful, and I believe and am sure, most pure and noble woman, who sat by my side, enjoying all my enjoyment of these new emotions.

The sublimity of Niagara is like that of the ocean and the stars, but more concentrated.

Our boat was swept down by the torrent, and made its landing among the rocks, where, refusing the proffers of accommodating Jehues, we walked gaily up the road built on the side of the almost perpendicular precipice. But, at every few steps, I stopped, and turned to get a new view. The sun was now shining full upon the whole long line of the falls, whose height seems lost in their extent. From the middle of the great Horseshoe, where I could see that the mid channel of the river lay, there rose a cloud, like the smoke of a furnace, high in the heavens. The white gulls were sailing in the air; and the scene grew in beauty, as it lost in the terrors of proximity.

My friend looked on it all, calm, silent, pointing to one feature or another with finger or parasol, saying few words, but, as I saw and felt, watching my features, as if to see how they reflected the scene; sometimes she laid her hand upon my arm, sometimes on my shoulder. Once, when half way up the cliff, her enthusiasm broke forth, but not at the cataract. "Oh! my dear flowers," she exclaimed, and in an instant she was clambering up the steep side of the cliff, I could hardly tell how, and eagerly picking the wild flowers that grew from the clefts of the rocks, where the moisture was dripping from every seam of the limestone strata.

When she came down, with a hand full of lovely little flowers, her eyes were bright and moist, and her cheeks flushed.

"Here they are, the dear ones!" she said; "the same that I found here ten years ago. They are not only sweet and beautiful, themselves, but fragrant memories cluster round them."

"You were not alone, then;—nor with indifferent company?" I remarked.

She looked in my eyes with her clear, open look, and said : "I was with one I dearly loved—but a true friendship is not indifference. Do you feel it so?"

"I shall be very grateful," I said, with real humility, "for whatever you can give me."

She took my hand, and we walked up the rest of the ascent, hand in hand, like two children.

Here stands the Clifton House, the resort of most English, and many American visitors, with its pleasure grounds laid out too precisely to harmonize with the savage aspect of rock and flood around. We passed along the margin of the great gulf, stopping at many points to get new views of the scene, until we stood on Table Rock ; and then, from the very margin of the descending river, followed its torrents down into the chasm into which they plunged.

She stood alone with her thoughts and memories, her face now calm and pale ; her eyes looking either back into the past, or forward into the future. She had advanced to the edge of the over hanging rock. I knew there was no danger to her steady nerves and well-poised spirit; but the rapid fall of the water, as I looked past her, made her body seem to rise, and I remembered, with a shudder, the fate of the young girl, whose fall, a few rods from this spot, has found affecting record. I sprang forward, and caught her firmly by the wrist, to ensure her safety. She turned with a sweet smile, and said :

"The spirit-world is beautiful, and I have some dear friends there, but my work here is not accomplished. This life has come to be too rich in blessings, to be thrown aside. We need not be in haste to meet the future, because of the eternities."

O Clara ! how precious seemed to me this calm and beautiful faith in the unseen world.

"But this life," I said, "is so poor, in its hopes and possibilities, and worse than poor in its realities to most, that they can scarce be blamed for flying from the present if they have any reasonable hopes of a happier future."

"Suicide," she said, "is a violence to nature, only justifiable as an escape from something worse. It is sometimes a right, in a world, whose imperfect conditions admit only a choice of evils. But all destinies are onward, and the fruition of all our hopes is before us. Century by century this river eats its way through these rocky strata. The mountains crumble, and the valleys are filled up. The tree grows from its germ to its destined strength and beauty. Humanity also grows and advances toward its future."

"True of the race, or the races," I said, "this may be; but how of the individual victim to the imperfections and wrongs around us?"

"The eternities are ours, and justice is the supreme law. You ask God to be merciful. He will not be what he is not for your asking; but it is enough, if He is just. He is accountable to all His creatures. Evil, privation, discord, are stages in progress; they have their uses to the undeveloped spirit; but let us be thankful that we are emerging from them; and that the time has come for truth, riches, and harmony. Happiness is the universal aspiration, and the universal destiny."

"Happiness for all?" I asked. I can not tell you, Clara, with what a look of angelic pity, mingled with surprise, she turned to me.

"For all!" she repeated softly. "Can you believe there is in all God's universe, one human soul destined to an existence unworthy of his goodness?"

I have never felt so ashamed of a creed which dooms our brethren and sisters to utter and eternal despair. But my mind was darkened with other doubts.

"You talk," I said, "of happiness on the earth. Are we worthy of such a social state, as some of our sanguine reformers have imagined. Is humanity yet good and pure enough to live in a harmonious society?"

She walked away from the brow of the rock on which we were standing, a few steps; then turned and stood before me.

"Look at me," she said; "I am, as I told you yesterday, a human sister of yours. Am I good enough to deserve happiness? Were you as good as you believe me to be, do you not think we could live harmoniously, purely, and happily?"

"Were all like you, I could believe any thing," I hastened to say.

"It is not a question of all, but of some. There are those, who are wiser and better than I, living nearer to the life of the heavens. There are many who, in various degrees, are so far freed from ignorance, error, and evil habits, physical and spiritual, as to be able to live in the harmony of a true life. I am but one of many loving women, who enjoy upon the earth, a foretaste of the freedom and harmony of the beautiful life of the heavens."

I was impressed with the simple truthfulness of every word she uttered; yet, it was so strange, so different from what I had ever heard. I looked around, to be sure it was no dream; but more than the fact of my wakefulness was a testimony in my spirit, that what she said not only might, and should be true, but was a living and present reality.

A group of fashionable ladies from the Clifton House passed by us; and their coquettish airs, and frivolous conversation, offered a contrast which deepened my impression.

"You have excited my curiosity, and my hopes," I said. "Will you not enlighten me further?"

"I have said too much, not to say more," she replied; "but this world requires such things as breakfasts. If you please, we will take a carriage here, and go round by the Suspension Bridge. It is an example of human achievement in one direction. Let us not undervalue ourselves.

We entered a carriage, and after an interesting drive, and a view of that beautiful work, and its surroundings, came back to the hotel with an appetite.

Night.—The evening of my second day of absence from you, O beloved One, has closed around me; the evening of a day full of new sensations and new emotions. How much of life is sometimes crowded into a single day!

After breakfast my guide went to her room to write some letters, and I wrote you the account of our morning's ramble. When I had finished, I went down, and found her ready for our visit to Goat Island, which separates the American from the British fall; though, as the boundary line of the two countries runs in mid channel, it gives us the whole of the lesser fall, and more than half the greater.

The mid-day had grown sultry, and I found my guide dressed in a charming robe of light blue stuff, which floated in ample folds of unstarched gracefulness. I am not good, you know, in describing costumes. I could never answer your question, "what kind of a bonnet had she on?" I only know that, in this case, the entire dress seemed as clear and pure an expression of herself, as her language or gestures. She gave me several letters, in the most tasteful envelopes, directed to gentlemen and ladies in various places, in a handwriting full of elegance and character, and sealed with a seal of curious device—a peculiar ring, encircling nine stars. I afterward saw such a ring, on the third finger of her right hand; and she wore a broach with nine golden stars, set in a peculiar fashion.

Going toward the rapids above the falls, which themselves form a spectacle of great power and beauty, we passed over the bridge, which spans several piers; how built, passes my engineering skill. Near the further end we found a group of ladies and gentlemen, looking at the place where the poor man clung so many hours, and then went over. As we passed along, meeting groups of visitors, I saw several gentlemen salute my guide, with great respect. She returned, or rather invited their salutations; but no one approached to speak to her.

"In heaven's name, who are you?" I would have exclaimed, but I was held, as by a spell, from making any obtrusive inquiry. We walked slowly through the walks of this beautiful, and though much visited, still, secluded place; for the island is large, nearly covered with forest trees, with cool walks among them. At the best points of sight are seats for the accommodation of visitors.

As we sat on one of these, where we had watched the adventurous little steamboat, the Maid of the Mist, with her deck load of mummy looking passengers, dressed in yellow oil-cloth cloaks and hoods, to save them from the showers of spray, while she ran boldly into the foam-gulf, and then fell off rapidly down the tumultuous tide—as we sat here in the deep noon-tide, after seeing this wondrous voyage, without caring to make it, she said:

"It is time, my friend, that we were better acquainted. Can you shut out the old world of forms, customs, and prejudices, as these torrents separate us from the lands on either side?"

"I can try," I said, with a curious sense of a Robinson Crusoe isolation, in very pleasant company.

"Well, try. First of all, how do you like me?"

The question took me a little by surprise. I am afraid I blushed, and hesitated; but, remembering Robinson Crusoe, I summoned courage, and answered:

"I admire you more than any woman I ever saw; I respect you deeply, and am ambitious of your good opinion and friendship. I hardly know how to answer to the word like. It seems too weak an expression, for the kind of devotional feeling you inspire."

She smile a gratified smile, which was not one of vanity, but of hope; not of pride in herself, but pleasure at my frankness of expression, and perhaps my power of appreciation.

"In investigating some things," she said, in her quiet and unpretending manner; "it is needful to begin with the outside, and work inward; but with the human character, it is best to begin at the center, and work outward. Will you tell me of your loves?"

O Clara! I have a faint suspicion that I blushed again. But she sat, holding my hand in hers, like a dear elder sister, and looking so sweetly kind! Once, and not long ago, I think I should have fallen on my knees, and said—O, divine angel of my life, I love you, and you only. But that was before I knew my Clara. So I answered bravely:

"I love the dearest and most charming little girl in the world. We are engaged to be married next spring; meantime I go with what means I have saved, and a little my mother left me, to find a home."

I thought a shade of sadness passed over her countenance. It might have been the remembrance of my mother. It might have been the thought that so many such anticipations of happiness as ours, have never been realized. She said, then:

"Does it seem to you, my friend, that this love, and this union, will fill up the capacity of your loving life? Do you feel secure and

3

justified in making the irrevocable vow, to love this dear one, and no other, "till death does you part."

"It seems to me," I said, "that this love so fills my being, as to shut out the possibility of another; and I hope that even death may not part us."

"If it is a true and integral love, it will not," she said; "but every passion asserts its eternity. No one, until taught by bitter experience, ever expects a love to change. But they do. The love that seems to fill our desires and capacities, at one time, in a few years may seem poor and mean; and expanding souls find a capacity for more loves, than they can often find to fill them. Will you tell me what idea you have of freedom?"

I will not try to tell you my answer, Clara; for I just then caught sight of the "meteor flag of England," on the opposite shore, and launched out into some apostrophe to liberty worthy of a ward meeting. I was checked by a droll look of surprise, and my lady said:

"We are not talking of such external matters, as they discuss at Tammany Hall. Our political freedom is well as a step in progress, but not much to boast of."

Now I had boasted of it so much, even in the sacred precincts of Old Tammany itself, where I have inhaled so much bad air, gin, and tobacco, in "our country's cause" that I felt it necessary to vindicate myself. So I said—

"You will allow that this is a free country, I hope."

"Not very," she said, with a smile of provoking assurance.

"Do not the people make their own governments, constitutions, and laws?"

"With some slight exceptions, perhaps. A few millions of negroes do not vote."

"They are represented by their masters and owners."

"All the women."

"They have their husbands and brothers to vote for them and protect them."

"Yes—I read of a case of this protection, a day or two ago, in the papers. A man killed his wife with a club. But this is not all. Leaving out all slaves, and women, and children, who seem to fare pretty much alike, a majority governs, and the minority is governed. And even of the majority—are you not politician enough to know how wire-pulling, caucus nominations, and party discipline reduce the number who govern to a few individuals, self-appointed, and not the most worthy? Does it surprise you that a woman should know something of politics? I have associated with men, and lived at times, in the heart of this turmoil."

It was all too true; and I concluded to let Hail Columbia sing itself, as best it could.

"Now, let us come back to my question. Have you the freedom in your spirit, to always do the right yourself, and to allow his rights to every human being?"

"This involves the question of what is right?" I replied; "is that settled?"

"The first right is the right of each one to settle that for himself, and to pursue his own right, in his own way, so long as he does not interfere with the equal right of every other. The Declaration of Independence asserts the principle crudely, but well enough—in the Right to Life, Liberty, and the Pursuit of Happiness. It is a tautology; for either term includes the others. The right of Life, includes all the conditions and uses of life; Liberty includes all freedom of thought, passion, and action. The Pursuit of Happiness means, that happiness, being the true end of existence, no one has a right to deprive us of its means, which are in a freedom to follow that attraction which is proportional to destiny."

Do I tire you, my Clara, with these details? I know I can give you but a faint impression of the eloquence, with which all this was uttered; but I wish to write it down while it is fresh in my mind; and I wish also to fulfill my promise, in giving you a full account of every incident of my journey. I shall wish to read it all over again, on my return. So, patience, love!"

"What I wish you to think of," she said, after a little pause, "is whether you, who are, in many respects, so pure and intelligent, have the idea of a true freedom, which will not allow your soul to be bound, nor allow you to bind another. Are you tolerant of human deficiency and error, while you have a standard of absolute right? Can you leave even this loved one whom you wear on your heart, free to love another—if another love should come to bless her—or would you make it a curse? This is the first central question for you to solve. Study it well."

"I will try to do so," I said, with a feeling I never had before. Clara, we must try to leave each other in freedom. God forbid that even my great love should be a bond to you.

We walked in silence, broken only by the musical roar of the cataract, the tenor of the rapids, and the basso profundo of the Falls; walked away from the latter, and past the former, to the upper end of the Island, where the glassy river ripples calmly against the shore, in beautiful contrast to all the foam and tumult, heard in softened murmurs from below.

Here we sat down on a grassy bank, by the water's side, secluded from observation by a clump of evergreens, which also protected us from the sun.

"Is it not beautiful," she said, after looking up the river. "I have a friend who crossed up there," pointing up the eastern channel, "when the 'Rebels' were on Navy Island yonder, and the loyal troops were raining shot, shell, and rockets among those trees. A very fine spectacle at night, he says, with the sound of the cataract for an accompaniment. Happily, the trees sustained all the damage. But a truce to all wars, great and little. To-morrow we go on our journey; is it not so?"

"Do we?"

"If you choose to accompany me, we do. Have you any settled route; or selected destination?"

"I had thought of going to Wisconsin; crossing to Minnesota, and then south through Iowa, and perhaps to Kansas, and back by the rivers—or even round by New Orleans and the sea."

"A good route enough. But let us see if I can induce you to vary it. I go up the lake to Cleveland; then across Ohio to Cincinnati; then down the Ohio and Mississippi, to my home. Has it ever struck you as a possibility that a home which makes me happy, might answer for you?"

"If I knew where it was?"

Can not you trust me to take you there? Then, if you do not like it, or me, the world is all before you, save what you leave behind."

Though couched in a playful badinage, I felt that there was an earnest good faith in this invitation. I held out my hand, and let a beneficent destiny, as I believe it to be, lead me onward."

"You are very good," she said, with an expression of joy; "you do well to trust me—better than you now imagine. Oh! my home; if this were there, and you were one of ours, do you know what I should be doing? Stop, I'll show you; will you please unlace my gaiter?" and she held her little slender, foot to me, just as your little sister Flora might. - And, with a trembling hand, and, I confess, a throbbing heart—for I am not so good as I wish to be—I unlaced the pretty boot, and took it off, and then the other.

"Thank you!" she said, with the utmost simplicity; and then, while I wondered, she carefully unclasped her garters, and pulled off a pair of most gossamer webbed stockings. I don't know what made me tremble, or how I could doubt. I am ashamed of myself. I am ashamed of the world in which I have lived. But my doubts were soon ended. Laying her things by my side, she took up her skirts, as gracefully as possible, raising them nearly to the knees, and walked into the river, and stood there, dabbling her white feet and most beautiful limbs in the cool water—a picture of radiant happiness. She seemed to me, Clara, not a Venus new risen from the sea, but the goddess of a holy freedom, that had just descended from the shining heavens.

When she had enjoyed the coolness of the pure water, which had come all the way from the Great Superior, and the Lake of the Woods, she said, expressly to wash her feet, she came and sat down in an attitude a painter, or even a sculptor, would have loved to copy, and let her limbs dry. As I admired them, she looked at them, and then at me with such a happy look.

"I think they are pretty," she said. "I am very glad my body is beautiful;" and after a moment's pause, she added softly—"I am also very glad that you are so good. Say to your Clara, that she has much right to love you, for you are worthy, and will be more so."

I write it, dear Clara, just as it was said. Then she dressed herself without my help; and I knew she had given me another trial, and was thankful, very thankful, that I had borne it so well. And then she put her arm in mine, and we walked slowly back, scarcely looking at the Falls or rapids, to dinner.

And dinner, I would have you know, is rather a sublime affair at the International. So I dressed for it; that is, I dressed as much as our fashions allow a gentleman to dress. And when I went into the drawing-room to escort this newly found sister of mine to the table, I found her superb as a princess. I will try to tell you "what she had on." Her hair was dressed, rather simply, away from her forehead, with a knot of the little wild flowers of the morning, which she had kept fresh. Her dress was a very rich brocade of pale lilac, trimmed with falls of rich lace, and made just within the fashion. Her white round shoulders, and beautiful bust are all her face and contour promised. She wore diamonds and turquoise; but every ornament seemed to have some special use and meaning. I have the idea that she dressed, not for the company, not for any impression she might make on a crowd of visitors; certainly not for admiration, but *for me.* It was another lesson—to show me that a true life includes the beautiful. That if we would win people to knowledge, virtue, and happiness, we must not begin by outraging their taste. How many reformers have made this grand mistake.

When I advanced near her, I know not how the feeling of familiarity had vanished, but her style, elegance, superb beauty, and more superb manner—impressed me as if she were a queen—not an actress queen, putting on haughty airs of royalty, but a queen of nature, born to her sphere, and living in its constant recognition and use. Do not think it strange, Clara, that my heart swelled with great throbbings, as I approached her, and I bowed to her with a genuine humility. Her pure, calm eyes surveyed me, from head to foot, and with an approving smile she extended her hand to me. The gong sounded its brazen summons with its most civilized dissonance, and she took my arm, and we went to dinner.

I wish I could do justice to that dinner. It is a large, high room;

at the end a recess, in which was stationed a band of music. A regiment of colored waiters, drilled into a droll, stiff, imitation of military evolutions adapted to a dining-room, brought and removed the courses, with great pomp and ceremony. The band played some appropriate march at each remove; then there was a waltz for the the soup, and fish was eaten to a polka. It was a little tiresome, perhaps; it made our unsophisticated country friends stare a little, but they soon got reconciled to it, as we do to every thing. I was very much amused, and commented freely to my companion.

"You see attempts every where," she said, "at order and harmony. They are often imperfect and grotesque, but they show the direction of our aspirations.

"Here is a collection of strangers, inharmonic and discordant, whose only safety is to hold themselves apart, in little knots and coteries. How few here, have any real knowledge of, or trust in, much less any love for, those around them. We are played to by a hired band; we are served by hired waiters, who labor under the burden of caste. It is cold, discordant, or at best indifferent and mercenary.

"Can you imagine, in a far more beautiful room than this, a company of free, pure, and loving men and women—all acquainted with each other, all harmonized in groups of friends and lovers; genial, hopeful, happy; the music by an artist group playing with enthusiasm, and rewarded by plaudits; and the table served by those with whom it would be a labor of love, so that every dish would come with its own blessing? Can you not imagine such a dinner as this?"

"In heaven, perhaps;" I answered, almost bitterly.

"Whatever can be truly conceived of the Earth-life," she said, "is possible, and practicable. Ideas were given for realization. I see that I must make a personal application. Do you not think that you and I are capable of being members of such a society?"

"I believe," I answered, "that you are capable of any good that is possible. As to myself, I am not sure that I am good enough."

"Could you not cheerfully play in the band that furnished music to such a feast, and feel rewarded when I, and those younger, and more beautiful, and dearer than I, thanked you for that portion of the repast?"

Such a question did not need an answer.

"Can you not fancy yourself very happy to stand behind my chair, and supply my wants, and those of others you might admire more and love better?"

You know it would make me happy to be of any service.

"Others have devotion, enthusiasm, friendship, love, as well as you. Civilization, with its bigotries, false methods, and discordances, tends to cultivate isolation and selfishness in us, and to make us believe there is little else in others; but it is not truly so, my friend. Humanity is better than we give it credit for. There is more devotion, more heroism, all around us, than we reckon. There are fifty men in this room who would risk their lives to save mine; who would brave great perils to save a house on fire—who would volunteer on a forlorn hope in any great emergency. There are few women here, frivolous as our social habits make them seem, who are not capable of great exertions, and great devotion. The human heart is full of heroic qualities and aspirations, seeking for spheres of action."

I shall tire you, dearest, if I go on giving you these conversations; but they had an inexpressible charm for me.

Our dinner itself, was of little account. I have long been half a vegetarian, and the flesh of most dead animals disgusts me. It is but a modified cannibalism; and some of these dead bodies, set on our tables to be eaten, I know had better be in the cemetery. I am not satisfied with myself when habit, or some remnant of savageism in my nature, tempts me to eat food worthy only of a savage or a beast of prey. I could not imagine this pure and lovely woman, putting flesh between her lips. She quietly waved away the soup, declined fish, asked the waiter to remove the side dishes nearest us, and took a potatoe and some maccaroni; and afterward some pudding, and fruit. Of course, I followed her example. I could not have done otherwise, had I wished.

But here is a difficulty. I felt that for me to eat flesh, in the presence of this woman, in my present relation to her, would be an indelicacy approaching sacrilege. It seemed to me in the strength of her pure presence, that I could never taste it again. But how shall I reconcile this conscience with politeness, when I sit by a lady who devours pork chops and sausages? But this was a question not to be discussed at table, and I postponed its further consideration.

Remembering the little draught of delicious wine in the cars yesterday, I turned to the long wine list, on the bill of fare, and passed it to my friend. She ran her eye over it and said, " it is not needful, unless you require it. The water is good, and wine belongs to occasions. If we are to have any to-day, it will be furnished us."

What this meant, I could not conceive; but a few moments after, a waiter came with the compliments of a gentleman whose name I did not distintly hear, and filled our glasses with a beautiful hock wine. She said, in a low tone, " that elderly gentleman, near the head of the table; he is Mr. ———, Senator from ———."* He bowed to us with much dignity; and my friend raised her glass to her lips, with a sweet recognition of his friendly attention. But, though the wine was excellent, she drank but little. Later, another gentleman sent us champaigne wine. I recognised him as one of those who had saluted us on Goat Island. She tasted this as before, but would not permit me to order wine and return the compliments, as I wished to do. And I see now that it was a very "snobbish" notion that made me desire it.

"It is natural to wish to return presents, compliments, and hospitalities; but if you reflect a moment, you will see that it is not delicate to do so at once. It is as if you were anxious to discharge a debt. If you meet these gentlemen, at any future time, you will have the right to reciprocate, *after* I have introduced you. You are not too old or too proud to have a mentor."

---

* In the revision of these letters for publication, I have thought proper to carefully erase or change every personal designation that might compromise any one.—*Editor.*

"No," I replied, as we rose from the table, "I am only too happy."

In the evening we had music and a dance. When I entered the drawing-room, I saw my friend surrounded by a group of ladies and gentlemen, among whom were the two whom I have mentioned. I did not go to her at once, respecting the mystery which enveloped her. It was her supreme right to be incognito, if she chose, and as long as she chose. In casual glimpses, I saw her engaged in an earnest conversation with the group that had gathered around her, and who listened to her with an affectionate respect which gave me much pleasure. Pretty soon she invited me with a movement of her fan, to approach, and introduced me to the ladies and gentlemen.

"This is my brother," she said, "who has been very kind to his unknown sister. Mr. ———, said she, turning to the senator, will you introduce me? The best of *men*, even, have some curiosity."

The gentleman took my hand with a benevolent smile, and said, "Mr. Wilson, I have great pleasure in presenting you to my dear friend, Miss Elmore.*

I did not feel any better acquainted, though the name solved many mysteries. I had heard my mother speak of her very lovingly, and of her family.

Music interrupted further conversation. A professor of the pianoforte displayed his skill, playing with a facility of habit, but a lack of feeling.

A lady sang, in a manner that showed long and careful training, but it seemed to me with a superficialness and meretriciousness, that gave us only the mere shell of the compositions she essayed.

Mr. ——— asked Miss Elmore to favor us and the company, and was warmly seconded by the rest of the group—all but me. I confess that I feared that she would not succeed—that in some way she should fall from the pedestal where I had enshrined her. She made no excuse, but looked around to see if no one else wished, or

---

* For convenience sake I substitute, in print, this name, for the real one, of a woman, whose relations might object to such publicity, and for other reasons which will become apparent.—*Editor.*

was invited to play — then took the arm of her friend, and walked with the most perfect, simple dignity to the piano-forte. A murmur of inquiry and approbation went round the room ; which a moment after was hushed in a silence so profound that we could hear the ticking of a clock, and the sound of the cataract. She stood so poised and graceful ; her movement in taking off her gloves was a tableau; she sat down—I know no other word—regally. I saw a gleam of pride in the deep eyes of Mr. ———. I never waited for music with a more excited expectancy.

She began by a light, trickling run ; then struck several chords of very unusual combinations, and fell into a prelude, which was an evident improvization, and took up little passages of several operas, as if she were thinking over with her fingers, what she would choose. Finally, she struck thrillingly into the prelude of the cavatina in I Puritani. I can not tell you of voice, or execution. She seems perfect in both ; but the soul, the feeling, the spell of power, with which she gave this noble composition, was so far beyond any thing I had conceived of, that I can not pretend to describe it. It may not have been to others what it was to me. But the group in which I was, sat spell-bound, and I saw tears run unchecked. When the last note died away the hush continued—there was not a sound. The clock ticked, the cataract murmured ; and it was not until she rose, and bowed with a bright smile, that there came from every side tumultuous plaudits and encores. Gentlemen pressed around her, and begged her to favor them again—to sing some thing, any thing, even to play if she could not sing.

She sat down, and all returned to their seats. She commenced a series of graceful variations on the air of Home, Sweet Home. " Sing it ; Oh ! sing it," came to her in appealing murmers. She looked at me with a happy smile, and sung the dear old song, as it could only be sung by one whose memory and heart is filled with a home of beauty and love, and happiness. And this time, there was no lack of tears, and no attempt to conceal them, and no stint of the plaudits which followed, in the midst of which she glided gently back to our corner, and received our congratulation.

III.

BUFFALO, AND A PILGRIMAGE.

I WRITE to you, angel of my life, from the bosom of Lake Erie and the cabin of a steamboat, whose motion must account for any peculiar eccentricity in my chirography. The noble boat rolls gently on the swells of this blue inland sea. The passengers have retired to their state-rooms, and I write by the cabin lamp, alone. In twenty-four hours I hope to have a letter from you. You are well and you love me, but none the less do I wish you to tell me both.

I took one last, lingering look at Niagara from the verge of the American fall; reserving for my final view, that which is the first to most visitors. After breakfast, we took the cars for Buffalo, bidding good-bye to some pleasant acquaintances, who, 1 hope, may be our friends in the future. Senator ——— shook me kindly by the hand, and said: "You are highly favored, Mr. Wilson; and it will be your own fault if you do not have a very pleasant journey. I wish you much happiness."

"I hope, sir," I replied, "that I may be worthy of my good fortune and your good wishes;" and so we parted.

Miss Elmore had been very kind to me all this morning; but there was a musing sadness in her looks, and a tender melancholy in her tones, which interested me. She said little, during the ride of twenty miles, and we were soon in the heart of a finely built, enterprising city, and took an omnibus to the American Hotel.

"1 stop here," she said, when we were in the parlor, "to make a pilgrimage. You can join me, or not, as you choose. It may be neither pleasant nor interesting to you."

"I shall never lack interest or pleasure in your society," I answered. Now, Clara, it was not a compliment. This is not a

36

woman to be flattered. She accepted what I said, just as I said it— as the simple, frank expression of my thought. If she had thanked me, or made any similar acknowledgment, I would not have spoken in this way again.

"Oh! here is my old friend of ten years ago," said she, going to a piano-forte in the corner, and striking the keys; "but it has changed in that time, or I have. I played and sung to him, and with him here, in this very room, and with this very instrument. I remember what I sung;" and she struck with a beautiful feeling into that beautiful and once favorite song—·

"O, Pilot, 'tis a fearful night,
    There's danger on the deep;"

and when she came to the lines

"Fear not; but trust in Providence,
    Wherever thou may'st be,"

she sung them with an expression that thrilled me.

"I sang it to *him*," she said, rising from the instrument, and going to the window, opening on Main street, "and he has had reason to trust. We will make our pilgrimage. It is not every one I would allow to go with me, but you will know him one day, and you are worthy."

I gave her my arm and we went into the street, walked round a few squares, passed through the little enclosure of an old Court House, and came to a prison.

Here, then, was the pilgrimage. I was curious, but Miss Elmore is not one you can ask questions of. I was very sure that at the proper time, she would tell me all that was needful. On my knocking at the gate, the jailor came and opened it. She passed before me, saying, "We are strangers, and wish to see your prison." The man, with a droll, puzzled look, seemed to have no especial objection; but asked, "is there any particular person you wish to see?"

"No—not at present," she answered. "A friend of mine once had the good fortune to be a guest of your establishment. I have the curiosity to see a place he has described to me."

We were admitted without further delay; first into the yard, then through another door into the jail. There are four ranges of small cells; two on the ground, two reached by galleries. The cells open outward toward the walls. The windows are cross-barred with iron, and the doors of the cells the same. The light is faint, and the air foul with that sickening fetor, which belongs to the emigrant ship, the hospital, the prison, and the crowded homes of poverty and ignorance. The cells were full of vagrants, small thieves, burglars, counterfeiters, accused persons waiting trial, and witnesses. As we went in, a chorus of prisoners in the further cells was singing with great unction a highwayman's song, beginning—

> ' In Dublin city I was bred and born,
>   On Stephen's Green I die forlorn ;
>   'Twas there I lear'nt the saddler's trade,
>   But was always counted a roving blade."

We followed the jailor round the lower tiers of cells, then went up to the narrow gallery that gave access to the upper tiers. When we had come to the further cell on the right, it was empty.

" Will you permit me to enter this cell a moment," she said, in a low, tremulous voice, to the jailor.

He unfastened the door with the customary professional joke, and she entered. It had been papered at some time, and was in better condition than the other cells ; but of the same size—about four feet by eight. After a glimpse of the interior, I called away the attention of the jailor by some inquiry, leaving her in the cell. In a few minutes she joined us, looking pale but serene, though I saw traces of tears. As we went out, I saw her silently give the jailor a gold dollar; and as we walked up the grassy slope, she turned and looked a moment through the window, covered with dust and spider's webs, opposite the further cell.

I drew long breaths as we gained the pure free air of the open street. We passed a theater not far from the jail, opposite which she paused and looked up a moment, then smiled and said—" now we will take a pleasanter walk."

So we walked down Main street, which is the Broadway of Buffalo, down among the warehouses near the harbor, and going up the creek, passed over a bridge, looked at the fine array of shipping—steamboats and propellers—and then soon found ourselves walking on a hard sand beach by the side of the lake, whose waves were breaking musically at our feet. Then we clambered up the outer shelving side of the long government breakwater, and walked along that and the pier which forms the outer side of the harbor, until we passed around the little light-house at the end, and then sat down on the smooth rocks in its shadow. The beautiful city lay fair before us, and all its hum and clatter came softened across the water; while westward stretched the blue lake, north opened the Niagara river, its outlet, and opposite on the Canada shore, could be seen the grassy mounds, which mark the site of Fort Erie.

"It is a famous place in border story," said my companion and guide. "In the war of 1812, the little village that was the Buffalo of that day, was burned by the British troops and their Indian allies. They have different allies now, but the same mode of warfare. They still burn unoffending and defenceless villages.

"Over there they had a little experience of Yankee valor. The fort was taken by storm; I believe it was blown up, and some gallant men were buried in its ruins; but I confuse the stories of these old quarrels. Let me tell you of one of a more recent date, and of more personal interest."

I changed my place and sat at her feet, prepared to listen. I find myself *looking up* to this woman, just as naturally as I would look down to some others. There is a sphere of freedom surrounding her, which permits every one to take his proper place; and there seems also a sphere of power, the action of forces, which harmonize all around her, by bringing all to their true relations. So I sat at her feet and listened.

"Nearly twenty years ago, before you were old enough to care much about politics, an ambitious lawyer was elected governor of New York. I remember it well, for my father was an active partizan on the other side, and his frankly expressed opinions of the man were not in the least complimentary. I think he has not changed his opinion of him; and I am certain that I have not.

"Buffalo was then a city of less than half its present size, but its leading men were a set of unscrupulous borderers, and at the head of the dominant party in this district. They secured this man's nomination, and he paid the price. The price was to aid them in sending a much better man to State Prison, and keeping him there. He was elected. It was a triumph, and the victory was celebrated by a grand illumination. Buffalo was in a blaze, cannon thundered, and rockets rose. But, as sometimes occurs, the elements took part in the performance. All day a gale from the southwest had been increasing in fury. The waters rose in the harbor and in the streets. In the midst of the festival, the glare of the illumination lighted a scene of terror and death. The heaped up waters swept over all this point of land, where was then a little village of dwellings. The celebration was interrupted by the crash of these falling houses, and the shrieks of crushed and drowning victims. The sailors of the harbor, the hardy steamboat men, gave all the aid they could; but when morning came, it lighted up a pitiful scene. The wreck of houses and furniture was floating in the harbor; a score or more of the stiff corpses of men, women and little children lay in the watch-house, under the market yonder; vessels were stranded high up the streets, others, attempting to gain the harbor had been thrown on the beach below. Afterward the general government built the brakewater.

"I said that this governor paid for his nomination. His friends, here, had been trying for two years to send a man to the State Prison. He was a contractor, builder, financier; one of those who build cities. A man of great constructive and administrative power; upright in intention, I should think. In a financial crisis, in his efforts to continue his work of making this the city he foresaw it must be, he made himself, or was made, amenable to the laws. With or without his knowledge, the persons who managed his finances, multiplied the endorsements of his co-adjutors here—men whose fortunes he had made—by forgery. When this became known, he placed his property in their hands, to pay his creditors; and trusted to their professions of sympathy and promises of aid.

They seized on the millions intrusted to them, and then he refused to leave the country, or submit to this robbery, they threw him into jail, kept him a year in that cell, and then failing to convict him here, after several trials, took him to another county, where, with their own judge to try him, their own jury to convict, their own nominated governor to give his personal presence and influence, they secured his civil death, and their safety. It was a bold strong game. They had money and political influence, and were unscrupulous in the use of both. An amiable, able, and I think essentially an honest man, was torn from his wife, and sent for five years to Auburn. There was great sympathy for him, and petitions were sent from the whole State, but he was very safe, as long as their own man was governor. A pardon would have endangered every thing."

"And was it your sympathy for this victim of a mercenary treachery, that made you visit that prison?" I asked, for, though a hard case, it was only one of thousands as bad, and I could not see in it the element of a personal interest.

'Oh! no," she said, seeming to read my thoughts; "this is but the introduction. The honest felon, the crafty governor, and his clique of alternate employers and tools, are little to me. They have their reward. One of them has been President; another hopes to be. But there was here, at that time, a volunteer Knight Errant, whom you will know hereafter; and you may as well learn now, this little passage in his history. It will be a good introduction."

Ah! thought I, here is the center of this mystery. When a woman speaks of the man she loves, there is no mistaking. She speaks of him, as she can speak of no other. I wished to see how she would bear the test of this revelation.

This is not all, dear Clara; I must tell you all the truth. When she spoke of this man, with the consciousness that she loved him, there came a deep, dull pain into my heart. I tell you the fact. I do not try to account for it. I feel it yet; but I will tell you the whole, and you may understand it.

"Mr. Vincent," she continued, pronouncing this name as if each tone that made it was precious to her, "came to Buffalo, when he was twenty-one years old. He came here, it seemed by chance, for he left New York without any plan, but to see the world. He was

4

a student, and at this age a philosopher, and a man of letters. Soon after he came here, he became editor of a daily paper; as such, he made a thorough exposure of all the iniquity I have narrated, and, of course, brought upon himself the vengeance of these men. He fought them step by step, and so excited the public that they were obliged to admit their prisoner to bail, and to take him to a distance to convict him.

"I don't see how he went through the contest that came. He was very young, for such a position. But he was an eloquent writer and speaker, and his personal qualities aided him. I am partial, perhaps, but he was called handsome then; you will see him and can judge. He walked these streets, I have been told, as if he owned the city; I know that many loved him. Too free, or too prudent to marry; too generous and honorable to injure any one; he rather avoided love than sought it. But you will know him and I need not describe him.

"The contest was fierce and unequal. It was right against might. A youthful adventurer with his pen, against all the wealth, and influence, and consequent respectability of this city. His society was tabooed, until ladies who would have him, were obliged to make up special parties, when he was invited. The contest raged everywhere; this city, where it is now forgotten, was divided into two parties of his friends and his enemies. He had numbers and honesty —they had wealth and position.

"He was attacked in the streets by hired ruffians, but fought with spirit enough to beat them.

"At another time, an organized company of men came, in the day time, posted sentries at the door of his office up Main street, and marched into his editorial room, picked and prepared to inflict upon him a personal chastisement. He received the delegation with a grave courtesy; inquired their business; and when it had been stated by their spokesman, and he had respectfully declined the honor they intended him; just as the men deputed to seize him were gathering around, fifteen to one, he drew two little brass pistols from his vest pockets, and pointing them at the nearest, gave them such an earnest assurance of receiving their contents, that the meeting adjourned.

"When it was found that he was not to be bribed at any price, nor intimidated by any means; a gang of desperate ruffians was hired to tar and feather him, and destroy his press and types. The conspiracy was deliberately formed, money contributed, and the ruffians were disguised, partly intoxicated, and paid to do their work. A large wagon and two horses were provided to carry him off, gagged and helpless, into the forest; a rope to bind him to a tree, and tar and feathers to complete the outrage—which would, undoubtedly, have ended in murder, had not a providence watched over him.

"It was before the day of spiritual manifestations, but it is, perhaps, as remarkable as most of these. While this gang, concealed in the shadow of a building, at ten o'clock in the evening, where my friend was accustomed to pass from his office to his boarding house, was waiting for him—he was walking home alone, in the moon-light, without a thought of danger. He was on the very block, round the corner of which the blackened men awaited him, with gag and ropes, and their wagon was in the next street.

"Just then he met an acquaintance, a clerk in one of the banks, who passed, then turned back, stopped him, and asked him to turn and walk back. As they went, he said: 'You must go home with me to-night, I have something to say to you. I don't know how it is, but something is wrong. I was at a party on the street below; it was a pleasant party, I was dancing, and engaged to dance again. I never left such a party before, but to-night I could not stay. Every one wondered, and pressed me to stay longer, at least to supper, but I could not. There was no reason, only I was compelled to come. When I passed the building below, I saw some men hiding in its shadow; I remembered that you boarded in the street, and in a moment I met you.'

"Mr. Vincent would have gone back to investigate this mystery, but his friend pursuaded him to go to the hotel where he boarded. The next morning it was found that the gang, though foiled in part, had completely demolished the printing office."

"But was nothing done?" I asked.

"No; the conspirators were not known until long afterward. They had influence enough to hush up investigation. The mayor of the city, it was afterward proven, was at the head of the conspiracy.

"Finally, a grand jury, mostly from the country, was found to indict Mr. Vincent for libel. He had called one of these lawyers the tool of his employers. For this, he was tried; a corrupt, and drunken judge, who owed them money, tried the cause, and an ignorant and weak-minded jury was persuaded to bring in a verdict of guilty. He refused to leave, even at the request of his own bail and counsel, and was imprisoned four months in the cell to which we made our pilgrimage."

"But what said his friends, and the public?" I enquired; "was no effort made in his behalf?"

"There was no lack of sympathy and indignation. A mob surrounded the jail and would have torn it down. The Sheriff asked him to speak to the crowd, and he sent them peacefully away. Still he was treated with cruelty. Presents were stopped at the door, and visitors often could not gain admittance. But he had books, and his violin, and his writing materials were smuggled in, and his manuscripts out, in spite of the jailor. It is quite a romance. The people paid his fine by a complimentary benefit at the theater we passed. They offered him an ovation; but he declined it. They would have elected him to any office in the popular gift, but he was not ambitious. He had done his work, and had another destiny. The wrong was exposed, and the power broken; he had the trial and the discipline of the imprisonment in that foul dungeon; and the world has had the benefit of that experience. Some day, when I shall sit on one side of him, and you the other, you will see what it has done for him. To labor well for humanity, one must see all the phases of its development."

We walked back along the pier.

"Here," she said, "he used to ride on the beach, his horse's feet washed by the turf. One day he rode along the pier, and round the light-house. The waves were dashing over the pier; the way, you see, is very narrow, but a horse feels the will of his rider. One strong will may govern many."

"Has this man such power as to control those around him?" I

asked; wishing to know how much my companion might be under such an influence.

"I think he *has* such power," she said, "but I do not see that he makes often voluntary use of it. He wishes all men and women to be free, and to act for themselves. In those days, he experimented sometimes. He had a magnetism that could excite or paralize. He could throw an impressible person into a two-day's trance. He cured the blind, and many diseases. I think he tested the power to make one love him; but that he has ever since refrained from using it. I can not find that he ever used it harmfully.

"This city, and the hills and waters here, are full of associations with his adventures. When the frontier war broke out, his friends were engaged in it; but he went from camp to camp, as if it were only a study. When a man has a distinctive work to do, a real destiny to accomplish; he has years of practice—he makes many studies and sketches. The world calls his efforts failures, but they insure success. To succeed in any thing but the real life work, would be a failure indeed. To fail in lesser enterprises, or have them prove fruitless, is often the condition of the final success. Mr. Vincent could have been Mayor of Buffalo, Member of Congress or have risen to any political station he might have desired; but at every turn he put aside such ambitions, and kept to his far higher mission. Of that you will soon know, and be able to form your own opinion."

We passed the rest of the day pleasantly, with conversation and music. Two or three gentlemen called, and conversed with Miss Elmore earnestly; but I was not invited to join them. She seems to be consulted, looked up to, and reverenced; but there is a mystery I can not fathom. Were we in Europe, I should think she was a secret agent of a revolutionary society. Here, her mission evidently has nothing to do with politics; yet it is certain that she can have no narrow or selfish object.

We came to the boat in the evening and stood upon the deck until we came round the light-house. She took a long look at the city, a look full of loving remembrances.

As she stood by my side, in the soft twilight, I said—

"You have been very good to me. I thank you for your confidence. You loved Mr. Vincent much."

"*Loved!*" she said, with a glow of feeling; "loved? I love him *now*, and ever shall."

I stood silent. The dull pain sank on my heart. I did not say one word, Clara; but she must have felt me.

"My dear friend," she said, taking my hand, and holding it between both of hers; "I love this man with more devotion than any other. But it does not hurt me that others love him as much or more than I do. I have my own place in his heart and life; as he has in mine."

"It is nothing to me," I said, "whom he loves, or you." I was angry at myself, and therefore rude to her.

"My brother!" she said, softly; "you must not be unjust to yourself or others. All pure and true loves come from the Heavens to bless us. They come singly or in groups and clusters of loves, and all in harmony, and all to bless. Why should we shut our hearts against them? *I* shall not. Good night."

She glided quickly to her state-room. I walked up and down the deck a few moments, let the night breeze cool my fever, and came here to write to you.

My heart throbs like the engine of this vessel which bears me from you. I have been frank to you, dear Clara, but I can not explain, for I do not understand. Pardon me, and pity me, if I need it. I wish to be, and to do, right. I know that I love you; for in the thought and hope of you, I find rest.

Blessing of my life, good night!

IV.

CINCINNATI.

My blessed Clara!—When I recorded my name on the register of the Burnet House, this evening, your precious letter was given me. I was shown to a charming room, with a large bath-room attached. The hotel is grand, spacious, and luxurious beyond my expectations. I took a bath and then read your letter. It is unromantic, I know, but after a long day of dusty travel, I did not feel that I had a right even to come into the presence of your written words, until I was in a condition to enjoy the ineffable sweetness and purity that breathes in every line you have written. The letter and picture will lie together on my heart to-night, and I shall sleep happily. Thanks and blessings for all the love you send me.

When I entered the name of Miss Elmore, after my own, I observed the expression of the bland countenance of Mr. Coleman, whom I knew at once by his resemblance to his brother, in New York; I was glad to see an added gleam of sunlight; and, I doubt not, I was provided with a better room, and treated with more deference, than if I had been a solitary traveler; for a man is judged, if not always known, by the company he keeps.

After landing from the steamboat, at an early hour this morning, we have traversed the great State of Ohio, from its northern central meridian, to its south-western extremity. The sun rose to us over the blue waves of Lake Erie; its setting beams were reflected from the beautiful river Ohio. It was my first salutation *a la belle rivière*. This is called the Queen City, you know. Her majesty is a little sooty, and wears a crown of smoke. I shall pay my respects to her to-morrow. It is Sunday and we remain here until Monday But now I must give you an account of the day.

47

After writing my long letter of last night, I slept soundly, rocked by gentle billows, and soothed by the regular working of the machinery, and did not wake until it stopped at the dock at Cleveland. When I came into the saloon, I found Miss Elmore, bright, rosy, and smiling, waiting to walk the short distance to the railroad depot.

"You will not see much of this pretty place," she said, "for we have much to do at Cincinnati, and I have promised to spend our Sunday there."

"We," and "our." Well, Clara, they are terms that may include many. All of life is before us; all is new in the future; all our relations are to be defined. I feel that we must be brave, and true, and shrink from nothing that is right; as well as be careful to do nothing wrong.

And so "we" took our places in the cars, and were soon whirling across this great, fertile, and well peopled State. You will find our route on the map. We took the line by Columbus, the State Capital, and the Little Miami Railroad. I shall not describe the cities and villages through which we passed, because I saw but little of them, and because it is better done in the Guide Books, and Gazetteers.

But the face of the country, alternately rolling and broken, but with no mountains in sight, and the evidences of abounding fertility attracted my attention. I called the State well peopled, and so it seems to be on the census list, but when you look over it, you can see that it would support twenty times its present population.

As we went south, the country grows richer, the forest trees of a more gigantic growth, and the corn-fields more magnificent. Oh! these corn-fields of the West; none of your little patches of a few rods square; but we passed through miles and miles of bright waving maize, and great fields of wheat of golden richness, ripening for the harvest. The wealth of this fertility is wonderful. A Quaker sat behind us, as we passed through the great Miami valley. He took a quiet pride in my exclamations, at these glories of the wealth of nature, and volunteered some information in regard to it.

"Do you live in this region?" I asked him.

"Yes," he said, "I have a little farm of three hundred acres, down here by Loveland."

There's a name for you, Clara; but they have a right to love such land.

"What is this land worth an acre?"

"Well, about fifty dollars, on an average."

"Is it under high culture?"

"I don't know as I understand what thee calls high culture. We get about as much off as we cleverly can."

"Oh! I meant rotation of crops, and manuring, and all that sort of thing," said I; for you know, Clara, I take a great interest in agriculture, and read the reports of the meetings of the Farmer's Club, with much assiduity.

"I suppose I ought to manure my land some," said the bland Quaker, "but I never have; I never could find time. As to rotation, I have grown corn on one bottom every season for fifty-two years, and it still grows from fifteen to twenty feet high, and I have to reach up to get at the ears. I am afraid that if I went to putting on goo-an-no, I should have to use a ladder."

The group of farmer-looking men sitting around confirmed the old man's testimony. One had a corn-stalk twenty-one feet high. Another had climbed into a weed strong enough to bear his weight. Others had raised crops of wheat, corn, and Irish and sweet potatoes, which I can not pretend to remember.

"No wonder that people go West," I said to Miss Elmore, who had been listening to this conversation with a quiet interest, which took in and comprehended every thing.

"And they continue to go West," she said. "They come from New England to Ohio and Michigan. They go from these new States, with their forests unfelled, and their lands uncultivated, to Wisconsin, Iowa, Minnesota, and Kansas, and from beyond the Mississippi to California and Oregon."

"And why?"

"The reason commonly given, is that the lands are cheaper. Great tracts of land in these settled States have been bought as investments, or for speculation. Prices are high; but they are ruled by

5

markets and other conditions. But this is not all. Emigration is the protest against the institutions, customs, and conditions of civilization. It is the blind search after a better social state; it is the universal pursuit of happiness, the right of which is bravely asserted in the Declaration of Independence."

"Is this pursuit ever successful?"

"You will not wish me to say no, because you are one of the seekers. But how can it be, when men carry about with them the conditions of their discontent? They might as well try to escape from their dyspepsias. A man moves with his family, his bonds, his habits, his diseases, his ignorance, and selfishness, and bigotries. Ah! if he could leave all these behind, there might be hope for him. Of what account is a little more or less labor, a few bushels, more or less of produce? These form but a small part of the elements of happiness. Wherever he goes, he sees the same sun, and sky, and stars, lives on the same earth, and mingles with the same humanity. The same restless fever of unsatisfied desire burns on. They change the place, but keep the pain."

"What would you have? What is the remedy? Are men to be content?"

"By no means! Content in bad conditions? Content with ignorance, poverty, disease, and all forms of slaveries, within and without? O no! To be content with evil is the condition of despair. Discontent is the first sign of hope. Emigration, change of place, is an effort, which will lead to others. The more discontent with the present, the nearer the hope of the future."

"But what are these conditions of happiness, for which we are all blindly seeking?"

She smiled at the question, as if it was ridiculous not to know, or absurd to ask.

"You must excuse my ignorance," I said; "I have neither read nor thought much of all this, and I need to be instructed."

"I hesitated to answer," she replied, with a sweetness that was the best possible answer to my last remark, "because it was a question which might require three words or three volumes. Reading might not have made you wiser; and few think in the right direction.

"Look at it. For two thousand years, religion has been preached as the panacea of social evils; and when the Church has embosomed as much discord and misery as can be found out of her pale, then we are told that we are not to look for happiness in this life, but only content. As if the good God had decreed all miserable generations here, and eternal torments hereafter!

"Social happiness has been sought in political liberty, and its result, in the present forms yet achieved, has been only to awaken men to a keener sense of unhappy conditions.

"A few seek happiness in honors or wealth. Honors and wealth are beautiful and good; but not a social state in which they are the result of intrigue and injustice.

"Property is plunder; position is an imposition; and power is usurpation. The world is a society of Ishmaels; every man has one hand upon his neighbor's throat and the other in his pocket. All are robbers and all are robbed, but the strongest and most cunning get most of the spoil. All are oppressors and all are oppressed; but the weakest, the ignorant, the women, and the negroes somewhat the worst. The picture is strongly drawn; but if you consider it, you will find it true."

She turned to the window, and gave me the next hour to consider; and I did, honestly and faithfully. Clara, it is all too true. How can God answer for such a world?

She must have known my thoughts; for when she turned to me again, she said—

"The Eternal Justice will be satisfied, and the Infinite Love will be made manifest, in the law of growth. If this were the beginning or the end, we might doubt and despair. But much allowance must be made to an infantile race. When humanity shall have arrived at the stage of manhood, we may expect something better."

This was a little vague to me. I wished to know what were those social conditions, which would make men happy, and therefore content.

"The first condition," said she, "I have told you, is freedom. All seek it. The fugitive slave runs away to Canada in search of it, but it is not there. He changes the form of slavery and not the fact. The fugitive wife runs away from her husband—or *vice versa* —but society holds her in a severer, though perhaps a less repulsive bondage."

"But is this really so? Are men and women so enslaved?"

She looked incredulously at me, as if distrusting my seriousness in asking the question; but seeing that I was truly in dead, stupid earnest, she said:

"Are you free to go and speak to that lady yonder, though you knew that she desired it as well as you? Is not every woman guarded by her husband, or father, or brother, or by 'what will people say,' against all freedom, as much here as in Turkey?

"What are the natural rights of woman? Are they not personal freedom, genial companionship, the free exercise of her intellect and talents, love, maternity? Does society allow her these rights?"

I have never thought much of this, Clara dear. I have heard about the woman's rights women, and read their droll proceedings in the papers. I went to hear Mrs. Rose, and Lucy Stone once. They want to be lawyers, and doctors, and preachers, and vote, and run for office. But this idea of women being free, in any such sense of freedom as Miss Elmore speaks of, I had never thought about. And yet I see that she has this freedom, and that on it depends much of her wonderful fascination. Beautiful as she is, good, and true, and noble, as I see and feel her to be, I can not conceive of her as the wife of any one. She seems a heroine, who might command an army; I think she would preside in a Senate with admirable dignity; I doubt not that she is loving and faithful to the deepest life of love; but still, Clara, I can not but see how far removed she is from all the women I have ever seen. She enjoys my astonishment very much.

Here, then, we are, in the Queen City of the West. In the morning we are to take a little ride, and look at the city from one of the surrounding hills. I shall also try to get a peep at the river and steamboats. Good night, darling; I will finish my letter to-morrow.

Sunday Morning.—"And this is the great city of the West," I said, as we stood on the brow of a hill to which we had ascended up zig-zag roads, in a carriage from the Burnet House, an hour after sunrise. The sky was clearer than I expected, for the chimneys of a thousand manufactories and furnaces had ceased to belch out their clouds of bituminous coal smoke. I could see all the compact, well built city; the river skirting in a semi-circle beyond, and then passing off to the south-west; the Kentucky suburbs of Covington and Newport, and the circle of hills that surround the city. Miss Elmore surveyed it all in silence, and then, remembering her office of guide, said to me:

"This is Cincinnati, an embodiment of thrift and piety, a city of manufactories, ware-houses, steamboats, and churches. There is not a public square, park, or parade ground, in the city. The ground is all built over. There is a noble Cathedral in the Grecian style, and you see the cross glittering on many a spire. A third of the city is German, and two-thirds of the Germans are Catholics; nearly all the Irish, of course. That tall misshapen spire belongs to a Presbyterian Meeting House. It is very characteristic, dark, ugly, pretentious. The yellow excrescence on the top is a fist."

"A fist?"

"Yes, a doubled hand, with the index finger pointing upward. It is generally mistaken by strangers for the representation of a yellow washed ham, a symbol of the chief trade of the city. The building is surrounded and shut in by stores. The Catholics keep commerce at a more respectful distance."

"But, excuse the question, Miss Elmore, this pork trade you spoke of?"

"It is very quiet now. Those large buildings by the canal yonder are the pork-houses. In the winter three hundred thousand hogs are driven or brought on the cars and steamboats, killed in the suburbs, drawn into the city, and packed in those ware-houses. Then Cincinnati deserves its name of Porkopolis, and its offense is rank, and smells to heaven. A very unpleasant smell it is. But it is a part of civilization, and thoroughly characteristic."

"Why do you say characteristic?"

"Because the animal, in his filth, gluttony, diseases, and destiny, is a representative of the impure, sensual, selfish, and miserable lives of most of those who fatten, buy, sell, and eat him. O Moses and Mahommed! ye lived in ages of darkness, but ye knew better than to eat pork. Let us change the subject."

"Excuse me; are the people of Cincinnati more hoggish than civilizers in general?"

"Oh! by no means! In many respects they are a very amiable people. I know them well. They mingle southern warmth with northern prudence; and eastern thrift is softened by the rough, large-hearted, whole-souledness of the West. I should like the Germans but for their tobacco, in which they are steeped."

"And the *lager bier?*"

"Oh! that is not a very bad concoction; far better than whiskey. But these people are so genial, familiar, and good-hearted. There is a sphere of friendliness, you find in no eastern city; an outflowing humanity and benevolence which reconciles you to every thing. Boston has more intellectual culture and refinement, New York more dash and splendor, New Orleans more fascination, but for genuine, unaffected, honest goodness, commend me to Cincin nati."

There, my Clara, as an impartial traveler, I send you the result of my second-hand observations; and the little experience I have had confirms their truth. Every one you meet looks as if he would be really glad to render you some service; and would take it as a favor if you would stop and talk with him.

We drove around what is called Mount Auburn; saw some very beautiful villas and gardens; and on the hill sides, some of the vineyards, for which the city is famed. The wine made from the Catawba tastes a little harsh at first. I thought it not so good as the ordinary Rhine wines, but after a little you get to like the flavor; and every patriotic Cincinnatian is ready to swear that the whole world does not produce such wine.

When we returned into the city, the driver, an Irishman, took good care that we should see what he thought its most attractive portions. Going down Vine street, Miss Elmore pointed out the

German Theater, and three other public buildings, which are spacious, and convenient enough, but not very ornamental.

"Yonder," she said, "is the Turners' Hall, where the young men, by gymnastic exercises, combat the ill effects of coarse eating, beer, and tobacco. There is the Liberty Hall, owned by a society of fifteen hundred infidels, who glory in their negations. The Canal is a sort of boundary between the German and native populations, and this northern quarter is called ' over the Rhine.' Yonder are the People's Theatre, and Mechanics' Institute—curious specimens of Italian and Gothic architecture—but if you look about among the better class of private residences you will find many evidences of graceful art." I forgot to say that our Jehu, whose Christian name was Patrick, went out of his way to drive past the Cathedral, and though the same space and cost might have been more imposing in Gothic, it is a credit to the Church and an ornament to the city. I don't know how it may be, in fact, but it seems as large as both Grace and Trinity.

We had good appetites and a charming breakfast. When we sat at the table and looked over the bill, my companion, who likes to play guardian and guide, called the waiter, gave him a small paper package, and some very careful, but inaudible instructions. Can you conceive of a woman, whose whole appearance and manner, though full of gentleness and almost infantile loveliness, is yet so full of a sweet charm of power, that every one must obey her, with a most cheerful obedience? I see it, even in the waiters at the hotels; I feel it in myself, so that I am compelled to analyze this feeling. It grasps me like a fate; but it seems also like a most benevolent and beautiful destiny. And, Clara mine, I know and feel, through all my being, that I love you, not less, but more, for this influence.

The waiter came with some beautiful corn-bread, French rolls, and two cups of the most delicious chocolate I ever tasted.

"It is a little pet weakness of mine," she said, when I looked round with admiration at the rare beverage. "It comes to me from a dear friend in Havana. I have no doubt it is the best in the world."

"But the flavor."

"There is a very slight addition of orange flowers and vanilla."

"But is not this indulgence against your principles?" I asked.

"Pray, sir, do you happen to know what my principles are?"

I thought I knew, but I found myself at fault. "I supposed," I said, "you objected to the use of all stimulants."

"Oh! how mistaken the young gentleman is. Have I not been indulging in your exhilerating society for four days past?"

"But I mean pernicious stimulants."

"I certainly do not drink whisky. You have not observed me smoking. Coffee is harsh and acrid; there are black teas of delicate flavor and not very harmful, as an occasional luxury. You saw me drink wine. I think I take a pint a year. Each stimulant, if pure, has a specific action; it goes to a particular organ or group of organs. Chocolate, such as this, with the added flavors, excites gently, but very perceptibly the faculties of beauty, love, and music."

"Then you will sing," I said, hoping for more of the happiness I had tasted at Niagara.

"Not this morning. I have visitors and business after breakfast. You will write or walk. We will meet at dinner."

She went to her room, and I have written this continuation of my letter. This business and these visitors? Well, they are none of mine; so I will go and see the steamboats.

Good by for a little.

Night. — Blessings on Phonography! How should I ever be able to write you all I wish, without its time-annihilating aid? I was never so thankful for having learned it with you as to-night. You will see why. But I will go on all orderly with my narrative. What a thing it is to travel!

I took my walk down to the river. The beautiful Ohio, just here, is not the most romantic looking stream that meanders over the planet. Did you ever think how these long rivers run over its circumference, and what a droll figure they cut, when contemplated horizontally, and philosophically? The color is a bluish brown, like weak coffee and skim-milk. By the way, I found it the same in my bath-tub this morning. They filter it for the table, and it compares well with the Croton.

There is no mistake about the chocolate ; it is musical. I found myself singing, and even whistling ; but I had a rival in the latter accomplishment, in a steamboat, which came down the river with the water foaming at her bows, and her tall pipes vomiting blackness. She came round handsomely, so as to make her landing with her head up stream, in the orthodox fashion, in the meantime blowing a signal that might, I think, be heard to Lake Erie. It is like the scream of a locomotive, but compares with it as the ophicleide does with the piccola ; or a cannon to a pop gun; or better, as the steamboat to the locomotive.

If you shared my passion for steamboats, I think I would describe these that lie, in a long line, side by side, each with its nose resting on the shelving bank of the river. There is nothing in or around New York at all like them. The steamboats of the western waters are *sui generis.* The lake boats are large and lofty. They partake of the characteristics of the Hudson river boats, the ocean steamers, and the Ohio and Mississippi boats. But these : they are flat bottomed, so as to draw as little water as possible, and glide easily over the bars. Their bows, instead of being sharp, like ours, cutting the water like a knife, are flat and rounded like a duck's bill. There are no wharves, as the river rises and falls, at its own good pleasure, twenty or thirty feet; and the boats haul up, or spar off from the shore as it rises and falls. Their guards are close to the water. All the smaller boats have one broad wheel at the stern, instead of two at the sides. They have two smoke pipes, not near the center, but close to the bows, like two great ears or horns ; and a row of long, high-pressure boilers under them. The hold and lower deck are appropriated to freight, and the deck hands and passengers ; the main deck has a long cabin, with a range of state-rooms on each side, over which is the promenade hurricane deck, officers' room, pilot house, &c. There, that will do for steamboats.

As I stood on the upper deck of one of the finest—and really a magnificent boat of this kind—I saw four ferry boats, two above and two below, plying rapidly, backward and forward. It was droll. Each passage was a letter S, for even the ferry boats, with their little wharf-boats on each side, were obliged to make the landing with their bows up stream. So when they started they went up, turned, went down, turned, and by a series of graceful curves, came heads up again; and as the river is narrow, these curves constituted the entire voyage.

I crossed on the lower ferry, to Covington, walked up the bank of the river toward the government barracks, at Newport, crossed a very handsome suspension bridge, over a small river, which, running in a channel out of all proportion to its present size, looked like a small boy in his father's great coat, and came back by the upper ferry; my first visit to the State of Henry Clay, and the Mammoth Cave, and the "hunters of Kentucky." But I saw none of the latter.

But all this seems very trifling. What I liked better was the great steam engines that pump the Ohio into a reservoir, for the use of the city. A steam engine is such a human thing. It is the embodiment of the mind of the inventor, and the muscular power of all the men that dug, and smelted, and cast, fashioned and finished, the iron of which it is made.

We dined sumptuously, calmly, delightfully. Among my many faults, darling, is that of eating, not wisely, but too much, and too fast. But it is not possible to do any rude or unrefined thing in Miss Elmore's presence. She is a refining spirit, toning and tempering all to her own pure standard. I find myself unconsciously doing as she does, copying her manners, and not so much trying to please her, as resigning myself to the influence of the beautiful sphere that spreads around her. She was dressed in a rich light blue, trimmed with white, and wore pearls instead of diamonds. An elderly gentleman, a resident of the city, was her guest, and sat on the other side of her. He, too, ate only beautiful food. When we came to the dessert she said to me in a low tone—

"Now you can pay your respects to Cincinnati, and compliment our guest, by sending for a bottle of sparkling catawba." So I called for a card, and ordered a sample of Mr. Longworth's vintage."

"Ah!" said the old gentleman, when his glass was filled, with a glow of very visible satisfaction—"you are going to try some of our native wine. We think no small deal of it; and our Ohio Legislature, when they passed the Maine Law, made an exception in favor of the native article."

" Which has led, I presume," said Miss Elmore, " to a pretty extensive naturalization of less favored potables."

" Well, I believe there is some adulteration going on," said he; but this is the genuine catawba," he added, looking at his glass lovingly, and sipping off the bubbles as they rose.

" It is very well," Miss Elmore said, tasting her glass delicately; " but it does not taste like ours. You must try mine after dinner. This has something of the harshness and discord of the civilization which produces it. How do you find it, Mr. Wilson?"

I had tried the still catawba before, this was sweeter and softer, and the sparkle and carbonic acid make very common liquids palatable. " When I can shut out the remembrance of my first love, the delicious Widow Cliquot," I said, " I think I may get up a small flirtation with this ruddy squaw, Catawba."

Our Cincinnati friend was amiable enough to credit this as a jest worthy of his favorite wine; and after a merry dessert, we adjourned to Miss Elmore's room, which I found to be an elegant private parlor, with a bed-room adjoining. I had not asked for such a room, but they knew her here, and she may have written to announce her coming.

" So you go to-morrow," said our Cincinnatian, with a tone of sadness. "It is an angel's visit; we get a glimpse of brightness, and it is gone."

" My dear old friend," said Miss Elmore, laying her hand tenderly on his shoulder, as he sat beside her, and looking in his face with an expression of confiding love, "we must get off to-morrow, so as not to keep our friends waiting for us, and you must work clear, or cut loose from these civilized bonds, and come and be happy with us."

" My work is here, for a time," he said. " I must stay while I can do good to the cause, and help to prepare others to join us. In a few years my active life will be over, and then the old man will come and take his rest, and enjoy a calm and happy sunset."

"Your place is ready whenever you can come, and if you can gather a little group of true ones to come with you, they will be so welcome. The hard work is over, and we live in plenty and peace."

"And Mr. Wilson, our young friend, here, does he go to join you?"

"He goes with me," said Miss Elmore, "but with no bond upon the future. I have tried, and can trust him. If our life proves to be his, he will be with us; if not, there will be no harm. We have been very careful about visitors, and to avoid intrusion; but we are now growing strong enough to venture something for the good of others. So long as our life was an experiment, I think we did well to keep it in all secresy. Now, that it is a forever assured success, which nothing but some great convulsion can destroy, we may begin to give the world an idea of the happiness that awaits it. If Mr. Wilson does not belong to us, he will make a good report of us.

"I have only one stipulation to make," she said, turning to me, "and that is for others. I could trust you, for myself. You will promise *us*, in your letters, after we leave the Mississippi, not to give localities. All the rest you are welcome to give to your friends, or to the whole world."

I gave the required promise, and was glad to know what I might properly communicate to you, and, if it prove of interest enough, to all who may choose to read; for as I go on with this narrative, as I remember each day more clearly, and write it down in these rapid characters with more facility, I turn my thoughts to the many who may be as interested as we, in what promises to be a curious adventure, for I confess the mystery increases hour by hour. Each hour develops something new in this admirable woman, and I have already grown impatient to see a society in which, though she must be a ruling destiny, there must yet be those who are worthy of her beautiful dominion. I was not sorry to learn that we take the first boat down to-morrow.

"Now, sing me one little song," said our visitor, "and I will go and get ready for the evening."

Miss Elmore, with that cheerful promptness with which she does every thing, and which adds a charm to her kindness, opened a cabinet piano-forte, and sang, in low, sweet tones, Mrs. Hemans' little song—

> " Come to the sunset tree ;
> The day is past and gone,
> The woodman's axe lies free,
> And the reaper's work is done."

The thoughts of one, and the hopes of the other, I could feel, were in the home of which she had been speaking, and which I, before many days, am hoping to see. When the last tremulous note sank into the repose of silence, I saw that her long lashes were wet, and the tears were running unchecked down the other's furrowed cheeks. I will not swear that my own were dry. He rose, grasped her hand, and as she bent toward him, he pressed his lips to her forehead, and with a fervent "God bless you!" left us.

"The dear old man!" said Miss Elmore, as she came and sat at the window beside me. "For twenty years he has worked and hoped for some kind of social reorganization. He was a sanguine disciple of Fourier, and believed that all we required was the power of wealth to make harmony out of discord. He saw a hundred poor, meagre, and, of course, abortive efforts; but he hoped and believed through all. Now, what he has so long wished has come, and though not in his fashion, he is happy in the fact of success, and in the hope of spending his last years in the personal enjoyment of something approaching a harmonic life."

"And then, so soon to die!" I said, sadly; for I thought how little time he had, after a long life of toil and disappointment, to enjoy this happiness.

"Not so soon, perhaps. Our friend is sixty, with a vigorous constitution, and living a pure life, as one can live here, where the very air is loaded with impurity. If he will come to us, we will give him twenty years of calm, restful life. And when, in the wise and voluntary separation of the spirit, in the death of age, and the birth to a higher life, we shall lay his form away, and cover it with flowers, his spirit will be with us still, in a more intimate communion.

"Please don't wander off again. I would like your company this evening;" she continued; changing her manner to its usual play-fulness; and I took this as a signal to leave her. As I passed the office, a gentleman, and two ladies; brother and sisters, apparently, inquired for her, and were shown to her room. I went down into the reading-room, and read the newspapers till tea time.

Just at twilight, we walked out on Vine street, and up toward the center of the city. We entered a large, square building, ascended two flights of stairs, and found our excellent old friend waiting to show us into a neat hall, capable of seating two hundred people. It was nearly filled, with an audience of old and young, but mostly of those not yet past the meridian of life; intellectual, tasteful, aspiring and hopeful. The sexes were about equally divided.

At the end of the hall was a raised platform, with a desk and chairs for speakers. Behind, on a higher elevation, and extending across, was the choir of singers, with a melodeon for accompaniment. Over this platform, was painted on the wall, what I took to be a symbol of this society. It was a golden crescent, on a ground of blue, in which was a triangle composed of three golden stars. Around them were budding branches—symbols of growth. Over them was a scroll, on which was inscribed with golden letters on a white ground, the words, "FREEDOM, FRATERNITY, CHASTITY."

As we walked through the room, a murmur ran over it, and every eye was turned to Miss Elmore. Our friend conducted her to the raised platform, which she ascended; she looked around with a happy smile of recognition, bowed graciously, and took her seat. I was shown to a vacant one in the corner, where I could see all.

Our friend, who seemed the presiding officer, now rose, placed upon his breast a scarf of blue, embroidered with golden stars, and said, "*In the name of our Sacred Orders, I open this meeting for Harmony, Growth, and Aspiration to the True Life.*"

I took my note-book, that I might lose nothing. There was a small choir of four male and two female voices, besides the leader, who accompanied—a musical group of seven. The leader took his seat at the instrument, played a delicate prelude; and the choir sang a quartette, doubling the tenor and bass, with a perfection of time, harmony, and style, I have seldom heard equaled. It had the true effect of music, harmonizing the whole audience to one common feeling. The outer world was lost to us. The president then said : " Are there any candidates present for the Order of Growth?" A young man, of nearly my own age, and his two sisters, came forward. The youngest did not seem more than twelve years old. They stood before the stand.

"Do you come in freedom?" was asked of them. They answered, " We are free."

" Do you accept, and will you endeavor to order your lives by, the principles of equity, progress and harmony, that have been unfolded to you ? "

" We accept, and will endeavor."

" May all good spirits guard, and guide, and strengthen you in the Order of Growth, with whose symbol I now invest you;" saying which, he presented to each a symbol of the order, and continued:

" My children ! be faithful to the trust that is now given you, and the work in which you have engaged. Cultivate all your faculties ; improve all your gifts ; let the vigor of your lives flow out in all uses, that none stagnate or waste. Develope your whole beings in harmony ; aspire to all purity of thought and life, obey the monitions of your guardian spirits, and so prepare for the True Life on the Earth, and the transcendant Harmonies of the supernal Heavens. May all good angels bless you."

As they bowed reverently, the choir, which, with the audience, had risen during this most impressive ceremony, sung a song of welcome, which was a rhythmical rendering of the charge just given.

The little group took their seats together, with a glow of happiness, and a moment after, Miss Elmore rose, and stood before us.

Not when she came to me first, a forgiving angel ; not when she stood on Table Rock ; at no time had she seemed so beautiful as now. There was a flush on her pure cheek ; a light in her eye ; a divine radiance all around her; yet her manner was calm, and full of dignity and sweetness; and her voice low, rich, and without a tremor. I could not help looking at her. I forgot myself, and lost some sentences, and no transcript of words will give you any idea of.

the charm of her manner; but I must send you what I can of her address, though I know well that it is like a pressed flower; its beauty half preserved, and all its freshness and fragrance wanting.

"*Dear Friends!*" she began, after looking round on all, with a loving regard, "I am very happy to meet so many of my human brothers and sisters, who, amid this Babel of a discordant and oppressive civilization, can respect their interior attractions toward a purer, freer, and nobler life than civilization affords.

"Long and earnestly, through all the ages of our progress, humanity has aspired toward the true life of the Future, that now dawns upon us. Failing to find it here; growing faithless of its possibility on earth, the good have looked for harmony and happiness only in the life of the Heavens, and while they have daily prayed, 'Thy kingdom come, thy will be done, on Earth as it is in Heaven;' they have either prayed without faith, or looked forward to some mystical, and illy conceived millennium.

"The kingdom of Heaven is its life of Freedom, Harmony and Happiness; and that Life we can enter upon here, whenever we can place ourselves in its conditions. The Earth, our home, is adapted to the exercise and satisfaction of all the faculties we now possess, and therefore to the enjoyment of all the happiness of which we are now capable.

"I speak, dear friends, no longer as a theorist in Social Science; no longer do I reason of possibilities, and assure you that the attractions of the Human Soul are in proportion to its destinies, as the axiom which proves a True Life and a True Society practicable. I have a happier duty to perform : to tell you that the problem is solved ; that our millennium is begun ; that there exists, even now, not only the germ, but the well grown, vigorous plant, of a healthy, social life.

"I no longer say to you that such a life is possible for us; I say that it now exists for us, and opens its loving arms to receive those who are ready to enjoy its blessings ; and to enfold, in the bosom of plenty and peace, all who can come out of the discordances of civilization.

"The Life of Harmony, which has come down to us from the Heavens, is like a tender plant, to be cherished with care; and great secrecy has been deemed needful to guard its earlier unfoldings. But I am the witness and the proof that such a society exists; and though I am not ready, even here, to proclaim its locality, or to subject it to the risk of an incursion of crude and undeveloped persons, who might bring discord into its harmonies; I can, and do tell you, that all who advance truly, in the orders of harmony, will realize all that they can hope, and more than they can now conceive of in the life of our society.

"It is a home of freedom. The limbs and organs of your body are not more free in all their functions, than are the members of our society. There is no government, but the self-government of developed and harmonized faculties. As in the heavens, attraction is our only law. Each one finds his place, and work, and enjoyment, in obedience to his spontaneous desires; for health is the law, and disease the rare exception. It is a freedom of which you can hardly conceive; but we have found it the first and most absolute condition of harmony, and every attempt to impose the life or thought of one, as an authority to control another, has produced a discordant jar, which we hastened to remedy. We have found, as we were taught, that there is no truth but in freedom; and that freedom is not only consistent with, but an absolute condition of order.

"Our home is a home of plenty. The earth seems blessed with an abounding fertility. Our granaries are full. Our trees and vines are loaded with fruitage. Our active, spontaneous, irrepressible industry, has accumulated all the necessaries of life, and many of the luxuries of art. Our surplus has a convenient market, and we readily exchange all we do not care to use.

"It is a home of love. In the exercise and outflowing of all faculties, attractions and ambitions, we still find that the central life is the life of the heart. Our love is as free as our thoughts and lives. Raised above the plane of sensual excess; our energies flowing out in industry and art; in the daily intercouse of life, giving from all faculties to all faculties;" our purified, ennobled,

6

and emancipated loves, become to us only sources of good. These relations are thus made sacred; and not, as over the earth, sources of disease, evils, and sufferings innumerable. Our children are the pure and beautiful offspring of wisdom and love; never the deformed, diseased, discordant progeny of ignorance and disgust. We are happy in our loves, and very happy in the children that bless them, and who promise to bless the world by being born and nurtured in the harmony of a true life.

"I bring you a cheerful greeting from the heart life of this home; and I tender its welcome to all of you who may become, in all respects, worthy to become members of our society. But we must be patient of growth. You would not wish to mar our harmony, by coming before you were ready. It is better, for the time, that we be assured, beyond all doubt, that each one who comes to us is in every way worthy to become a partaker of our life. Whatever is not of us, must be cast out. We can not assimilate crude and hurtful materials. A selfish, jealous, discordant civilizee would be to us like a mote in the eye, or a sliver in the hand. He would be like an unskilled player, or an untuned instrument in an orchestra.

"Dear friends, if you would be worthy of all the freedom and happiness of a harmonic life, purify and harmonize your own beings, attune your lives to our harmony, which is but the harmony of your own true natures. It is a spiritual unfolding of the inner life of man, now comprehended, now possible, now realized by a few, and ready soon to be extended to all who can partake of this life of the heavens."

So far, I have taken down what was said and done; but at this point, her eye sought me, and by a glance I understood, placed the seal of secrecy on what followed. It related to certain movements of the general organization, of one of whose branches I was a guest, and I can no more divulge what I understood to be confidential, than I could visit a family and betray its secrets.

At the close, when Miss Elmore had taken a most affectionate and affecting leave of them, in words that filled all eyes with tears, in which there was more of hope and joy than sorrow, she went to the instrument and sang a song worthy of the home of which she had told us. The choir then sang its parting song of benediction; and in a moment she was surrounded by a group of those who pressed to touch her hand, and to express some hope of a future, to which she was the guiding star.

We went home in the fair moonlight. We then went to her room, when she brought a curious little decanter and glasses, and said:—

"My father, I said you must taste our vintage. It bears the aroma of the home to which I hope soon to welcome you. You must bring along those beautiful and loving hearts that are forming and clustering here, and all come together as soon as they are ready. I see that you can not be spared here yet. But the time will come and your reward is sure."

We drank from the delicate glasses to that hope.

"Here," she said, handing him the little decanter and our fairy glass, "keep these in our remembrance; and now to our business."

She held out her hand to me; it was my signal of good night. I took it, and pressed it reverently to my lips and heart. She looked at me with an earnest, inquiring look, as if she would read my soul, but said not a word.

And I came to my room and have written. And now, dear one, the morrow takes me further on this journey. Day and night we shall move on down the current of these great rivers. But I shall write you every day, and give you faithfully, oh! most faithfully, the life that comes to me.

May the angels guard you from all pain and sorrow, and keep your love pure as mine.

V.

THE OHIO AND THE MISSISSIPPI.

"Once more upon the waters," dearest Clara. In some former phase of my existence, I must have been a water fowl. Now we are "Going down the river—the O-h-i-o." I surrender myself to all the idleness of this week's voyage, very happily; but let me proceed with my orderly narration.

I wrote late last night, but still I did not sleep. I thought and lived over the day and evening. The sweet voice still sounded in my ears; the life portrayed to us, excited my imagination, and the world of civilization seemed such a sordid, miserable sham. I needed no Thackaray to draw it. After a time I fell asleep and dreamed that we—you and I—were the inmates of this home; but it seemed far away in cloudland, and I looked down on the groaning earth with a great pity.

We made a late breakfast. Miss Elmore was calm, and a little pale. I think she longs for her home, and for the society of those she loves. I have a very humiliating consciousness that my company is but dull to her. But she was kind, delicate, and almost tender, in her voice and manner. I offered my services toward any preparation for our journey; but she found nothing for me to do.

"We can take our choice of boats," she said, pointing to the list of those up for New Orleans. "The river is high, and one of those will suit us as well as a packet—so we shall not need to change at Louisville."

Before breakfast was over, our good friend made his appearance, very glad to see us, and bringing intelligence of a fine boat, nearly loaded, going in the afternoon, and so sure to suit us, that he had engaged two state-rooms.

63

So, after breakfast, we went down to the public landing, and there found the "Effie Afton," with steam up, colors flying, freight coming on board merrily, and every appearance of a speedy departure.

"You will allow me to arrange for our passage," said Miss Elmore. Two minutes after, I think the captain would have placed his boat and himself at her disposal. I don't see but a fresh water sailor is as gallant as a salt. Captain Hardstein is as pleasant as a pet Walrus. Very confidentially, and as a special favor, he informed us that though the bills said twelve o'clock, five would answer every purpose.

Miss Elmore had her own work to do; but I am fit for nothing, after a passage is engaged, and before the hour of starting. It is only to wear away the intermediate time. So I lounged in a reading room, and bookstores, and a meager picture gallery, and a horrible museum. I sauntered by the river and the canal. I went into lager bier gardens, and looked at great manufactories. At last came dinner time, and I went joyfully to meet the happiness of our last dinner here. All the morning, in my lonely saunterings, I compared the life I saw, with the beautiful life that may be; and the women I saw with this woman, who, at least, is no dream, but a living reality.

"You have been a truant," she said, as she held out a frank hand to welcome me, when I entered the drawing-room. "Are you enamored of Cincinnati, that you have deprived me of your company, all this morning?"

"I do not forget," I said, with a humility, which had no pretence in it, "how little I can be to you, and how kind you have been to give me so much of your society."

"Well, have I any other? Besides, I have much hope of you. I have been at work this morning; but we will make much of the coming days; for it will not be long now before I shall have rivals, who will dispute my claim to you. You are to prepare yourself, like a gallant knight, to defend your fortress."

This seemed absurd enough, but she appeared serious. I see that there is one; but I have no expectation of finding other women like this.

We dined, and at five o'clock shook hands with our Cincinnati friend on the steamboat; then backed out into the stream, came round handsomely, and pointed our bows toward the setting sun.

And here we are on the river, and here I begin the record of this voyage—of the length and duration of which I am in a state of blessed uncertainty—but what matter, so it be blessed?

I began my letter last evening, sitting on the guards or balcony outside my state-room, and writing by the red light of a western sun-set, while we glided past the panorama of the Indiana shore. As the light faded, Miss Elmore came and joined me. I put up my writing, as she sat at my side, and began to tune a small, sweet-toned guitar. Soon her fingers swept over it, and brought out the harmonies I love. She seemed to muse and meditate in music, which became the expression of every thought, emotion, and memory Soon she began, in a low voice, to sing old familiar tunes—the airs of her childhood and ours. It was very pleasant to hear the old songs we have so often sung together; and I ventured to join in them. And so we glided along.

We were alone, but not unobserved. Forward, there was a group of the colored waiters, listening in silence and with great enjoyment; nearer were passengers, but all at a respectful distance. There was not an ill-mannered remark, nor the least intrusion. It was no repulsion, or haughtiness of manner that kept them thus apart from our little communion; but a perception of that sweet dignity and purity, which commands universal respect and admiration. I could see it in the look and manner of every one. As the night closed round us, she laid the instrument down; our friendly visitors retired, and we sat conversing.

"We are now fairly embarked on our voyage," said she. "You are the first person, not initiated into our society and principles, who has been invited to visit us. But we grow strong, and secure in our strength. You are to be trusted personally; and the time approaches when the world will be ready to reap the benefit of our work. You will see things which will seem very strange to you; but if you can lay aside the prejudices of education and custom, I think they will not seem false or unnatural."

"I can not feel that I am so prejudiced, as to think our society perfect;" I replied, "or to condemn another which secures in a greater degree the true objects of society; the improvement or happiness of all who compose it."

"Society perfect!" she said, with a voice of deep scorn, softened by pity. "Perfect! This society that produces and perpetuates ignorance, poverty, disease, sensuality, bigotry, and all despotisms and slaveries? A society where the rich plunder the poor; where the learned oppress the ignorant; where disease, wickedness, and crime are the support of three great learned professions; where birth is a curse, and life a burthen; where nine-tenths die premature deaths of exhaustion, and the diseases of evil habits; where body, mind, and heart are alike enslaved, and where there is not the first condition of happiness in a true freedom? I shall show you something better than this."

"You speak much of freedom, as a condition of happiness. Do you think freedom compatible with civilization?"

"Every human condition has its own laws. The selfishness of civilization requires the isolate household, marriage, the slavery or ownership of woman, jealousy or the property feeling, applied to her as well as every thing else, and so on. If you will think it over, you will find all social moralities belonging to this civilized condition."

"And does a different state bring different ideas of morality?"

"That is not a very wise question. Are not all social morals conventional, and related to the system which they guard? For example, it is very moral and highly respectable, in the polite Empire of China, to have twelve wives; in Turkey, four; Solomon is nowhere condemned for his family establishment, which the morality of the age sanctioned, but for worshipping strange gods. England has one code of morals and respectability; Italy another. In France, maidens are recluse, and married women free; here liberty belongs to the unappropriated."

"But still, there must be an absolute right, above all these customs and conventionalisms!"

"Ah! that is what you have to find, and what we have found. Now think out for yourself, what this absolute right is; and then

you will see how near we have come to its realization. Good night,
and happy dreams. Will you help me to see the sun rise?"

With a kind pressure of the hand she left me, and retired to her
state-room. I went forward to the bow of the boat and enjoyed the
freshness of the evening breeze, and the music of the gurgling
waters that foamed around our prow. Soon I saw a cloud of smoke
below; a line of glaring red lights; then two tall chimneys, and
soon an upward bound steamer, illuminated like a floating palace,
rushed roaring past us. And I retired to my berth, to think and
dream.

On a boat, the bustle of the day begins early. A bell is rung to
waken all drowsy passengers. But I did not wait for the bell. I
heard the dash of water in the state-room next mine, and sprang
from a wide and comfortable berth, enclosed with musquito nets,
to perform my own ablutions. I found Miss Elmore fresh as the
rosy morning, on the hurricane deck. We were gliding through a
fine country on both sides of the river—Indiana and Kentucky—and
in the distance were the spires of Louisville, where we arrived just
after breakfast.

A traveler should give some account of manners and customs.
Those of a western steamboat are unique.

The great cabin of our boat, (and all these boats are much alike)
is, perhaps, two hundred feet long. The first thirty feet from the
forward entrance is liberty hall. Here is the clerk's office, the bar
or saloon, as they call it, and the barber's shop. Each is a state-
room; and drinking and shaving are both done in the space forward.
Here the floor is bare, or covered with coarse matting, and spittoons
are plentiful. Then begins a carpet, and the extension tables of the
great cabin, which are closed up in several divisions, after every
meal, and where parties sit playing the favorite games of the West,
euchre or poker. The last thirty feet is the ladies saloon, furnished
more pompously than the rest; but not separated until 10 o'clock
at night, when folding doors close up this sanctum sanctorum.

When the first breakfast bell rings, the captain or clerk, generally
the latter, takes his place at the head of the table, which is, of course,
its after extremity. On all water-craft, the head is the tail, and

precedence is to come last. All the ladies, and gentlemen attending
ladies, seat themselves near the head of the table, but the whole
double line of forlorn male bipeds remains standing, until every
lady is seated; and if any one can not get her curls arranged or her
collar pinned in season, they all wait with the most wonderful
patience and gravity.

When the master of ceremonies is satisfied that every feminine is
in her seat, he gives the signal for the second bell; and the un-
privileged male passengers sit down and fall to without further
ceremony.

We stopped at Louisville two hours to discharge and receive
freight, and Miss Elmore accompanied me on a tour of observation,
but we saw little peculiar or worthy of notice. A northerner looks
for some sign of slavery, but I could not see that there were any
more negroes than in New York, or that they differed materially in
their condition.

I asked Miss Elmore about it. "There are great hardships
incident to slavery," she said, "but travelers can see but little of
them. Slaves are sold, rather oftener than our free girls at the
north. I am not sure that they find harder masters, or that it is
more difficult to get away. Year by year, as many wives are killed
by their husbands in New York city, as negroes by their masters in
the whole south. Children are whipped, abused and starved, by
bad parents at the north, as negroes are by bad masters at the
South. Every Legree here, can be matched by some sensual,
drunken husband and father there. A good man is a good husband,
parent, or master. A bad man finds the means in either place to
wreak his badness on some one under his control."

"But the law affords relief in one case, which it does not in the
other," I said.

"Are you quite sure of that? In how many cases does the law
interfere to protect wife, or child, or apprentice from the cruelty of
a brutal husband, father or master? There is law and custom,
public opinion and humanity, here as there. There is but little
difference. When men and women are far enough advanced to own
themselves, they will not be owned. When they can govern them,

7

selves, they will not be governed. In New Orleans the relation of
master and slave is usually very mild. I know a bookseller, whose
smartest clerk is a mulatto slave; and he wears diamond shirt
studs. I know a large cotton house, whose head clerk is the
property of the firm; and I have seldom seen a more competent or
gentlemanly man of business. He lives in a neat cottage, and has
a wife and family. *All* slaveries are wrong, and an evil, but it does
not appear that all wrongs and evils are concentrated in one. I,
who believe in universal freedom, rate them all alike, differing only
in degrees of misery, as circumstances make them differ."

We returned to our steamer, now ready to start. The abundant
rains had swollen the river, and our captain had decided to save his
toll by "running the *chute*," instead of going through the canal and
locks, which in the three miles between Louisville and Portland, raise
or lower the boats a hundred feet. There was a mile of swift, and,
in places, foaming rapids; but our big pilot took the center of
the current, and with a full head of steam, the smart "Effie" went
over flying. It was grand. We were forward on the upper deck,
and had the full enjoyment of it. It was good railroad speed, but
that on a steamer seems very different. The falls of the Ohio are
not much as a cataract, but very good boating, when there is water
enough—short and sweet, and soon over.

After this little excitement, I turned my thoughts homeward, and
have written thus far on a letter which I will send when it is full.
I sit and write, and think of you and home, so far in the northeast,
and then of the unknown home which I long and yet almost fear to
see and know. This fear comes of a selfishness, I find, in my heart.
I can see your right to the freedom that is said to reign in this
home; but I cannot think of you as enjoying its possible results.
You are *mine*. But I also find myself growing selfish in my friendship for Miss Elmore. I am disturbed at the idea of seeing her
loving and being beloved. I *see* that this is absurd, and wrong, and
hateful. I *see* that she and you, and every one should be free from
every bond on your spirits—free to love all that is lovely to you;
and I *know* that I would not have the love that was owned as

property; and yet I cannot get rid of the feeling which men have for whatever they claim as their own.

During the long, sunny day, the passengers either clustered around the card tables in the cabin, or on the shady side on the guards, in groups. They fell into conversations on various subjects—they discussed the Maine Law, Kansas, the Eastern War, Knownothing-ism, Spiritualism, and all the exciting questions of the day. Free Love and Woman's Rights included. A country Magistrate gave his opinions as from the bench of justice; an itinerant lecturer on various reforms was fanatical on all, and some gentlemanly, but hot-blooded young southerners felt bound to flash fire at every slur on the peculiar institution.

It was as good as a play. A pale methodist parson, of the Church South, defended slavery and denounced rum; preached piety and put down the "isms," with a warmth that was very amusing. He had so many sides to combat—repelling now the assault of an abolitionist, now of an infidel; and whipping his little testament out of his side pocket to quote chapter and verse on every subject. When it came to a dispute on any question of fact, he offered to bet a Bible!

But he seems a very innocent man, and one we should call rather green, in spite of his white neckcloth. A lovely little girl, five years old, the daughter of a radical passenger, bound for Minnesota, gets into his lap, and talks with him. She was curious to know what book he was reading. He told her it was the Holy Bible.

"Oh!" she cried, "I have got a *leetle bit* of a one at home, and it is full of the *silliest* stories!" Here her mother interfered, and put a stop to her heresies.

Once, as they were gathered near our state-room, the discussion grew warm on the "isms of the day," as the preacher termed them.

"There's the Woman's Rights question," said he, "that a set of infidel and abolitionist women are agitating. Its all against the Bible. Read what St. Paul says. He preached the true doctrine. He says, 'wives obey your husbands,' and he would'nt allow a woman to teach." And out came the little testament. "Now, who are the women that are lecturing about Woman's Rights? Why, they are a set of infidels. Mary Wollstonecraft, that wrote the first book on Woman's Rights, was an infidel, and opposed to marriage. Fanny Wright was an infidel and an Owenite. Mrs. Rose is a rank infidel and makes speeches at the Tom Paine Festivals in New York. Lucy Stone is'nt much better; for she got married under protest. I tell you they are all infidels, free-love folks, abolitionists, and spiritualists."

Miss Elmore, who was standing near me, looked round at me with a benevolent smile, which the preacher took for an approval of his sentiments.

"That's so, is'nt it, marm?" said he.

"Do you wish to know what I think about these matters?" she asked, quietly.

"Yes, I should, for you seem to be a sensible woman, and when I meet a sensible woman, I always like to get her judgment."

"Then you differ a little from St. Paul, I think, for he did'nt allow women to teach."

A roar of laughter at the minister's expense showed the sympathies of the audience.

"Yes, marm; but giving your opinion will not be the kind of authoritative teaching, which the apostle intended."

"Perhaps so; but if my opinion should happen to carry conviction with it, how would it be?"

"I think it would be very well, marm, if it was the right kind of an opinion."

"But St. Paul says nothing about a woman teaching truth or falsehood—he says she must not teach."

And here was another laugh, at the preacher or the apostle, I could'nt tell which.

"Now," she continued, "when you will allow that a woman's opinion may be as good as a man's, and that she has as good a right to its expression, I will give you mine."

This was a poser, which divinity could'nt get over; and amid the laughter of the delighted audience, he was compelled to withdraw his appeal.

When we were alone, I asked Miss Elmore why she refrained from the expression of her sentiments on these subjects.

"The good I could have done," she said, "would not have compensated for the inconvenience, and it would have been bad economy. This poor little parson would not have been benefited; the rest are working their way out to the light very well, as it is. My views would not satisfy the partisans of any faith, and their expression might make our voyage unpleasant. What I did was as well."

"But you will not refuse to tell *me* your thought on these subjects," said I.

"Oh, no. You are my pupil; and as you believe in the divine mission and right of women to teach the most interior truths, I shall not refuse you. If men originate principles, women give them form and vitality. The law of sex applies to the intellectual and moral world, as well as the physical.

"Abolition is the protest against an evil, seen more clearly, because distant. Men labor to abolish negro slavery and neglect their own, for the same reason that they send missionaries to convert the heathen, and neglect the pagans of their own parishes.

"The Maine Law is a futile effort of a democratic majority to usurp and exercise the powers of a benevolent despot, and force people to do right against their inclinations. The agitation will do no harm in the end; for though it may be established that the right to drink whisky is guaranteed by the constitution of the state, it will be found to disagree with that of the individual. The struggle tends also to freedom; for in defending the individual right to do wrong, men may stumble also on the idea of a right to do right."

"But can there be a right to do a wrong?"

"Not in the abstract and ultimate; but there is the right of individual conscience, and every one must be left free to do what he *thinks* right, so long as he does not interfere with the same right in another. This freedom is the condition of experience and knowledge. As men come to the understanding of principles, they can seize upon the absolute right."

"The absolute—that always confuses me. In human actions every thing seems relative. The right of to-day becomes the wrong of to-morrow. What is right to do under certain conditions, is very wrong under others."

"That all falls under the law of relations, which is as infallible as mathematics. All principles are absolute, immutable, eternal. Proportions, relations, and adaptations have their laws. A wise expediency is the absolute right. We carry out absolute principles, by truly measuring relations. In building, the level, the plumb line, the measure and square, never vary; but we apply them to produce all convenient forms and relations. In our conduct, we have one object—happiness; the means are the adaptation of our faculties and passions, to the objects of their satisfaction within our reach. You will think this all over, and it will come clearly to you. Work it out like a problem in geometry. You will find that all sciences are exact sciences when you know them. Rather, you will find that there is only one science, and when you get to the central truth, you can see clearly all the circumference."

Thus, dear Clara, does this woman talk with me. Thus does she instruct me; and yet there is not the least pedantry or pretension in her manner. It is so calm, gentle and loveful; her eyes beam in mine with a light so soft and clear; her smile is so sweet; her tones and modulations so musical, that I am charmed, and yet there seems no possibility of my having for her a sentimental, much less a sensual, passion. I try to analyze my feelings. I try to tell you the actual truth; but I think that I do better in giving you these details, and allowing you to form your own opinion. Whatever my present feeling, or future relations to her, I know that I have never loved you more dearly than now; and I never seemed to myself to be so worthy of your love.

I rose early this morning, waked by the rushing steam. We had made a landing at Shawneetown, a lively little river port in south-eastern Illinois. We were to stop some hours, and the engineer blew off steam, and damped his furnaces. I will go on with our voyage.

Last evening a group of passengers gathered round the table in the ladies's cabin, which, though a part of the long open saloon, and free to every one, so far as I can see by any printed regulation, is held sacred to the lady passengers, and their friends, and is scarcely ever intruded upon by any other. The more quiet and studious men occupy the tables nearest; the card players are further forward, and those who drink toddies and tell stories are at the forward extremity. If the Captain went through the boat every evening and pointed out each one's place, they would not be better arranged.

We were sitting, reading and conversing on general trifles; a sweet pretty Irish woman was exulting in the hope of meeting her soldier husband in St. Louis; a Kentucky lawyer was carrying on a desperate flirtation with the bar-keeper's wife, a plump Bowery beauty with a turn-up nose; I was making studies of the party, and comparing them with Miss Elmore, who held in her hand a volume of Tennyson, when I heard angry exclamations from the other end of the boat. There were oaths, a movement, and then a sharp pistol shot. I started to my feet, and involuntarily looked round to where Miss Elmore was sitting. She was gone—she was half way up the cabin. I followed her as quickly as possible. The passengers were many of them pale; some were escaping through the state rooms; others were gathering about two men who were clinched in what seemed a deadly encounter. One was armed with a bowie-knife and the other with a revolver. One shot had been fired, when they closed, but in such a way that neither could use his weapon. But the man with the revolver, a powerful man, threw off his assailant with the bowie-knife, and raised his pistol with a quick but deliberate aim, when Miss Elmore glided between them, raised his hand so as to make the shot harmless, and at the same time holding up her other hand, awed back the man with the knife, who was preparing to spring upon his antagonist. The Captain was just in time, as he rushed into the cabin, to see this *tableau*. But there was no necessity for his interference; and Miss Elmore, by a look or sign, checked his advance.

" *Gentlemen!* " she said, with a very deliberate emphasis—"You surely forget that you are in the presence of timid women ! "

"There is one here, brave enough," said the pistol man, "and I honor courage any where."

"Then you should honor this gentleman," said she, pointing to his opponent, who had put up his knife; "for he has no lack of it. You are both brave, strong men; and you know what belongs to gentlemen, for you can respect a woman. Now," said she, with a smile, "I do not find gentlemen so plentiful, as to allow them to be wasted. If there is any wrong between you, you know how to right it. A brave man can atone for a fault as well as avenge an insult, and, under the circumstances, and considering the scarcity of men who are honorable enough to do both, I think you had better do the handsome thing."

"Madam!" said he with the pistol, "I will do any thing under God's heavens you wish me to. I may have been mistaken about the play, and wrong; but I can't take the lie from any body."

"No body should give the lie," said she, looking at the other, with her clear, calm look, "where a mistake is possible."

"I was hasty, Madam, and I apologize," said he, with a quick frankness.

"Enough said," replied the other, offering his hand. "I was likely as not wrong about the play. It's no consequence any how, but as I had my shot, I'll stand treat."

"And you will play no more to-night? said the beautiful peace maker.

"Not a deal; if you will take a glass of champagne with us."

The glass was brought. She raised it, and said, "gentlemen, you always mean well, but you sometimes forget yourselves. I wish you better memories!"

The toast was drunk, and applauded. Miss Elmore had just tasted her glass, and now returned with me to the ladies' cabin.

The fainting lady had so far recovered as to be in a comfortable fit of hysterics; and the passengers who had escaped from the cabin came back in time to get a glass of the peace-offering.

"*Are* those men gentlemen?" I asked Miss Elmore, when I got the opportunity."

"Yes and no."

" Does the question admit of both answers ? "

" Almost every one does. It depends on what you understand by the term gentleman. These men are brave, frank, generous, sensitive, and honorable, as they understand honor."

" But they seem to me to be two professional gamblers."

" So they are ; but why not gentlemen, as much as lawyers who help fraud and oppression for a fee ; preachers who teach doctrines they do not believe, for a salary ; speculators who gamble in stocks and staples ; financiers who loan capital to usurers and swindlers, and share their plunder ; soldiers who make a business of slaughter and kill according to orders ? Why may not a gambler, who stakes his living on either chance or skill, be as good a gentleman as these ? "

" But why call any of them gentlemen ? "

" A man may have the elements of a gentlemanly character, and not be strong enough to control his circumstances. So we must be charitable, and call those gentlemen who might and would be, if they had the opportunity."

The scenery of the Lower Ohio has elements of beauty. The foliage is of great richness ; the grass of a deep vivid green ; but I miss every where the noble back ground of mountains, lifting their blue summits against the sky. But the sun-sets are glorious. At times the bluffs on the river side are high and picturesque. The boats we meet and pass, give animation to the voyage. The flat boats loaded with coal, or lumber, or corn, which glide down with the current, have their interest. Sometimes you see a corn sheller at work—sometimes a fiddle is playing. Still it is all an idle, monotonous life enough. I do'nt know what we should do without our discussions, which seem to be a school of popular education.

The parson still attacks the " isms of the day," but upholds his own with great fervor. He is a great advocate of total abstinence.

" But how about that advice of your friend Paul, to " take a little wine for the stomach's sake ? " asked an objector.

"Medicinally; we allow it to be prescribed as a medicine," said the preacher.

"Oh! then Paul was a doctor," said a Hoosier; "I wonder where he got his diplomy?"

"He was an inspired man," said the preacher, "and knew what was right."

"Look here!" said a quiet, slow spoken man, with a twinkle in his eye; "St. Paul, we are told, cured a great many people of their diseases by praying for them, laying on of hands, and even by their having handkerchiefs and aprons brought to them, that he had touched. Now, I should like to inquire why he did'nt cure Timothy's dyspepsia, and other infirmities, when he liked him so well, instead of ordering him to take his bitters, and setting such a bad example to all posterity?"

The preacher was entirely unprepared for this question; and as he stammered and hesitated, the free thinking crowd did not restrain their triumph at his discomfiture.

So we glide along. I walk on the upper deck; or stand on the bows; and I think of you all the hours, and of the fast increasing distance that separates us; then I think it is the same sun that shines for us both; the same bright stars, the same blue sky that bends over us, and the same Providence that enfolds us.

————

We made Cairo, the great city of some dim future, at the junction of the Ohio and Mississippi, late in the night. I looked out but could see little in the misty moon-light. Our St. Louis and up river passengers went ashore here. The rosy little Irish woman, whom every body was in love with, came past my door, as I stood wrapped in my dressing gown, looking out upon the scene. She held out her hand to me.

"Good bye, you little darling, God bless you," said I, with more warmth than I should have used, had I ever expected to see her again.

Her reply was eloquent and characteristic. She said never a word, but as quick as a thought, or the impulse of a loving woman,

hold up her pretty lips to be kissed. And I kissed her as I would
a very nice fat baby; and she ran off without a word; but turned,
and waved her handkerchief to me and the rest, as she went up the
landing.

In the morning we were steaming down the great, turbid, mighty,
monotonous Mississippi, through which flow the currents of a thousand rivers to the distant sea. I can never tell you of its melancholy
grandeur.

You will look on the map and see its windings, and fancy us
steaming down—down those long reaches, going at times three
hundred miles to gain one. The great, impetuous river, filled with
the energy of all the thousand torrents, of which its life is made,
goes tearing along through interminable forests. In its windings,
it washes away the banks on one shore, uprooting great trees, and
filling its bed with snags and sawyers; while a vast sand bar is left
on the other side to be covered in time with the cane brake jungles,
made of those long, slender, jointed reeds, you see in New York
sold for fishing poles. The great fields of these are of a beautiful
light green; but the sad havoc of the river on its banks, is a melancholy ravage. And such sameness. For hours and days the
only change is in finding the perpendicular wall of undermined earth
and forest, now on the right hand, and then on the left, as the river
bends to the west or the east. If I go in the cabin, and stay for
hours, when I come back it is the same. The only change is that
the foliage indicates a more southern clime. The moss hangs pendant from the boughs of the cypress, and on the shore I see the palm,
whose leaves supply us with fans and hats.

I have promised to write no particulars of time or distance below
Cairo. I can not, therefore, give the days; not that I do not trust
you, but for fear of accidents.

We pass the hours in reading poetry, aloud; in music, when we
feel musical; and in long conversations, of which I can give but a
meager record. But I must finish one, of which I have given a
part. It was renewed at intervals, for my fellow voyager is sparing
of conversation, and leaves me much time for reflection. Every day
I see how wisely and beautifully she has taught me.

"You began," said I, "to speak of these 'isms,' our clerical friend is so fond of denouncing. Will you tell me further about them?"

"I will tell you all you can hear," she said. "He spoke bitterly of this question of Woman's Rights, and its advocates. Mary Wollstonecraft, the wife of Godwin, and the mother of Mrs. Shelley, was a beautiful and heroic spirit, not very wise. She loved much and suffered much; and had an instinct for freedom and a true life. Few more lovely and feminine spirits have ever lived. She rejected the popular theology, as did most intellectual persons of her time. But she also repudiated marriage, and the slavery of women. When Thomas Paine wrote his Rights of Man, she applied the same principles to a vindication of the Rights of Woman.

"Frances Wright had a more manly spirit. She was a woman of heroism and benevolence; a better logician, I think, but less instinctive, and affectionate.

"The estimable ladies who attend Woman's Rights conventions are doing their work of agitation, from various motives. The love of distinction, the hope of success, the consciousness of power, and the want of a sphere for its exercise, have their share as motives. But they all shrink from the central wrong in the lot of woman—her being owned and appropriated in marriage."

"And here," said I, "you come to the Free Love doctrine, I have seen so much discussion about."

"Any question of freedom will bear discussion. So long as men live in the isolate dwellings, and discordant selfishness, of the society of civilization—each robber in his den—woman must be appropriated, and owned; and custom and law must guard this ownership, as slave laws guard the ownership of slaves. But in a true society, woman can be free, and of course love may be as free as thought, or belief."

"There is one 'ism' more—Spiritualism; I wish to know more of that," said I, at our next conversation.

"What do you know already?" she asked, with a fine lighting up of interest in her expression.

"Very little, that is satisfactory. I have read of the phenomena, and went two or three times to hear the raps. The communications

seemed vague, and the phenomena of doubtful origin. I could not
see the use of it."

"Do you believe in the continuance of individual consciousness,
after the death of the body?"

"I hope it."

"Hope in the possible is a good basis of belief. Attractions are
proportional to destinies. The testimony of spiritual phenomena is
abundant. Immortality is as possible as life. I have as good evidence of the existence of spirit friends, and intercourse with them,
as I have of your existence, and of my conversation with you. It
would be just as hard to disprove one as the other. But you will
probably soon have better opportunities of testing this for yourself.
Our society lives in open and constant communion with a spiritual
society, with which it is in Harmony; and it is to the earth, what
that society is to the heavens. If you come into the life of our
Harmony, you will find spirit-friends, and spirit-loves in the
heavenly society. We will not argue about it or speak of it more,
now. We will wait and see what is for you."

———

On and on; running down those long, interminable, forest-lined
curves of the river, swept our good steamer, night and day. Sometimes we brushed over the branches of a tree, whose root was
anchored in the bed of the stream.

At last, one bright but very warm afternoon, I saw a little town
in the distance; and laying at the landing a beautiful little steamboat, with a single smoke-pipe. Miss Elmore was standing on the
upper deck, forward, by my side, looking through a pocket spy-
glass. She held out a white handkerchief, and let it flutter in the
wind. In a moment a broad white flag, with a golden star, made
of nine other stars, rose from the deck of the little boat; and at the
same moment there was a burst of blue smoke; and soon came
booming up the river the roar of a cannon.

The booming echoes had scarcely returned the sound, when there
burst upon the air a peal of triumphant music such as I never heard

before. It was like a bugle, but many times louder, coming with a power and sweetness of sound which enveloped me in extacy. It was like no earthly music, but seemed poured upon us from the clear blue sky, a torrent of melody. I looked round in surprise to my companion, and she, delighted at my astonishment, pointed where the fairy little boat was throwing off a jet of steam; and I saw now that it was the boat, herself, welcoming her expected passenger. Instead of the usual shrieking whistle, she was provided with a full harmonic chord of musical tones, so that she could give bugle signals to a great distance. The single tones were wonderful; but when the chords were given, it was like a tornado of harmony; grand, overpowering, indescribable. It was like musical thunder, or a harmonized Niagara. Not the " voice of many waters," but the voice of steam.

Miss Elmore looked up to the wheel-house and nodded at the pilot; and said to me, " come, my friend, our voyage here is ended."

I went to my state-room and hastily packed my things. We said good bye to our friends, and went on shore, and the Effie Afton plowed on her way.

I finish my letter at the little Post-office here. and know not how soon I can mail another. Good bye, my dear love. Love me and trust me.

VI.

DEAR CLARA.—Each day of absence falls with an added weight upon my heart, and almost every day has increased our distance. You are so far away! I cannot forget the convexity of the earth that rolls up between us, nor that, when I look at the sunset, its last light had faded from you more than an hour. Nor can I forget the long days that, even with the most rapid modes of transit, must elapse before this letter can reach you. But I will be patient, and trust you with the Providence that hath guided me to this home of our Future, as I now believe it to be.

I have much to tell you—so much, and so important, that I can only hope to tell you all I wish, by beginning where my last letter ended,—and continuing my narrative, as if I were writing a history.

The little Steamer "Fairy," you will remember, was fired up and ready, and gave us a musical welcome. I deposited my letter in the post office, which occupied a small corner of the bar-room of the tavern and grocery, and went on board. Miss Elmore had gone directly from the Effie, and was at home in the beautiful saloon, where I found her seated, with a boy, five years old, in her lap, and two young girls kneeling, one on each side of her.

She held out her hand to me, her face radiant with some great joy, and introduced me first to the boy Vincent, and then to the two girls, one a petite brunette Laura, the other a fair girl, of the medium height, with blue eyes and chestnut hair, named Eugenia.

"You will soon know these dear ones, who have come to welcome us," said she, "and now I must introduce myself. In the world of civilization, I am Miss Elmore, or whatever name is con-

87

venient. Here and in our home, I am called Melodia. The name
will sound strange at first; but you will soon grow accustomed to it."

"And this young gentleman, Master Vincent—is he the son of
the friend you told me of?" I asked.

A strange, bright smile came over her face, and was reflected by
the two younger ladies. Melolia simply nodded assent, but made
no further observation; while the handsome boy, who had been so
careful not to interrupt our conversation, now began a series of
ingenious questions respecting our travels and adventures, and
before they were half answered began to tell his own.

I went on deck to look at the gem of a boat. With no misplaced
finery, she is the perfection of every thing at once strong, light,
and graceful in steamboat architecture. There was exact order,
neatness, and polish every where; and every thing about her
showed how use can be joined to beauty. The pilot house is a
domed octagon lanthorn; her high chimney is as graceful as a
column; the arrangement of her little saloon and state rooms the
perfection of convenience and elegance; and her few ornaments of
carved shell and coral work, with paintings of water lilies and
other aquatic plants and animals. Below, a compact boiler furnished
steam to an engine worthy to propel such a boat. The freight was
carefully stored; every thing was in its place, and when the Fairy,
with her starry flag flying, rounded out upon the turbid Missi-sippi,
fired her parting gun, and waked the echoes miles away with her
triumphant melodies, I felt proud to step on such a craft.

But I must not forget her officers and crew. There were but
five, besides the young ladies in the cabin, and the boy Vincent,
who was every where, and equally interested in all departments.
As soon as we were well under way, steaming down the river. Miss
Elmore, or Melodia, as I must now learn to call her, came and
walked around the boat. I looked in vain for servant, chamber-
maid, or any common boatman. The five men on board were
dressed nearly alike, in light caps, blue jackets, and duck trowsers.
There was no captain or command. They seemed equally capable
of taking turns in the pilot house or engine room, so that only two
were on duty at a time, leaving the other three at liberty to rest,

or sleep, or amuse themselves. They changed at intervals of two hours; and the one who had been busy with the furnace and engine, was next walking on deck with one of the ladies, or playing the violin with a guitar accompaniment, in the saloon. We were ten in all, little Vincent included; and I had never seen any family where I felt so soon and so happily at home. Laura, with her sparkling black eyes, glossy hair, and piquant *n z retrousse*, told me all about their trip to New Orleans and their visit to the French Theatre; and then sung, I am sure, half the airs of the opera, while detailing the plot. The more sedate Eugenia, whose hair was all ringlets and wild flowers, which she had gathered where we came on board, and who might have stood for a Flora, if the goddess of flowers had ever taken passage on a steamer, asked me of New York, where she had once lived, and knew how to pity all who were condemned to live there, she said. Her frank, confiding, sisterly ways made me acquainted with her at once and always.

The leading spirit of the group of young men who united in the duties of navigating this boat, is Mr. Alfred. What surname he may have borne formerly, I know not but it is not mentioned here; and he may have chosen Alfred or accepted it, as more appropriate than the one given at his christening. I must introduce him, for I hope you may become better acquainted. When Melodia brought me to him, he looked from her eyes to mine, seemed to take me in at a glance, and held out his hand as if I had been his best friend, returned after a long absence. With them all I felt as if I had returned, not come. When I asked Melodia of this she said that to know her—to become acquainted with the spirit of her thought and life, made me also acquainted with all who lived the same life.

Alfred, a man of perhaps thirty years, strong, manly, vigorous, with a clear grey eye, and brown beard, is the impersonation of energy. He impressed me as a man who would infallibly accomplish whatever he undertook, and be able to command all men and means necessary for that purpose. I felt a great reliance on him; a trust that could not be shaken, for integrity was the expression of his life.

I saw that Melodia, as I soon learned to call her, leaned upon him as if he were an Atlas, and trusted him, as one trusts an unfailing spring.

The youngest of our sailors, except little Vincent, was Edgar, a blue eyed son of mirth, always sparkling with good humor and merry conceits. But I must not prolong these introductions. We have a little voyage before us, and I will do my best to give you a good account of it.

An hour after we came on board there was a musical signal for supper, which we found served up in the little saloon. All came but the pilot and engineer for the time being. Melodia took the head of the table as by natural right, and gave me a seat on one side while Alfred took the other. The pretty Laura sat next me, the fair Eugenia opposite; next Eugenia sat Edgar, and next Laura a young man who seemed more thoughtful and poetical than talkative or mirthful. Little Vincent sat at the foot of the table; and I could not avoid seeing the striking resemblance he bore to Melodia. Such was our group.

The table was set with a delicate repast of rice and southern hominy, bananas and oranges, with guava jelly, and lemonade reddened with claret; add some light warm biscuits and fresh butter, and the supper was complete.

I cannot describe the geniality of this group. It was evident at a glance,—it was palpable to my feeling that it was a loving group, full of tenderness and devotion. There was not one there who would not have died for Melodia, no one who was not devoted to Alfred. Stranger as I was, just escaping from the discords of civilization, I could not but feel the beauty of this harmony of a purer life.

I could not but see how quietly and beautifully it had arranged itself. I would not have been any where but where I was; the two persons most attractive to me on either side; and it was the same, I think, with every person there

The supper was eaten with a delicate deliberation, but also with great enjoyment. Little Vincent sent his plate for a second portion of guava, remarking that the sea air always gave him a famous appetite. He also made a brave attack on the bananas.

The conversation at table was marked by as much propriety, as geniality of feeling. A rough jest; a rude remark; any boister ousness would have been discordant. The tones were low and sweet, and even the humor of Mr. Edgar was toned to the precise key of the circle. In the general conversation there were occa-sional duets; and I could not but remark the delicate tact, which yet seemed unconscious and habitual, with which Laura addressed some sprightly remark to me, when Melodia was listening to some matter of home interest from Alfred; or with which Eugenia asked a question of him, when she turned to me. It was the same with the others; a fitness and adaptation, which seemed perfect; yet I fe t assured that no one had planned it; but that the group had formed itself in the most spontaneous manner.

Long before we rose from the table, Edgar went and relieved the engineer, while Laura's friend took his place at the wheel: and yet this change did not mar the harmony. They seemed just as well adapted to their places as the others: two genial, cultured, well mannered young men, proud of their duties, and happy in their society. Master Vincent pitied them for having waited so long, and urged upon them all the dainties of the table as a compensation.

After our little supper, to which the pilot added the music of his steam organ, which, controlled by the valve, was capable of soft as well as loud tones, and wondrous modulations, we all went upon the promenade deck, when I saw that we were no longer plowing down the broad Mississippi, but were stemming the current of a much narrower stream — one of its western tributaries. The country was low, the scenery melancholy, with the cypress forests, and pendant mosses; but away in the northwest I saw the outline of hills in the distance; and the steam organ pealed out the familiar music of "Home, Sweet Home," and all turned their eyes in one direction with looks of love and joy; and as we stood in a group, forward, near the pilot house, the voices joined in a perfect harmony, accompanied by the softened organ notes, in singing the dear old song, the full, clear tenor of the pilot joining with the rich, mellow bass of Edgar, who was playing engineer below, while the fine baritone of Alfred harmonized lovingly with the noble soprano of

Melodia. The scene, the circumstances, not less than the perfect harmony and feeling of the music affected me to tears. I tried to join in the song, but my throat swelled, and I sank upon a stool and gave free vent to my emotions.

When the song was ended, the pilot turned on a full head of steam, and roused us from these soft memories, with the grand song of *Liberta*, from *I Puritani*. You may judge how grand its effect must be, so given. It was as if the Heavens were singing to the Earth a song of Freedom.

Then we had more music: beautiful songs, and duets, and choruses, while the shades of evening were descending. Old songs linking us to the past, with many sad or pleasing memories: and new songs, carrying me into the spirit of the future, with which I had now begun to make acquaintanceship, and which, until now, has always seemed so distant.

As the sun sunk in the west, the full moon rose and silvered the waters in our wake, playing upon the broad lily leaves of the river margin, and the backs of the sleeping alligators. Our little Fairy glided along noiselessly, all but the murmur of parting waters, and the cascade-like sound of the swift revolving wheels. And now a mist rose from the waters and obscured the banks; and the moon was veiled in the fogs below. The channel was too narrow and difficult to go on in darkness; so the pilot sought an eddy in the stream; a small anchor was dropped, the furnace damped, steam blown off, and we lay by for the night.

I sat by Melodia. She held my hand silently in both of hers, as if she would feel out my emotions; then said: "We near our journey's end, my brother; to-morrow will take us to our home. You see here a little group of our family. How do they seem to you?"

"As if I had always known them."

"That is well. It is the home feeling. Where a true affinity exists, and we recognize our own, nothing is strange to us. We seem to have found those for whom we were seeking, and from whom we have been only for a little while separated."

"It was my feeling," I said, "when I found you." She smiled

a quiet smile, which said as plainly as words could, "And
also?"

"But this is not all," I continued. "I must confess that I have
no claim upon you, and no possible right to feel as I do: and yet I
am disturbed, and almost jealous. I perceive all the merit of this
brave, manly, energetic, handsome Alfred: it seems quite natural
that you should love him. It is evident that he has gone on this
expedition, and taken charge of this boat, and the business of the
voyage, expressly to be with you a few hours sooner. Still I am
troubled. I find my heart growing heavy and bitter, when I
seem to have less of your society and sympathy than when we
were alone.

"You do well to be frank, my friend;" she replied. "though I
do not need the revelation. I knew it, and had foreseen it. The
habits of a very selfish civilization cling to you. Its thoughts
and feelings are in your life, like the taint of disease, or the poison
of malaria. You must become clear and free from all this. We
seek only true relations; we earnestly wish to avoid all false ones.
This is our freedom and our happiness."

"But to know the true."

"The test of a true relation, is the unmixed happiness it gives to
all who are truly related. The sentiment I have for Alfred is
painful to you, either because it is false in itself, or because it meets
some element of falsehood in you. Which do you think it?"

"I know it is my own selfishness," I replied. "Forgive me.
It is absurd and ungrateful, and I will overcome it."

Just now, Alfred himself came aft and joined us. Holding me
by one hand, Melodia extended to him the other, and drew him to
her side: "Here, Alfred," said she, with sweetness, "is a young
gentleman, who pays you the compliment to be jealous of you."

Alfred laughed heartily, and grasped my hand as heartily,
exclaiming: "Well, Mr. Wilson, which do you think has most
cause to be jealous, you or I? You have been journeying together
all the way from New York; spending one day amid the romance
of Niagara; another in a pilgrimage to Buffalo; sailing on Lake
Erie; spending Sunday at Cincinnati; and then steaming, with

abundance of solitude to sweeten as best you could, down the Ohio and Mississippi. Now, I ask you, as a sensible young gentleman, am not I the one to be jealous, and call you out, and insist upon walking on shore with you with a case of pistols, at daylight?"

I could not but laugh at the absurdity of my position.

"But instead of that," said he, with the most perfect frankness in his tone and manner, " I have to thank you for every kind word, and every affectionate thought you have had for her. My love is only equalled by my trust "

"This is the perfect love, that casteth out fear," said Melodia, softly; and when she gently pressed my hand, I knew that she also pressed the other, and far more fondly, and yet I felt in my heart such a confidence in the entire nobleness of both, that all bitterness went from me. Had we been two brothers, with our loved sister between us, we could not have been more at peace.

The pleasing reverie in which we sat was broken by the light roll of a drum ; and the next moment we were greeted by the music of a band, playing exquisitely on four saxe horns, with the drum most delicately beaten by my little friend Laura, who seemed to throw into it all the charm of her lively manners,—and a silver triangle, skilfully handled by Eugenia. It was a new surprise. They play as well as the Dodworths, in the perfect chiming harmony of family music, but with a more pure and tender feeling — with a more loving unity than I had ever heard. I sat entranced.

But the mists creeping out from the shore, and enveloping us, warned us to retire to the little saloon, where Melodia sang to us, accompanying herself on the pianoforte. Alfred leaned over her to turn the music, and sometimes joined his voice to hers.

"You love music," she said, when she rose from the instrument, and came where I was sitting. " There is much pleasure in store for you. It is the perpetual aspiration for harmony in the world you have left, and the perpetual expression of it in that to which you are going."

"To which I have come," I said.

"Our group here, is but a little fragment; but a very happy one. To-morrow night we shall all be happier. Now, good night!"

she said, stooping to press a pure kiss upon my forehead ; "good night, all my dear ones ;" and she gave a hand to each, and each one kissed the fair hand reverently.

The little Vincent had become so tired, helping to work the boat, that he had been asleep in his berth hours before. Melodia went and kissed his little rose bud lips ; and charging Laura to show me my state-room, passed to her own.

They all retired but one, who took his lamp and a book, to keep wa ch in the pilot house. Laura sat on a cushion at my feet. Though fatigued with the emotions of the evening, I was far from being sleepy. I sat, thinking of you, who are never out of my thoughts whose image ever lives in my deep heart ; and still, darling one, I so felt the sphere of affection around me, and was so softened in its influence, that my great love for you seemed only to open my heart to other sentiments, tender and beautiful ; but whether of the same kind, I confess myself at a loss to determine.

And as I mused on this, thinking of my distant home with you, and of this near home, to which I feel myself so lovingly welcomed, Laura was looking up into my face, with her dark eyes, as if she would read my soul. There was tenderness, sympathy and curiosity in her looks. I stooped toward her, and she put up her hand, and pushed back my hair from my forehead, as if she could better read my thoughts. Her round, plump arms were bare to the shoulder ; her dress of perfect neatness, so appropriate to the voyage that I had not noticed it, made modest revelation of a beautiful bust. She seemed very charming. Her manner was so sisterly and confiding, that I offered her a kiss. It was no passionate impulse, but the expression of a brotherly regard. She drew back gently, gravely shook her head, and said :

"No, my friend, you must not be in haste, and you must make no mistakes. We do not kiss idly or profanely. A week hence you will know better whom you have a right to kiss. It may be me ; but I think not. At least, I must be sure, first, that you will not repent it."

"Do you think that possible ?"

"With you ? yes. Not often with us."

"But imagine me your brother."

"Were you a thousand times my brother, I should not kiss you
if I did not love you; and if I loved you, I should kiss you all the
same."

' Are you sure you do not ?"

"No: I have been feeling you. You are too mixed. You do
not recognise your own emotions. You are liable to make mistakes.
You are selfish. You must wait. Come, sleep and dream of me."

She took my hand and led me to such a cosy little state-room,
with a nice bed in it—not a berth—with a lace musquito bar,
and everything in the neatest order; and bidding me a cheerful
"good night," went to her rest.

n the early dawn, a southerly breeze dissipated the fog, and the
Fairy was under way long before sunrise. Our group assembled
on the promenade deck, to greet each other, and the world's
illumination A l nature was rejoicing in the opening day. If a
tender and pensive thought of you, so distant and so dear, made me
less cheerful, the rest were happy in the hope of seeing those they
loved in a few hours. As we stood aft, in an interlocked group,
watching the changing sky of the dawn, and the first ray of sunlight shot across the scene, our grand organ pealed out a song of
welcome to the sun, as sublime as his uprising; and after the
prelude, our voices joined in singing a glorious morning hymn—
religious in the deepest sense, and yet in harmony with all around
us, so that it seemed to combine the songs of birds, the lowing of
herds, and all the music of nature.

Then all went joyfully to their duties, all but Melodia, Alfred
and m , who remained on deck, to watch the growing splendors of
the scene. We were passing through a broad, lake-like opening of
the river; water fowl were flying over it; birds were caroling on
the shore, and beyond the fringe of trees, we saw the smoke of
distant plantations.

Alfred and Melodia wore the aspect of serene happiness; bu
there was a perceptible difference. He seemed to be in possession
of what he most valued and desired, and to be supremely blessed:
while she looked forward with a joyful hope to a still greater

happiness. I watched well the countenances of both. It was evident that she was to him the "bright particular star" that centered his fondest aspirations; but, while it was apparent that she also loved him, with a fond trust and tender reliance, I knew well that she loved another with a still deeper devotion — that while she was a sun to him, her soul revolved around another center of loving life.

And yet, dear Clara, I could see, and I could feel, no jar — no discordance. We have seen such things, in our world, causes of strife and misery. Here all these attractions seem accepted, harmonized, and a means of increased happiness. I have been absurdly selfish; I have felt even the pangs of jealousy toward Mr. Vincent and Alfred, but I feel them no longer. They are unworthy of that great true soul, whom I both reverence and love. I have said it, O my Clara! May you so enter into the harmony of this love-life, as to be able to accept with me this reverential love, which I feel ennobles me, and makes me more worthy to be yours.

After a little Melodia went below, to kiss the slumber from the eyelids of the little Vincent, and prepare him for breakfast. Alfred took my arm, and we walked the deck together.

"You feel your welcome, I trust, Mr. Wilson," said he, when we had taken a turn in silence. "Your love for Melodia makes you a brother to me, if you can accept such a relation. This is the spirit of Harmony—that of the discordant society we have left would make us vengeful foes."

"It is new to me," I replied, "but very real. I am at peace. I feel the love-life of this little group circulating around me. I see how it is all combined, knit together, and harmonized by these interlacing attractions."

"You see well," said Alfred, smiling; "you will soon see more. The same harmony of a sweet passional life pervades all the groups of our society. The same loves are every where a bond of unity instead of a source of discord, because every one is free, and we hold no property, either in the bodies or souls of men or women."

I have thought much of this expression, Clara. No property in body or soul. I fear that I have very selfishly held you as my property. body and soul—but I can do so no more. You must be your own ; and what of you, or the expression of your life, is truly mine, must flow freely to me, wi hout clu ch or claim, or bond or chain. The immortal loves must be free as the immortals ; not the helots an l slaves of civilization. I see so cl arly, now, in the light of my recent experience, and in contrasting the sphere of th s life of harmony, on which I am entering. w th the selfishness of our rapacious social dissonance, that Freedom is the condition of Order, and Harmony, and Happiness.

When I said this to Alfred, he took my hand, and pressing it warmly, said :—" My brother, I claim the right to welcome you to our family and home. You are mos? nearly rela ed to me, because you love the one I most love on the earth. This is a bond of true fellowship, and I shall claim the right to serve you every way in my power, while you remain, and to see to the preparation for your joining us in the future."

As I accepted this frank proffer of friendship, the s gnal for breakfast was given, and we descended to the saloon, where we found an excellent repast, prepared by the skillful l ands of the sprightly Laura, and the calm and beautiful Eugenia, who welcomed us to their hospitable an l elegant board, for such it truly was, containing a meal of various edibles, all harmonizing to the taste. and presenting the best materials for nutrition. The orange and banana, of which there was a large s ore on board, were fresh from the New Orleans market; the ripe figs from tl e same place were delicious ; the cream was preserved in the ice house, in the hold.

We sat as at the evening meal, only that Laura and Eugenia l ad changed places. Vincent still felt the influence of the sea air on his appetite, but was also very happy in the prospect of joining his playmates, and giving them a circumstantial narrative of the adventures of his voyage.

But I sl all make this letter too long, even for one of mine, if I wri e every circumstance and conversation of this quie t, but not uneventful day. I wandered over our little craft, admiring every portion of it. It seemed every where a labor of love. The carvings are exquisite. The paintings were done with a wonderful perfection of detail, which never could have come from mercenery labor. It was evident that the artists had loved the boat, and had done their best to beautify and adorn it. And it was the same with the finish of every part. It had a cheerful and harmonizing sphere, and might well "walk the waters like a thing of life," for it seemed permeated with vitality.

"Isn't she a beauty?" said Melodia, as I stood admiring her, and the ease with which she glided over the water.

"She seems fit to bear you and yours," said I.

"She was built for and by us and ours. I doubt if there is one of all our family, old enough to do any thing, who has not done some work on our Fairy. So she is a pet, and we all love her like a living thing,

"And what did you do?" I asked.

She led me to one of the most beautiful paintings; a cluster of marine plants, with two fishes lying in the clear water under them in their shadow, looking so alive and real, that you stood still for fear they would be frightened, and dash away.

"This is mine; and I helped to arrange the upholstery of the saloon, and contributed the pianoforte, because I had two, and this was just large enough. Alfred modeled and helped build the hull, and wood work. Mr. Vincent planned the engine, and every one was emulous to do some thing for our little Fairy. It is so of all our work, as you will see."

Laura showed me the little model kitchen on the boiler deck, with steam pipes from the boiler, for heating water and cooking. It communicated with a little store-room and ice-house, in the hold. The water was carefully filtered into the most translucent purity; and so, on the whole craft, everything was in the most orderly perfection.

As we ascended the river the navigation became more difficult, but our boat was of light draught, and abundant power, so that she went over the bars handsomely; or if she ever stuck fast, her reversed wheels took her off in a moment, and she tried again. With conversation, music, and a restful life, the day glided on.

Advancing westward, the country became rolling, and in parts broken, with romantic glens, and bold bluffs on the river. We were appro ching the hills we had seen in the blue distance. The eyes of the loving friends around me were bent upon them with looks of joyful hope. I had never seen Melodia so lovely as this day. Soft fires were burning in her eyes, which some imes brimmed wi h tears; her cheeks were flushed, and her voice deepened to a tenderer melody. The Fairy boat glided on, up the windings of the stream, which every hour displayed new beauties.

Our dinner was more pensive than joyous. But it was easy to see how happy were all, in the hope of soon reaching the home, which was so linked to the deepest life of all. All but me; to whom it was a new world, to which I was then a stranger — stranger to its localities, almost to its life; but not quite; for had I not lived in the sphere of one of its most potent influences, and was I not then the friend and brother, and welcome guest of a group of its noble spirits?

Therefore I did not falter, but hoped like the rest. I s udied Alfred. It seemed to me, at first, that he would not be in haste to convey Melodia in o the presence of an attraction deeper tl an his own. But I saw no evidence of any selfish desire to keep her with himself. He seemed to sympathise cordially with every hope and wish of hers.

At last, as we were walking together under the awning. after he l a l been at the wheel two hours, through some difficult navigation, I said to him:

"My friend, will you allow me to tell you my thoughts?"

"Why no ?"

" We are approaching Esperanza."

The joy-light spread over his handsome, energetic face, and he grasped my arm more tigh ly.

"You carry thither her you adore, where there are those whom she loves as much as she loves you."

' Well!" he said, with a still deepening joyfulness.

"Have you no desire to keep her a little longer?"

He looked at me a surprised moment; then with a quiet smile, answered:

"Wherever Melodia is, all she has for me is mine; and were she with me alone, banished from all humanity, she could give me no more than what belongs to me. My place in her heart is sacred to me. It is a true love, that no true thing can destroy. I wish, more than every thing her happiness; and if I secure it, by carrying her as soon as possible to the arms of him she loves as I love her, have I not my reward? There are other loves for me, as for her. Our lives are too rich for the jealousies and meannesses of passional starvation. Be patient, and you will see how, in the harmony of a true life, the good of each one is the good of all, and the general welfare consists in the happiness of each individual. The world of sacrifices is the old world we are leaving behind us."

I could not doubt his sincerity; but how nobly unselfish is this love! O my Clara, does it come to your heart as to mine? Can you accept, for this earth, a life that has seemed to us fit only for the angels of heaven?

The sun was descending toward the west, and we pursuing his flight, and nearing the range of highlands. There was with all our group the excitement of expectation added to the calm joy of a return to a home, where friendship and love, and all endearing ties were centered. It was an hour before sunset, when the Fairy turned suddenly and shot into a narrow branch of the river we were ascending. The banks were close wooded, and there was scarcely room for our smoke pipe between the over arching trees. One might pass the place easily without suspecting a navigable passage. But a few rods further up, the creek widened, and as we glided along, our triumphal chords echoed among the hills, followed by the booming of our little cannon, whose reverberations came back to us with wonderful distinctness in these quiet solitudes. All listened a moment, and there came, not an echo now, but the booming of another gun, and our friends knew that their signal was heard, and that their friends knew we were coming.

Our boat sped on, through a narrow channel, improved by art, until after a turn around a rich grove of cotton wood trees, we came in sight of a large saw mill and factory, driven by the stream we were ascending. On a flag staff, over one of its gables, floated the starry emblem of Esperanza. The labors of the day were ended; but we found a joyful group to welcome us, and open the single lock that carried us up the falls. When the gates were closed and secured, and our friends had come on board, we steamed up the creek a few rods, rounded a point, and with a triumphal steam song, and the sound of our small artillery, shot into a broad clear lake, upon whose shores was displayed a scene of such enchanting beauty as I had never imagined, and can never in all my life forget.

There, in the golden light of a most gorgeous sunset, rose the lovely edifices of ESPERANZA. The Fairy took a circle in the lake, to give us a fairer view. Our steam organ filled the scene with the melody of home; Edgar and little Vincent were busy with the cannon forward, firing a rapid salute, which was answered from a mimic fortress on the shore; sail boats were hastening toward us across the l ke; the broad white flag, embroidered with golden stars, was floating from the tallest spire, and through my tears I saw a goodly company gathered on the sloping lawn to welcome us.

Our music ceased, our prow turned toward the landing. I surveyed the beauty of the scene before me—the noble towers, the graceful arches, the embowered porticos, the varied and beautiful architecture of a Unitary Home. It was simple, yet grand; chaste, yet most beautiful. Trees, and vines, and flowering shrubs, and dark ever greens were scattered around, with a consummate art that made a new creation; beyond were the stone houses, and granaries, and the great fields and orchards, and vine yards, and the green pasture lands stretching up the hill sides.

When we approached the shore, as we did slowly, there suddenly rose into the sun shine, the play of many fountains, throwing up their silvery jets: then came a burst of grand music from a noble band, on the great terrace in front of the central tower.

Melodia stood at my side; calm in her manner; her voice without a tremor, but I knew her heart was beating. I s w the fl is' ing of her cheek; her bosom swell with emotion; and once she stretched out her arms as if she would have flown. But in a m men she was calm again, and smiled on us—Alfred and me, through the happy tears.

The Fairy rounded to her little dock, and blew her steam into the wa er. with a dull roar. We went on shore. and were met by a torrent of little girls and boys, who first surrounded us and then took little Vincent prisoner and marched him off in triumph; and as we wa'ked up the graveled ascent of the lawn, the more you h- ful and im e'uous l astened to join us; but the music quieted an l harmonized all demons'ration- of joy, and in a moment more I saw Melodia clasped in tle arms of him who had waited calmly to receive her. It was Vincent. Ta'l. erect, pale, calm and almost cold in his seeming, he yet folded the beautiful one to his heart, and pressed a kiss upon her brow; and then gave her to the warmer embrace of a delicate woman at his side, who kissed her m iry times with a passionate fondness.

It was a moment in which the breath stops, and the heart almost forgets to beat. In the embraces of these two, Vincent and Harmonia, all loves and all welcomes seemed to center in a perfect sympathy.

Next they welcomed me. kindly and affectionately, not as a stranger, but as if I too had come back to them, and then all of our little company; and now as we stood so grouped and clus'ered togetl er, in the glow of the sun set, the band struck a prelude, and a l undred voices of men and women and the rosy children, joined in a song of welcome. And as the last notes went up to heaven, the evening gun was fired, the great white and gol len flag des- cended, the bugle signal for the evening meal was given, and we all went to the great banqueting hall, where tables were set for every group, and adorned with flowers, whose delicate perfumes filled the air, while an invisible instrument, playing at intervals, stirred it wi h the vibra ions of exquisite melodies.

The supper la ted an hour. The f od was of the most simple and delicate kind. The flavors were like the odors of the flowers:

not coarse and obtrusive, but fine and penetrating. Gastronomy, I saw, was a science ; and none of the senses were neglected. The chairs we sat in were the perfection of comfort ; the table service of a pure quality and elegant forms. The room was painted with cool tints and exquisite designs, while a tinkling fountain cooled the air, which was also changed continually by a scientific ventilation, which filled the room with refreshing zephyrs. There was every where the hum of happy voices talking in quiet, subdued tones. Even the groups of children, old enough to leave the nursery, and eating by themselves. with only one or two of their most especial friends at each table, were gentle and quiet, and harmonized to the spirit of the scene.

It seemed to me that there was a pervading unity ; yet each group was distinct. Only at one moment were all united. Vincent rose at the head of the table of his group, where he sat between Harmonia and Melodia, and said, "Friends; a toast! Welcome to those who have returned to us, and welcome to our guest."

The toast was drunk in the crystal water, as the head or center of each group, even the children repeated it. I rose, with the others so welcomed, who were scattered in the groups to which they belonged, and we bowed our thanks. Then the band, whose members had quietly left their seats a moment before, played exquisi ely for a few moments, and the supper was ended.

Scattered groups now gathered on the lawn, in the soft summer twilight. They clustered in little companies, sitting on the soft grass, in twos and threes, or dozens, each group far enough from the others not to interfere with their conversation or amusements. Some sang low, sweet songs, with guitar accompaniments ; some were relating stories, as in a new and purer Decameron ; some were planning work in industry or art, or amusement for the morrow, and all seemed happy.

Melodia sat awhile between Vincent and Harmonia. Alfred and I completed the group for a time. Others came of whom I must speak hereafter Melodia recounted her journey : then she took my arm and guided me among the groups, pointing out, and sometimes introducing me to those I might wish to know. But formal introductions were little needed, as all—even the young ladies and the children, came to me as frankly as if I had been an old acquaintance.

The shades deepened, the holy stars came out. I saw boats stealing out from their little harbors, to a small island before us in the lake, which is laid out as a garden, with an elegant pavilion. Soon we heard a slight explosion, and saw a gleam of light. Many colored stars seemed shooting into the sky. Then followed a flight of rockets, and such a pretty exhibition of scientific pyrotechny, as delighted us all, and sent the children to their beds extremely happy.

Then the windows of a large saloon over the dining-room, were in a blaze of light. We heard music again sounding its cheerful strains; and all ran gleefully to prepare.

"They welcome you with a festival," I said to Melodia, "like a princess returned to her dominions."

"Oh! no: We have fireworks often; music and happiness always. They are happy to see us, but are making no extraordinary manifestation."

We went to the music hall; listened to some admirable instrumentation; heard a new chorus, just composed by one of the cultivators of this divine art, who came forward and directed the performance; and then there was a dance in which all mingled beautifully and happily for an hour, during which I saw that the musicians were more than once relieved that they might take part in the dancing.

You may well suppose, that in all I have narrated, there were many things entirely different from our accustomed life. There was much more than I can tell you now, and yet the whole did not differ so much from the most refined societies as you might suppose. It was more natural, beautiful, loveful. There was an inexpressible charm of repose in the midst of gayety, of which our fashionable languor is a coarse imitation.

At the end of he last dance, which finished at ten o'clock, there was a Good Night Carol, merry and cordial, and all retired to their apartments. Melodia led me to a charming little bed-room, in her own suite, furnished with a bathing room and every convenience, and adorned with the productions of her graceful pencil. The window opened on the scented lawn; fragrant odors were round me. The moon was rising over the silvery lake, the stars were gleaming with their angel glances, and with a tender good night in my ear, and a dewy kiss upon my cheek, I sunk to rest.

I had slumbered an hour—I was dreaming happily of you, sweet one, so far away, when soft music mingled magically in my dream, and slowly awakened me. How delicious it was. I knew it was meant for Melodia, but it was no less, ah! it was even more beautiful to me. And with all I could have of it, and all that was mine. I sank into a profound and dreamless sleep, surrounded by a sphere of happiness that wanted only you to be complete.

VII.

I woke very early, yet entirely refreshed. The life around me seems full of invigoration, and time is lost in sleep. Ah, my Clara! we shall never wish to kill time here. O that you were with me now, to see and feel with me the life I can but faintly portray to you!

The light had just begun its struggle with darkness, and the eastern stars grew pale in the conflict. I heard those little warbings of the birds, which are the prelude of their morning songs. Then came the crowing of many chanticleers from the poultry-house. But as the dawn grew rosy, and the light diffused, there came other music. There was the roll of a drum, first low, and then louder; and then the call of a single trumpet; next a trombone, and then came music like the light, full, rich, inspiring, that roused me from my couch, and I listened to one of these glorious bursts of melody, for which a full band of enthusiastic artists only can find expression. I looked out upon the lawn, and saw Mr. Vincent leading the band with the cornet- -piston; playing as you would wish such a man to play—without pretense, without effort at execution, but with a grand power of expression.

As this noble *reveil e* ended, I heard the rush of many waters; and, taking a refreshing bath, I was ready to join the groups gathering at the parade for sunrise. It was on the eastern slope; and nearly all were gathered. The youngest children, and their nurses, and the few aged or weak, alone were absent. The groups gathered silently, or exchanging greetings with low voices. Harmonia stood at the side of Vincent, and welcomed me with a pleasant smile; Melodia held out her hand to me, and as I gave one

107

to her, I extended the other to Alfred. Eugenia and Laura were in
near groups. The children formed in separate groups of their
own, and all knew their places, or took those they liked best. There
was order, but no constraint, and a harmony that seemed the result
of something higher than discipline. Vincent stood in the center,
facing the east, with the band behind, and our group around him ;
the other groups spread off, right and left, forming a crescent, opening to the east, where the firmament was now glowing. All was
silent—then a ray of sunshine shot across the scene ; a cannon fired ;
the white flag with its symbol stars rose gracefully to its staff ; the
band played a grand prelude, and men, women, and children
joined in a noble chorus, to salute the day.

When it was ended, the crescent closed into a circle around
Vincent, who read the Orders of the Day. The first was the Order
of Industry, consisting of an enumeration of the work most needful
to be done, naming the leader of the day in each department, and
calling for a certain number of volunteers for each work. First
came the household, or domestic duties ; such a lady and so many
assistants for the kitchen ; so for the laundry ; a leader and a
company for the harvest field ; others for the orchards and gardens,
poultry yard and dairy ; others for building ; and the mill and
factory. All the work was laid out, and as each leader was called,
he or she stepped forward, and was promptly joined by the first
relay of workers—so promptly, that it was easy to see that it had
all been canvassed and arranged the night before, so that each one
had chosen his work and companions, and wore the badge of his
group.

The leaders of the harder or more repugnant labors were men ;
those of the lighter and more agreeable, women. Laura, for the
day, was mistress of the group of confectioners, or preservers of
fruit. Eugenia had charge of the flower garden. Boys of ten or
fifteen, and young misses, were chiefs of groups of industry, and
took their positions, and gathered their adherents around them with
a flush of pride. I saw that the groups were composed of both
sexes ; those for the harder toils and out door duties being two-

thirds or more of men ; those of indoor employments, mostly, but not entirely, of woman.

All this was arranged in less time than you take to read it ; when the Order of Recreation was called. This was for the afternoon ; a regatta on the lake ; music practice ; artist work ; rehearsals of drama and opera, etc. These were under more permanent direction, and the leaders known. The time only was given.

Finally, an opera was announced for the evening ; when the band played a lively air which set all in motion. Those whose duties were immediate, as the groups for preparing breakfast, feeding animals, etc., repaired to their functions ; the rest to the lecture-room and lessons of the morning. As all this had been arranged in twenty minutes, there was left more than an hour, either for quiet reading or study, for conversation, or for the morning lecture on some branch of science, or practical lesson connected with industry or art.

I went with Melodia to the Lecture-room. Most of the younger, and more intellectual had gathered there. It was itself a panorama of science ; a circular room with a dome of blue, admitting a soft light through itself, and the constellations of the northern heavens. The walls, or rather a continuous circle of wall, was painted to represent the various climates and scenery of the earth. At the north and south are icebergs, white bears, seals. East and west, the equatorial regions of the eastern and western hemispheres, with their vegetation, animals, and peoples, and the temperate regions in their places. It is charming as a work of art, and perfect as a scientific representation. The fore-ground is boldly painted, so as to represent geological structures, minerals, and rare animals and plants. There is land and sea ; calm and storm ; here a water spout, and there a tornado. Ships sail the summer seas ; steamers cloud the sky. My eye wandered over every part with surprise and pleasure.

Mr. Vincent gave the morning discourse on the Unity of Nature ; treating all sciences as portions of the one science, and giving the analogies which pervade the universe many illustrations. "A principle, which can be demonstrated as such," he said, "is universal in its application. The laws of harmony in music we find to

be those of social accords.   Chemical affinities are no more ruled
by inexorable laws, than the relations of friendship and love. Every
atom in the universe is distinct from every other, as is every individual spirit —and the social order we have achieved is by having
every soul-atom free to follow its own attractions and repulsions,
and to place itself. and not be placed.   Our freedom is the freedom not to disobey any law of our beings; our freedom not to be
placed where we do not belong.

"Science is not a thing apart from life.   We do well to know the
universe, and our place in it, and relation to every other part.   If
the soul of our planet is conscious of us, it must feel new vigor and
hope with this germ of social harmony, and as it extends, we may
hope for serener skies, more equable climes, and a more abounding
fertility.

"We do well to know the earth, and all its countries and peoples:
we see how much work there is before us, for all must be won to
our harmony.

"We do well to make ourselves acquainted with all vegetables
and animals, that we may find uses for all the good, and extirpate
those which belong to the sphere of discord.

"Above all we are to study the Life that informs and unfolds all
things: that glitters in the crystal, and palpitates in the heart;
that works out beauty in man and woman, and unity in all who
can unite in a true life.

"We will work on patiently, hopefully, joyfully; for the time is
near, when our experiment will be ended, and the true life of man in
society will be seen to be, not the idle dream of a benevolent enthusiast, but the practical realization of purified, enlightened, and
spiritualized humanity.

"Let us live this life, then, in all purity, not for ourselves alone,
but for the Earth, our Great Mother; for the Humanity to which we
belong; for those who have gone before, and who now look down
upon us; and for those who shall come after, and bless us."

I give a few sentences of this discourse, omitting the scientific
facts and illustrations.   The audience rose, filled with the earnest
feeling of the speaker, and broke into groups of persons who

conversed together, and walked through the library and reading room, and we soon heard the signal for breakfast.

A vegetarian breakfast, on a large scale, is a beautiful thing. This was not wholly so. Animalized substances, as eggs, and the products of the dairy, were on many of the tables. But the staples of consumption were the various preparations of corn and wheat, in bread, mush, and cakes, and fruits, fresh and preserved, or in marmalades and syrups. There was no more haste than at a festival. It was a cheerful meal. From the younger groups came bursts of laughter. In twenty minutes, the tables were cleared: and a few minutes after, I stood in a balcony and saw the parade of the groups of Industry. Their costumes were adapted to the work of each. The young and robust women and girls, who had volunteered for the harvest field and other out door labors, wore blouses and trowsers, and could be distinguished from the men only by their smaller limbs, and more delicate figures. They were rosy and happy, every one.

I have not spoken of the dress here. It is so remarkable, that I wish to give you a full account of it. The working dress, however, is nearly uniform, of a strong light colored material, easily washed; and as it is used in the common labors, it comes from a common stock. The dresses of the afternoon and evening are suited to the taste and fancy of each, and are as varied as the characters of the wearers, each trying to make in dress, as in every thing, the truest and best expression of individual character. The effect s indescribably beautiful, and can scarcely be conceived by those who have only seen all men and women dressed nearly alike, and in accordance with the prevailing fashions.

Even in the working dresses, the bands, badges, and ornaments a e varied and characteristic. The children carry this to a picturesque excess, indulging in quite a fantastic display of personal adornment. But the taste of those who are most respected, the artists and most cultivated persons, gives tone to all, and keeps all in harmony.

The bands marched out, one by one, each singing its own song; and the day's work had begun. Melodia led the way up a stair

case in the tower, and knocked at a door, which, in opening, admitted us to the study of Mr. Vincent. It is an octagon room
with seven windows; and as it is above the roofs of the buildings, it
afford a view of the whole domain. I saw it spread out before me,
on every side; front is the lake with its forest on the opposite shore,
supplying timber of which I soon saw a raft, which some happy
boys were sailing toward the saw-mill. In the rear are the orchards, and vineyard, and the great garden, filled with a profusion
of berries, fruits, and vegetables. The vines, trees, and cultivated
berries climb high up the hill sides, where a stream, fed by mountain springs, and which supplies the domain, is led along the slope
and affords water for irrigation. To the right and left stretch the
great fields of corn and wheat, and pasture land for horses, cattle
and sheep. Around the central buildings, all is a garden of flowers
and shrubbery; walks, fountains and groves; the work of loving
workers, in the groups of recreation. I tell you what I saw first;
but I must now introduce you to him whom you have recognised
as, in some sort, the presiding genius of this scene. The room is
plainly furnished—its only luxuries consisting of some pictures and
other keepsakes. A few books were on a shelf— mostly standard
scientific works. There were some volumes of Fourier, with his
autograph in one of them; and a portrait of the noble Harmonist,
in crayon. There are also portraits of a few other masters in
Science, Literature, and Art, and of some lovely women. There
was also a violin, a flute, a cornet-a-piston, and a melodeon.

He was sitting at his table, with writing and drawing materials,
and music paper. He did not rise, to receive us, but held out a
hand to each. He drew me to a chair, near him; and Melodia sat
on a cushion, and leaned upon his knee. He is a little taller than
I am; his hair and beard brown, his eyes hazel; his face thin and
pale, mostly grave in expression, but with smiles often playing
among lines of study and care. His forehead is severe, but the
mouth genial, with a pleasant, but not melodious voice, a pure articulation, and a frank address. He is slender, and erect, and as
to his age, any where from thirty to forty-five—simply a man at
maturity, without any mark of decay. .

" We are glad to have a visitor, Mr. Wilson. You are welcome to Esperanza. I hope you had a pleasant journey," he said, with a grave courtesy.

" You know my company," I answered; and his eye fell with a proud tenderness on the beautiful woman at his side.

" I think you could scarcely have found better," he said; " and now we must be hospitable. If it is agree ble, I will be glad to show you our home, and to give you the chance of a general survey, and then you can pursue any details you may wish at your leisure. We will have horses, and find one to accompany us." Speaking through a tube, he asked for some saddle horses, and then went with us to the apartments of Harmonia. He knock d lightly at the door, and a fair rose-bud girl of ten years bid us enter, and putting her arm around her papa, deman led a kiss.

We were in the presence of a woman of scarcely the medium height, her face thin and pale, with delicate little hands and feet, but with arms and form well roun led. Her eyes are of a heavenly blue, her hair dark, glossy, and curling in ringlets; her forehead intellectual; and though there are lines of care upon her face, and silver in her hair, suffering and disease, rather than years, have made them.

She kissed Vincent and Melodia, and gave me her hand, over which I bent reverently; for I stool now in the presence of the center of the heart-life of this home; the chosen medium of the spirit-love, that has formed upon earth one sphere of rest and happiness, the one whom all here revere and love. I felt the influence of her pure loving life around me. The whole room seemed filled with it. It was furnished with a singular, but fitting elegance, and with a harmony of forms, colors, and arrangement, such as I have never seen. It seemed to me, that if one article had been removed or displaced. it would have marred the harmony. The colors were buff, blue and rose; the picture frames and furniture carvings of oak, and light mouldings of gold. Vases of blue and gold were filled with odorous flowers; the offerings of affectionate devotion. A canary and a mocking bird were singing emulously among the roses in a bow window. A large music box lay on the

10

carved octagon table in the center of the room, which played airs of Massanaella and William Tell, her favorite operas.

" We are going to show Mr. Wilson our home," said Vincent, with a tender deference of manner, which one does not expect from a husband, " will you give us your company ? "

" With pleasure—but you must let Angela have her pony, and ride with us ; for I have promised her the morning."

The little face that had saddened a moment before, at the idea of losing this precious morning with her mother, now brightened, and she ran away to prepare, and summon her little steed.

The ladies were soon equipped for the saddle with riding skirts, and plumed caps ; four glossy saddle horses were brought to the door by as many happy boys, and we saw in a moment after a round and roguish little Canadian pony come bounding up, with a boy of a dozen years on his back, who assisted the blue eyed, rosy, and most beautiful Angela into her saddle, as if she had been a princess, and he her own true knight. Vincent helped Harmonia to mount, and I gave my hand to Melodia ; but when we were ready, Harmonia signed me to ride next her ; while Melodia led off with Vincent, and Angela was on all sides of us by turns.

First we rode along the hard beach of the lake, across which a cool breeze was blowing ; then in a road through the wheat harvest, where over hundreds of broad acres, heavily laden with the bright grain, two machine reapers, each drawn by four horses were doing their rapid work. The near horse of each span was ridden by a boy or girl ; the machine was followed by a group of binders, and the sheaves were loaded in a waggon at once, and conveyed to the threshing barn, to be further ripened in the sun, where they could also be sheltered in a few moments from a passing shower.

In the center of the field was a grove, affording a pleasant shade for men and horses in the intervals of labor; with food and drink. Here they took their intervals of rest, and here reposed the relays of those who did the hardest labor, or those who were exchanging from this to some other group. There was a spring, a cheer, and enthusiasm in the work of this group, such as never comes from mercenary task labor. The will and the love were in the work; and it w s a real festival of industry.

To the right of the wheat spread out a vast field of bright Indian corn, through which a little squadron of horses were drawing the cultivators; each horse ridden by a boy or girl, with their plumed sun-hats, who went on in a merry company, singing as they went, while the men, who guided the cultivat rs, often joined their deeper voices to the merry songs. Beyond, a field of oats was ripening, and we saw up on the hill si.le, and beneath the picturesque groves, the horses not in use, and the cows, and goats, and sheep.

" Here," said Vincent, as we halted under a grove to look upon this lovely scene, "you see the staple of our industry ; that which gives us the s'aff of life. Bread, or some form of farinacious food, and fruit. form five-sevenths of our nourishment, and these are the first to be provided. There,"—pointing to the gardens and orchards which rose back of the hou-e— "is the source of the most beautiful and best part of our food ; and that which gives us least labor and most pleasure in the cultivation."

We rode on to the end of the domain. A spur from the hill here shot down nearly to the lake, and the interval was crossed by a high strong paling, with a gate, strongly locked against the outside worl l. A rough road leads off some ten miles to the nearest settlement in that direction. Putting our horses to an easy gallop, we swept around by the hill side, skirting along the pastures to the orchards and vineyards. The apples, pears, and grapes were swelling with their riches; and the peaches and plums were in their full harvest. Here we dismounted and joined the groups, composed chiefly of women and girls, gathering the ripened fruit. Here the children were at work with great enthusiasm, performing their full share of labor. They stormed the trees with their scaling ladlers, and shook the fruit from the branches into the large funnels of cloths spread underneath, and opening into the baskets. Others managed the little waggons drawn by goats, rams, and ponies, which drew the fruits to the store houses, where other groups were engaged in sealing them

up in air-tight cans, preparing them for drying, or making marmalades and jellies. Others were at work in the gardens. It was
a busy time—but evidently a happy one. I did not see one sickly
looking, or sorrowful, or discontented, or idle person.

As we rode along, group after group saluted us with a joyful
welcome. The children offered fruit or flowers to us all, but
particularly to Harmonia. Angela was at home every where. Not
less so our beau iful Melodia, in whose presence every eye beamed
with a brighter luster. I noted the different influence of these two
women on myself and others. Melodia excited to energy and
enthusia m, and inspired admiration and devotion ; Harmonia was
the center of a most reverential love. I saw how each was related
to Vincent, and to each other, and, even with my cru le ideas and
unharmonized feelings, I could see no ground for jealousy. nor can
I detect, with the most suspicious watchfulness, the least sign of
such a feeling in any of those around me

As we came to the buildings, we found Alfred at the head of a
group of builders, hard at work with hammer and trowel, laying
the walls of a new wing of the home, which was enlarging for
new groups of members. I saw here how the whole pile had
grown, like the growth of a tree, every addition increasing its
beauty. The larger portions for general uses ; the Banqueting
Hall ; the Festive Hall ; the Hall of Science ; the Library ; these had
been bu lt of a sufficien size at first to accommodate seven hundred
persons. or were adapted to an easy ex'ensi n. So the nurseries for
infants, the unitary kitchen, laundry, cellars, store houses. and work
shops, were all on the large scale—not the fu l scale of Fourier,
but the modified scale of a model home; for, though eighteen
hundred person of all grades may be necessary to a full harmony,
a much smaller number of carefully selected and adapted ones,
may produce equal results.

We passed through the frui'-preparing room, and saw the groups
of skilled men and women preserving their stores, which were
packed away for future use. Then we went through a laun ry,
where two men and three women, wi h s'eam-power and machinery,
were doing the entire washing of the home, where clothing is

abun lan:, an l cleanliness the first of virtues. This is no idle
department. A thousand towels a day ; bed-linen and clothing for
day a d night ; all the common work is done here ; but there is
an other place for the fine and ornamental work, which is arranged
differenly.

Then we visi ed the kitchen an l bakery ; and having lunched,
to in down the lake to its out-let, where water power drives saw
mill, fl ur-ing mill, an l the heavier work of various manufactures
On the way we passed fields of peas, beans, asparagus, tomatoes,
a1 l the sweet and Irish potatoe. The yam, plantain, and banana, and
o ang: are cul iva ed in places sheltered from the nor.h, and where
t ey can be protected in winter ; while the great glazed hot house,
or winter garden of the central court, affords tropical fruits and
fl w:rs a: all seasons; an l in the winter, and in rainy weather takes
the place of the lawn for parades and festivals.

I ha l now ha l a general survey of the industry of Esperanza
an l ha l learned, in the conversations held alternately with each of
our party, and by my observation, something of its economies
Every where was order—every where the best adaptation of means
to ends in labor-saving machinery and processes ; every where a
loving harmony and enthusiasm.

As we returned slowly to the home, riding up the slope through
a garden of shrub- and flowers, we opened upon a group under a
grove of sprea ling chesnut trees, the most charming I ever saw or
imagine l. An old man of nearly eighty years, with hair and
beard white as frosted silv r, resting in an arm chair, was the center
of the group ; around him were gathered the youngest children and
babies, with tl eir nurses and care takers. The older children, not
yet old enough to join the groups in the fields, but very useful
with the babies, who were their dolls, were gathered around him,
and had crowned him with flowers Two chubby cherubs were on
his knees, playing with his beard. The children of three to six
years ha l formed a ring, and were singing and dancing around
him ; while the babies were rolling and crowing on the sward, or
in the arms of their nurses, or riding around in little carriages. We
paus d a moment to contemplate this truly Arcadian scene; then

alighted, and as some boys flew to hold our horses, we approached the Patriarch, who laughed heartily as the ring opened to let us enter. The ladies kissed the old man on his cheek, and inquired of his health, and introduced the stranger to their good father.

"Well, my darlings," said he "never better, never so well. Here are the companions of my second childhood. I grow younger and younger, you see. More and more a baby. So they are my proper play fellows. I shall go soon, you know, where they have so lately come from; so it is quite right we should know each other."

"O, but father," said Melodia, "you will stay with us a good while yet. This is a pretty good heaven, you know, and we will make you as happy as we can."

"You are angels that would make heaven in a less beautiful place than this—but I am old, and not very useful here; I think I shall not be long with you; is it not so?" he said, turning to Harmonia.

"Yes, father," she replied, with a calm joy. "Our friends expect you soon. We shall attend you to the portal of the beautiful world, and they will welcome you."

Angela, who was standing by her mother, burst into tears. "I don't want our good father to go from us!" she exclaimed.

"I shall never be separated from those I love," said the old man, with a tremer in his voice; but I can be happier and more useful where I am going. You know that, little darling," he said, laying his hand on Angela's head, who had nestled to his side.

"Yes, good father, I know it will be better for you, and that your spirit will never leave your children."

"God bless you, no; my little one. I will be with you always. You have made my last days happy; I shall not forget you in the other home."

"You will do well," said Vincent, "to watch over your own. All goes well, father; and we are preparing to welcome more to our harmony."

"Good! — I don't know whether I want to stay most with you, or to go and see our friends who labored so long for this result.

I shall be very willing to go. Young man, you are welcome, now," said he, courteously to me, "and welcome back again; for I see that you will not be long away from us."

"No, father," said Melodia; "your eyes serve you well."

"Oh! the old man has n t lost his senses," he said, with a happy laugh. We departed, and the little ones again took possession of him, and replaced the wreath he had removed when we came, by a new and more magnificent diadem, and the old man tried, with his trembling voice, to join in the chorus they were singing, as they danced around him.

At ten o'clock, three hours after the day's work begun, there was a pause for rest and refreshment; and at this time there was a general interchange of employments. Many of those who had been at work indoors went to the fields; others came from the fields to the store houses and work shops. The builders and quarry men went to the harvest, and all the groups re-arranged themselves for the next session of work, when all went on with the same harmonious enthusiasm, with the added charm of new companions. I wrote my letter of yesterday, describing our voyage on the Fairy, and our reception here.

At half past one o'clock a signal gun suspended all labor, and the bands returned merrily from field and orchard, garden and workshops, and all put off their working clothes, bathed, and dressed for dinner. This was a more elaborate meal than supper or breakfast. We had an abundance of sweet corn, sweet and common potatoes, green peas, eggs in various preparations, puddings, jellies and fruits. The tables were arranged and dressed with exquisite taste, each group vying with the other for the best display. Music summoned us to this repast—and when it was over, we had a delightful concert for the repose of digestion, while little parties sauntered in the shade of the trees or buildings, or reclined upon the grass.

Then the drum beat; and the lesser labors or recreations of the afternoon began. The boats were filled for an excursion across the lake, and a swimming party. There was a rehearsal for the evening's opera. The artists repaired to the ever attractive labors of the studio; each one joined the group that pleased him best, and did what was his highest attraction. The labors of the first class, those of necessity, were ended; and each one worked or played as he chose, until the signal for the evening meal.

This was served partly in the great saloon, partly in the parlors of the groups who wished to be more secluded. There were a dozen little festivals, and I had the happiness of taking a delicate repast, and enjoying a beautiful society in the group which clustered around Harmonia. It consisted of ten persons. Vincent and Harmonia sat opposite each other; at Vincent's right hand sat Melodia; at his left, Serafa, a woman or girl, a few years younger than Melodia, and less beautiful, but one who impressed you as a person of rare endowments, and a highly poetical temperament. She seemed plain till I found the depth of her gray eyes; and her low voice was full of enthusiasm. She is the poet of this home. The opera performed last night was her libretto, all but two or three songs by Melodia. I sat next her, and at my left was Evaline, the eldest daughter of our hostess; smaller than her mother, pale, with light hair, a lovely figure, but a face capable of the whole range of expression from ugliness to beauty, and becoming quite dazzling with the excitement of enthusiasm or pleasure. She is an artist, and somewhat of a musician, but art is her supreme attraction, and she works with great enthusiasm, and also with great patience, instructing all who will learn, and having around her a large group of loving and devoted pupils.

Opposite me sat Alfred, and at his right hand Eugenia, who develops more character, and a higher beauty each time I see her. She is so calm and wise, that the most turbulent might find her presence a repose, and the weakest find strength in her firm will. Next her, and at the left of Harmonia, sat a sculptor and architect, who has designed most of the buildings and ornaments, of which I shall give you a description hereafter; and on her left a man who impressed me with his integrity and reliability, and who, I understood, fills the important place of balance holder, accountant, or an embodied justice in the domain — the referee, the reconciler; a man of equity, who has the faculty of making the right of every case so evident, that there is never any wish to appeal from his decision.

I felt the beautiful sphere of this company like a rich harmony around me. I knew that a most loving life circled among them ; and I could feel no discord — but I had evidently the place of some one who would have completed the circle, and sat in my place, between Evaline and Serafa.

"Who do I keep away?" I asked of the latter, when we had become a little acquainted.

"Oh, no one that would be here. Our Paul has found a tree, or a rock, or a bit of moss, that holds him by too strong an attraction. He is doing very well somewhere, and our gallery will be all the richer for his absence."

So Paul was also an artist and an enthusiast, somewhere at his work.

Our repast was slight, and very simple. Boiled rice with banana syrup, a quince jelly, some little crisp cakes, and a single glass of the purest white wine, delicate, aromatic, and almost sweet, something like the finest champaign, without the sparkle, was all that was taken. There was conversation, in low, quiet tones ; a repose of being that was very beautiful to me. There was not the least constraint or excitement, or effort at display. The news of the outside world, particularly the literary and artistic news, was discussed. The opinions expressed of authors and artists, and the leaders of movements, were singularly just and appreciative. Nearly the whole conversation was general. Scarcely for a moment did any two subside into a *tete a tete*. You can imagine such a circle of refined, cultivated, intelligent persons, adapted to each other, without a single one discordant or tiresome ; but can you imagine such a company, all loving each other, in perfect harmony, and with the happiness of this love increased by this harmonization ? I could not see that my presence was any bar to their enjoyment. My acceptance by one seemed to have made me at home with all ; and though I am but a neophyte, on my probation, they feel assured, as they well may, that I shall never be satisfied with any other life than this, of which I am allowed a

11

foretaste. If I doubted you I should not enjoy it—but how can I doubt that you are even more ready than I for a life of truth and harmony, and that you will joyfully escape from the world of falsity, selfishness, and discordance, which you see and feel around you?

After our half hour at supper, we heard a little trampling of feet and then a gentle knock at the door, when our circle was enlarged by the entrance of the two lovely children, Angela and the little Vincent. Vincent carried a bouquet of fragrant flowers to Harmonia, while Angela gave hers to Melodia.

"Didn't you mean this for papa?" asked Melodia.

"Yes, I meant it for both of you, and for all; but only one can hold it, and you are the one who should hold flowers." Then she sat in the lap of Vincent, and reaching over tò Serafa, said, "but I have a kiss for you."

"And what for me, my sister?" asked Evaline.

"Love for you, always, for teaching me so patiently to-day. And Melodia has taught me music. Oh! mamma!" turning to Harmonia, "one tune on your music box, please. Mr. Frank, are you musical?"

"A little, my dear."

"When you come and stay with us, you shall be my lover in an opera, and sing you are jealous, and stab me, or I'll stab you, just as the foolish people do—"

"In operas," said Harmonia, interrupting her.

"Oh, no, mamma; not in operas only, but in the world. I have been reading history, the past week, in the library, and there is plenty of such savagism."

And now, as the sun was descending, we heard the music of the band, and joined the groups, who were assembling to give him their adieus.

"It is so hard," said Serafa, who had taken my arm, "to think that all round the earth he will not shine on such a Home as this!"

"We must be patient of growth," said Vincent, who was near us: "all the future is ours, and the work is now begun. Think of the time when the sun will shine only on homes as happy as ours."

"But a whole planet to be transformed!"

"Yes, and a whole planet once had to be formed. Our ancestors, some centuries back, were painted savages, ferocious as the beasts they extirpated. Now they are civilizees."

"Are civilizees so much better than savages?" I ventured to ask.

"Yes; it is worse to knock a man on the head than only to pick his pocket. It is progress; and the way from savagism to harmony is through the discordance of civilization; and a high harmony cannot come without it; for civilization has given us all we have of industry, art, and their capabilities. They are worth all they have cost."

It was the evening parade. The sun sank in glory. The music repeated the golden clouds, and the deepening shadows, and all the mild and softening splendors of the scene; and the magnificent choral, as the last rays fell athwart our assembly, was in keeping with its tranquil grandeur. The evening gun was fired, and the flag descended.

The groups lingered a little in the twilight, and watched the coming of the early stars; but all were soon busy in preparing for the evening's amusement, the opera, which I must now attempt to describe to you. This, you know, is the crowning triumph of civilization. It is, indeed, a partial harmonization; a composite pleasure, adapted to refined and cultivated tastes, and combining a great variety, and a high order of enjoyments. The opera gives us poetry, music, painting, dramatic situation and action, dancing, often military evolutions, and such forms of life, energy, beauty and passion, as the poet and composer may combine.

As the night closed around us, all but the youngest children, their care-takers, and the first relay of the night watch, repaired to the opera. The large assembly-room had been changed into a beautiful theatre, with an ample stage, orchestra, and all needed appointments. A band of twenty one musicians, led by Vincent, played the overture, and the curtain rose on a performance, less powerful and effective, perhaps, than some that we have seen and heard at the Academy of Music, but more interesting and beautiful to me. Melodia was Prima Donna assoluta; next her was Evaline,

who proved a charming contralto, and Laura ; the male characters
were supported by the truant Paul, a delicate tenor; Alfred,
baritone; Edgar, buffo; and Manlins, a noble basso. It was in
two acts of an hour each with a most vivacious and sociable intermission ; with dancing in each act, executed by a small, but very
nicely trained *corps de ballet.* The chorus was full and effective—
perfect, indeed, in time and harmony.

Thus there were eighty persons engaged on the stage, and in
the orchestra, including twenty boys, who figured with great eclat,
first as a corps of soldiers, and afterwards as fairies ; and who
marched, and performed their evolutions and exercises with
wonderful precision.

The audience was as interesting to me as the performers. They
were dressed with elegance, and taste, but with great freedom and
variety. Close around the stage, in the front seats, gathered the
juvenile portion ; and their enjoyment was the keenest, and their
plaudits and encores the most vociferous ; and when the encore
was not sufficent, their exclamations of "O, once more," "please
once more !" were exquisite. I sat with Harmonia, who, not musical herself, enjoys music with all the capability of her sensitive
organization—exquisitely sensitive both to harmony and discord—
to pleasure and to pain. Serafa and Angelo, the sculptor, were near
me, and I was pleased to see that the poet enjoyed as well as any one,
her own creation, so far as it was hers, for she assured me that it
owed almost every thing to Melodia, who had written the best
songs ; to Vincent, who, with her, had composed the music, and to
the suggestions of others. I will not describe the plot. It opens
with a scene in civilization. There are three lovers, each loving
by turns, or all together, three mistresses, which leads to jealousy,
quarrels, attempts at assassination, poisonings, prison, and misery
enough. The first act ends very unhappily. But an enchanter
takes the affair in hand, and in the second, they find themselves on
an enchanted Island, a scene in fairy land, where the queen of the
fairies, by a potent spell, allays all jealousy, and after a few efforts
and some relapses, they all concluded to love each other, after the
fashion of Fairy Land, and all ends happily.

This was worked out with a delicacy and truthfulness of which you can have little conception. The scenery and appointments of the stage had been prepared with care, and the whole performance was full of the enthusiasm of real artists. The performers were called out in due form at the close of each act and pelted with flowers. Then the composer and author were called for, and crowned. It was a genuine ovation; after which all went happily to rest.

I accompanied Harmonia to her apartments, with Serafa and Raphael. Soon came Vincent and Melodia; she still in the costume and jewels of the stage, and wearing her crown of flowers. Never had she seemed more radiant than now. Vincent was sparkling with a refined wit; and both put their arms around the modest Serafa, and congratulated her on the success; but while she accepted their praises, she gave them all the credit they deserved. In our world, artists and singers are too often selfish and jealous, for these subverted passions are every where, poisoning all relations—but I saw none here. Alfred and Eveline, Laura and Paul, now joined us, and all brought stools and cushions, and gathered around Harmonia, and talked over the evening's pleasant work. Vincent made chocolate, Laura brought some cakes, and we supped together; and as quiet succeeded to the excitement of the evening, all joined with clasped hands and blissful tears, in a simple, gentle good night song, and all went, I could not doubt, to a blissful repose.

And I to mine, my Clara! Alone, but very happy;—alone, but ensphered in the harmony of the loving life around me, —alone, but resting in the hope, that not many months will elapse, before you will be here, to rest in my bosom, and share with me this paradise.

VIII.

My Clara ;—I wish to give you, as freshly as I can, and before one emotion has obliterated the impression of another, each day's experience of my trial of this new life. So I write on from day to day, and shall send the package by the weekly mail, sent by a messenger to the nearest post office.

My slumbers had not been disturbed by any seranade, unless it were the music of the opera, which came back in dreams ; and I woke with the first clear bugle note, the salutation to Aurora, bathed, and joined the parade at sunrise. I am not an early riser from habit, and a sunrise is a novel spectacle ; but I find here an impulse and attraction which I cannot resist. There is a fresh spirit in this morning assembly, a vigor of vitality, which inspires me. Is it the magnetism of the *esprit de corps* which animates every member of this society ? No regulation demands the presence of any ; there is no compulsion, any more than there is to labor—no external force, but in each case an attraction of abundant potency. No discipline demands it ; no roll is called ; there are no fines assessed, or penalties inflicted ; yet you can see and feel that no man, woman, or child of sufficient age, would willingly be absent.

Each day is a new life, and has new achievements. The order is also different for each day. This morning, for example, the band had another leader ; the morning choral was different, and the order of the day was called by Melodia, with different leaders in nearly all the groups of industry. The groups also, were all freshly arranged ; and if any one had failed to be present, his place would have been filled by some ready volunteer.

I observed that the hardest and most repugnant labors were sought as posts of honor, as the bravest soldiers volunteer for the
126

most dangerous duties. Approbativeness finds here its legitimate action. The night-watch, and other posts of responsibility, are also places of honor, to which only the most trusty and devoted are elegible.

As Melodia had directed the music, and the Order of the Day, she also gave the morning lecture. It was a beautiful statement of the political and social movements, tending to the progress of humanity, which she had observed during her recent journey. Many eyes sparkled, as she told of the rapid spread of the principles of their organization. · She inspired the enthusiasm of hope in those who wish to see the happiness they enjoy extended to all humanity, as fast as men can be prepared to receive it.

Even in our latitude, we know how delicious are fruits in the morning. It is even more so here, or else the fruits are of a richer flavor. Those which loaded the breakfast tables were fresh and delicious ; and I made my breakfast almost entirely on melons, peaches, and plums. After the groups of industry had gone to their labors, I wrote to you, until it was time to meet an appointment with Harmonia, who had invited me to make her a visit this morning.

I found her in her own parlor, study, or boudoir, for it is all combined. She held out her left hand to me as she laid down her pen with the right, and when I sat on a low ottoman beside her, she laid her thin pale hand on my head, and said : "Are you a good boy to-day ?" I think young men do not usually like to be called or considered boys ; but I was very grateful for this maternal recognition. I only kissed her other hand, and looked up with a smile.

"And do you think the little one you have left is as good as you?" She asked, with a serious look.

It was you, Clara, she meant by the little one. I told her of my great faith in you, and my great love for you. "Yet it is a hard trial," she said, "for the absent one. She is lonely and desolate —you have the excitement of new scenes, and the interest of new friends. Have you been quite frank with her in your letters ? It is well that you have," she continued, when I assured her that I had written every thought and feeling to you; "for though the trial may be sharp and difficult to bear, neither of you can afford the expense of deceit."

"I have been true as truth," I said.

"And you hope," she continued quietly, "that she has borne it as well as you would have done, were she now here, and you at home in her place."

O my Clara! I was rebuked and humbled by the consciousness that I could not have borne this trial as I have wished you to bear it; and were I not sure that you are better than I feel myself to be, I should fear that I have made you suffer more than I can tell; for it all came over me in a moment—all the loneliness, all the fear, all the agony, I might have endured. And yet, O beloved! I have been true to the deep love of my heart for you all the moments. May you so feel it.

Harmonia saw how troubled I was at the thought she had suggested, and said with a smile, "We, who are children of Providences, are not tried beyond our strength to bear. The angels who have led you to us, have filled the loving heart with the consolation of trust. If she is to come to us with you, she, like you, must have her preparation. She must understand, and lovingly accept our life of truth and freedom. Do not fear to be as frank to her as you have been hitherto. Let her know all our life that comes to you, that she may accept it as you accept it."

"I accept and welcome joyfully all I see and comprehend of it," I answered; "but how it has come to you, and how it exists, I do not yet understand."

"This is the lesson you have come to learn, and all here will be your teachers. Shall I begin my lesson?"

"I would drink at the fountain," I answered.

"The rains, and the hidden sources supply the fountain," said she; "I have been but the instrument of this work. The thought and the love were born; and the world groaned with its great needs. Civilization, with all its progress, and all its triumphs, had never satisfied the social wants of man.

"At last, the harmony, sought in vain on earth, descended from the heavens. The angels, in the higher spheres, live in harmony: and the germ fell into the hearts of a few who could receive it humbly and joyfully, and give it the conditions of growth. We sought for freedom and truth in all relations, and especially in the relations of love, and all that cluster around them. With a single devotion to this work, we accepted for it the consecration of our lives, receiving into our group only those who could join in this consecration. Our lives were thus made pure and fitted for harmony; for we had seen that there could be no social harmony, until the faculties of the individuals composing it were first harmonized."

"It is of this harmonization," I said, "that I wish to know. By what process was it attained?"

"We endeavored to free ourselves from every thing discordant in our lives, and to put away all hindrances to harmony. Our minds were freed from all prejudices and superstitions, so that we could receive the truth. We rejected the false gods, that we might accept the true. Individual freedom came to us, as the first condition of this purification. To be able to do any thing, we must be free to do it—free in ourselves, and free from all control or influence of others. So we became self-centered and self-governed beings. We sought physical purity, or health, by pure habits, and the disuse of all diseasing aliments. So the germinal group became purified."

"And all bonds were severed?"

"All false ones fell from us; all arbitary restraints of law and custom we put away when we passed to a higher plane of life, where they were no longer of any use, but only encumbrances. Thus marriage, as a legal bond, had no more use to us. If a love relation was a true one, we needed no legal bond—if false, we could not be compelled to live the lie. Our higher law was to live the true life—in all things to cease to do evil, and learn to do well.

"In the consecration of our lives, during this period of probation and germination, when the central group of this society was forming, and when all the energy and power of our lives was needed in the work of growth, our love became spiritual, to the exclusion of the sensual element, or the material union. We formed a sacred vestalate. It was necessary that the harmony of love should come to us on the spiritual plane, before we could be fitted for it on the material. In all this we were guided by the wisdom of the Heavens, which we received with reverence and lived to with devotion. So it was, my friend, that those who came to us were of the same life, entering into a perfect accord with us, in a loving harmony, the fruits of which you see around you."

"And there came no jealousy — no discord ?"

"Jealousy and discord were severed from us, or they severed from us all who were not ready for harmony. The selfish only are jealous. It is the passion of claim or ownership. When we renounced all claim to, or ownership of, each other, there was no longer any ground for jealousy ; and when this principle had been extended to all things, there was no cause of discord. When the harmony was established in our little group of earnest and devoted lovers, they drew others to them, of whom other groups were formed, until we were strong enough to seek our Home which Providence had given us."

"And all came here ?"

"First, the central group, and a band of pioneers, to build, and plant, and prepare. Then the groups who were harmonized with us. You will better learn the details of the work from others. My work has been to harmonize the interior life, and to be the medium of the spiritual society, in the heavenly life, which it is our work to represent in the Earth-Life."

She sat a moment in silence — then binding a fillet over her eyes, she held my hand. A tremor passed over her, and she smiled and said : "A lovely woman is standing beside you ; she is tall and graceful, with blue eyes and curling auburn hair : she has a deep dimple in her left cheek : she bends over and kisses your hair. She says she is your mother ; that she guided you to Melodia, and so to us ; and that she will not leave you until you are one of ours. She watches over the beautiful one at home, and consoles her, and is preparing her, with your help, to come to us. She says there is a good work for you to do in the future, both in the world and in Harmony, and that you will be the instrument of bringing many into the True Life: and Earthly Harmony, which is but the prelude to the Grander Harmonies of the Life of the Heavens. She kisses you, and she smiles upon us — and I see her no more."

I did not doubt that it was the spirit of my dear mother. True, there was no test — she might have had her description from Melodia — but there was the internal conviction of truthfulness and reality which was worth all tests. My mother still lives; surely, if living, she comes to her child; and why should not this woman, so pure, so spiritual, so gifted, be clairvoyant enough to see her. It is but one spirit seeing another.

She removed the fillet from her eyes, and said, "I am very glad your mother has come to me, for it confirms our acceptance of you, and our belief in your usefulness. Use your time here diligently; see all you can of our life, and try to live in its spirit. Live in unity with those you most love on the earth, and in the heavens. When we taught freedom, a sensual world accused us of licentiousness; you will find in it the removal of all hindrances to the highest and most heavenly life. Our life here is not perfect, but progressive. Every day it grows more beautiful."

"Ah! but the great world, and all its miseries. Can you enjoy all this plenty and happiness, and not think of others?" I asked.

"We *do* think and we act. It has been our high mission to show mankind the possibility of a harmonic society, free from all the cares, discords, and miseries of civilization. The work is nearly done. The experiment, or working model of such an association is accomplished, and, after an earnest trial of five years, you see its success. Could we have done so well for the world by any other means?

"We cannot open our doors to unprepared and discordant civilizees, with their present habits and vices of thought and life. It would peril all. Could we have a flesh-eater with his butcherings; a tobacco user, poisoning our atmosphere; a bigot with his persecuting spirit, willing to commence on earth the tortures he believes to be in store in future for all who are not of his creed; a domestic despot, holding property in a wife or husband — in the life and soul of another? Do you not know that a single untuned instrument, or unskillful player, will make discord in the finest orchestra? So would it be with us. We cannot destroy our work, but we can perfect and extend it; and we shall be ready soon to receive such groups as are forming and attuning themselves to our harmony; and when our number is complete, you and others will be ready to form the germ of another association. Meantime our thought is finding its way to many minds, and the love of a pure and integral freedom to many hearts. Many will soon be ready to graduate out of civilization, and the movement will go on with an accelerating momentum.

"But nothing must be done hastily or rudely. We do not give concerts with a band of beginners in music. And we must guard with care the tender plants of harmony. You can see well, how all previous attempts have been failures of necessity. There must be no more with us."

"I know that all have failed, but I have not seen the reason."

"In every case there have been many causes of discord, any one of which was enough to drive asunder those who wished for harmony, and not an aggregation, and aggravation of discords. Disease is a burthen, and all civilization is full of disease. Marriage and the family, the central institution of civilization, is unsuited to any other social state. A single family here, living in the usual relation of husband and wife, parents and children, would destroy our harmony. In a true society, self-ownership and self-governmuet, and the mutual adaptation and responsiblity of each to all, and all to each, must pervade the whole body. We have no married couples; no family jars; no education in discordances. But you will see all this better than I can tell you.

"Well, does this hurt you? Do not be troubled for the little one. Her instincts are more to be trusted than your reason. Have you a confession to make?"

It was not strange that she asked this question now, for my head was bowed in a profound sorrow. I told her, frankly, that I had thought of you, and that I could not endure the idea of your loving another.

"No," she said, with a tender smile, "you want the dear one all to you self. Well, find a nice cottage, with a pretty garden, a horse and cow, and have it as you will. If she were here, she might love Vincent, or Angela, or Alfred, as much, perhaps, as you love Melodia, or might love Serafa, or Evaline, or me, even — who knows?"

I laughed. It was too ridiculous. I was ashamed of my inconsistency and absurdity.

"Come, we have talked enough here," she said, rising from her easy chair; "you shall go and help me work now."

We went to a portion of the garden, where a multitude of roses, of the most fragrant kinds were blooming. A group of young girls and children were busily and merrily at work, gathering the petals of the fully opened flowers into baskets, which, as fast as filled, were carried into a room, for the manufacture of perfumery. I saw that the roses, and other odorous flowers cultivated so profusely were not alone for ornament, but were converted, by a pleasant and most attractive industry, into many rich and delicate perfumes, which yielded a handsome revenue. So we worked, picking roses, and one of the young ladies, an adept in botany and vegetable chemistry, ex lained to me the processes—how some odors were separated by the fixed oils, and others by distillation, and how they were combined to form the various mixtures of the toilette.

Farther on were groves of the sun-flower, so arranged as to give great richness to the landscape, and whose seeds, gathered by a group of juveniles, and submitted to a hydraulic press, a mysterious power they were delighted to exercise and explain, yielded a large supply of a pure oil, for various uses ; after which the seed cakes was conveyed to the poultry yard.

Flowers, useful for show alone, were cultivated sparingly, but the odorous one in great abundance. We found great beds of the heliotrope, the white lily, the lemon verbena, and the sweet voilet, all used in perfumes. Here, also, were groves of the magnolia, and flowering lo ust, whose blossoms they make as profitable as the fruit of other trees ; while they are, in their season, the glory of the landscape.

After two hour's of work, which Harmonia counted for four to her, since I had helped her, we went to meet the returning harvesters, with whom Vincent and Melodia had been at work. How rosy and beautiful she looked, in her blouse and trousers, with her broad hat wreathed with wild flowers, intermingled with heads of wheat. She welcomed us, like a queen returning from a victory.

And now the returning bands gathered to the home, and the waters flowed, and all were dressed for the dinner festival.

As we ate our strawberries, which by a careful culture and irrigation are made to produce fruit the whole season, and I sat by Evaline, Harmonia said to her: " My dear, I think that Mr. Wilson and I will pay you a visit this afternoon, if agreeable."

Evaline looked at her mother, and then at Vincent and Melodia, before answering ; then, as if the scrutiny were satisfactory, she said : " I shall be happy to see you."

" But you did not seem quite certain," I said, in a low tone, fearing there was some reason why she did not wish me to come.

" I was not—because I have not had the opportunity to know you, as these have ; so I must take their judgment of you until I can form one of my own. Our Eugenia has been more fortunate."

I looked across the table, where the beautiful Eugenia was blushing rosy red—but I did not know why, then. I was fool enough to think that she had expressed some partiality for me, which she blushed to have expressed to me.

After dinner, came a musical repose, with all the gems of Norma, exquisitely rendered ; and then I prepared to go with Harmonia, who had given the day to my instruction and amusement.

She conducted me to the Art-Gallery, which is also the studio, where we found several groups of artists and students, engaged in various departments of their beautiful work. I saw here the center and source of the tasteful decorations and fine works of painting and sculpture, which adorn every portion of the edifices of Esperanza. I have written of the decorations of the Fairy, and of the Banquetting Hall, and the scenery of the Opera ; but I have not yet given you an idea of the art-beauty which enriches every thing. Here I found how it has been produced.

Near the entrance of the long gallery we found a group of young students, taking their early lessons in drawing, and who should we find as a leader or teacher, but our lovely Angela, who sat in the midst, drawing an urn of flowers? Others were drawing different objects, and all were at work happily.

A little further on were some older and more advanced students, standing at their easels, and drawing from casts of antique statuary. Another group was modeling figures in clay. Around were the best works of their classes or groups, each with the name and date — mementos of progress.

Further on we found Evaline, Paul, and the group of painters, painting landscapes, historical or alegorical pictures, etc. It was still a school, but the work was of such a merit as to command a ready sale.

Harmonia had taken my hand as we advanced, and when we came where several were painting the same subject, she turned with me to look at what I supposed to be a picture they were copying. It was a scene of some fairy land, a happy group reposing under trees, eating fruit, and weaving garlands of flowers. The design, composition, and coloring, all struck me as wonderful, and I stepped forward to get a nearer view, when I found myself looking at, not a painted picture, but a living composition. The figures were models chosen from the most beautiful forms; the fruit and flowers were real; the background had been sketched from nature in distemper, like scene painting, with great truth and effectiveness, and the drapery was arranged with an artful carelessness, that was truly charming. The repose of the positions was so real, that the *tableau vivant* could remain an hour without fatigue, and the result, I saw, would be five grand pictures, each a copy of the model, yet each original in execution. It was a friendly competition, which must bring out the finest powers of each artist; and when all were finished, the one selected would be kept here, and the rest sold f.r the mutual benefit of the artists and the Home.

At the far end of the gallery I saw the sculptor Angelo at work upon a statue, while one was standing near him, on a pedestal, in all the purity of truth—a statue, but living, I found, like the picture. I hesitated—but Harmonia laid her hand upon my arm, and I went forward. The undraped and most beautiful model whom I did not recognize, so accustomed are we to look only at faces, held out her hand to me, and with a start of surprise, I saw that it was Eugenia.

Well, I took her hand as if she had been only the loveliest statue in the world. She blushed no more. Enshrined in the purity of art, there came to her pure spirit no thought or emotion of evil. The sculptor worked on with his copy, soon to be moulded and cast in alabaster; while others were taking advantage of the presence of the model, to make exquisite drawings; and two or three advanced students were modelling ·busts, or statuettes.

The long room, with its soft, cool lights, its groups of earnest students and artists, its stillness, broken only by low murmurs, and the pictures and statues along the walls, seemed to me a sacred temple for the worship of the Divine Beauty. All art schools and artists, I know, have models, such as they can procure; but they are usually such as serve for hire. Here were those who gave themselves to the uses of art, with a real enthusiasm; who entered into the spirit, and could give the very expression of each subject. I cannot doubt that pictures and statues, produced under such circumstances, must have a peculiar value, and I can well believe that no other industry yields more revenue to Esperanza than the works of her artists.

Pictures and statues are multiplied, to a limited extent, by the means I have described; but engraving and lithography are also employed for this purpose, and to aid in the mission of the beautiful.

"I thank you!" was my exclamation to my friend, as we descended from the gallery. "You have afforded me much pleasure."

"And you have also given me some. 'Blessed are the pure in heart.' The rest of the verse is, 'for they shall see God.' Perhaps if you read for they shall see *good*, it will be as well. I do not think we are likely ever to see God, but as we see him always, in all the universe; but the pure in heart see good, where the corrupt find only evil."

"I have never seen evil in works of high art; they have always seemed to me to be elevating and refining in their influence."

"You have been fortunate in your birth and your culture; but there are thousands in our country, of Pharisaic pretension, who are much less fortunate, and but few in the world of civilization, not accustomed to the sphere and methods of art, who could have passed so well through this ordeal. In our life, and with our thoughts and feelings, clothing is a convenience, a necessity of climate, or an ornament; not a moral necessity, as in civilization. Madame 'George Sand' once said, when her friends were talking enthusiastically of the establishment of association — the Phalansterie of Fourier — 'Gentlemen, I will tell you when it will be possible to realize association. When a woman can walk out into the street naked, and excite no more attention or remark than if she were dressed; then, and not till then, may your dreams be realized.'

"It was a profound truth. What is needed for harmony is that moral purity, which comes from the development and equilibrium or harmonization of all the faculties. It is here — here where woman may wear any clothing, as you see, or none, without offence or injury to any."

"Is the studio I have visited to-day," I asked, "open to every person?"

"Assuredly, it is open to every one of us at proper times; but our principles guard us against intrusion. Eugenia, or Melodia, or whoever might be the model, would not be troubled at being seen by any who would wish to visit the studio. If there were strangers, they must be such as we know, and could welcome into our family."

I expressed my thanks for this confidence; but I confess, dear Clara, that I was not quite satisfied. It is not easy to say why one may not look at a woman, beautiful as she came from the hand of nature, with the same feeling with which we may look at the picture or statue of one, such as may be seen in all of our galleries;

12

and it may be that there is prejudice in one case, as there has been in the other. But though I was reconciled to having my divinities seen by a few, I did not wish to extend the privilege to so many, and I expressed these doubts to Harmonia, who said:

"You are still a little prejudiced and unjust. The rules, and customs, and restraints of civilization may be necessary to the conditions it creates. Here it is not so. All who are here have come through the gate of consecration; and though some have less of culture and taste than others, all are honest, and have a right to the refining influences of both nature and art. Beauty exerts a holy influence on such souls; why should you deprive them of the highest beauty? The legend of the Lady Godiva, while it records the devotion of one woman, also records the conscious unworthiness of all the men of Coventry to look upon her, as well as their honest self-denial in refraining from looking unworthily."

"But, dear madam," I said, "you would not have sensual eyes gloating on the beauty of those you love?"

"I would not have sensual eyes around me to gloat on any thing. Where there are such, beauty needs protection. But when fashion tells your New York ladies to uncover their arms or bosoms, do they ask any questions about sensual eyes?"

"They do not: but I have never felt satisfied that any one I cared for should be exposed to such rude gazings."

"You were right, I think. Sensitive natures feel the influence of the emotions they unwittingly excite. Your shrinking from it is a true instinct — but were all men and women pure and honest, could you have such a feeling? We do not hide ourselves from the angels, nor from any that we love and trust."

"But would you have Eden back again?"

"Perhaps not; certainly not until the race improves in beauty. There are few of us who do not need clothing to conceal our imperfections. Beauty, now, is the exception; it will soon be the rule, and then universal. When that comes, Eden, if you will. At present, I should beg to be excused, for the sake of my own eyes, as well as those of others."

So our strange conversation ended; and I walked down to the lake-side, thinking of it all, and surveying the beauty of the scene, until the bright Angela came running to invite me to take my supper with her sister, and the group of artists to which she belongs.

It was served in Evaline's apartment, where she sat at the head of the table, as hostess, while I had the place of honor as her guest.

It was a delightful party. We had Melodia, Eugenia, and a bevy of bright girls, with the charming Angela; and for men, Angelo, Paul, and their brother artists. The conversation was of beauty, and tasté, and I saw evidences of both all around me.

I wish I could describe this room of the gentle, artistic Evaline. It is the more outer covering or clothing of herself. Its walls are of her choice colors, in which blue and rose predominate; and though delicately painted in fresco, they yet admit of many gems of art, pictures of her own, portraits of her friends, and the works of her brother and sister artists. There is a library of her choice books; and with her pianoforte and guitar, a music rack, filled with her favorite music. The furniture is of carved wood — each piece of some different device, and each the design and work of some one who wished to be remembered. Every thing has its story, or its memory. The room opens into a sleeping room, with its closets, bath-room and dressing-room.

Every person here, who has arrived at the age of twelve years, has his or her own independent suite of rooms, with the simple necessities of furniture, at first, to be added to afterward, according to taste and ability. Each apartment is sacred to its owner, and free from all intrusion. Parent or friend cannot come without knocking, and no one asserts claim or authority. Privacy and entire individuality are thus secured.

So the tasteful Evaline was here in her own home, and those she chose to have with her she took here, as she might have taken them into her bosom. She had dressed for the little fete in colors harmonizing with the room; and her guests had each dressed for the occasion in varied, but graceful costumes. It was a refined adornment of natural charms, like a fine setting of gems, or a fit framing of pictures. Conforming to no tyranny of fashion, each one was a separate study in character and becomingness.

So in our little feast, while all was gentleness and courtesy, there was an entire absence of all formality. When any thought of a story to tell, it was told; and if a song or an air was spoken of or thought of, some one would run to the pianoforte to sing or play it. This gentle revel, so full of wit and soul, lasted until we heard the music of the band on the western lawn, summoning us to the parade at sunset. It was a moment of sublime beauty. The descending sun, sinking in the golden west; his beams reflected from the windows of the Home; the grand music of the full band, and a chorus of two hundred voices, all produced an effect of sublimity, until the evening gun boomed over the waters, and came back in echoes from the forest coves, and the flag descended, and the day was done.

I could see the harmonizing influence of these morning and evening assemblages, in which all were animated and inspired by one common emotion, in one common act. As the last echoes died away, the sacred emblem was folded with religious care, and brought to Harmonia. She gravely thanked the pages who had brought it; then others came, took it in charge, and conveyed it to its place of deposit, to bring it forth in the morning to be raised at sunrise, with similar ceremonies.

When this was done, the assemblage, which had been formed in crescentic order, broke into groups, and spent the next half hour of early twilight like innocent sportive children; and then all went to prepare for the evening festival.

It was a concert and ball of an entirely informal and unpretending character. The evening was warm, though freshened by the lake breeze; the toilets were light, gauzy, but very graceful. The music, mostly of stringed and light wind instruments, as the flute and oboe, was of a soft exhilaration, while the dances were of a gentle, graceful character, such as we seldom see in our assemblies.

After a little practice, I found this style of dancing very agreeable. In a quadrille, where the sets change so that you dance with many partners, it was pleasant to be acquainted with every one, and to need no introductions. It was better to feel that every one treated me with entire confidence. I saw no sadness here, such as one sees with us in the gayest company, and felt no distrust. There was the most perfect freedom, without riot or disorder. A refined courtesy, a gentle politeness, a self-possessed, and yet deferntial behavior, was universal. There was no haughtiness, and no intrusion. Groups clustered by spontaneous attraction. If I looked at a lady wishfully, as if I would speak or dance with her, she held out her hand to me, or signed with her fan or bouquet to invite me to approach her. And I have observed here, that at all times, in the fields, shops, or assemblies, no one ever risks intrusion by approaching an individual or a group, without an invitation. So, if you choose, you may be in the most perfect isolation. I have seen no rudeness, coarseness, or impertinence of speech or action, such as we have seen but too often, even in the most fashionable assemblies.

In the intervals of the dancing we had two or three stories, recitations, or speeches; and some choice vocal music; and at the close, one of those grand chorusses, which seem to melt all into the same harmony. So the merry evening closed with a calm happiness, and Harmonia, who had given me the morning, now came to bid me good night. We walked out into the moonlight, and down through the soft odors of the night to the sands of the lake, and sat there by the silvery ripple of its waves.

"Two days with us, my friend," she said; her hand resting on my shoulder, "two days of our life. Will you tell me how it now seems to you?"

"It seems like dream-land.'

"It has been a dream—but all such dreams come to be realities."

"But is there no fear that some calamity will befall this happy scene; that these gathered groups may be scattered again into the discords and isolation of the outer world?"

"We have no such fear. What is to scatter us?"

"If you and Vincent were to die."

"As we must, soon. There are many ready to stand in our

places. The harmony clusters around the central life, but that belongs to no individual. And each group has its own center, as well as all the groups a central group. All are educated, and are being every day more educated in this life. Nothing but some convulsion of external force can destroy us. From that the Providence that has brought us so far, will guard and defend us."

"Amen!" I murmured reverently. "But I have much yet to learn. You now, sitting with me alone in the night. Does no one wait for you?"

"Do I belong to myself, or to another?" said she, with energy. "But I can pardon the question and the thought, for I have lived in all the slaveries of civilization. I know what it is to be owned. But now, and here, I am free, as every one here is free. No woman here is owned by husband, or parent, or lover. She lives her own life, accountable only to her own interior sense of right— to the Divinity of her own being. So, if I should sit all night by the lake shore, alone, or with another, there is no one to call me to account, or to criticise my conduct."

"And Vincent?"

"Is he less his own? Look!" She pointed across the lake, where I saw a boat with its white sail, and in a few moments we heard first a few clear bugle notes, and then a glee of three voices, in which I recognized Melodia, Vincent, and Evaline. The boat sped on, and the music died away in the distance.

The lights had been extinguished, one by one, until the home was lighted only by the clear moonbeams, a picture of wondrous beauty; a cluster of buildings, which have spread out like the banian tree; a symetrical variety, every addition adding to the picturesqueness of the whole mass without marring any effect

"Our life is three-fold," said Harmonia, when I had looked some moments at this scene; "the life of the individual, of the group, and of the whole society. Our life secures to us the most absolute individual freedom. Every one consults his own tastes, chooses his own employments, and disposes of his time, labor and affections as he wishes to do. Every one finds those with whom he can group in the relations of friendship and love, and all groups join together in those enterprises and amusements which are for the common good. We have a beautiful home, plenty beyond all care, a healthful and attractive industry, a growing and refining art, means for intellectual improvement and enjoyment, freedom and love. Heaven is very near us in this Home. With our own present and future assured to us, we only ask that others may be prepared as fast as may be to join us, and then to form other Homes like this, until the world will be filled with riches, beauty harmony and happiness."

"Will it be soon?" I asked, as if certain that she could tell me.

"Not soon, if we reckon by our wishes," she said, "and yet sooner than would be reckoned by our fears. It is a question of progress or growth. But few of the present or passing generation can be developed up to the plane of harmony. Our work is with the young. We are preparing the means of education for vast numbers, who will come to us soon, before the habits, and vices, and bonds of civilization have gathered around them. The older, who can become as little children, may also enter this kingdom of Heaven."

"You have a goodly number here; and persons of all ages."

"Yes; yet they are mostly young. And these have been gathered from a large territory. They have come, many of them, out of great tribulation, and with the sundering of many ties. It required years of progressive development, before they were ready even to form the first groups of harmony. But the great want and the great love conquered, and when Providence opened the way, we came, and our groups gathered around us; and here we are, the only free society upon the earth."

"It seems to me," I said, "that if I could present simply and truly the fact of this life to our society, they would receive it at once, and that the whole world could be revolutionized in a few years!"

"So thought Fourier. He believed that if some great monarch or great capitalist would only advance the means to form the first Phalanstcrie, it would not be more than seven years before the whole human race, even the barbarians and savages, would come

into the harmonies of the combined order. Enthusiasm is very
credulous. Think what men must abandon before they are fitted
for the first step. Man must be freed from all their prejudices.
They must give up all sectarian bigotries. A man cannot live in
harmony with those he believes to be totally depraved and destined
to eternal perdition. Men must give up the selfishness of personal
ambitions, the lust of wealth, the lust of power, the lust of appetite;
they must be cleansed of all lusts, and come into the consecration
of all faculties to the work of development and the purposes of
harmony."

"Leave all, and follow the Divine Truth?"

"Leave all that is inconsistent with the practice of the truth. A
man may not necessarily leave father, and mother, and children;
property and friends; but he must be ready to do so, or there is
no true consecration. Think now, if you know many persons
ready for our life."

I thought earnestly, my Clara, and I could only think of you,
and of you hope, not without trembling. It asks for so much, and
yet it seems to me but the most simple, natural, and beautiful life,
and one every body ought to live.

We heard now a song stealing over the waters; a sweet low
song of love and happiness. I recognized, even in the far distance,
the voice and guitar of Evaline. Soon the sail whitened in the
moonbeams and the boat drew nigh. We rose and Harmonia
waved her handkerchief, and the boat, obeying her signal, soon
grounded on the beach where we were standing, the sail was
furled and a party of six came on shore. Vincent put his arm
around Harmonia; Melodia came to me, and we went slowly up the
gravelled walk, through the heavy perfumes.

We all went to Melodia's apartment, when each one drank a
single glass of wine, as if it were a sacrament; then, with a kiss
of peace they went to their repose. And I was left with Melodia,
alone, at midnight.

She sat upon a couch, and I sank at her feet — the beautiful feet
of her who had brought me glad tidings. Lovely as I had
thought her, when I first saw her; beautiful as she was to me on

all our journey, she had never appeared so beautiful as now, in the heart of her Home, and among her loved ones. She did not wait for me to speak first, but said:

"Have I done well to bring you here?"

"I can never thank you as I wish," I answered.

"I am thanked and paid, if you come back to us."

And I said "Oh, beautiful one; my life is here. I shall come, for I love you."

She took my hand and held it a few moments in silence. I would have spoken, but I could not. I felt a subduing power, which calmed me. I wondered how I had said what I did, but I could not take it back. It was not needed. She said very softly and tenderly to me —

"I know that you love me; and this love, which must live a a sacred thing in your heart, will help to conquer obstacles, and bring you here again. When you have come, and have passed through the portal of consecration, you will find all that is truly yours. I accept the love with a devout thankfulness; you must trust me as you love.

"Is it so hard to wait?" she asked, responsive to some look or thought of mine. "You must wait with an entire patience, until you are in the harmony, before you can know what the harmony will bring to you. I accept your love as a prophecy, which may help to accomplish its own fulfilment. I thank you for your love, and I give you *hope*."

She rose as I did, put back my hair, and with an inexpressibly sweet, tender dignity, pressed her lips to my forehead, and I went from her presence as reverently, as I would have parted from an angel.

13

IX.

My Beautiful: I imagine myself with you, seated at your side, and telling you all that I write. Would that it could be so! I know that you would ask me many questions, and bring out by your inquiries, a hundred details I may forget to give you.

The basis of all true life is industry; and the product of industry is wealth. In our civilization, many are idle drones; and the labor of vast multitudes is wasted or unproductive. I have long seen this, but never clearly as now. Here all work, from the infant of five years to the oldest; and a large portion of this labor is productive of wealth. I walked around yesterday, almost the entire day, except the hours in which I wrote to you, and inspected many details of this industry, which is the basis of so much happiness.

The first material wants of this society are food, clothing, and shelter. Grain, fruits, vegetables, milk, eggs, honey, are produced in superabundance for every want, and some in large surplus. Of wheat and corn, those great cereal staples, for example, there is always a three years' supply in the air tight granaries. Of fruits, there is a large stock, dried or preserved. The finest vegetables, as green corn, green peas, and tomatoes, are also kept in large quantities. There are a thousand hens, and a hundred swarms of bees. The eggs are preserved both in vacuum and by drying to powder. A few hours' labor each day, through the growing season, not only supplies every want, and fills the granaries and store-houses beyond all fear of want, but leaves an abundant surplus, which the Fairy takes to a ready market at New Orleans, Memphis or Vicksburg.

This surplus is exchanged, in part, for sugar, rice, etc., and in part for the materials of clothing, both for the general stock, and

146

for individual requirements. This clothing is made up during the winter, and on rainy days, when out-door work is impracticable. The general clothing, and bed and table linen, is made up by groups of workers, in the sessions of general or communal labor. The private wardrobes are made up in the groups, in the hours of individual work or amusement. A lady who has dresses to make for herself, or for some one she loves, invites a group of skilled artists to assist her, and she assists them in turn. Great skill is thus developed, and a wonderful beauty and variety of costume.

The shelter, or dwelling combines every needed convenience. The suites of rooms, consisting of parlors, bed-rooms, bath-rooms, and closets, are clustered in groups, the parlors of a group opening into each other, so that several can be combined, where a group gives a party, and invites the members of other groups. At the same time the privacy of every individual is most sacredly respected. The whole is lighted, and warmed in winter, by gas, and cooled in summer by a most perfect ventilation.

The large saloons have self-acting ventilators, which open and let out the warm air, and admit the cooler, at a certain temperature. The outer walls are all double, for protection against both cold and heat ; and a blower attached to the steam-engine throws either warm or cold air, as needed, through pipes, to every portion of the buildings

So the three physical wants have a beautiful and abundant pro vision : a residence of excellent adaptation to every requirement of comfort and taste ; clothing for use, cleanliness, and beauty ; and food in abundance, healthful, nourishing, and satisfying the demands of an esthetic gastronomy.

But the supply of these physical requirements, even on a scale of luxury and refinement. requires but a small portion of the industry of this society. There is a varied and active work in manufactures and art, adding to the wealth, elegance, and luxury of the Home. Of these I will hereafter give you some details. There is abundant work, and also abundant leisure ; but the work, performed as it is here, is more attractive than rest, and I see that the busy instinct of humanity here finds its normal action. Every work, by skill and combination, is made amusing.

It is curious to see the industrial force of this society, and the prodigies it performs. I spoke of this to Alfred, yesterday, as I watched the progress of the addition to the building, whose walls are rising day by day, and where men and boys, and even a few girls, work on like so many beavers, impelled by the same instinct.

"We have nothing else to do," said he, "for we are not obliged to take care of each other, as in the society we have left."

"For example?" said I; willing to see the case he would make.

"For example, we need not deduct from the effective industrial force of our society, a parson to preach for us; a doctor to cure us of diseases self-produced; a lawyer to help us quarrel; police to keep us in order; soldiers to fight for us; sick people and their attendants; financiers to fleece us; traders to buy and sell for us; thieves and paupers to plunder us; and so on to the end of the long list of the civilized drones, leeches and parasites."

It was a good enumeration, but not yet half filled out. In New York, every working man does enough labor every year, in paying his rent, to build a good house, which would last him his life time. If he works three hundred days a year, two hundred and fifty or more are for other people. Yet what a life! How poor, enslaved, meager and miserable it appears, in comparison with the free, buoyant, happy life around me.

"There are other economies of labor here," said Alfred, "which may be worth considering. If the men are set free from the useless occupations of civilization, or the necessity of supporting those who follow them; the women are quite as free and available to productive industry. In the isolate and discordant disorder of the prevailing society, our women would be either fashionable idlers, or housekeepers, or domestic drudges. Here we have neither. A small group is in the nursery; others in kitchen and laundry; and all free to assist in some productive or beautiful industry. Our force is four or five times as great, therefore, as with the same number of persons in the old society, so that we can easily accomplish double in half the time."

"And the enthusiasm counts for something?"

"It nearly doubles the product again. Twenty of our boys and girls, working together, with the vigor of health and the excitement of an emulative contest, will often do more work in two hours, than the same number of hired laborers would do in a day.

"There are other economies than those of labor. For instance, it would cost three times the labor to build separate dwellings, for as many families as our population would compose. They would burn six times the fuel. Their separate cookings, washings, bakings, etc. would require ten times the labor. Fifty barns, granaries, cellars, sets of fences, kitchen furniture, implements, etc. and all this, to secure less privacy than we enjoy, less comfort in every way, giving us a thousand cares and annoyances, and not a tithe of our means of happiness. Civilization is a miserable state of toil, vexation, and enslavement, under the best conditions. You have seen what it may be under the worst."

The hideous picture of the life of poverty in our city, came to me, in the light of this contrast, as it never came before.

I walked away thoughtfully, and came soon where a noisy group of children, from three to ten years old, were engaged in picking and shelling green peas. They were stripped from the vines with great rapidity, and carried in baskets to two dog carts, the contest being to see which cart would be soonest filled by its group. There was also a spirited contest between the pickers and shellers, and it was no empty victory, for the members of the triumphant groups have the right to wear the badge of their triumph at the evening parade and festival.

It had been beautiful weather for several days, but the gardens required moisture. I went with Vincent to see the opening of the sluices for irrigation. The canal winds along the hill side, with an embankment skirted by the osier, or basket willow, which is also a staple of industry for the winter; the willow furniture of all kinds made here, being light and graceful as fairy work, and finding a ready market at high prices.

In the arrangement of the grounds, more than four hundred acres can be watered from this canal, which is fed by a mountain lake and living springs. If these were to fail, Vincent said, they could readily send the water up from the lake below. As we passed along the dyke, opening the sluices from point to point, it was beautiful to see the waters go rushing and dancing down the slopes, and we heard the cheers of the children, as the rivulets reached them. In a little time the whole region was well moistened. Where the lands are out of the reach of this irrigation, there are watering carts, filled by backing into the lake, and then distributing their showers like the watering carts in Broadway.

Among the favorite amusements or attractive occupations of the young people of both sexes, is the training of horses to beautiful exercises, on a part of the grounds, well fitted for this purpose. As there are fifty horses and ponies, there is no lack of material; and the children not old enough to be entrusted with horses, have their pet goats, dogs, and sheep, under excellent subjection, so as to go in the saddle and harness, and perform many uses.

This life, you see, is not simply utilitarian. It is not to get the greatest possible product out of a certain amount of labor, or a certain number of hands. The higher object is seen every where, of making the life best worth living; a means for the exercise, development and enjoyment of all faculties. These equestrian exercises, I could see, were well adapted to give strength, energy and a certain boldness and self-possession of character. There is, also, on this play ground, a gymnasium for old and young, much used in the winter, and at all seasons when the regular work does not furnish sufficient exercise. This has done much, I am told, to give the men and women the fine and full development which I cannot enough admire. We have seen this, even in the city, where the pupils of a few teachers of gymnastics show a remarkable contrast to the pale cheeks and undeveloped forms which fill our drawing-rooms with objects of pity, and the grave-yards with victims of consumption.

I am indebted to Vincent for many of these observations; for he accompanied me in my walk, pointing out any matter of interest, or giving any required explanation. He had been a physician formerly, I knew, and I asked him respecting the health of Esperanza, for as yet I had heard of no sickness.

"My office of physician is a sinecure," said he; "we have left the causes of disease behind us. With pure food, cleanliness, exercise, freedom from care, and happiness, what should make us sick? We have had no death here, and scarcely any illness. Many brought out of civilization the results of its evil practices, but every day of this life has purified and strengthened them. The children who came with us have passed their purgations, such as measles and scarlatina, almost without confinement; those born here, we hope may not need them,"

"Do you think uninterupted health possible?"

"Why not? Health is the natural condition; disease the unnatural. Men earn their diseases. Even where there is malaria, or a poisoned atmosphere, one whose life is pure and true in all other respects, can resist a single cause of disease. People who eat no flesh of dead animals; who take no such poisons as opium, tobacco, hops, or whiskey; who do not exhaust their lives by any immoderate or unnatural indulgence; who are pure and chaste, have a vigor of life which triumphs over many evils. Harmony of the system is health; and where is each body and spirit so likely to be in harmony, as in a harmonic society? We have solved the question of disease. For us, then, is no more sickness."

"Have you ever thought," I said, "of the possibility of a continual recuperation?"

"Of an earthly immortality; yes. It cannot come, I think, to a fragment of humanity; but when the whole earth is harmonized, I see no reason why life should not be prolonged indefinitely, if it were desirable; which it is not, at present. The argument to the contrary is from analogy—and all analogies fail under new conditions."

"Will you excuse some questions, which may not seem needful to you, and may even seem invidious?" I asked.

"I wish you to be entirely frank with me and all," he said. "Ask freely, and you shall have as true answers as can be given. We would cheerfully make our life an open book, to all earnest seekers after the truth."

"Will you tell me how you deal with crime?" Vincent looked in my face with a curious, puzzled expression; then smiled, and said:

"I was near forgetting where you have so lately come from. I have told you that we have no disease. The mental disorder, or discordance, which results in crime, finds no place in harmony. What crime, for instance? Theft, where every one has all he wants? There is no inducement to any crime against property, where all have an interest in the common-wealth. There is scarcely a possible motive for a crime against the person, and a pure and healthy life is a good security against the insanities of passion. There is the same security against sensuality. If a crime were committed, the criminal would be pitied as an insane or diseased person. All would try to cure him."

"But if a man or woman were wicked or perverse?"

"If this were not also disease, there would be, first, coldness; then withdrawal of all sympathy; then expulsion. It would be like the sloughing off, or excision of a mortified limb. But I apprehend no use for such surgery. A healthy body does not lose its members. No more does a healthy society."

"If, at any time, or for any reason, a member wishes to leave?" I said, not without a sense of some absurdity in the question.

If any member wishes to travel abroad, there i sentire freedom. Each one has an individual property, as well as an interest in the common wealth. The society is like a bank, where property is deposited for safe keeping."

"I have asked you in regard to crime. It is true that I see no temptation to fraud or violence; but it is difficult to conceive of a society where there is never idleness, wrangling, or any other disorder. It seems necessary that there should be some government or authority."

"The prevailing spirit of our society is activity. It is our fashion; and approbativeness and self-esteem, no less than conscientiousness incite to industry. How can a man with any self-respect, or feeling of justice, or regard for the good opinion of others, eat the bread of idleness? The social wants of sympathy, friendship, and love, can only be satisfied here, by earnest right doing. Paul said, "if a man will not work, neither shall he eat." With us, it would need no authority to enforce such a rule. A man would be ashamed to eat, who did less than his full share in producing our food. As to wrangling, whoever should begin it would wrangle himself out of his group, and out of all sympathy and enjoyment. There is nothing to wrangle about. The healthy and happy are not quarrelsome.

"You ask of government. The individuals are self-governing; the groups are self-governing; and the society, which is a group of groups, also governs itself. How is that tree governed, or your own body, which is, perhaps, a still better type of a true society? Each leaf does its own work; each organ performs its function, and the result is harmony. We have our central group, which is in some sense governing, but it governs only by attraction. It is the central wisdom and the central love. All offices are functional. For example, Manlius is an accurate calculator of relations and equilibriums, and an orderly and exact accountant. Should there arise any question of justice, in business matters, every person here would wish to refer it to him, and would be satisfied with his decision. We do not need to appoint or elect him to this office. It is his, because of his fitness. So all other matters. If a discord arises in our harmony, every nice ear detects it, every one wishes it corrected, and it is. The central group governs, but as unconsciously as the central nervous life in your body. It is the center of the pervading life, or harmony of the spirit."

"Does the pecuniary success of this enterprise equal your expectations?" I asked.

"Look!" said Vincent, with a wave of his hand toward the home and domain, which we now overlooked, from a little eminence. It was in truth a glorious sight. Fields, gardens, groves, vineyards, edifices of an architecture like music, the fairy steamer, a little fleet of boats, the mills and factories in the distance, the groups of gaily dressed and happy men, women, and children, some with horses and carriages, some on the lake, some bathing in its waters—for it was late in the afternoon, and in the hours of recreation—all these made a scene of enchantment.

"Pecuniary success," said he, "is not a very high consideration, perhaps; but it is a fundamental one. We owe nothing, we own all you see; our granaries, stores and cellars are well supplied. We can spare a large surplus, and our mills, manufactures and arts bring us a good income. We shall soon have the means to found another home; we could do it now if we could find people who were prepared for it. But we must risk nothing by haste.

"But the true success is the securing of happiness, in the harmony of all relations. Our life gives exercise and enjoyment to every faculty. Our eyes see beauty in nature and art, and are not pained with deformity, and the spectacles of poverty and misery. Our ears are fed with music, and speech, which improves in purity. We breathe a pure air, and have done something to gather around us a harmony of odors. The natural taste finds its highest satisfaction in our fruits. The sense of touch is never violated by uncongenial contacts of false relations. So much for the satisfaction of the senses.

"Small as our society is, it affords a career for a true ambition. The approbation and love of our own, are what best satisfies us. The applause of strangers, and people with whom we have little genuine sympathy, is a very hollow thing. I need not tell you that our loves are true, free, and beautiful. You have seen our children. It is a new generation of humanity, which will complete the work we are beginning, and in due time spread peace, plenty, and harmony over the earth. Then our armies will be armies of industry; our wars will be with the deserts and morasses, which will be conquered into fertile domains. The wilderness is to blossom as the rose; and all prophecies are to be fulfilled."

"Then you believe in the millenium?"

"*It is here.* This is the cloud no bigger than a man's hand. It is the 'kingdom come.' We are beginning to do the will of God on earth as it is in the heavens. As all prophecies are fulfilled, all prayers, also, are answered."

"All?"

"Yes. Those which are not fulfilled — or answered, are not prophecies or prayers."

"Do you look for cities in this new order?"

"Yes, magnificent cities—but not such gatherings of avarice, voluptuousness, poverty, crime, and all miseries, as London, Paris, or New York present—those aggregations of all the infamies of civilization. I can imagine the bay of New York surrounded by a hundred homes, with extensive gardens, each the palatial residence of two thousand persons, largely engaged in manufacturers and commerce, and certain arts which flourish in concentration. Here the museums, libraries, art-galleries, and theatres would be upon a grand scale, and hither would tend a constant stream of visitors for improvement and pleasure from the rural homes, scattered over the country. But this is for the future. The present cities are concentrations of the present civilization. The cities of the future will be the magnificent emporiums of the future society. We are in its germinal period ; but there is no conceivable condition of riches, grandeur, and happiness, which may not be achieved by a harmonized and spiritualized humanity."

We walked slowly homeward, along one of the nice graveled roads, which run to every part of the domain. On each side were beds of odorous flowers, and masses of berry-bearing shrubs. The raspberry, the blackberry, currants and gooseberries grow along these roads in profusion, and all the grounds are so laid out as to combine use and beauty. Thus the merely ornamental trees are rare ; but an abundance are growing which will be useful, such as the sugar maple, the common and Spanish chestnut, the English walnut, and all kinds of fruit trees, set in lovely groves, wherever the ground is more suited to that than to other culture.

"These are our workers," said Vincent. "Every leaf is at work, collecting from air and sunshine the materials of our wealth. Our bees are seeking honey in every flower. We could turn everything we touch to gold, if we choose: it is better to turn every thing to improvement and happiness."

At a turn of the road, where it winds round a mound planted with a grove, we heard happy voices, and pushing through some thick foliage, we came upon a group of young people and children, surrounding Serafa, who was giving them a lesson in Botany, and the analogies of plants and flowers. With a subtle, penetrating, poetic power, she seemed to read the secrets of every flower brought to her, and to find in it some characteristic development, either of civilization or harmony. As we came near. we paused, but she held out her hand, and the circle opened to admit us; so we reclined on the soft carpet of the grass besides her, and amid many shrewd and curious questionings, she concluded her lesson; which had been appointed as one of the recreations of the day, in in the order of the morning. When she had finished, a cry arose from the girls and boys of ···'The poem — now the poem!'"

"Ah! a poem is waiting?" said Vincent.

"Yes, she has promised us a poem at the close of the lesson," said Angela—"a poem of flowers, and fairies, and dreamland."

"I should think that more in your line," said Vincent. "You generally contrive to exhaust all the riches of fairy-land, so that nothing is left for other poets."

"Papa! you are always laughing at my poetry," said Angela, re-provingly: "When you were at my age did you make any better?"

"Oh, no! much worse, I believe, and no verses at all; but let us have the poem."

Serafa made no apology; but, shading her eyes, thought a moment, while all were hushed in a profound silence; then she began, slowly and in low tones at first, and afterwards more rapidly, to weave a fairy tale in rhyme, which I could scarcely believe an im-provisation. Her audience hung on every couplet with breathless delight, and when it was finished some were clapping their hands, and some laughing through their tears; and then they gathered around her, and threw their arms about her neck, and kissed her all over.

She gently disengaged herself from these fond and admiring caresses, and joined us in our walk home, taking my arm as frankly as if I were her brother or her dearest friend. I asked if she wrote down these inspirations.

"No," she said, they were not worth it; and it was better to make new ones when they were wanted." But I thought that if I were in the way again, I should try to save something for those who have no poet-improvisatrice at hand.

We parted from Vincent, and continued our walk alone, along a shaded and odorous path, bordered with the sweetest flowers. Serafa is not beautiful like Melodia ; she has not the piquant charm of Evaline, but a grace and loveliness all her own. She reminds me of those birds of modest plumage, which excel in song. Serafa is the living spirit of gentle poesy.

"Will you tell me," I said, "something of your experience of this life ? "

"Gladly !" was her answer. "I came with the first group, and have seen our harmony expand to its present development. The germinal period, when we struggled in the darkness of the old, was one of devotion and consecration. We worked out our development in trust and hope. Even that was a life of happiness. But here we struggled up to sunshine, and put out leaves and tender twigs, and so, gathering the elements of growth around us, we have increased to our present period of flowering and fruitage."

"Did your education fit you for this work ?" I asked.

"By contrast, perhaps," she answered. "I was nurtured in the severest school of Calvinistic orthodoxy. Poetry came and set me free. I read Shelley and the mighty bards, and in the light of their inspiration, the dense fogs of superstition vanished. I was brought by angel ministration to the heart life of our group, and in it found my home. All life, all hope, all worthful work centered in this cause, and when providence opened the way, I found with them my happiness, and here, the life you see, but as yet only an external view. The interior, spiritual, and love life is for you, I hope, in the future."

"And you are happy ? "

Her radiant look answered me, but she gave expression to the emotion that spread over her not beautiful, but most charming face, a gleam of sunshine.

"Happy !" she said, her eyes moistening : "have I not every thing life can give or be. Home, rest, work, congeniality, friendship, love ? What is there more ? "

"A poet might ask fame."

"I will not affect the modesty of disclaiming the title of poet. I have the consciousness of the divine gift, and feel myself an instrument by which the poetic element finds a certain expression ; a weak and uncertain instrument, yet giving my notes cheerfully· I have the dearest appreciation here ; and I know that what I may ever give of living poetry, will not die. I look to a bright future, in which the works of these first workers for harmony will be es; timated, perhaps above their intrinsic merits.

"As for the world outside, I care little for its opinion of me, but wish to do it what good I can. We have a little volume of my poems now being electrotyped, and they will soon be sent to some publisher, to take their chance in the world, and do the good they may."

I may not have mentioned that a printing office, small, but very complete, is among the means of industry here. In it are printed all labels of perfumery, preserves, seeds, and various manufactures ; also a monthly magazine, and circulars which are required to send to the groups of preparation. There is also printed and distributed daily a miniature journal, containing news, criticism, satire, drollery, and a curious variety of articles of general and local interest. I will enclose you copies of some of these, which will give you a vivid idea of the freedom and good feeling which prevail. This paper is a perpetual source of expectation and amusement. The articles are anonymous, and the little groups every day try to guess out the authors, and criticise them without mercy, and often, of course, to their faces. Here appear the poems of Serafa, criticisms on the artists and public speakers, and the musical and dramatic entertainments.

I have spoken of the refined manners, and the ease, and even elegance, of deportment and conversation, which are universal here. I could not understand it at first, but it was easy to see how those who gathered, group by group, around the refined and delicate spirits of the central life, would naturally take on the tone of their manners. The whole society is a school or a university of daily culture. Coarseness is soon polished by contact with refined natures ; and a pure harmonious life develops into every expression of beauty. The stage, dramatic and operatic, is also a school of manners, and conversation ; so are the daily assemblies ; and the works of art have their own refining influence.   The little journal is a sharp but friendly critic of any deficiencies ; and I have heard in all the groups of old and young, railleries, full of wit and plea- santry, but quite free from bitterness, on any awkwardness of speech or behavior.   These seem a natural or spontaneous means of education and improvement.

I have looked for the feeling or reproach of aristocracy or ex- clusiveness, but it does not appear.   Each group seems to cluster together by its own affinities, and the groups are interlocked by many interests, in labors and pleasures.   Scattered in all the groups are persons remarkable for particular qualities, or for skill in particular branches.   For instance, the fashioning of costumes brings into request the skill and dexterity of those who have been tailors and dress-makers.   A good shoemaker is an acquisition.   A blacksmith finds himself the center of a group of ambitious pupils ; a skilful mason is looked up to by all who take their turns at building, and so on.   Every talent finds its place, and the real uses of life are held in due respect.

But I must finish the story of my walk.   We sauntered by the shore of the lake, talking of many things in this life, and its contrasts with the constraints and evils of the old society.   Our path wound round a little cove or bay shaded with over-hanging willows, a retired and lonely place, where we heard the merry voices of children.   Coming to an open space, we saw a picture, worthy of some tropical Arcadia, or a new Eden.   Harmonia, Vincent, and the venerable patriarch I have spoken of in a former letter, were on the bank, sitting on a mossy seat, while a large party of the children, from three years old to fifteen, were bathing in the crystal water .   The bottom is of pure white sand, and the shores gently sloping, so that each one found his depth.   It was a beautiful sight.   Foremost among the swimmers, in beauty and skill, was the lovely Angela, whose perfect form had been the study of all the painters and sculptors.   The exercises of industry, the menage, and the gymnasium had developed both boys and girls into a perfection of contour seldom seen.   Their skins were rosy with health, and I seemed to be looking upon a group of the water genii, or the cherubim of the classic painters.

As I came in sight of this group, sporting in these clear waters in all the innocence of nature, stranger as I was to such a scene, I looked for some disturbance; but there was not the least. Angela hailed us with joy, and led off a series of aquatic gymnastics for our amusement, in which she was followed by all her companions. They swam and sported like so many mermaids; while some were teaching the smaller children, and aiding their efforts; until Vincent and Harmonia rose to join us, and then all came out upon the bank, wiped each other with towels, and put on their clothing. I thought of the virtuous indignation of one of our policemen, at such a spectacle. His feeling may be right enough for civilization — but here, I could not detect the least indication of a thought of impurity. Why need we be worse, in this respect, than the savages, or even the partially civilized inhabitants of tropical climes?

We supped with Serafa; a quiet, genial, soulful repast. She had asked those she wished to meet; not those who might expect an invitation; those whom she might benefit, as well as those who could be a pleasure to her. Of our old friends we had Laura, Edgar, and Endymion, a brother poet, who, you will remember, was with us on the Fairy. We had bread, a *blanc mange* of sago, honey, and pear marmalade that was perfectly delicious, and strawberry ice cream.

There was a pleasant and exciting anticipation of the grand fete of the evening, which was to be a masquerade — that most piquant metamorphose which our morality has mostly denied to us. The cabalistic spirit I found in full play. Every one had a secret, for the grand charm was to be able, by an entire change of costume, manners and voice, to either maintain a perfect incognito, or, better still, by an imitation of peculiarities, to pass for another person, and then, in the assumed character, to say and do things that would afford a week's amusement. All this was explained to me by Laura, who offered to assist me in disguising myself and to keep my secret, while she defied me to find her out before ten o'clock, when all unmasked and all deceptions were exposed.

The sunset hymn was sung, and the day stars taken to their rest, when all went eagerly to prepare for the evening.

When the band sounded the call, and I went to the large and brilliant assembly room, the spectacle that I encountered was one of the most grotesque and picturesque that could be imagined.

The saloon, besides its permanent ornaments of painting and statuary, is freshly decorated by a group of artists, for each new occasion. Now it was hung with the flags and emblems of all nations, and the costumes and masks represented nearly all peoples, civilized, barbarous, and savage. I found myself in an assembly of Japanese, Chinese, Tartars, Hindoos, Persians, Turks, Arabs, Russians, Germans, French, Spaniards, English, Irish, Scotch, Africans, North and South American Indians of the primitive nations, and South Sea Islanders. In all these, the costumes, male and female, were carefully copied from the best authorities, even to the color of the skin, and imitations of elaborate tattooing. Not only was geography thus represented, but history, for we had the finest costumes of Greece and Rome, and the ages of chivalry. Laura had procured me an excellent dress from the wardrobe of the theater, and I appeared as *un beau Chevalier*, of the period of Louis XIV., and with a little change in my voice and gait, mostly escaped detection.

The effect, *en masse*, as the whole company marched around the room to the music of a full band, such as we seldom hear, was indescribable. In each group were children, dressed in corresponding costumes. I must leave the scene to your imagination.

After the first set of quadrilles, the band played the music of all nations, beginning with the most barbarous ; while groups executed the corresponding dances. Thus we had the Greek and Roman dances, such as we see in bas relief and pictures, the dances of the Bayaderes of India, the dancing girls of Otaheite, and the Marquisas, savage Indian dances, and the polkas, waltzes and mazourkas of Europe. I was thankful for skill enough to execute, with some applause, a version of the *minuet de la cour*, with my pretty partner, who, with her powered hair, patches and train, and gentle coquetry, might have been taken for Ninon de L'Enclos.

14

In the intervals of the dances, all mingled in conversation ; but there was nothing but persiflage, mockery, and drollery. Every one was laying plans to entrap another into some betrayal of identity, and at the same time guarding his own. I thought I recognized Harmonia as a Roman Vestal ; then as a Hindoo Bayadere ; then a princess of Ancient Peru ; but I was each time mistaken. She spoke to me several times in her natural voice, but when I turned to see her, it was to confront a group in which I could not distinguish her in the least.

At ten o'clock, in the midst of a quadrille, the word was given to unmask. In a moment every mask was removed, and all bowed gravely to their mystified partners ; and then burst a roar of merriment, as all the mistakes of the evening were at once detected. But as the mistakes were all innocent ones, and involved no bad consequences, the dance went on happily.

Then came a supper. On ordinary occasions, no refreshments are served in the evening, each group making its own repast, if needed. But as this was an extraordinary festival, a supper was spread in the hall below at eleven o'clock, the tables being set as at our public dinners, with presiding officers, and toasts prepared for the occasion. The representatives of the various ages and nations were called on to respond to appropriate toasts, which they did in keeping with the characters assumed, and I had an opportunity to hear eloquence, wit, and humor, with a freedom and elegance of elocution, which was a constant surprise to me. I saw how completely this whole society was one family, and a school of the most thorough education.

The lights in the ball room had been extinguished ; the band, which was at the supper, took their instruments at its close, and as the great clock on the tower rung out the musical midnight chime, all struck into a grand good-night chorus, and soon after all was in profound repose.

X.

I HAD been wondering, my Clara, how we Harmonians should spend our Sunday; but I did not inquire. I waited, sure that each day would bring with it its own life.

In this home, where every day is a holy day; where the noblest and purest religion is incorporated into the daily life; where labor is prayer, and festivity praise; I did not expect the puritanical observance of Sunday to which we have been accustomed. In a society, where men cheat and plunder, and war with each other in the hard battles of commerce and finance for six days of every week, it may be proper enough to confess themselves "miserable sinners," and listen to sermons, and draw on sanctimonious faces, on the seventh. But I did not expect it here.

The Sunday morning ushered in a day of jubilee. On no morning was the band so full, or the music so exhilerating. It had a grandeur of movement and a sublimity of effect, such as I had not heard before. The softest bed could not tempt me to prolong my repose. It was as if every nerve was galvanised to life, with the spirit of the music; so I sprang from bed to bath, and dressing with some regard to the day, I soon joined the sunrise parade.

All were in festal attire. I saw that there was to be no labor. And the band was now swelled to over a hundred performers. All who have musical ears play on some instrument. Those who have only the sense of time, beat drums, triangles, cymbals, and even the Chinese gong joins its wondrous dissonance to the tempest of sound.

I know not if I have said that our bands are composed of both sexes. The flutes, piccolas, oboes, violins, small drums, triangles

163

and lighter instruments are played by women and girls; while the clarionets, trumpets, bassoons, trombones, ophicledes, double basses, and larger drums, are retained by the stronger sex.   This was one of the novelties of the opera, as of our parade bands.   Often, the light quadrille bands are more than half composed of women and girls, while the out door bands have a larger proportion of men.

On this morning, the order of parade was different from usual. The crescent, in which the beautiful assembly first formed, closed at a signal given by Vincent, and, as the music proceeded, became first an ellipse, and then a circle.   There came then a Song of Light, given with all the power of a hundred instruments, playing in full harmony ; and here occurred one of those effects, which we have heard faintly given sometimes in our ball rooms, and in the concerts of Jullien.   When the full band was playing, without notice or pause, their voices took the places of their instruments, and gave the words with a choral power and a thrilling effect which I had hitherto but faintly conceived.   And amid this grand anthem—now of a hundred instruments, now of more than a hundred—voices, now of voices and instruments mingled,—up rose the golden sun, and the cannon fired, timed with the music, and with the light, and an emblazoned flag of larger field and grander device rose above us, and received our salutation.

The Order of the Day was now given by Harmonia, who seems consecrated to the best work of this life.   It proved to be a review day, in which the achievements of the week were brought forward, and a new beginning made in the life of the future.   It gave me a fuller idea, than any observation had yet given me, of the variety and perfection of existence here.

The morning lecture, given by Harmonia, was very fully attend-ed. Its subject was the spiritual significance of the facts of science. She opened to us the soul of nature, and showed us the relations of spiritual and material ; finding even in the laws of ultimate atoms, the principles which govern the life of the soul.

After this discourse, which was of a wonderful spiritual beauty, and which seemed full of the inspiration of a higher or more in-terior life, I heard the drums beat, and the bugle sound a call ; and every one went quickly from the halls of science ; and in wonderfully brief time assembled to the vigorous rappel, on the lawn, armed and equipped for military duty ; a beautiful little regiment of two hundred, or five companies of forty each. Of these companies, two were composed of the strongest and bravest women ; but as they were dressed in masculine costume, they could scarcely be distinguished from their male companions ; but their shorter statue, more delicate forms, superior elegance of dress and ornament, and martinet precision of drill soon marked them to the careful observer.

It was the first I had seen here, of preparation for military defense. True, there was the cannon on the Fairy; the guns for salutes at the landing ; the morning and evening guns, and the soldierly care of the flag ; but here, on this festal morning, was a solemn parade of the whole effective force of this peaceful society, armed and drilled for deadly contest. I have been familiar with the drill of our "crack companies ;" I have witnessed the reviews at West Point, and of some of the finest regiments of our own and the British armies, but I have seen nothing like the celerity, unity and graceful beauty of the evolutions of this corps. The music was serious, grand, and full of sublime energy. The companies marched down the lawn by the lake, and fired rifle vollies at targets, one for each company, anchored at proper distances on the water. The cannon shots boomed across the lake, fired at a more distant target. Finally all paid a marching salute to the groups of spectators, were reviewed by Vincent and dismissed. It was, in all respects, a religious ceremony ; and I could see that no duty of life could be more solemn, than this preparation for defense against whatever violence might assail the life of their society.

Then a breakfast, crowned with an unusual display of flowers, and festal appointments. Thus, at eight o'clock we had enjoyed four beautiful scenes — the sunrise parade, the morning lecture, the military review, and a festal breakfast, each of which would have been a rare event in the dull life of civilization. And now the whole day was before us, to improve and enjoy ; a day of rest, of freedom, and sacred to the highest uses.

From eight to nine o'clock, all occupied or amused themselves, singly or in little groups. Some sat in the groves; some read in the library; some sailed along the shaded margin of the lake; some walked apart in quiet contemplation. I walked with Laura and Angela to a cool grotto, hollowed out, partly by nature, partly by art, in a limestone cliff, on the margin of the lake, and ornamented with shells and petrifactions. The wavelets rippled on a pebbly beach, close by the entrance, round which grew climbing plants. Within are mossy couches, on which we reclined and drank the crystal waters of a cold spring that gush from the living rock and tinkle down a series of minature cascades. It is a lovely place, cool in the warmest day, and the gentle singing of the gushing rill lulls to repose. Were you but with us, I thought, I should be completely happy.

We returned a little before nine o'clock, to be ready for the Review of Industry, which I was not willing to lose, as it would give me a better idea than I had yet obtained of the labor-life of Esperanza. This weekly congress of workers, men, and women, and children as well, met in the large assembly room. Alfred presided and opened the session with a brief address, very manly and straight-forward. He then made report of the progress of building, awarded the credit due to the best workers, not forgetting the girls and boys who had aided efficiently in carrying stone, mortar and other material; a work which was genuine play to them. I looked round and saw cheeks flush and eyes sparkle, as name after name was called, of those who had aided in this work.

The next report was from the recognized chief of the group of gardeners, a lady of great skill in this department. She also named, and praised in a few choice words, her most skillful, active, and zealous co-laborers. The harvest fields, the mills and manufactory, the kitchen, the laundry, the service of tables and chambers, all departments of this complex industry, were represented in this review, progress noted, defects complained of, criticisms made, and honors awarded.

I had a better opportunity than before to notice the ease, freedom, and entire self-command, with which every one spoke his thought, and also the clear enunciation, pure elocution, and choice phraseology, which have become habitual in the whole society. There was not a harsh tone, uncouth expression, or any vulgarity of speech. It was a school of graceful elocution. How beautiful it seems to me to have all the children here growing up amid the teaching of such examples. There were in this assembly, twenty little speeches made, of from one to five minutes duration, by men, women, and even the older children. My little friend Angela, for example, gave a very pretty report in the Floral department.

This session closed with a statement by Manlius, of the general results or proceeds of their combined industry. These results were surprising to me, and very animating, I could see to those interested. The wheat harvest, just completed, had added six thousand bushels of the surplus wealth, allowing so much to be sent off on the Fairy, ground into flour for the market of New Orleans. The stocks of preserved fruits, perfumery, oil, etc. were also of considerable value; while the great work of the harvest had diminished the results of manufacturers. The feeling of this wealth and abundance was not one of greed; but of strength, and freedom from care—of power and peace. Riches, I saw, gained by labor, and the product of nature and industry, were not despised, but held in proper estimation. It is beautiful to see a whole community living in perfect honesty; fed and clothed by sun, air, and earth, and their own free, voluntary, and harmonious labors. No one plunders or is plundered—no one has any occasion to do or suffer any injustice. Whatever is sold to the outside world, is sold at the market price; but it is the best of its kind, and always what it purports to be. Whatever is made is done "upon honor," and is of more worth than the usual manufactures, and will in time command a higher price.

At eleven o'clock there was an Educational Review, which interested me even more than the review of industry. Vincent presided at this; for to this important work he has given his chief attention. From the first, all had to be educated. All, the elder as well as the younger, needed to come under a thorough training, and, beginning at the elements of science and mental discipline, put themselves in the path of progress.

I found now how this work was done, at intervals each day, without confinement, without severe labor; but with attraction and enthusiasm. The groups of education were like the groups of industry. The most capable were alternately leaders of groups, in sciences and various branches of culture; and these reported progress. Exercises were also given in elocution and declamation. The groups or sections of the sciences were large; the same person belonging to several groups. In this way are cultivated geometry and the mathematical branches; astronomy and the natural sciences, going up to general and human physiology, phrenology and psychology. Brief essays were read, giving the study of the week in each department. In all this, the old and young were alike interested. It was beautiful to see a man or woman of fifty learning Greek in the same class with a child of ten. I inquired of the progress of these elder scholars, and am satisfied that amid the awakening and invigorating influences of this life, age is no obstacle to improvement.

The modern languages are cultivated with assiduity; particularly French, German, Spanish and Italian; and it is arranged that the children now growing up shall speak all these as well as the English.

Dinner was served at noon with festal display and ceremony. The band was larger than on other days, the music of a higher character. More flowers adorned the tables; the toilets were more beautiful. Every thing marked the day a solemn festival. The pure wine of Esperanza was drunk in moderation, and more as a symbol of this loving life than as a mere beverage.

So passed the morning hours, my Clara, in a succession of interesting and beautiful spectacles. It was all religion; all worship; all devotion; but of that character which belongs to life; active and real.

Melodia came to me after dinner, saying, "My friend, I have an hour for you," and giving me her hand led me to her own apartment. The mid-day was warm without, but sheltered by these double walls, and with the system of cooling ventilation, there is no languor within. You may graduate your room to a degree of the thermometer. The beautiful one reclined gracefully upon a couch, placing cushions for me at her side, and held my hand. Do you not feel how much I thanked her for this trust in me? Is it possible to be other than good, under such an influence? Were I ever so base, or sensually depraved, this would purify and ennoble me.

She held my hand in silence a few moments, first with her eyes closed, and the long, shining lashes penciled on her cheek — then looking into mine with an expression of trust and hope. I uttered no word—not even my gratitude.

"You love me?" she said, at length.

I kissed the beautiful hand I held in mine.

"You feel sure it is love?"

"I have no other name to give it."

"Yet you love another; others, perhaps. Look into your heart and see how these sentiments compare."

I tried to do as she desired. I felt my love for you, my precious one, as clear, as earnest, as much a portion of my life, as since the hour it came to me, a vivifying flame. I cannot be mistaken in this. It is a pure, and it seems to me, a deathless love. But I saw and felt no less, that I love the beautiful one, who has brought me hither, and introduced me to this enchanting scene. I find also that I have a tender reverence for Harmonia; that my heart yearns fondly to the spiritual Serafa; that I am deeply charmed with the lovely Evaline; and I grew alarmed at myself, as I recalled my real feelings toward Laura and Eugenia.

But I have determined to live the true life, and to be utterly honest to myself, and to all with whom I am in any true relation; and I owe this honesty to Melodia more than to any one but you. So I told her, with perfect frankness, and in as fitting terms as I could find to express my emotions, what I have written to you.

"Were you compelled to choose the love of one of these, and reject the others, can you see what your choice would be?" she asked me, with a look that seemed to penetrate the depths of my spirit.

15

"What I ought to do in such a case, is evident enough," I said; "but it is not so evident how I could do it. I can conceive of no power which could compel me to such a choice."

"If Clara were to demand it?"

"She could not and would not. If she is in that unity with me, which makes her lovingly mine, she must understand and sympathize with my feelings, and would ask nothing false to them. A demand of exclusive love to her, and an exclusive right to me, would prove that she did not belong to me. So, either way, there is no such thing possible."

"You have learned much genuine heart lore," said she, " since you first saw me."

"I have had excellent teachers."

"It is not so much that. The instinctive life of the heart demands only freedom, that it may attain to the highest wisdom. I have done little for you, but to set you free, and introduce you into a society where the emotions of the spiritual heart are as free as the movements of the material circulation. Here, removed from all outward control of habit and custom, you have been free to think and feel. The ideas come into your mind, and the loves into your heart. But there is a trial before you—how severe, I cannot well predict. When you go from us, the sphere of the old life will assert its power. Should the one you love join with that, to hold you in a selfish and isolate bondage, we may lose you."

I knelt by her side, dear Clara; I pressed her jeweled fingers to my lips, and I promised for you as for myself, that nothing would ever enslave us, but that we would live the life of freedom now open to us. Was I not right? Must we not live this true life of our spirits? It is true that I tremble, and that my heart shrinks when there comes to me the fear that this may not come all lovingly to you; but in my deep heart I have an undying trust in your truth and goodness. Forgive me, dear Clara, if even this assertion seems to imply distrust.

"She will come with me," I said. "I can answer for her as for myself. She will come to our thought, and life, and our beautiful home, and you will love us!"

"We shall all love you, as you are able to attract our love. The earth draws all things to herself, according to their capacity of attraction. In freedom, love is attraction and obeys the same laws.

"You will leave us soon — we cannot hope to detain you many days longer ; but you will come to us again, and not alone ; and you will come very happy, and both will find your happiness increased. Live but our life, in its truth and purity, and the earthly heaven opens before you."

She bent forward and pressed her lips upon my cheek — then rose to change her toilette, and I went also to prepare for the afternoon and evening, and whatever they should bring to me.

———

At two o'clock, all who chose to do so, and nearly all must have so chosen, visited the gallery of art. The drawings, pictures, carvings, and statuary, finished during the past week, took their places in the gallery, and were inscribed with the names of the artists. The visitors brought single flowers, bouquets and little garlands, and each one hung flower or garland upon the picture or statue he liked best, or which showed most improvement. It was an ovation to art. Some were not content with marking the works of art in this way, but also crowned the artists with garlands or enriched them with bouquets. So I found the gentle and tasteful, and now, in the excitement of this triumph, beautiful Evaline, walking in a cloud of perfume—incense to her art genius. Melodia had saved a few of the most fragrant, but had resigned most of her honors to younger aspirants ; and as tastes are various, and friendship and encouragement go for something, all who had made earnest endeavors found their reward.

From the Gallery of Art, we went to the Hall of Science, dedicated for this hour to the muses. Here, in a deep hush of delight' Serafa read a noble poem, which was greeted at the close with plaudits and laurel crowns. Next came Melodia, with an ode, not yet married to music, but which almost sang itself in the purity of her reading. Then Harmonia read one of those wonderful inspirations of the spirit life, which give, in themselves, the best evidence of their divine origin. Serafa and Melodia give us their own best life in verse; but Harmonia gives us the pure life of the heavens. They crowned her with a garland of white lilies.

I have not transcribed these poems for you. You must read them here.

We rested until four o'clock, when the only service of the day, which would be considered specially religious, found place. It is the hour devoted to general communion with spirit life. In a circular hall, lighted from above, with a subdued light, the whole assembly sat in a profound silence. Melodia went to a beautifully toned seraphine, and sang an invocation, which, if it had failed to call spirits from the heavens, would almost take us there. We sat there still, in a silence broken only by sighs, until Harmonia rose, and in a manner, very different from her usual one, spoke to the assembly with a power of eloquence, a depth of love, and a wisdom, transcending any thing I had ever heard of mortal utterance. It seemed the Heavenly Society speaking to the Earthly, lovingly, earnestly, reprovingly, and, withal, still encouragingly. If an angel spoke not, it was still an angelic utterance. But no one here doubted for a moment, that the thought and love was heavenly. It was an earnest exhortation to purity, to integrality, to progress in the Life of Harmony; a promise that faithfulness to every duty, and the highest love of the spirit should lead to a continual expansion and elevation of this life, and in consequence to a continual increase of happiness.

She ended with a serene benediction, and the whole assembly rose and sang a hymn of solemn joy.

The remainder of the afternoon was devoted to many little festivals of groups, composed of persons drawn together by the most intimate sympathy; groups of friendship always, often groups of love. I found myself with those who have become so dear to me, and was glad to be accepted as one whom they could trust, and whom they might love, should the future prove me worthy. In our little company I saw more of Vincent's social qualities than heretofore. He talked, sang, and enjoyed a restful repose; laying aside the care which has become habitual to him and bringing out those genial qualities which have surrounded him with a loving devotion.

Each group made its Sunday supper, either in a private apartment, or in the groves, or on the shore of the lake. Some made gipsy parties in the woods, and cooked their suppers in the most primitive fashion. The more central the group in this society, the more simple the food. Our group, to-day, ate only farinacecus food and fruits, believing that the spiritual love life is best nourished on these pure viands. These, with a little wine and sugar, made our repast. It was a genuine love feast, in the sentiment of which all participated ; or, if I am still an exception, it is not wholly so ; and I fervently hope will not so remain. It was a harmony in which I could detect no discordant tone—a loving unity where every heart throb found its response in every other bosom.

The sunset hymn has always the religious element, but it seemed more strongly expressed this Sunday evening than on other days, or I was more fitted to its appreciation. The glorious image of creative power and love, sank in mild splendors. The festal flag which had floated in the breeze all day, was now deposited in its sacred place, for the week ; and all prepared for the musical review which was to be the fitting close of this day of rest and joy.

I found the great Music Hall freshly decorated with evergreens and flowers. The review consisted of the past week's progress and achievement. First, there marched into the room a corps of little fifers and drummers, boys and girls from six to twelve years old, marching in very creditable time, playing simple airs, and beating their parchment with remarkable precision ; and as cymbals, triangles, and tambourines were not wanting, they made a very enlivening music. They marched around the center of the hall, were handsomely applauded, and took their seats, in the great orchestra.

Next came a class of musical pupils on various instruments of a higher grade, forming a band, as yet of moderate attainment in execution, but showing excellent training and zealous practice.

After these came solo performers, vocal and instrumental. Songs newly learned, and original songs and music came to us in all their freshness, and were applauded according to the impression they produced. Some of these were full of local allusions and home feeling; they were sung with a beautiful abandon, and responded to with an enthusiasm, glowing, but never boisterous.

Finally, we had two new chorusses, one for the morning, the other for the evening parade; a grand march, and a glorious symphony, which was a musical revelation of the life and work of Esperanza.

Melodia had composed it, and now directed its first public performance. In it was expressed the break of day, the musical awakening, the play of the fountains, the gathering to the parade, the sunrise hymn, and the morning gun; then the departure of the groups of industry, and all the scenes of the day. The children's band of fifers and drummers was introduced with beautiful effect. As the symphony proceeded, it gathered warmth and richness, corresponding to the pleasures of the afternoon. Then came a musical rendering of the delightful supper parties. This was a gay and lovely passage; then the gorgeous sunset hymn; and the finale of the evening festival, which was indescribably light, joyous, and enchanting, closing with a few soft chords, full of repose and loving sweetness, as if sinking into dreamy slumbers, ending with a pianissimo passage of a delicious serenade.

At this ending, the whole house, which had sat eager and breathless, rose, spectators and musicians alike, and applauded Melodia, who stood by her music stand, pale and agitated. Vincent, who had played in the orchestra, came forward to congratulate her. He picked up a wreath that had been thrown to her, but before he could place it on her head, the lovely head sank upon his bosom. She threw her arms around him and burst into tears.

But the plaudits recalled her from the one to the many. She raised her head, and now radiant with a flush and a smile of joy, thanked the musicians for their performance of her work, and all for their generous applause.

The festival was ended, and its queen, crowned with flowers, then came among us, and received our individual congratulations. I did not press forward, where so many had an older if not a better claim; but she soon came to me and held out her hand. As I pressed it to my lips, the scenes of the brief past flushed through my memory : the first meeting in the cars ; the hours at Niagara ; the pilgrimage and the journey by lake and river ; our beautiful voyage on the Fairy, and now the life of Esperanza.

Oh Clara, were you but here to live this life, and partake of all this happiness ! Patience, oh heart of mine ! Patience and Hope !

How rich and beautiful, O mine, is every phase of this life ! What a contrast has this day been with the dull, tiresome, solemn Sundays of our puritanical Pharisees, who "for a pretense make long prayers !" It has been a day of rest, but not of idleness ; a day of repose, but not of a miserable solemnity ; a day of recreation, full of joy in the present, and blissful anticipations of the future.

All the days seem long here, so filled are they with uses and pleasures. At night, I think over so many pleasant events, that it seems as if they must have required a week for their occurrence. And this Sunday, it seems like many great festal days combined in one, and each event is crowded with delightful memories.

And now a new week opens to me—one more week of absence from you—one more week of the enjoyment of this earthly paradise. I have the hope that you will be content with the delay, and have such sympathy with my enjoyment of this life, and such a desire to know all I can learn of it, that you will not wish me to be in haste to leave it, only that you may the sooner come with me. I have a week to learn the deepest workings of this life. I have given you its external aspect ; something you may have gleaned of the heart-life already, but that I have yet to penetrate more fully, for I feel that it is in the heart, or love-life, of this society that reposes its divinest charm. The dear friends here, I am sure, will hide nothing from me.

XI

ECONOMICS.

My CLARA ;—I resolved to devote the remaining days of my
sojourn here to a more careful investigation of the details of this
life, both by personal observation and inquiry. I wish to know,
not only the external economics of wealth and its distribution, but
the nature of those internal relations which are the chief sources
of happiness. As all here know and trust me ; as I am recognized
as a friend and brother, not only in the central group, but in the
entire body, from the noble and venerable Father Gautier, whom I
have described to you, to the infant that hides its little head in my
bosom, all this life is free and open to me.

I have talked with Vincent, Manlius, Alfred ; with Harmonia,
Melodia, and Laura : and many others have answered my inquiries
upon particular points. Some of the great problems of political
economy have here found an easy, because a natural, solution.

"First of all," said Vincent, of whom I made my earliest
inquiry, "the Domain is ours. We pay no rent or interest for the
air we breathe, the water we drink, or the earth we cultivate. It
has come to us all, a free gift, as it came to man from the Creator.
Father Gautier, a Frenchman of New Orleans, a pupil and friend
of Charles Fourier, was led by Providence and his own generous
impulses, twenty years ago, to explore this region, and to select and
secure this tract of country, as the domain of a future association.
He became acquainted with us, through our Melodia, who found
him. when she was spending a winter in New Orleans. Next to
him, she has been our good angel, for she was the inheritor of a
considerable fortune, the most of which she devoted to building
our home. We had all saved what we could, during the years of
176

our probation, so that we began our life here with prosperous conditions. Our father has found a beautiful home and a great family
of loving children. It is not the Phalansterie of Fourier, as he
planned it in his Earth-life, when he so ardently longed to see its
realization ; but it is the growing harmony, over which he presides
joyfully, as one of its guardian spirits, in the life of the Heavens.

"So much, then, was provided ; and we entered upon our domain
with the means of comfort at hand, and ample security against
immediate need. Socialists have adopted two theories of economy.
They have been either communists, having no individual interests and property ; or individualists, with personal or joint stock
interests. We did not feel like making an utter surrender of
individual rights and freedom, as in the communities of the early
and some of the later christians, as the Rappites and Shakers ; nor
yet could we willingly enter upon the complicated individual
accounts of the Phalansterian Association. So we stopped all
planning and calculating, and let the economies settle themselves.

Our family is a body, composed of members, involving general
and particular interests. There are the common wants and necessities to be supplied ; and also individual tastes to be gratified. A
natural method provides for all. The land is ours by a perpetual
free lease. The buildings belong to us by a like tenure. All the
improvements belong to all—that is to us, in our unitary capacity ;
and out of this common store, all common wants are abundantly
provided, by the common industry.

"So far, this was well ; but beyond this are the wants of the
particular life of the individual ; and for those also, there has been
made a satisfactory provision. Many of our members have the
savings of former years to expend upon their individual tastes—but
more often for the general happiness. For instance, we buy musical instruments, books, pictures ; or we use our leisure time in
decorating our theater or assembly rooms ; or we indulge in some
luxuries of dress and personal adornment. It is not for ourselves
alone, but for all others."

"But you have accounts of labor and wages, and of articles pur-
chased for individual use ?"

"They are few and simple. To credit each member with so many hours of labor, and charge him or her with so many weeks board, and so much clothing, would be useless. Ours is a family in which all work according to their ability and the general need, and all receive according to their requirements, and our abundance places us above the necessity of any meanness. In civilization, millions of idlers and drones are supported by those who labor. Shall we trouble ourselves, here, where all work from attraction, and labor, as you see, is full of charm, because the weak and the young cannot do as much as the strong and mature? No—in our life the strong man glories in his strength, and gives of it freely for the general good, just as the tasteful woman gives her beauty of work or life. We all work, more or less, in the needful works of industry; we all do what we can also for the beauty of life. You can see that the strong worker in the field or shop, who works from impulse or attraction, must be proud to put his useful labor against the genius and skill, which delight him in music, in the theater, and in all that embellishes the life of our society. It is so even in civilization. What man, who loves his wife and daughters, and toils for their support, but rejoices when he comes home at night, and one plays and sings to him, another shows him some beautiful work, and another reads aloud for his amusement? In our large family this feeling is much stronger."

"Then I see no use of accounts, at all." I said.

"We try to keep on the safe side, and just reckonings do no mischief, and may sometimes be a useful check to individual extravagances."

"And you find no difficulty from selfishness, which is the bane of civilization?"

"No. Selfishness is balanced by the corporate spirit. Each individual finds himself richer here for all practical purposes, than he could ever hope to have become in civilization. Melodia, for example, could not possibly have expended or invested her wealth in any way, to so much advantage. Few monarchs have so many sources of pleasure as are here the right of all. The individual selfishness, acquisitiveness, and the monopolizing spirit which poisons the life of society, has gradually subsided here. With plenty has come a spirit of generosity, which tends constantly to equilibrium, like the radiation of heat by physical bodies. Every one asks, not, what can I gain, or get? how can I secure my happiness? but what can I give, and how can I promote the happiness of others? In the world's poverty, material and spiritual, all are beggars or thieves; in our wealth, external and internal, all are seeking to bestow something on others. And as every one who has any good or beautiful thought or thing, wishes to bestow it on one or many, —all are thus enriched. It is a condition in which it is better to give than to receive; and in which all are givers and all receivers."

"And there is no difficulty in securing the necessary labors of the domain?"

"There is a pride in doing more than is needful. As men offer seats, or service to women; as the strong protect the weak, every where, by a natural instinct, where humanity is not utterly depraved; so, here, the constant tendency of the stronger is to take on more than their share of the common burthen. We are obliged to plan attractive amusements to prevent excessive labor; for when industry becomes an enthusiasm, it will run into excess, if not balanced by other means."

I left Vincent to the work of the morning, which was the correspondence of the Home, in which he was assisted by Harmonia and Estelle, a radiant girl, with a fine talent for literary work, a strong good sense, and an earnest devotion.

Looking toward a field of green peas, I saw a group—mostly of children, engaged in gathering them, to be preserved in large cans for the winter's supply, and for sale.

Laura presided over this nice harvest, and the little carts with dogs and goats, and the tables of the little shellers were in full and gleeful activity. It was easy to see that the field would be exhausted, before these workers would begin to weary—Laura found no difficulty in overlooking this work, and talking with me as I assisted in the gathering.

"Mistress Laura," said I, "how would you like to be rich?"

"I have never thought about it. I have all I want; and if 1

wish to make presents, what is better than a wreath of flowers, or something I can make?"

"But this diamond ring, that Melodia gave you?" said I— "would you not like to give her something of equal value?"

"What! to neutralize her gift, and acquit myself of a burthensome obligation? That would be the world's way; but I love her too well, and am too happy to be obliged to her. She is happy in being able to make such presents, but I do not see that I am not just as happy in receiving them. She is rich; but not for herself. We all partake of her riches; and she has only a little more care. No—I think I had rather be as I am. I have all I want."

I found no element of dissatisfaction in my lively and lovely friend; so I went to one of the work shops, where a group of musicians were making musical instruments, a favorite and profitable branch of manufacture. In these shops an account of work is kept, and a certain portion of the proceeds of the sales are distributed to the individual workers. And here, as in the other departments, those who choose to work in the hours of recreation, have the net proceeds of their industry. I found here a musical German, who has succeeded in making some violins of great value. These, like other works of art, are sold, and the proceeds are equitably divided between the general and the individual claimants. Thus, a violin made in three or four weeks, with the care and skill required for a fine instrument, is sold for from one to two hundred dollars. If the maker has given his whole time to the work, there is deducted from the sale, the equivalent of his proportion of the common labor; but if he has performed his usual work besides, he can receive the entire proceeds, less the cost of sale. And this German was working hard, to get money to bring two sisters from Germany, with whom he had corresponded, and who wished to join him here.

Manlius, who has a special talent for arranging equilibriums, settles all these accounts, and with such an evident justice, that no one can be dissatisfied with his decision.

I spoke to him to-day about the little property that is coming to you; wishing to know what disposition he would advise, or what would be customary respecting it.

"She can do as she likes," he said. "It can remain in stocks or mortgages, and bring her interest, which will be her individual property: or it may be invested with us, in buildings or machinery. But we can pay no interest or usury to any. No such burthen can be thrown upon us. Capital advanced, may be withdrawn; but it must not be a burthen upon industry. If civilizees choose to bear such burthens, paying the cost of houses and lands twenty times over, and binding themselves in a perpetual slavery to a constantly `` growing capital, we cannot help it. They may as well be enslaved and pay this tribute to you as to another; but we must not enslave each other. The most of us have our capital invested here, as loans, without interest, liable, but not likely to be recalled."

"But is it just?" I asked, with all my financial prejudices; "Is it just to use the capital of another, without paying him for its use?"

"I will answer your question," said Manlius, "by asking you a few others, and so put you in a way of answering it for yourself, which may be more to your satisfaction. Is it just for a man to take possession of the earth, and compel those who till it to give him a share of its products? Is it just that a tenant of a house, in fifty years, should pay rent enough to an idle landlord, to build five more such houses, whose tenants also are in like manner enslaved to him? Is it right that a man, who, by inheritance, or some fraudful speculation, or by aggregating the petty thefts and spoils of miserly accumulation, should be able to command the whole time and labor of ten, or a hundred, or a thousand men, to enable him, not only to live in luxury and idleness, but to still further accumulate the means of enslaving his fellow men? This is the financial system of civilization."

"But in the system of Fourier," I replied, "the proceeds of industry are divided between capital, talent and labor."

"It is true. Fourier was a financier. He wished to interest capitalists, as such, in association. He offered it as a good investment; but the money lenders were wiser than he. They saw that talent and industry would not long remain in a useless servitude to money.   We devote ourselves, our lives, our talent, our industry, to the life of our society.   Shall we not devote to it our accidental possessions ?   If the money we chance to have is returned to us, when required, we lose nothing, and no one is burthened.   To pay interest, rent, or usury, is a necessity of civilization, but can have no place in a free and harmonic society."

As I passed across the lawn, I saw the aged Father Gautier, sitting in the shade, alone, save a little girl of seven or eight years of age, who sat at his feet, quietly, as if to attend to any want. The wind played with his white locks, and his eyes seemed looking into the future.   As I came near, he saw me, and with a wave of the hand, signed me a gracious invitation to approach.

"Good day, my young friend," he said, holding out his hand, feebly.   I took it and remarked that his face had changed.   It had less strength than when I saw him last, but a more serene happiness.

"You have been ill, *mon père*," I said.

"I am old, *mon fils*," said he.   "Old, and with a life, wasted in the struggles of the world.   But I have no regrets.   This," waving his hand toward the Home, "pays me for all.   No triumph is like this.   The earth has no such glory.   I thank the benign God, that I was permitted to choose and secure this Home for the dear ones who were ready to enter it.   'Now lettest thou thy servant depart in peace, for mine eyes have seen thy salvation.'"

The tears of joy ran down the old man's face, and my eyes, too, were moistened.

"And you are satisfied with your family?" I said, cheerfully.

"Satisfied?   Ah, yes.   They are all good children.   They live in peace, and love, and harmony.   It is the Eden of which we dreamed.   I remember, when we used to talk of such possibilities, how we were ridiculed and satirized as visionaries and fanatics.   I wish I could see them here—but no.   They would spoil our paradise.   They are not worthy ; and it could not come until there were those who were worthy.

"Is that my child, Melodia, coming?" he asked, with a brightening eye.   My poor senses fail.   I shall not be here long, so I must have all I can of my dear ones.   Call her, my Constance ;"

and the child ran to bring the queenly Melodia, who had already turned to come to us. Constance took her offered hand and led her to the good father.

"How does my beautiful one to-day?" asked the old man, as she knelt beside him and put his feeble hand to her rosy lips.

"Very well, Father, and very happy; but I wish you were better."

"I shall be better soon, my dear," he replied with animation. "Very soon I shall be as lively as any of you, and as handsome, perhaps. And have a finer home than this, and more lovely scenery."

"And better children, Father?"

"Ah, well, I don't know. Dear ones are waiting for me there also. My earliest love, my beautiful Marie! I saw her last night in my dreams, a radiant angel, with her blue eyes and golden hair, like thine, my pretty Constance. She smiled, and said, 'a little longer.' It will be but a little now—but do not weep, my children. Your father will be ever near you."

Constance wiped her eyes, smiling through her tears. "I know it, dear Father," she said. "You will go and find just such a beautiful home for us, in the other world, as you have in this."

The old man did not reply, but his face lighted with a smile of joy ineffable.

I spent the day, my Clara, save when writing to you, in such inquiries and observations as I have briefly noted. I visited the shops of blacksmiths and wheel-wrights, of cabinet makers and makers of agricultural implements, as well as the studio of the artists, and the makers of musical instruments. The dignity and attraction of labor, here, consists in the use or beauty—which is but a higher use, of what is made. In every department, the work is constantly inspected, and improvements sought for. A council of construction will sit on a plow, or rake, or axe helve, to seek the perfection of each. So it is with every manufacture. I have never seen implements combining strength and lightness, beauty of form and perfection in use, as here.

And these workmen, uniting science with taste, and the individual with the general interest and welfare, work with an enthusiasm which our ordinary methods are not fitted to inspire. In our great manufactories, what can be expected but that the capitalist will be anxious only to make as cheap, and sell as dear as he can, and the operatives will all try to slight their work, and earn their wages as easily as possible?

I have paid three or four dollars for a pair of cloth gaiters from a Massachusetts or Connecticut manufactory, and had the entire sole peel off in a week, as if it had been put on with paste. Whole cases, doubtless, were made in the same manner. What self-respect can workmen have, who are engaged in such fabrications? But here, every shoe is an honor to its maker, and every workman takes pride in his work.

As I stood beside one of these fine spirited and intelligent mechanics, in the group of wheel-rights, I said:

"Well, Mr. Frank, is this life altogether to your liking?"

"There may come a better," he said, "in this world or the next; but this will do for the present."

"But have you no want unsatisfied?"

"None out of myself. I wish to know more, and be more; but that will come. I am growing all the time. I learn something new, and feel myself somewhat better, every day. We must wait for growth."

"Very true. But is there no feeling of a desire for independence?"

"How of independence? I have all I want. Food, clothing, shelter, society, study, amusement, friendship, love; and all in the most absolute freedom. What can I have or wish more? I can choose my own work, and my own time for working. I can be alone, or find congenial society. I can go or stay at pleasure. Perhaps you think we are under some constraint. I can put on my coat, go strait to Mr. Manlius or Vincent, draw for a thousand dollars, in New York or New Orleans, and go where I please. I think, sometimes I will take a trip to Paris, but I can never make up my mind to leave those I love here, long enough for the voyage. I go to New Orleans with the Fairy sometimes, for a taste of civilized dissipation; but a taste is enough. After our life here, it seems very flat and insipid."

"And you are satisfied on the score of wages and profits?"

"Bah! wages and profits. I am a master workman, and have no wages, I make as much as I choose. As to profits, we get good prices for every thing, and I have my full share. here is not a man, woman or child here, who does not have more than they could get elsewhere, unless they went to robbing. The satisfaction of being honest, and plundering nobody, is something."

Frank was working away all this time o n a wheel, which excited my special admiration, it was so light and strong and beautiful. There was not a shaving of timber to spare in any part, and it was wonderful to see how the carving away of every superfluous portion had left the wheel of the most elegant form possible. The outer rim of the wheel was of one piece of oak, bent to a circle by steaming and machinery; a great improvement on the felloes. The spokes were light and tough as whalebone, and the hub light and shapely as an Etruscan vase. The entire carriages, buggies, etc, turned out here, are of the same perfection, and finished, painted and trimmed so tastefully as to bring the best prices. A group of more or less skilled workmen begin on a carriage of a certain construction, of which they have made or procured plans and drawings; and they work on with great zeal and industry, until it is completted, perhaps in competition with another group, trying to excel each other. In this contest they often work greatly beyond the ordinary hours of labor ; but this time is carefully credited in their individual accounts. But the profit, or gain, so far as I can perceive, is never the motive to this exertion. It is the pride and happiness of achievement. It is the spontaneous activity of the spirit, finding manifestation in works of use and beauty.

I am satisfied on the score of economies. Production is ample ; distribution is equitable ; kindness and generosity tend constantly to equilibriums ; labor is from attraction, and all are free and happy. There is no repugnance to labor ; no wearying monotony ; no loneliness of spirit ; no corroding cares for the future. No man is weighed down with the care of a family—feeble wife and help-

16

less children, whom his illness or death may plunge into destitution
Esperanza is an escape from all the worst evils of civilization, and
this is much.   It is a realization of some of our highest capabilities for improvement and happiness, and this is more.

Viva Esperanza!

The spirit of Justice reigns in this society, as the basis of its
economies, but over this is the spirit of Love, which renders a
resort to justice unnecessary.   If the love prompts to too lavish a
generosity, to an excess of devotion, justice, holding the scales of
an exact equilibrium, restores the balance between the rights of
the individual, and the demands of the social body, and allows
neither to encroach upon the province of the other.   The reaction
from the personal selfishness of civilization is to the other extreme
of a single communism ; and this is the first form of social organizations.   But men cannot dwell in extremes ; and the individual soon
asserts his rights, and the old selfish spirit returns in full and de-
structive force.   The golden mean is the exact balance of the
individual and general good ; each tending continually to perfect
the other, as they must where they are in entire harmony.

Thus the great problem of the social life is solved for me.   The
centripetal balances the centrifugal.   The earths revolve in their
orbits, by these combined forces of attractions and repulsions, in a
sublime equipoise, and a glorious harmony.

Again, *Viva Esperanza!*

XII.

THE CHILDREN.

My Sweet Clara :—Some years ago, I visited a Shaker village. As I look back to the strange scene their life presented to me, and compare it with the rich and beautiful life around me here, the Shaker society seems a dim, faint outline, with no light and shade, no effect, or warmth of coloring, a pale, cold skeleton.

I remember how the uncouth and ugly costumes of men and women, contrived to make them look as hedious as possible ; their thin forms and pale faces, coming from a spiritual, not a physical starvation ; their soft "yea" and "nay," and simple, child-like language, affected me. And what a contrast is here ! There were fertile fields, abundant crops, noble barns and granaries, substantial houses, and plenty and peace. But all was designed for the most simplistic, naked, and homely use, without beauty or ornament. No pictures, no flowers, no music, no beauty, except that which cannot be shut out. They cannot shut out the glory of the heavens ; nor the green woods or fields. They only mar and make ugly all they can. No flowers bloom in their gardens, or adorn their walks. You see no where ,roses and honey-suckles, and morning-glories, nor even the modest heliotrope, and mignonnette. It was enough to make one's heart ache to see a whole community striving to shut out the beauty of God, and crucify the faculties of enjoyment he has given us ; shutting out also, and crucifying, the deeper corresponding beauties and fragrances of the affections.

But here, O Clara, while the necessities and uses of life underlie all, and have their true value recognized, beauty also adorns every thing. A dead tree is either cut away, or covered with some climbing plant. Flowers bloom all around us, and beauty and fragrance ravish the senses with delight. Carvings and ornaments, statues and pictures embellish and adorn every appropriate situation. The costumes of both sexes combine the highest degrees of use and beauty. The working clothes, even of the strongest and coarsest materials, are perfect in form and fitness: while the varied dresses of festal occasions are beautiful, separately, and of indescribable effect in the *tout ensemble*.

I have felt my esthetic life expanded and satisfied here, as it never has been before. Beauty is in the thought and life, and in all its manifestations. The forms and movements of men and women seem moulded into grace by all the graceful influences around them. The carriage is free, active, and of an easy dignity, inexpressibly charming. There is a fine poetical gesticulation united to the pure and musical modulations of their speech. There is not an awkward, sheepish, bashful or constrained person here.

And yet there is no sameness or mannerism, but a wonderful variety of individual development and manifestation. Neither in manner nor speech, more than in personal appearance and adornment, are any two alike; so that there is the most interesting variety; but each one is free to work out his own distinct individuality. One might have supposed that a noble and beautiful woman like Melodia, so admired and beloved by all, would have found many imitators. Not so. There is but one Melodia. No one imitates or copie another, but each one strives to develop his own best life.

I devoted yesterday to an examination of the education of this society; that, at least, was my plan; but my account of it will scarcely equal your expectations.

"Our whole life is a school," said Vincent, "and all our labors and pleasures are educational. We pay less regard to the accumulation of the facts of knowledges than you may think. To be, is more than to know; and when the mind is free and active, it seizes upon the mental food it requires. There is no need of systematic cramming, according to the civilized system. Our children are not educated to prepare them for life; it is the life itself which educates.

"For ten years, our members, who were bred in civilization, have had more trouble to rid themselves of error, than to acquire truth. Free the human mind of the errors which cramp and fetter it, clear away the obstructions from the avenues of knowledge, and truth will flow in like the light, from every portion of the universe. Science, in the human mind, is but the picture of the universe; and the universe is the expression or manifestation of the wisdom, power, and love, of the sublime Intelligence which pervades its infinity, and which men, in their feeble conception, call God."

We walked together to the Hall of Science, of which I have written. It was occupied, just then, by a company of children of from five to fifteen years, one of the oldest of whom was giving a lecture on geology, illustrating it by the paintings on the wall. The young professor, who had evidently read up carefully for the occasion, was listened to with interest, and when he was particularly eloquent, was well applauded. But if he fell into any error, or supposed error, he was interrupted politely, and, as Vincent was present, he was appealed to. He gravely and courteously explained the difficulty, and the lecture proceeded.

We passed on into another room where a class of different ages was being exercised in the elements of vocal music. We found another group arranging a cabinet of botany, from specimens which they had collected and classified. Other students, in the long afternoons, gathered in the library, and the little conversation rooms adjoining, and pursued favorite branches of study or investigation. There are hours also when the most interior subjects are discussed, and when our philosophers and their disciples hold converse in the groves of a new Academa.

"Every one follows out his attraction in these studies," said Vincent; "but the real school is the life of industry, art, and social enjoyment. The best way is to give conditions of growth, and then allow the whole being to expand harmoniously and beautifully. We endeavor to do nothing which will cause an expansion of one part of the being at the expense of another part. We aim at integral development, or the development and perfection of the whole man. And we, who have so lately progressed out of civilized imperfection and discord—we strive not to perpetuate our incompleteness and imperfections, by having them repeated in the education of the young. Our great law is *give from all faculties to all faculties.* This is the law of spiritual and passional equilibrium, and the condition and result of integral development.

"But, if you wish to get a true idea of that in our life which corresponds to what you call education, you should go a little farther back, and begin, if possible, at the beginning."

He turned and ascended a wide stair-case, and I followed him to a large, airy and beautiful apartment, which proved to be the nursery of the Home. We were welcomed by Harmonia. "You find me among my little ones," she said, with a smile of maternal tenderness. In this room were all the babies, of three years old and under, attended by a little group of mothers and nurses. There were grand-motherly women, so fond of children, as to find here their greatest happiness; mothers, who either took their turns in the general care of the nurseries, or came to give the infants their natural food; and young girls, whom a strong instinct led to volunteer in these pleasing cares. It was very sure that they all, like Harmonia, loved babies.

And such beautiful children! So rosy, fat and happy. They laughed, and crowed, and jumped, and rolled about, with a healthful activity and a perpetual joy; or slept the sweet sleep of a pure infancy.

The room is wonderfully adapted to its uses. It is large, well lighted, and perfectly ventilated. The soft breezes flow through it; fine nettings shut out all insect annoyances; the temperature is easily regulated; and the capacious baths, where the children bathe, and even swim, morning and evening, and oftener if needed, are at a comfortable temperature.

The ceiling is of a soft blue, like the heavens; the walls are a lovely, fairy like landscape painting. A musical clock plays pretty airs every quarter of an hour through the day. There is a profusion of toys and little furniture, and a world in miniature. The only punishment is to be banished from this infantile paradise.

"Here," said Vincent, "we receive the tender plants of humanity, and give them, from the beginning, the conditions of a healthy and harmonic growth.   Here every mother can nurse her child, and take just as much care of it as she pleases; without its ever being a burthen to her; since, if she is wanting in attraction for these natural offices, there are others happy to supply her place."

"But can others supply the love of a mother?" I asked.

"It is not needful.   Since no woman, in our life of freedom, ever has a child forced upon her, or against her wishes; since the love of offspring and the desire for offspring—the strong instinct of maternity—is the only motive and cause in action, it may be presumed that every mother must love the child of her fondest hopes and wishes.   But it is true that all women, even with the same love for their children, are not equally adapted to the performance of maternal duties.   Would you wish Melodia, for example, to leave her art life, and her sphere in our society, and devote all her time and thought to the care of an infant, that three-fourths of the time would be just as well cared for by those who would attend it with a great love and devotion?   Our children are never left, as so often happens in civilization, to indifference and hate.   They are never stupified into quietness by opium, or lulled into the insensibility of intoxication by beer or whisky.   Our mothers have not the fault of not loving their children.   It is only when children are forced upon women, against their wishes, or are born out of a low plane of selfishness and sensuality, that there is lack of love.   The danger with us is in their being too much confined to them for the good of either.   Variety of life, exercise and repose, are favorable to the health of the nursing mother, and of consequence are for the good of the infant."

On one side of this hall is adopted that pretty invention of Fourier's, for the young infants—the elastic net work, with a cloth covering, sinking in the interstices, in which the babies, with but little clothing, play with each other, or roll and tumble about without the least risk of injury.   The soft music, the tinkling fountain, the bland airs, the lovely aspect of the beautiful things that make this infant heaven, all contribute to harmony of being. From this room, often noisy with sports and childish, romping glee, we passed through a passage to another room, where silence reigns over the repose of sleeping innocence. I could have stayed here an hour looking at these cherub forms. Happy children, I thought, and happy mothers! Happy society, where every child has the beautiful care and conditions of health and enjoyment, which our civilization gives but imperfectly to the most fortunate, and which millions never enjoy. For this loveful care, this nursing from attaction and enthusiasm, is what no wealth or power can command.

Vincent went to his work; and Esperanza has few members who are more industrious. I was left with Harmonia, whose love of children is a strong passion. In the world, she could never pass a babe without wishing to take it in her arms; and many a sick child of an ignorant mother has she taken in her arms and blest, by her knowledge of disease, and skill in the healing art.

"Are they not all beautiful?" she said, as we sat and looked at a group of young children.

"When I think of the poor, sickly, miserable infants of the world, half dying before they are five years old, and then at these healthy and happy darlings of our home, I can hardly wait for the world to grow. It moves so slowly! Every year millions of little ones, born only to breathe out a few days and months of suffering, and then fill the little graves that are scattered over the face of civilization! Then the agony of ignorant parents is not lost to me. I have seen and felt it all. But the future has hope. If God can wait, I must wait also. One of the attributes of Divinity seems a sublime patience; but I do not believe that even an Infinite God can endure an eternity of evil and misery!"

"Do you tell me," I asked, "that these little ones are not liable to the diseases of infancy?"

"A few have them in a very slight degree; for we are not yet purified from the laid-up causes of these evils. But their sickness is light; it is for purification; and it is not into death. If a child should die among us, it would be because we had committed a great sin, and deserved a great calamity."

"Is it possible that you believe that the Almighty punishes our misdeeds by such a vengeance as killing somebody's child?" I asked, with undisguised astonishment.

"You mistake me, my friend," said Harmonia. "The sin must have been in the begetting of such a child. The child who dies of any disease of infancy, had no right to be born. The crime is that of generation, or gestation, or succeeding conditions. The healthily generated, born and nurtured child of healthy and harmonious parents, never dies of croup, or scarlatina, or cholera infantum. There are no effects without adequate causes.

"Supernal wisdom has revealed to us the laws of a wise and healthful generation; and those laws we must obey. Here is our reward.

"It has been revealed, and is moreover scientifically demonstrable, as Vincent will explain to you, if you desire it, that each child, born into the earth-life, has the sum total of parental possibilities, when generative conditions and gestative are equal."

"You mean that when the father and mother, in their functional capabilities are balanced, or harmonious, that the child will be superior to either, and equal to both?"

"Yes; such is the law of progressive generation, as revealed to us from the angel life. And the superiority of children to their parents, and of consequence, the progress of the race, is determined by the intensity, and integrality, or completeness of love unities, or harmonization in the parents."

"Then the finer the development, and the greater the love of parents, the better will be their children?"

"Doubtless: but you will not lose sight of the principle, that this development, in each, must be whole, complete, integral; from inmost to outmost, from all physical powers and functions, to the highest faculties of the mind and spirit. When two persons, so developed, meet in the unity of a pervading love, which joins them in all faculties, then the generative and gestative conditions are equal, and the child combines the sum total of parental possibility."

"But how is this noble and beautiful result to be attained?"

"It cannot be in civilization, where men and women, diseased and discordant, feel at liberty to perpetuate all their discords and all

17

diseases. It cannot be where the ignorant, and partially developed come together from interest, or caprice, or sensuality; where maternity is forced upon woman, without respect to her condition or desires; and where opinion, custom, and law bind men and women in the abhorrent bondage of discordant marriages.

"I have given you the law of progression, and life. Civilization supplies the conditions of deterioration and death. It is the divine energy that resides in humanity, struggling ever upward to light and life, that has prevented the utter depravation and annihilation of the race."

"And here," I said, " where I see these healthful and beautiful children; how have you secured the conditions, which, according to this law, are necessary to such a result.?"

" Our whole life is made up of these conditions. We perfect the plant by culture, and by choosing the most perfect seeds of the best perfected plants, we secure its progressive improvement. The love of humanity demands that none but healthful and developed beings, should reproduce themselves in children. We *produce* ourselves, by integral culture, before we venture to reproduce ourselves, in our offspring."

"Would you deny the right of the parental instinct to the diseased and discordant?"

" *We* deny no *right*. Nature, herself, forbids that we inflict disease, insanity, and all the miseries of an incomplete and discordant life on our posterity. Those of us who are consciously unfitted to wisely sustain the parental relation, conscientiously refrain from it. They do not the less love and care for the robust and beautiful children of those who follow their most divine attraction, in a wise exercise of their portion of the creative energy. "There is no compulsory restraint on any, but the whole intelligence, and the whole sentiment of our united body, is in favor of our giving to this life none but those who are fitted for its enjoyment. In the outside world all this is different. The laws and customs of society are in direct opposition to the teachings of science, and the dictates of common sense. Disease, deformity, insanity, and every form of mental and physical idiosyncrasy, are reproduced remorselessly and continually. Children are born in multitudes, one-half to populate grave-yards, and a large portion of the other half to insanities, idiocy, crime or poverty, disease and misery. It is this terrible civilization which Fourier has called a social hell, with its miseries unutterable; but not, thank God, unending."

"And here?"

"Here, even now, after a few years of progress, and the approximation to a harmonic life, you see how the spirit of that life incarnates itself in these rosy cherubs. The first law of this progression, given us from the higher spheres, was, that in the relations of the sexes: *material union is to be had only when the wisdom of the harmony demands a child.* All have come into this harmony through the gate of consecration to a pure life—to an entire chastity, which defined itself first as continence, and later as an equilibrium of the faculties, in which the physical senses are held under the control of wisdom and conscience, or the highest sense of right, in the relation of each individual to the harmonized society to which he belongs."

"This restraint and governance of the sensual nature, by an almost monastic discipline; is this consistent with the freedom you demand—the freedom of the affections, as well as of thought and belief?"

I did not need to ask this question; I could have answered it myself, but not so well as Harmonia.

"Freedom," she said, "is the first condition of our life. We must be free, to do right. The woman, held in marriage bonds, has no freedom. It may be abhorrent to her to be a mother. Sense and soul revolt; but she has no power to refuse. Her life is wasted, and she is made the involuntary and unwilling mother of a diseased and discordant offspring. The first condition and necessity of a true life, is, therefore, freedom: but being free, we can order our life according to our own highest freedom and sense of right. No one can come to us, but in freedom; no one can live our life truly, in whom it is not a free, spontaneous expression of the highest attractions. Fourier saw that *libre amour* the

'Free Love' which you have heard stigmatized by sensualists—
must be of necessity, the supreme law of a harmonic life. Here,
all love is free, and in its freedom, seeks the highest purity, and
noblest expressions and results. All our children are 'love children,' and the children of the most integral and intense unities of
the passion. And the child, born of the mutual love of two
developed and harmonized parents, who are free to follow their
highest attractions and divinest impulses, must most surely and
inevitably combine the same parental possibilities. Such are the
children of harmony, and of such is the kingdom of Heaven!"

Harmonia rose, gave me her hand, which I reverently kissed, and
we parted; she to some work of love, I to reflect on what she had
said to me.

This thought, and this realization of the freedom of woman,
opens to me as a new dispensation. In savagism, woman is a
drudging slave. In barbarism, a slave of appetite and luxury. In
civilization, still a slave, of fashion, custom, law, and the marriage
institution, in which her most sacred life is crucified, and which is
to her, so often, a hopeless bondage, full of constraint, deprivation,
and often outrage. I have seen all this. Now I see woman free;
and the results of her freedom, in a purity of life, a harmony of
interests, and a happiness, which I had scarcely imagined as an
earthly possibility. And I now see that no woman can be truly
noble, truly virtuous, only as she is truly free. It is only in perfect
freedom that every woman can exercise her highest of all rights—
that of choosing the father of her child. Vincent and Harmonia
began their work of human harmonization, at this point. They
said with Swedenborg, "there is no regeneration but in freedom."
They taught that freedom was the first and absolute condition of a
true life, and that no man or woman could begin even to live
truly, until they were free to do so.

They demanded, for themselves and for all, "absolute self-ownership, and the free disposal of one's time, labor, sympathies and
affections." It was a new Declaration of Independence, and a new
assertion of the Rights of Man, in which Liberty took on a broader
and deeper significance; for they asked nothing less than "Liberty,

of the person from all ownership, bondage, restraint, or imposed burthen; from all fraud or force; all despotisms of custom, law, or institutions; of the mind, from all arbitrary impositions of creeds, opinions, laws, or forms of social or religious dogmatism; of the heart, from the bondage that galls and wears, that paralyzes or breaks. A holy freedom to follow the dictates of nature, in her most sacred instincts. A sanctuary of love which no despotism can violate, and no power profane. The free Pursuit of Happiness, in the unconstrained exercise of all rights; in the following of all attractions; in the respect for all repulsions; in the full freedom of a true and natural life, which does not, in any way, limit the equal freedom, or encroach upon the equal rights, or wrongfully destroy the happiness of any other being."

"True Freedom" they define as "the right to do right;" and "there can be," they said, "no right to do a wrong."

These are the principles upon which this social organization is formed, and here they have found vitality, germination, growth, the blossoming of a blissful, loving life, and the fruition of a harmonic society, perpetuating itself in progressive generations.

Blessed children of Harmony! I exclaimed, as I thought of these happy babes, so embosomed in loving cares, and with the assurance of a life of peace, freedom and happiness, fitting portal to an immortal existence!

But as I walked alone, the prejudices of education and custom threw their shadows over my thoughts. That question, which expresses so many petty tyrannies, "What will the world say?" importuned for its cowardly answer. I even feared that you would be shocked—you, with your true, pure, womanly nature, because these children were born under the laws of heaven, instead of the institutions of civilization. As I walked moodily, wondering at the unreasonableness of civilizees in general, and at the strength of my own prejudices, the bright angel who had guided me to this paradise, met me, smiling as if she knew the source of my disquietude.

"He who contemplates a happy infancy," she said, "should look more joyfully at the present and the future. Can a clouded brow come from the cheerful nursery of Esperanza?   Or do you mourn that all children are not as blest as these?"

There was irony in the question, but it was suggestive, too.

"I have been measuring," I replied, "the power of those prejudices, which enchain the world, and keep its people in their miserable systems."

"Ah! that is better; and you found that measure in yourself?"

"It is true.   The old shadows darken me sometimes."

"Well that they are but shadows.   Open your mind to the light, and the shadows will disappear.   Does it trouble you that our beautiful children are not the sickly, unwelcome offspring of civilized marriages, born to die in their cradles, or to live and perpetuate parental discords?"

"No!" I exclaimed; a thousand times, no!   Woman *must* be free, or there cannot be a true maternity.   I see well that this is the only guarantee of social regeneration, and that the isolate household and the marriage of civilization have never resulted in the true family and the true society.

"Pardon me, who am so new to this life, if I do not understand all its relations.   I see these children, full of health and beauty, and surrounded by a most loving care and culture; and I see the life to which they are happily destined.   But I see also, that there are circumstances connected with their birth which would deeply shock the prejudices of civilized moralists, and which I find it difficult to look at like a philosopher."

"Are you in trouble about an imaginary taint of birth, when half the children born in civilization have the real taints of scrofula, and discordances tending to insanity?   Am I to tell you that the genuine legitimacy is the result of obeying the laws of nature?   Do you not believe in a higher law than those made by kings, or priests, or republican legislators?   You have seen our children: do you find them base-born?"

"The children of Esperanza," said I, "are beautiful as angels. I know that they are born of a pure life, and the most sacred relations.   Pardon me, if the sadness of a doubt has come over me for a moment.   You, dear Melodia, better than any, can tell me whether all the parental and filial instincts and wants are satisfied in this society."

"Better than they ever have been elsewhere, I believe. Every child born here is an answer to its mother's prayer. The father of every child is its mother's most sacred choice. The children of a mutual love, love both parents, and are beloved by them. They are loved also by all who love their parents. No child here can be an orphan, or want for the most loving care. These are conditions of human progress, and happiness, which no society but ours has ever provided, and which can only be realized in the freedom and harmony of the Unitary Home. Now, my friend, is there a place on the earth where you would rather have your child born and nurtured than here?"

I did not need to answer; and as we turned around a little copse, we came upon a group of children, so joyous, so beautiful, so loving to each other, so beloved by all, that all my troubles vanished like a morning mist. And the first who came to me, with his frank, brave greeting, was the little Vincent. He gave one hand to Melodia and the other to me, and told us the triumphs of his morning's work, and his evening's play.

"Master Vincent," said I, "who, of all these people, do you love the best?"

"Why, the same one that you do;" said the little rogue, looking up at Melodia.

"And who next?"

"Next, I love best the one she loves best. Then I love all who love them both; so I love you—*a little*;" and giving Melodia a kiss, he ran off to join his companions in their play.

O Clara, mine! shall not our children find their home and their loves in this beautiful Esperanza?

XIII.

EDUCATION.

O MY CLARA! How shall I unfold to you the interior beauty of this life, of which I have hitherto been able only to give you very imperfect glimpses? Words—the common words of our common speech, seem so poor—so inadequate to convey ideas of a life which must come in time to have a language corresponding to its dignity and beauty, its purity and bliss.

I have endeavored to convey to you an idea of the education here, which draws out every faculty of body and soul. It is a training which began years back, with an earnest purification and consecration of heart and life to this work. It was not a life of penance and mortification, but of resolute, high-souled endeavor to develop all that is manly in man, and all that is womanly in woman. It began with health, or the purifying and energizing of the physical system. All moral faults were at the same time systematically eradicated; and the whole life reduced to order and harmony. The adopted motto of the society in its formative stage was "Cease to do evil; Learn to do well."

It was an eclectic school of morals and philosophy; a school of the broadest tolerance and the most comprehensive charity. They looked upon all systems of religion and goverment as embodying some idea of humanity, and as having in it the germs of goodness. Hence they accept the goods of all systems. Brahmism, Boodhism, Judaism, Classic Mythologies, Christianity, Islamism, all creeds and institutions, were brought to the test of an all-comprehending humanitary philosophy, and the pure gold separated from the dross. Whatever was true, good, beautiful of all these outgrowths and expressions of the religious sentiment or esthetic life of man, this society has conserved ; and thus the whole progress of humanity in all its stages has been a preparation for this life.

The education here, and the life which educates all who are in and of it, is integral or harmonic. Never is it the development of a single faculty, or even of a few. In this large and varied life all talents, all powers, all faculties are brought into play. The senses, and perceptive faculties, the sentiments, and the instincts or passions are all held in balance. It is not as in our society, where one man is a laborer and nothing else, another a musician, another a linguist, another a teacher. Each life here, by its large and varied development, seems to include many lives, and the happiness of many lives is concentrated into its uses, and enjoyments.

I have asked of the discipline found needful to the ordering of this life from the crudeness and perversity of our depraving conditions ; and I have accepted for myself, and I bring to you this method of reduction to an orderly life. It is a work of systematic culture. In the novitiate and preparatory stages, each individual writes down from time to time the most prominent faults of his character, and rules of conduct respecting them ; and then for each fault fixes upon some suitable penalty—self-chosen and self-inflicted.

Most had tendencies to over-eating, and the self-inflicted penalty for every such transgression, and for many others, was to make the next meal on bread and water only,—at once a punishment and reminder of the fault, and a remedy for its consequences.

"And this practice of noting and marking all transgressions," said Harmonia, who gave me these details, " has had a wonderful influence in ordering and purifying all our lives. Some had bad habits of speech ; some were irritable, giving way to sudden bursts of anger ; some had inordinate approbativeness ; some were contemptuous of others ; all were more or less selfish ; and most of those born and bred in civilization have more or less disordered alimentiveness and amativeness. All this disorder it was necessary to clear from our lives, to make them clean and pure, even to the last fibre.

"Thus the first solemn pledge of the central group, in its most germinal stage, was to be chaste in thought, word, and deed. It was the central purification, from disordered and diseasing sensuality. And to all, even the purest and noblest, chastity came at first as continence. And now we all accept, as the law of our life, the principle that the ultimation of sexual love is justified and sanctified only by the desire of a wise maternity."

"And do all here accept, and live to this law?"

"All have accepted, and do accept, it, as a finality. No person could live in the blessed unity of our life, who wasted his existence in selfish, sensual, and enervating pleasures. I know well that a world sunk in sensuality, can not comprehend the beauty of such a life—but I may trust you with its most interior laws; the more as you are now an accepted neophyte. It is your right to know all that our life requires; and it is your duty to order your own life according to your highest perception of truth, beauty, holiness, or integrality."

I sought Melodia. She was in her own apartment, with her writing table near the piano, alternately playing, and writing out the score of a new musical composition. But she soon laid aside her work, held out one hand to me, and with the other drew a small ottoman to her feet, for me to sit upon.

"More trouble?" she inquired cheerfully.

"The life asks so much!" I answered.

"Do you think the life asks too much of purity, of devotion, of unity of being?"

"No: there cannot be too much; but I despair of the world, and almost of myself."

"But not quite. Do you not find in yourself a wish for all the purity of thought and action our life requires? Do you not wish for that ordering and harmonization of your own being and faculties, that shall fit you for our society?"

"You must be sure that I do. Is not my life here?" I answered.

"Then the attraction will work out the destiny," said she; "and you will be united to, and oned with, our life. Here you will find the satisfaction of all your faculties; here friendship and fraternity will unite you with a congenial society ; here your heart will repose in true and beautiful loves ; here will open a sphere for all ambitions ; here you will have respect and reverence for all above you ; you will influence and benefit all around and below you in the scale of development ; and here you may find the Home your whole being asks, and the conditions of the truest life now possible to us."

"Ah ! if I were but worthy of such a life !" I said with a profound humility.

"The attraction asserts the vocation. There is still a work to be done, in and for you, but not beyond the power to do, if you have the necessary humility and devotion."

"I am sufficiently humble, in the sense of my deficiencies," said I. "My education is imperfect ; my life impulsive, disorderly and selfish ; my will does not grasp my being with sufficient force, nor hold it with sufficient strength. I need help."

"You have it and shall have it, from within and without. Whenever any one makes an effort toward goodness, there stands some good angel ready to help. Lift at the wheel ever so weakly, and Hercules will come to your assistance. I too will help you. I will be your confessor and director. Can you trust me ?"

The joy that came into my heart, O, Clara ! how shall I express it to you ? Her face beamed in its pure beauty, like an angel's. I could believe that a radiant halo surrounded her, such as was seen around the heads of the saints. I looked up to her pure loving eyes, as the catholic looks to the holy mother, and felt peace and strength come into my heart.

"You shall be my confessor," I said. "I can open all my heart and life to you ; and you shall direct, order, and attune me to this harmony, so that no discordant tone of mine shall ever mar this divine beauty. I will perform all the penances you inflict. When I attain to any degree of goodness, you shall reward me."

She held my hand, looked into my face a few moments, with a solemn earnestness, and then said, in a low soft tone, "It is well. I accept the care of your life. It is my right, and my duty ; it is also my attraction. Come into unity with my being, and let all else come to you in that unity. Whatever in your thought or life accords not with that, is not for you, and must go out of your life. Bravely and resolutely put aside every thing that you feel that I would not approve—every thing you could not entrust me with in perfect peace. As bravely, and as resolutely strive to attain to all I would have you be. When that is attained, you can seek a superior direction and a higher unity."

It is right, dear Clara, that I should tell you this. I do it weakly; with a tremulous sadness in my heart, and with tears; for my faith is yet but weak, and I fear to hurt you. But I must do the right; and if you are joined to me in the right, then is our union blessed; but if the purest and highest right I can see separates you from me, then must I still accept the right and whatever it brings. But I have, even through this weak apprehensiveness, a deep and infinite trust in you; and the feeling that our love is a real unity, and that you will joyfully accept all the good and true that comes to us.

I sat there by Melodia, while she took the pen, and wrote down in a little book, the most prominent faults of my life, such as they now seem to me. To each of these I have affixed a penance, which I will religiously observe; and I have promised every evening to write in this book an account of my progress in overcoming any faults, which I am every week to transcribe for her. In all this, I feel a great peace, and an inconceivable help and strength in her sympathy and support. No more do I think confession a folly; I no longer disrespect penance; I see the wisdom and use of these ordinances, however they may have been abused.

"And you, my guide," I said to the dear Melodia; "have you too, your confessor and director?"

"Assuredly. We all help one another; and bear one another's burdens. Are we not all members, one of another; bound up in a sacred brotherhood; organs of the same body; notes in the same living harmony? The strong must support the weak; the wise must govern the foolish; the old instruct the young; the young give strength and life to the old.

"At first I laid the burthen of my life upon the bosom of Harmonia. I loved Vincent, but I also feared him. There was a reverence, or some such feeling, for which I have no better name—a kind of awe, which for a time kept me from confiding in him. It was not a want of trust. I felt that I could trust him utterly. I lived in his life; yet there was not the unity with him which I desired. I sought it through her, whose life was most intimately joined to his, and as my errors were dissipated and my life ordered and harmonized, I found myself more joined to him, until he became to me all that he is, and we three are now in that sweet unity of life which must be eternal."

"Do you not think all loves eternal?" I asked.

"Love is the expression or result of affinity of being. When this affinity is slight, extending to but one or two faculties, the partial unity is weak and transient. Most of the loves of the world are based on one or two faculties. Some are the simple sensual attraction—others unite to this vanity, or avarice. These partial unities can not be expected to endure. A love can only be permanent, when it is the expression of more integral unities. When the spiritual attraction corresponds to the material; when there is an interblending and harmony of many faculties and uses; then the love is full, satisfying and enduring. Then may we rest upon it, as on a sure foundation, for time and for eternity.

"For the time, provisionally, and during your novitiate, I assume the relation to you, which is a mutual attraction, and a mutual right. Your happiness in this will be just in proportion to the truth and use of the relation, and the future will take care of itself, if we are but faithful."

"And all here," I asked, "are they in this beautiful order of mutual help, all connected by these golden links to the central and the internal life?"

"All. None could be here who were not in the order of this harmony. Not that it is obligatory or compulsory in any external sense, but because any erratic, selfish, inharmonic action would throw the individval out of our life, as surely as a planet would be thrown out of a system, if it lost its attraction and relation to the central sun and the other planets. All belong to each, and each is joined to all, even to the remotest fibre or atom ; and as the whole body sympathizes with a diseased organ or atom, even so the whole body of our society would be pained should one of its members fall into any evil. And the whole body with a united effort would either cure the diseased member; or, failing in that, the line of separation would be formed, and the dead member would be sloughed away. So truly is the physical body the type of the social body—so truly are the principles of physiology those also of a true sociology.

"You have the maxim, in union is power. The more complete the unity, the greater the power. The principle of every unity is an orderly obedience to the common life. The power of a mob is in unity of purpose, the efficiency of an army is an orderly obedience ; the harmony of a society is in the obedience of each member to the central life or idea of that society."

"But is not this a despotism?"

"Yes, if you please to term it so ; but not in the proper sense of that word. Despotism expresses the exercise of arbitrary power, uncontroled by principle or law. The obedience which a true society demands is an obedience to law, an orderly accordance with principle, a harmonization with the controling idea of the life. Absolute freedom is the condition of order by obedience. The tree is free to expand according to the law of its life, but not otherwise. Every animal, in appropriate conditions, obeys its attractions and repulsions, which form its life. The planets move in perfect order, harmony and obedience to the laws of motion. The man who conforms his life to his highest sense of right, lives in obedience to its requirements. This is all. The freedom we demand and enjoy, is the freedom of each to live his or her own truest life."

As no work, no conversation, and no pleasure, is ever prolonged to weariness tending to exhaustion here, I now took my leave of Melodia ; rather we both walked out upon the lawn, where we met Vincent, returning from a short session of active labor. Its glow was in his cheek, and its moisture on his brow. He greeted Melodia tenderly; then, at a suggestive look from her, perhaps, he took my arm and walked with me to a shaded seat. For a few moments we looked out on the scene before and around us. There lay the lake, in its calm beauty, mirroring the heavens. Industrious groups were working in garden, orchards, and fields, and their songs came to us in softened cadences. Far across the lake we heard signal notes of a bugle. There was the hum of machinery and labor from the workshops. The fountains threw up their silvery spray, which fell in tinkling music. Gleeful children made sport of industry, or gathered around some one who both taught and amused them.

"The observation of our life," said Vincent, "teaches most of its lessons; but there are some principles which may not be apparent to a hasty observer. It is evident that we have escaped many of the evils of civilized society and morality; from poverty, and its depressing and debasing conditions; from competition, with its frauds and spoilations; from many evil and diseasing habits and circumstances. We have wealth, peace, competence, a cheerful co-operation, an attractive industry, a sphere of beauty and refinement, and the pervading charm of harmonic social relations; of friendship, which unites us all in a common brotherhood; of a true recognition of qualities which awards to each his proper social position; of love, which is the happiness of every true and noble heart, and of the tender relations which subsist between the gradations of age.

"All this you have seen, and you know, doubtless, natural and spontaneous as these blessings here seem to you, that they do not exist, only as exceptionally and fragmentarily, elsewhere on this planet. Esperanza is the emergence of order out of confusion; harmony from discord. It is our hope and faith that from this germinal point it may spread over the earth; that the human race may become one grand associated family; and that man may fulfil his destiny, as lord of the domain of nature, and harmonizer of the globe."

"You spoke just now of those principles, which I might overlook, in the observation of so much material prosperity and social happiness," I observed.

"Yes; it is due to you, who will soon be separated from us, that you should know the interior of our life, and how much it differs from that which you have been accustomed to observe. It differs in causes, as in effects. If you would know the sources of the evils 'n civilization, you must look for them to the principles on which it is based.

"Thus the wrongs and evils of excessive individual wealth and general poverty; of universal conflict, fraud and robbery, come from the prevailing systems of commerce and finance, and the laws and institutions respecting property.

"The social discords and miseries find their center and source in the monogamic, indissoluble marriage and isolate household, with its selfishness, deprivations, and moralities.

"So of the political and religious systems—an evil tree cannot bring forth good fruit. A trial of thirty centuries has given but one result—thirty centuries of toilsome progress have only prepared a few of the foremost of our race to accept the idea; and a few to enter upon the practice, of harmonic relations.

"There was no possibility of a half way reform. Every effort at a partial harmonization must necessarily fail. A society, with separate individual interests, is a school of selfishness. A society, with the social moralities of civilization, contains the seeds of dissolution.

"It was required therefore that all who came into our life, should come, first as distinct, separate, utterly free individuals. The husband, the wife, the parent, the child, as such, and as having any legal, or arbitrary claim upon or power over each other, we could not recognize. Each began our life as a free and independent human being, as if such relations had never existed. That a man or woman acknowledged any claim or right of husband or wife, because of the customary or legal relation, was enough to exclude them from our life; the very first condition of which is absolute freedom.

"Thus freed from these entangling alliances, disintegrated, and brought into the rank of independent human beings, all had that work of individual purification and harmonization of which you have heard, and the method of which has been revealed to you.

"The man or woman, so made free, pure, and equilibrated in all faculties, is now ready to form true relations in friendship, love, and that grouping of congenial natures which forms the true family or group of affection. These groups are formed by a harmonic law, on centers or pivots; thence branching or radiating outward, like the groups of all organic formations, and in virtue of the same laws of order and harmony.

"The central passion of harmony, is that of Love, which defines the relations of the two great divisions into which humanity is divided. Love, or the sexual passion, in civilization, is the direct or indirect cause of its deepest evils. In a false moralism, all falsities cluster around this central falsity. Even so in a true life, all true relations cluster round this central truth. All harmonies, material and spiritual, revolve around this pivotal harmony, the harmonic love. It binds us all in one. It is the key-stone of our social fabric—the key-note of our harmony. Whoever cannot accept this fundamental principle is not yet developed up to the plane of our life. There must be, with all who would live this life, the utter abandonment of all selfish or exclusive claim of woman to man or man to woman; the absolute freedom of all relations; but no less the absolute recognition of the laws of harmony in all relations. I wish to make this very clear to you, not only as a postulate, but as a demonstration. I would show you why this must be. I will take your own case. You come here, attracted to our life, or accepting the relation of a noviciate in its order. You come with a love, which you are not required to abandon, but only to purify from all taint of selfishness, and tyranny of claim and custom. You have to assert your freedom, not from, but in this love; and you have also to set this beloved one as absolutely free. You have found other attractions here, the germs, it may be, of the loves of the future. She whom you hope to bring with you to our home, and whom we shall joyfully welcome, if she prove to be one of ours, will also find her own attractions here. But all of these, in a true and pure life, are as much subject to principles and laws of relation as the harmonies of music, colors, or odors. Each love must be in harmony with the other loves. These separate unities combine to form the unities of the groups of love; and these groups interlock, to form

18

the series of our society. The threads can be traced from center to circumference, like the nervous system, which unites all hearts to the central love life and gives to us unity of feeling, unity of thought and unity of action. An injury done to the love life of the least of our little ones, is felt in the central life. It is thus that the good of each one is the good of all. And this love circulation is as unimpeded and universal, as the corresponding circulation of blood in the physical system ; this unimpeded circulation which is the condition of life to every organized being.

"You will study this, both here and in your absence. Give yourself up to the law of growth, and circulation. No ligatures, no compressions, no congestions, no starvations.".

Vincent left me, and with his springy elastic step, flew up the stair case to find Harmonia, whom one would think the object of his single adoration.

I asked her once—"Do you never wish that Vincent loved you with his whole heart ?"

"It is a great heart," she replied ; "but I think it is all mine."

"You think others have no share in it ?"

"I think love is one," she said. "I love with my whole heart always, and each one according to the unities which we have developed. In music, if I like Bethoven, does he lose anything of my admiration, when I come to appreciate Mozart ? If a mother loves one child with her whole maternal heart, is her heart divided into six pieces when she has six children ? Or, what is better, let me appeal to your own experience. Do you love your Clara less, or less wholly, since you have seen Melodia, or Serafa, or Evaline, or me ?"

With my whole heart, dear Clara, do I love you. I feel and know it. But I should be the meanest, most cowardly and most sacreligious of wretches, if I were to deny that with my whole heart also I love those who are so lovely to me, here, in this paradise, so soon to be a Paradise Lost to me ; but soon also, I fondly trust, to be a Paradise Regained.

XIV.

CLARA MINE : It is true—true to my inmost heart and life. I am thine, and thou art mine. I feel a sacredness in these words I have not felt before. I am not a property, a possession, a prisoner, a slave ; but a free, self-centered being. This is what I wish to be, and, with all the power of my soul, *will* to be. And I am thine, not in obedience to any clutch, or claim, or outward bond ; but as the spontaneous act of my free spirit. And so must thou be to me. O mine ! mine, in the inmost life.

I live here, hour by hour, in the sphere of a pervading, purifying love. It is a love that warms all hearts, and attunes them into the sweet harmony of this life. I melt into it ; I am absorbed by it ; and the old selfish, the miserable, craving, clutching, egotism of the isolate, discordant, and warring life, dies out of my spirit.

I do not give you the details of our daily life ; though each has its new interest and enjoyment. It is a life of continual progress— never of a dead routine. It is like a tree that is constantly expanding with its daily growth. The elements, indeed, are the same ; the laws forever the same, but the movement is onward, and each day presents some new achievement. Last night, for example, we had a comedy, full of droll, sharp, and yet genial satire, in which the little faults and peculiarities of half a dozen persons were ridiculed in such a way, as to amuse them more, perhaps, than any others in the audience. It was a little caricature, and every stroke told. It is by this means that many faults are corrected.

If a custom or habit begins to get ground here, some one writes a comedy or farce, in which it is worked out to its possible conse-

211

quences. It is the *reductio ad absurdum* in action. No one is hurt, and all are warned. The pervading love life—the affectional interlocking of all groups in this series, gives it the sensitiveness of an organized body. In our dislocated, dismembered society, some members suffer, and some die, and the rest are but little conscious of the evil. Our social life is paralyzed. Men and women are diseased, starved, depraved and cut off, without our perception.

It is not so here. The humblest member of this society is so joined to the central life, that his wants, his pains, his disorders, would be felt, and if possible remedied. And there is an embodied justice here, which all may trust, and an embodied love or philanthropy, on which all can securely repose. The society has the same faculties as the individual. As a whole body or organization, it has its benevolence, its conscience, its love. And while the individual never loses his individuality, he is still in entire unity with the whole, and the great problem is solved, of finding a social state in which the highest good and happiness of each, is not only consistent with, but promotive of, the highest good and happiness of all.

"If one person here were sick; or in any want, spiritual or material, or suffering any unhappiness," said Vincent, to-day, "every person here would be less happy. Every one, for his *own* good, if there were no other motive, would seek to cure the sickness, supply the want, or remedy the evil. It would come to the heart and head of our body, and help would come. What could resist the united love, and will, and power of a body so united. You know what the magnetism, and strength, and sympathy of one or two may be to you. It conquers pain and disease; it supplies our deficiences, or enables us to bear them. It compensates losses. It brings us the riches of life. How much greater might this power be when exercised by a harmonious society."

"I can see that this is true of philanthropy, benevolence, or the sentiment of paternity," I said; "but will you explain to me how far it is so of the more intimate and personal love of the sexual attraction or relation?"

"Yes; I will try; for I wish you to understand this; the more especially as you may have to explain it to others. You may bring it nearer to their minds than I can. It is well, often, that the teacher be not far in advance of his pupils. Our best teachers, in many things, are those one grade in advance.

"Our love life is composed of concentric spheres. The external is philanthropy, which grasps all humanity. The love of friendship or congeniality takes in numbers of both sexes, and of different ages. Each faculty has its own loves, which join together persons by similarity of tastes and pursuits. Thus scholars and artists flock together. There is also an attraction of contrast, or supply and demand, by which dissimilar persons are drawn together. We have the paternal instinct, special and general, by which we love our own children because they belong to us, or those we love, or merely because they are children. There is also the love reverence by which the young love those who are older than themselves. These loves combine variously, several entering into one combined passion.

"We find a natural or instinctive attraction, tending to unity between our young people and the middle aged; a relation of mutual help. So between infancy and old age. Naturally, the sexual attraction modifies all these loves, or relations. Other things being equal, men are more benevolent, more friendly, more tenderly parental, more reverent and protective toward women. And the reverse of this is true; yet men demand the manly, and women the womanly sympathy.

"In all these loves, or forms of love, there are certain laws of diffusion or exclusion, of relation, or want of relation. A man or woman may be joined to us by the sphere of philanthropy, but be excluded from friendship or any nearer relation. I may have a warm friendship for a woman whom I could never love with a tender, spiritual sympathy; and you may be able to conceive of having a very tender spiritual love for one, with whom you might never wish to come into the most intimate relation.

All these passions or sentiments are confused, distorted, or destroyed in the world of civilization. In that corporate Ishmaelism where every man's hand is against every man, there springs up a deep, pervading, offensive and defensive selfishness. The property feeling is applied to every thing. It is *my* house, *my* land, *my* friend, *my* wife, *my* children. This *my* becomes a word of terrible power. With us it is very much changed. We use the pronouns we, us, and our, much oftener. The little *my* has all its rights, but in a true subordination to the much larger *our*, which includes all the little *mys*.

"The policy in the world of civilization is that each man must have his own love, as his own exclusive property, and all teach, and many feel, that this is the natural law. That which is most craved, and most valued, becomes most subject to the property feeling, hence the claim, and right, and absolute despotism which men and women assert and exert over each other, in the civilized marriage, is the most oppressive and terrible of all the slaveries of civilization. Where it is mutual, it is mutually absorbant and balancing, and borne often unconsciously, supported as it is by custom, habit, opinion and law. But let its mutualness cease, and it becomes the most terrible hell to which man or woman can be condemned.

" This state does not belong to our life. It is utterly inconsistent with the life of a harmonious society, of which the love of the sexes must be the central harmonizing power. A selfish, enslaving, debasing property love, the love of clutch, claim, and exclusive right, must be an element of discord in every society, tending to the rupture of all other relations, and to a complete individual selfishness and isolation. Thus the individual, selfish, isolate marriage can never be an element of a true society. All have failed, and all must fail, which attempt to include this element. It belongs to discord, and not to harmony.

"Have you any objection," I asked, "to giving me your own experience in this matter ?"

"None, whatever," he replied, in a quiet, serious tone, as if his most sacred life was devoted to the great idea. " I was born in civilization, and experienced some of its evils ; but, either from a natural bias or from peculiar circumstances, I grew up in much freedom from its influences. My early studies were of a socialistic tendency. Nature and man were the objects of my investigations. I never fell into the social and domestic slaveries of the world around me. I grew more and more free.

"But I found in myself a hereditary taint of selfishness, which displayed itself in exclusive claim and morbid jealousy of those I loved. My reason, my sense of right, and my desire for a true life, have enabled me to overcome this depravity. I am content now to have of every man, every woman, and every child around me, what is truly and sacredly mine, just as I am content not to be a pirate, a thief, or a miser. The love that flows to me, freely, the spontaneous offerings of true and loving hearts, is mine by a divine right, and brings me the most beautiful happiness. The love that is claimed, clutched and enforced, by either a physical or spiritual despotism, gives no such happiness.

" The world shows us all grades of the debasement of love. The Australian, wanting a woman, knocks down and drags off to his hut the first one he finds, or fancies. Savages, a little more advanced, buy their women with skins, trinkets, and liquors.

"In barbarous countries, which include more than half the population of the earth, women are thus bought and enslaved. The civilizee knocks down his bride with fine speeches, and seductive behaviour, or buys her with position and fortune. In all cases, the freedom, self-hood, and spontaneity of the woman, especially, and often of both, are sacrificed and lost. The selfish and savage claim of a man over the heart and person of a woman is sanctioned by law, and sanctified by religion. This is the central Evil of the world.

" All this I have long since seen, and felt and deplored ; and I have done what I could to awaken thoughtful men and women to a consideration of this evil ; but it is a part and parcel of civilization, the center and pivot of its great system of wrongs ; and also its necessity. Only in a new and true social organization could a remedy be found for such a pervading evil. It is at once the bane and the necessity of the old society.

"In my present life, and in the life of our society, all this is swept away. So far from its being a necessity, we have to guard more carefully against selfishness and exclusiveness here, than elsewhere, because here it would be the greatest evil. Were any man here to assert an exclusive property claim to any woman, as wife or mistress, or any woman to assert a similar claim to any man, it would be felt as the violation of the rights of every other person in our society.

"There is, therefore, but one principle for us, and that is the absolute right of individual self-ownership, and the consequent absolute freedom of the affections. Living in the purity of a healthful life, with the development and exercise of all faculties, we find it entirely safe to leave the relations of love, as all others, to be determined by those attractions which are proportional to destinies. We recognize, as a principle, the self-ownership of woman, and her queenship in the realm of love—her consequent right to the bestowal of her affections and her person.

"It is our gallantry, our chivalry, to relinquish and secure to woman this, her highest right. Consequently, love, and its uses, and happiness, are in her keeping. It is she who regulates the sacred function of maternity. Never, with us, is a child forced upon a reluctant mother; and such is the sense of duty and responsibility here, that no woman in our society would have a child unless satisfied that it was her highest duty to humanity and to God.

"This secures the purity of all relations. The highest and most integral loves alone are ultimated; and love, no longer an idle, selfish, sensual passion, becomes the holiest thing in our lives. Love is our religion, and our religion is love.

"Marriage, in civilization, is, for the most part, a legal license for sensuality. We who have too many uses for our vital forces, to waste them in such sensuality, have no need of such a license; nor have we the selfish appropriativeness, that demands a legal claim to property, to which we assert exclusive ownership.

"You have asked my own experience. It is that of all. The freedom of love secures the purity of love. The purity of love permits its freedom. All good and right things act reciprocally—working together for good. You have been in the center of our life, and you know those who love me most intimately, and those to whom my whole life is devoted. I could not lose the love of any one without a pang—a great sorrow. But the life is more than the loves, which are the precious blossoms of the life; and if any one of these were to be false to the life, my love for her would die out of my heart: and if I were myself to be selfish and false, there is not one of these, I hope and believe, who would not exclude me from her love; or, rather, whose love, would not also die, with whatever regrets, but not the less die, and be buried as a dead thing, out of sight.

"Every heart has its own capacities and its own wants. I cannot speak for many, much less for all. I have never known man or woman, who, deprived of one love, would not seek another. I have seen few, if any, who were not capable of more than one love, or rather, of having more than one object of love at the same time. I have loves on the earth, and very real and sacred loves in the heavens; and so, I hope and believe, have most men and women. The number whom it is possible to love, with the intensity of passion, is probably limited by a law. All regular groups are restricted in the number of individuals composing them. In music a few notes compose the scale of harmony. In painting, a few colors. The heart of man finds its deepest and truest happiness in the harmony of loves."

Vincent sat a moment in a silence which I did not venture to interrupt—then went slowly away. I pondered his words; and that I might not lose them, came at once and have written them down as nearly as I can remember. Having performed this duty, I will pursue my investigations.

———

And to whom do you think I next addressed myself. Not to any man, for I had got the masculine statement from Vincent. Nor did I go to Harmonia, or Melodia, to the gentle Evaline, or the *spiritual* Serafa, nor to my piquant Laura, nor the calm Eugenia. I did not seek any one; but one came to me. I was walking near the house, when I was met by the rosy Angela, coming from the garden.

"O Mr. Frank," she cried, "I am so glad to have met you.

19

I have worked two hours, and that is as long as any one should work at once; and now I want you to be my beau, and walk with me, and amuse me, just as you do the young ladies in New York."

She took my arm with just such a demure look as I have seen a thousand times, and prepared herself for the customary compliments. I could only laugh.

"Well, Mr. Frank, is that the way you treat a young lady who favors you by taking your arm?" said she, with a pretty affectation of indignation. "Why don't you begin? Tell me that it is a fine day, and pleasanter than it was yesterday; but not so pleasant as you hope it will be to-morrow; that the country is delightful, especially in such pleasant society; and that the flowers are beautiful, but you prefer other beauties, you know; that the waves are sparkling, but not so brilliant as those corruscations which glitter —hem!—and that all the beauties and sublimities of nature are not to be compared to the—what-d'ye-call-em? You know, Mr. Frank. Why don't you talk to me in this fashion of nonsense? Oh! how stupid you are, to be sure!"

"Excuse me, Miss Angela," I said, "I have been talking and thinking on some serious questions."

"Such as— ?"

"Love."

The child's whole manner changed to me. She looked in my face with a serious earnestness. "Forgive me, dear Frank," she said, "I ought to have taken better notice of you. I saw you talking with my father; but it was an hour ago."

I wish you could hear this girl speak the words "*my father.*" I cannot tell you what there was of tender, reverent pride and affection in them.

"It was," I answered, "and I have been trying to write down all he said."

"That is right, Mr. Frank. My father is very wise, and you must learn all you can of him. He seems cold and abstracted sometimes, but he loves to talk with the young. Frank, you must love my father!"

"You need not tell me that—but to-day he was very kind, and gave me much information."

"And still you are unsatisfied?" said she; as if such a thing were scarcely possible, or a proof of a wonderful degree of stupidity.

"Yes, unsatisfied, if you please, Miss Angela; but not dissatisfied. Mr. Vincent's statement of the love relations, existing in this society, is clear and satisfactory; but I wish also to see how the same subject would seem to a woman."

"Because women are not philosophers; is that it?"

"That is near enough."

"Well, Mr. Frank, if I am not a woman now I hope I shall be, sometime. Suppose you ask me."

I was surprised at this—but why should I not seek wisdom from a child; one so clear, pure, and unperverted as this assuredly is? Without waiting for my questions, she said;

"I have seen a little of the world, and read history, poetry, plays and romances, in which it is more or less truthfully represented. And I think, Mr. Frank, that the human world is very poor, and mean, and bad. The trees are good and beautiful in their way; so are the animals, in theirs. They live their true lives. But men and women have lived very perversely. The loves of the plants are varied, and natural and beautiful. I read of them in Darwin first, and then I study them in themselves. How respectable all the animals are in their relations. Even the savage ones—you see that they act in character. Man only is a hypocrite—men and women both; and women most, just because they are the most enslaved.

"I am not old enough to have experience of love; but it comes first in idea, in the imagination; and I think it is as clear there, as it ever is. Now I can imagine myself loving you, a few years hence, very dearly; but I can never imagine myself bound to you in a civilized marriage. It might be that this love would satisfy my heart, if you were great and varied enough; but I could not live in the most sacred love that ever the pure heart imagined, if it was an outward bond to me.

"With us, each day is a new life. What I felt or did yesterday, does not bind me to-day. What I feel to-day must not enslave me to-morrow. That which is my brightest ideal this year, might next year become the most abhorrent slavery to me. So, Mr. Frank, if you are ever a lover mine, you will have to be good, and worthy, and attractive to me every day. No one can promise to love next week or next year. How stupid then to make a vow, or oath, or contract to love all one's life !

"The young girl, who stands at the marriage altar, promises to love, honor, and obey—an angel ; her ideal perfection. I mean if she is honest and is not selling herself like a prostitute. But in a month or a year, she finds that the man who claims to own her is not that angel, but a very common mortal, or worse. He is not the man she bargained for. He is not the man she promised to love, loved, or ever could love. You may say, she is bound to keep her promise, however mistaken and false. I say she cannot. It is a moral impossibility.

"Were I in the world I would make no such promise. Here it will never be required of me. No man or woman here promises anything, but to be true to themselves, and their highest sense of right, in all relations."

"And this life, my Angela, is full of promise to you ?"

"Oh, better than that, Mr. Frank. It is full of real happiness. Where in the world could I find so much ? Where such comfort and luxury ; so many friends ; such pleasant and varied employments ; so much exercise for my talents ; such opportunities for development ; such a home and such loves ? The dear life here is full af all beautiful things, even now. As my life opens, and our state and condition improves, there will be more happiness. I shall be able to help my dear father and mother ; the mother to whom we all owe everything in our life, and our glorious Melodia, and dear Evaline. Ah ! my friend, beautiful as I can believe that our life seems to you, it is yet more so to us."

"And the world ?"

"I know it a little, for myself ; and more from others. It is very poor and mean at the best. I read of it sometimes, not always with sadness. I have no desire to see it. It would be time lost and life wasted. I may join a little party to go to Europe to see the world of art, there; pictures, statuary and music; but that is all. We shall not be long absent; and the joy of our return may repay us a little for the deprivation."

" Will Mr. Vincent go ? "

" Scarcely. Melodia may, and Angelo, and Evaline. My father and mother would not wish to be separated—and our home could not well spare them both. It will be hard for any of us to leave. Perhaps we shall not go; but we dream and talk about it sometimes."

" Now, Angela, I am going to ask you a question. You need not answer it unless you wish. If you were obliged to choose only one person, of all here, to be with, and give your life to, who would that one be ? "

" My mother, always ! "

" Not your father ? "

" No—it is my mother; for though I may love my father most, or best, or however it is compared; I should best satisfy all my loves, even my love for him, and my sense of right by going with her. Thank God, their is no such alternative ! No, Mr. Frank, no child here is obliged to choose between father and mother, or between parents and husbands. Our family cannot be broken up and scattered, like the families of civilization, where parents and children, brothers and sisters are separated by the marriage system and the isolate household. Did you ever think what a tragedy of suffering it is ? "

" No, it is one to which custom reconciles us."

"Yes, like burning Hindoo widows, or christian heretics. Our family is sacred—sacred and imperishable. All its members are folded in its loving arms. The mind thinks, the heart loves, the hands work for all, and now I must go to my work too. Have you found out what you wanted ? "

Kissing her hand to me, she ran away toward the studio, where was her next labor.

Beautiful Angela ! what a treasure of rich, pure, loving life ! She is one of many here; but I could not help thinking that even this one would shed a radiance over this existence. I sat and thought of her life, her loves, her beautiful physical, mental and artistic development, and her relations to all here, till it seemed that no body in the world could be so fortunate and happy. Yet every one in Esperanza, in proportion to his capacity for employment, must be just as fortunate, and just as blessed.

Last night, I danced. We know very little of the pleasure of this harmonic exercise. You and I, when we have shut out others from our thoughts, have danced beautiful duets. But here we dance full harmonies. It is not only two lives that mingle, but many—many hearts and lives. It was a magnetism that entranced and up bore me. I seemed to tread on air. I moved to the glowing cadence of the grand music without an effort. It was like swiming in a sea of pure extacy. With the music still vibrating in my ears; still floating in the measures of the intertwining movement; still feeling the pressure of friendly hands, and warm beating hearts, I slept. May you, my beloved one, sleep ever as happily.

XV.

IMMORTALITY.

DARLING : My peaceful slumbers were broken, as broke the light of a new day, by the distant note of Vincent's bugle. It mingled with my dreams ; then I woke to the consciousness of the happy life around me ; then came the inspiring air, chased by the echoes of forest and mountain, nearer and nearer. It was repeated at intervals, until its full burst resounded on the lawn, and a moment after, it was joined by the band of instruments, in an awakening and inspiring harmony.

I thought at first that the seeming distance of these sounds had been the artistic effects of a skilful player ; but I found that our vigilant chief had mounted his horse in the first dawn and taken a gallop over the domain ; and that his bugle call had been sounded at intervals in his rapid approach to where the band stood ready to join him.

The morning parade has every day some fresh interest. A magnetic life is diffused through the whole society. In the music all are attuned. Discords vanish. The individual becomes so sweetly harmonized with the will of the body that all move as by one impulse of the pervading life, and find in that harmony the greatest happiness.

Never has the solitary, isolate life of the selfish individualist seemed so poor and mean, as it now appears to me. That longing of the soul for love, for sympathy, for unity, never wholly, and seldom at all, satisfied in our life, can only find its perfect satisfaction in the harmony of such a life as this.

When I entered the saloon of the morning lecture, I saw Melodia seated in the center of the platform, and on either side Vince and Harmonia. Vincent was calm, Harmonia pale and sorrowful. Melodia rose and stood silent a moment; and her upraised eyes filled with tears. Tears came in my own, though I knew not why. But soon a sweet smile and a slight flush came over her face, and in her low sweet tones she said:

"Dear Friends, what I have to say to you will sadden us for a moment; but there will come with it, also, a deep joy.

"Our good Father is soon to leave us, to join the noble and beautiful society of the heavenly life. Our dear Harmonia has been with him in the night watches; the spirits who watch over us have announced to him his speedy welcoming to the life of the heavens. He goes to join in higher accords of harmony; but he will still be with us and watch over us; and he will be able to be more to us, and do more for the great work of the redemption and harmonization of humanity than he can do here.

"Joyfully does he welcome the summons. He feels that his great love for all his children here will find a freer and better expression from the spirit spheres than it can from this. He wishes me to say, that before he leaves the bodily form, he hopes to see and greet you all. His strong, brave, generous spirit prepares to lay off the outer form of the earth life, as he would lay off a garment he needs no longer. His work is done. He is ready to enter with joy upon a new and higher form of existence, to which, when a few years are past, he will welcome all of us, his children.

"I, who have known him longest, and to whom he has been more than a father; I yield him cheerfully to the joys of the inner life; assured that while his external form seeks new unities in progression, his noble spirit, his best self, will be ever with us, loving, inspiring, and strengthening us.

"When the large bell of the tower, at whatever hour of day or night, shall strike nine strokes, it will be to summon us all to assemble here, to receive his parting benediction. Let us lay aside all selfish grief, and be prepared to bid him farewell as joyfully as the radiant ones will bid him welcome."

She was smiling through her tears. Harmonia took Vincent's arm, while Melodia supported her on the other side; and they breakfasted together--but all the rest conversed cheerfully, though in lower tones than usual. There was also a more perfect order of movement, and a greater earnestness visible; but no depressing grief. Faith in immortality is no pretense here, but a very real and sustaining assurance.

An hour later, when I returned from a sail across the lake, what was my surprise to see the good Father sitting in his easy chair, under the trees, with sunshine and flowers around him, enjoying the songs of the birds, and the beauties of nature. Harmonia held his hand, and Angela brought him the most odorous flowers. He saw my surprised look, and held out his hand to me. It trembled more than usual, and his face was more pallid. But there was hope and happiness in his blue eyes; and his voice, though a little fainter, was as cheerful as ever.

" *Bon jour, mon fils!*" he said, as he grasped my hand, " you expected to see the old man on his back. Oh, no! I prefer this. They are very good to me, and let me have my own way in every thing—my good children!"

" I hope you will recover, and enjoy their society many years," I said.

" Don't think it, or wish it. A few days at the most is all I have to stay now; and you are traveler enough to know that when one has made up his mind to go he does not wish to be delayed. I am satisfied and happy. All I have wished and worked for in life is accomplished, or will be, and I am content to go. You will join our family, and find here all that your mind and heart can ask. Is it not so, *ma fille?*" he asked, turning to Harmonia.

" Yes, Father. You have henceforth other duties and other joys. We are to increase, and you, with greater powers of vision and locomotion, can aid us. The little scattered groups, who are earnestly working in the orderly preparation for a harmonic life, may soon begin to join us, and enjoy its realization. You, father, will influence, guide, direct, and welcome them to the home you have chosen for them. Then, out of this, other homes are to be born, and you, who found this domain, will perform the same function in respect to others, and aid our spirit guardians in watching over the infant societies. So shall this new, harmonic man, increase, multiply, and replenish the earth."

The old man's eyes sparkled with joy; then he raised them reverently to heaven, and said in a low, soft murmer:

" *Que votre velonte soit faite sur la terre comme au ciel :*" with this sentence from the Lord's Prayer, in his sweet mother tongue, the old man closed his eyes, and there spread over his countenance an expression of ineffable rest and peace ; and, supported by the soft cushions, he fell into a slumber, as of infancy.

Vincent has managed for several days to give me, daily, an hour for conversation. In these hours he has listened to my doubts with entire patience ; he has answered all my questions, and thrown light on many subjects connected with the progress and destiny of our race. With very little of personal ambition or vanity ; with strong faculties of analysis and synthesis ; with a nature full of philanthropy and love, he has done his work of enlightenment, organization, and direction with so much fidelity, as to vindicate the wisdom which selected him for this work. That wisdom, dear Clara, I need not now tell you, I believe to be supernal. And he has had ever at his side, and in his deepest love, one who has stood between him and the angel life, and who has been to him the medium of its inspirations.

To-day we took horses and rode over every part of this domain, which is like the most beautiful garden, with groves, and shaded avenues, and lovely prospects, and pretty pavilions for rest and shade, scattered over it. I cannot write you all our conversation ; but I will put down the most important portion, both for you, and because I wish to record it while fresh in my memory.

"In what respect," I asked, "does your system differ from that of Fourier ?"

"It differs not so much in principles and ends," he said, "as in means Fourier saw the possibility of harmony, and believed that nothing was needed for its realization, but to bring a certain number of men and women together, under certain conditions. There is no experimental proof that he was not right—that is, that with means, and power, and science, and skill, men might not be harmonized *en masse.* But where is the means or power to do this ? Our system is that of growth, from the minutest germ to the mighty tree. And the preparation for germinal growth was individual development and harmonization. Fourier would have collected a thousand persons, in two or three years, in a phalansterie. I believe that there could not be selected one thousand persons in all civilized society, who could have formed such an association, or who could have been held together against their own repulsions except by some stringent despotism, without a previous preparation.

" We differ from the theory of Fourier, also, in not paying tribute to capital, and in giving less of external or pecuniary reward to talent or genius. These with us have their reward spiritually, and to a certain extent the material correspondent. We are somewhat more communistic than he proposed, while we guard, I think, better than he provided for, the special rights of the individual."

" Are you then nearer to the system of Owen ?"

" No: we reject a democratic communism as having no guaranties, either of order or individuality. A society is not a mere aggregation or agglomeration of individuals ; but a regular organization. It is a body which has its head and its heart ; its nervous centers and circulation ; its organs and members all united together, and constituting a united and harmonious body. Physiology gives us the highest type of a true society. Vegetable physiology approximates it, and, being more simple, is more easily understood."

" Have you examined the system of Monsieur Cabet ?"

" Yes. I wrote to him at Nauvoo, and he sent me his *Voyage en Icarie,* a magnificent dream of a National Democratic Communism, in which the government, that is, the central expression of the popular will, performs all functions, and provides for all wants, in a large country, with great cities, wealth and splendor. Men see something of the life of the future, but not the means to attain it. Hence all have failed.

" Yet the means are so simple, and so in accordance with all the operations of nature ! If any merit has been mine, it has been in

seeing this ; but I can claim none, for it has been revealed to me.
I have accepted and rendered practical, what Fourier himself has
revealed to me from the life of the heavens.''

" And this method — was it readily accepted by those whose
first impulse would probably be to denounce every thing which
seemed to them like a despotism ? "

"It was sometimes misunderstood ; but the rejection of our
method, for this reason, served to separate and keep from us those
disorderly persons who would have perilled our success.

"We taught that while freedom was a condition of a true life
of harmony, an orderly obedience was its most vital necessity.
We demanded obedience, not to us as individuals, but to the principles of the life. The lesson ever impressed upon us was that
there must be obedience, else there cannot be growth. In the tree,
every atom assimilated must obey the life of the tree ; in the
human body, every organ and every atom must alike obey the law
of life and its requirements. The strength of the heart and the
wisdom of the head can only be demonstrated by perfect obedience.
It is not by erratic action that the one gets power and the other
light. The heart and head of a man and of a society must be
corrected by consequences wrought out in obedience, and not by
disordered acts and efforts. Obedience is for a body and a society ;
and consequences are the only corrections. If there cannot be a
perfect and orderly obedience, then there is not unity ; and the part
that is extraneous or parasitic is to be cut off. And many were
severed from us.''

" Allow me to ask how you were able to satisfy people full of
protests against social tyrannies, of the truth of these principles ? "

Vincent smiled as he answered—"Their acceptance was not
so hard as you think. Most received them intuitively and lovingly.
The wise saw their truth and necessity. When it was proper to
make explanations, there was no lack of analogical illustration.

" I pointed to the director of an orchestra, whose function is to
guide every movement, and to become the central thought and will
of a body of musicians, where the most perfect and accurate obedience to the directing power is at once the greatest happiness of

each performer, and the necessity of the performance. I showed that the least erratic individualism here, would not only mar the general harmony, but destroy the happiness of the indivi lual. So in architec ure, every workman must work to the line of his speci-fications, and the directions of the architect and master builder, or mar the work, and his own delight in doing it. Every combined movement involves the same principle ; and that which is best for all, must always be best for each. Call this order, tyranny, des-potism—what you will—it is the absolute necessity of every har-monic movement, from the systems of the universe down to the smallest plant that grows.

" The conservative sentiment for the preservation of order is a true human instinct; but the order usually conserved is v ry false and costly. The true order, which is heaven's first law, never de-mands the sacrifice of the highest freedom and happiness of the individual, but secures both. The first qualification for our life is a tru humility; our first duty is a true obedience ; our first re-quirement a true order ; and these secure to us all the freedom and all the happiness you see us enjoying."

Vincent spoke a single word to his beautiful horse, and he bounded away toward a distant group of workers, whose labors he joined ; while I rode slowly h me, revolving all this in my mind.

I will not conceal that the words humility, obedience, order, have a harsh sound to me. Humility has seeme l a disease or a sham. Obedience has been the requirement of despotism. Order is the ex-cuse of tyrants. And yet I can see that throughout the universe there must be the humility which recognizes and strives to attain to the higher or more advanced perfection. The true scholar, artist, or poet must be a humble worker toward his ideal ; and the greatest men have ha l most of the virtue of humility. Away with vain pri le. It is the sign of a little, mean, and sordid spirit. I see, too, that obedience to laws and principles pervades all nature —every plant and animal living in obedience to the law of its life ; a oms and systems obeying the requirements of universal and eternal laws. Shall I be less obedient to the law of my own life? to the requirements of my physical organization, my moral nature,

and my conscience or highest sense of right? Surely not, dear
Clara ; and I accept the principle of obedience. And order : it is
a sublime ideal. It is the basis of all harmony. In architecture,
in music, in all that man has worthily achieved, it is the prime
element. It presides over the formation of snow-flake and crystal;
it is the governing principle of the Infinite series of worlds. Shall
it be less the controling element of the human soul, and of human
society? So I accept them all. May I live to them as I wish !

As I looked round upon the dinner groups of the great dining
saloon, I could detect no sign of sorrow. Beautiful as is the life
here, the life hereafter is seen and felt to be so much more beautiful, that the change has no terrors and no regrets. I think there
was less conversation than usual, but it was light and cheerful.
The old man had his chair wheeled out upon the balcony and enjoyed the after dinner music. He beat time with his fingers, and
looked round upon the groups of his children, and up to the serene
heavens with a countenance full of a calm joy. Melodia sat near
him, and they talked at intervals. He was giving her his last
thoughts and messages, as a friend who is going on a journey
leaves his directions, and then promises to write.

You shall enjoy with me, some of these bright days, the luxury
of this musical after-dinner hour ; almost the only one in which
all indulge in the *dolce far niente*. The necessary labors of the day
are over. Cares there are none—no cares nor sorrows, except for
the outside world, and the friends that many have left behind them ;
and for these there, is the hope of their sometime coming, when
their bonds shall fall off, or be broken asunder.

Then were formed groups of work, or study, or amusement,
which often combines both, for even the most romantic pic-nics are
made scenes of industry or of study. A group of artists goes to
the woods to sketch, and the afternoon's pleasure is an addition to
the stock of beauty and riches. The out-door conversations are
full of intellectual life. Children make groups around the wise or
imaginative, or people with good memories. Finally, there is no
lack of books.

I sat in one of these groups, to which I had been invited, on coming near,. and felt the calm flow of this restful life. It was a fraternal group of happy men, women and children, lying on the sweet grass under the shade of a broad spreading tree, discussing the future glories of the destiny of man, when this harmony shall have spread over all his heritage.

" It will not require so long as you think," said one. "Let but the most advanced minds now in the world have the assurance which our success must give them, and they will enter with joy and enthusiasm upon the needed preparation for our life. There must be hundreds, yes, thousands, scattered over civilization, now ready and longing for an exodus out of it. If we could but receive them here, the teaching, example and influence of our life would bring them into harmony. In two years we might form other associations, and so on in geometrical progression."

" Fair and softly, my dear," said a wise and gentle matron, who might have been his mother, but was not. "You have had but little experience of the life of the world, and know not the strength of its bonds. You do not understand how men are bound to their wives and families; and wives to their husbands and children. The church, society, business entanglements, debts, relatives, dependents, all these enslave vast numbers. So do all the common habits of life."

" But the young, the unmarried, and those not yet embarked on this dull and troublesome voyage," said he.

" The young have their duties, attachments and ambitions. The life of business and society is attractive to the young. They are full of hope, and do not see its cares and slaveries. Then there is much lack of courage in the young. I have known a college of hundreds of young men and women, as good as the average surely, held in the most abject subjection to the bigotries of two or three professors. It is a world of flunkies, my friend, with very little of genuine independence."

" But, if people are cowards, are they to be blamed for not having courage ?" asked one of the children.

" No, dear ; they are to be pitied. Cowards make despots, and despots confirm people in their habits of cowardice. It is a circle of error; and evils tend continually to reproduce themselves. Out of this slough of despond strong spirits rise, and inspire others with courage. They unite for strength; they come into orderly movement, and soon achieve the conditions of a noble life."

"But to me," I ventured to say, "it seems that so much depends upon conditions. For example, a tree on a high mountain, or in a high northern latitude, or where there is a scantiness of soil or moisture, attains but to a meagre growth. In Shetland, the horse dwarfs to a pony. Men require conditions for development. Here it is so easy to be good, brave, noble, heroic. Here all conditions favor the development of a true life, and true and beautiful relations; but in the world it is very different. All conditions and influences are false and evil."

"True; but you do not consider the sublime fact that man is a condition maker. He alone, of all beings, has the power of making his own conditions, and therein is the possibility of his destiny. The acorn must germinate where it is buried; the tree must grow where it is planted; but man, with his powers of locomotion, can choose climate, soil, food, and make for himself the conditions he requires, whenever he has the wisdom to know his needs."

I am surprised every day by the intelligence of the youngest and humblest members of this family. The facts and principles of universal science, but imperfectly known to our learned professors, and which they so often boggle over, are familiar to little children here; because they are common subjects of conversation. The intellectual light kindles and blazes here, from the proximity and harmony of so many minds; and the awakening and culture of all faculties.

The other day a group of children, tired of some active work, gathered round Vincent and asked him for a story. He sat down on the grass and they sat near him, two of the youngest laying their heads in his lap and looking up into his face.

He plucked a flower, and looked at it a moment—then began:

"Once upon a time the soul of a plant found itself flying through the air."

"Had it wings?" asked a little one.

"Perhaps it was in a balloon," suggested another.

"Souls are not very heavy," said Vincent, "but this one had its luggage to carry with it."

"A soul with luggage!"

"Yes, provisions, clothing, and other little necessary articles such as souls must have in this world; and these were all packed away very safely in a nice little case, large enough for the plant soul, and all its goods and furniture."

"Oh! but tell us what it had to eat."

"Yes; that interests you. You little folks are very fond of your victuals."

"Of course; because it is of our food that our souls are forming our bodies;" said one of the older children.

"You be quiet with your little wisdom," said Vincent, smiling, "it is not your soul that is now in question, but the soul of a plant.

"In this little case was carefully packed starch, sugar, oil, and some very fine matter, to manufacture into vessels and utensils. Plant souls are very carefully provided for. And this little carriage was flying through the air, upheld by wide-spreading silken wings, and borne along by the winds. It went high over trees and houses, in the currents of the atmosphere; then came a calm, and it settled down slowly to the ground, and fell in a moist, warm place, in a little crevice of the earth, and there it lay, all dark and still.

"So the plant soul rested awhile; but no soul is satisfied to be idle long; and as the warmth of the sunshine, and the sweet moisture of the dew began to come through the little windows of the soul's dwelling, it said, 'come, I must be at work. This idleness will never answer. I have a destiny to achieve, and I must be about it."

"So it went to work," said one of the little interrupters."

"Yes, indeed. It was all alive and busy, making vessels, and preparing to expand itself. But it had so little room. 'This will never do,' said the soul, 'I must get out of this, if I burst it open;' and as the shell grew soft and swelled out with the expanding soul, pretty soon it really burst open, and the little soul was free.

20

"How warm the sunshine was, how sweet the dew, and how pleasant the showers. 'Now I must grow,' said the soul. 'I must expand into all the use and beauty I am capable of. I am determined to be the largest, finest, and best that is possible to be. Let's see what I must do.'"

"Yes, I should like to know what a plant soul would find to do for itself," said a very young philosopher.

"'It will be a dry time soon, and I shall want plenty of water,' it said, 'so I must sink some pumps into the ground to suck it up.' So it began to make little fibrous roots, and push them down into the earth. 'And I must have more air and sunshine,' it said, and it began to build up a little tiny stalk, up into the light of day.

"But then its stock of food and materials was almost exhausted. 'This will never do,' said the soul. 'I must have food and matter to work with. Let us see what we can find.' It pumped up some water and examined it, and found some atoms of lime, and silica, and potash, and some old matter which other plant souls had no longer any use for. 'This will do very well so far,' it said, 'now let us see what we can find up in the light here. Oh! here is a plenty of good things. Carbon, and oxygen, and nitrogen, all in the atmosphere, and electricity, to work with, and a perfect shower of energising sunshine. What a rich and beautiful world it is for a little plant soul to expand and mature itself, and do its work in!'

"So the plant soul pumped up the water, and strained out all its solid matters to build with; and it made leaves with thousands of little cells to catch the carbon and oxygen, and nitrogen in from the air, and it inspired electricity, and drank in the sunshine, and worked away like a little bee, building its stalk larger, and its roots deeper, and making more leaves, until it had got a body large enough for its soul, and just as beautiful as it could make it."

"And then it rested, and had a good time," said one of the most tired of the little workers.

"Souls never rest long, and our little plant soul had now another work to do. It was to provide for a progeny of little plant souls, make their little cases, and provide them with just such a supply of food and materials as it had itself to begin the world with. So it set to work with a new energy and delight; and made such a nice, cosy little nest or dwelling, then set it all round with delicate leaves of bright colours, and gathered fragrant aromas from the atmosphere, and made up a stock of honey from the sweetest dews, and with much love and care, brought forth and nourished a whole family of little young plant souls, that the earth might continue to be beautiful, and the race never be lost. And in this last work was its chief glory and delight; and on it the plant soul expended all its powers; and then it was satisfied and content. Its work was done. Henceforth it was to live in the life of its children; or in the higher unities of the soul life of the universe."

You cannot think, dear Clara, with what a solemn earnestness these little children listened to this little story of the life of the plants and flowers. It is in this way that the children of Esperanza are educated. The whole world around them, every plant and flower, is full of life and wisdom.

The play at the theater last evening embodied humorous and ridiculous illustrations of the most besetting sins of our life. Three or four of the characters were personifications of pride, vanity, conceit, intolerance, petty malignities, gossippings, carelessness, bad manners, faults of speech, and queer gaucheries. I have seldom laughed more heartily. There was comic power, both fine and broad, among the actors and actresses, and they played with a perfect abandon, while the audience, down to the smallest children, enjoyed it even more than I, for many of the points were evidently personal enough to have for them a greater zest.

It seemed to me that the performance of this single comedy three or four times a year would do more to correct all the little faults and vices of any society, than the most careful and continual didactic teachings, and yet the serious portion of the plot was of absorbing interest, and also dependant upon the comic development. The use of the stage, as a school of manners and life, was never more apparent to me; and all its capabilities of use and beauty will be developed in the expansion of the New Social Order. When Esperanza shall number its two thousand souls, its Opera and

Drama will be proportionally expanded ; and when we shall have
clusters of such homes, and cities of Harmony, the grandeur and
beauty of Art will be beyond all our present conceptions, and the
scene of the most glorious of prophetic idealizations.

These dramas of the future !   How much more might they be
to society than those of the past !

Is it not time that we let the dead rest, and not be perpetually
digging up its mouldy relics, and displaying its hideous anatomies ?
It belongs to poetry to penetrate the realm, and shadow forth the
glories of the future — and why not of dramatic poetry ?   All art
seems to me the expression of hope, of aspiration, of an idealiza-
tion which looks forward into the future of our destiny, rather
than back into the past.   I would have the world look onward ; for
this perpetual retrospection cannot but hinder progress.   And
though the past, seen through the mists of time, may seem gigantic and heroic,—and even put on the semblance of a golden age, I
would still look for the grandeur and glory of a true life in the
future, which it is the province of all high art to reveal to us.

Every night I spend the last half hour with one or more of the
dear friends who are most in the life of my heart ; sometimes with
Melodia, sometimes with Serafa, or Evaline, or Eugenia.   As a rare
favor, I have a few moments before retiring to rest with Harmonia,
through whom the angel of my life, my sainted and adored
mother, comes to bless me, with the blessing of peace in all the
Present, and Hope in all the future.

XVI.

WE have much to do, my dear Clara, to make ourselves fit for, and worthy of, the happiness of this life. Perhaps I should speak for myself, and leave you out of the question ; but, however ungallant, I must believe that you have some faults to correct, as well as I, who have so many.

My habits have been disorderly and erratic—they must become orderly and harmonious. I have studied and worked by fits and starts, and without a steady, persevering industry, so indispensable to the accomplishment of any object. We must have a time for every work, and always the work in its time ; a place for every thing, and everything in its place. Every faculty must have its rights, and we must advance in the achievement of all our possibilities, in an orderly progression. Is it not so ?

Here, order, neatness and beauty, are habitual. I have not seen, for one moment, any person in an unsuitable or unbecoming costume. The dress is suited to the work. There is no where the least untidiness. In vain may you look through halls, rooms, saloons, and even the walks and lawns, for any object to mar the beauty of the scene. Dust, dirt, and disorder are banished. This care has become so habitual that it is not in the least a burthen.

There is a special group of cleanliness, which attends to the washing, sweeping, dusting, and general care of the halls and saloons, while each person cares for his own apartment, as for his own person and clothing. But every one has the habit of neatness and order, keeping every article in its place, and picking up every dead leaf, twig, scrap of paper, or any object unpleasant to the sight.

So there is a group or committee of temperature and ventilation, and pure air and agreeable warmth or coolness and pleasant odors are assured to all. These groups, like those of decoration and embellishment, are self-appointed by their attractions and fitness for these functions. And all the cares and duties of the home are so divided among those whose ambition and happiness consists in their performance, that they are done in the most perfect manner possible.

As I spoke of these practicalities to Alfred, who, trowel in hand, was working at the head of the building group, on the addition to the edifice, I asked him whether the more repugnant functions were readily performed.

"There comes in here," he replied, "the element of devotion. There is, in our best members, the most loving and the wisest, a strong desire to do every thing for the harmony. You may have seen, as I have, an accomplished musician, qualified to play the first violin, or direct the orchestra, beating a bass drum, or triangle, when needed, to secure the perfection of a musical performance. So here, Harmonia and Melodia are oftenest seen engaging in what civilizees would call the most menial labors; and Vincent and Raphael working in manures or ditches. It is the best and bravest soldier who volunteers in the forlorn hope. He who is chief among you shall be the servant of all. This devotion makes all functions honorable. If there is a duty more toilsome, repulsive, irksome, or dangerous than usual, it is sure to be most eagerly sought.

"This is the fact wherever exists the corporate spirit. Where is the post of honor in your fire department in New York? Nearest the fire, is it not, where the toil is hardest, and the danger greatest? so is it here.

"The orderly, faithful, heroic worker here, satisfies the most of his faculties, and enjoys the happiness which their satisfaction gives. We work from justice, benevolence, pride, ambition, love.

"All high motives here tend to goodness. Self-respect, a desire of the good opinion of others, friendship, affection, all stimulate to industry, to improvement, to elegance and refinement.

"In the old society of which you have seen something, it is honorable to be idle; and he is most caressed who is the least useful or the most mischievous member. The man who works is held in low esteem; but the aristocrat is he, who holds the power of compelling the largest number to work for him. In a social state so false, there are few motives to virtue, and many incentives to vice. In our society, and that we seek to perpetuate, all this is changed."

It is so true, my Clara! This is the place for us to be just as good as we wish to be in our best moments. And as there are here all motives to goodness and virtue, there are few temptations to vice or crime. Why should one ever do or speak a falsehood here, where all is truth? Why ever steal, either material or spiritual goods, where each one can have all that he has a right to have of either? Why should one ever hate, when love is the pervading element, or seek to injure any, where all are striving to be good and do good continually?

The passions and conditions which make the most terrible curses of civilization, here find no place. There are no brawls, riots, or tumults, for all is order and peace. There is no motive nor occasion for drunkenness, where all are free from care, and enjoy in the avocations and amusements of each day, a more beautiful exhileration than any stimulant can offer. Libertinism and prostitution are impossible, where love is without constraint, and the purity of woman finds its safeguard in the freedom of her instincts. Money is not here a temptation to the pretence of love, nor is the heart ever bartered for position or gold. The relations of affection are asumed with careful deliberation, and with a deep sense of their sacred character. There is no influence to induce man or woman to enter into a false relation; or to remain in one a single hour after its falsity is discovered; and the man or woman who should do this, would forfeit all respect; so much is the interior life—the life of the heart—guarded against all falseness and evil.

By our customs and laws, the woman is made subject to the will of man, in their most intimate relations. She is taught to submit and obey. It is not so here. Woman reigns supreme over the

realm of the affections, and with her finer intuitive sense, guards
the truth and purity of all her relations ; and every true man accepts humbly and joyfully the favors she bestows.   This chivalric
deference to woman, which is in our society so often a pretense
and a sham, is here a noble and beautiful reality.   The sphere
of woman, centering in the affections, is thus clearly defined, and
never encroached upon ; and the rights of woman are secured by
her having achieved her supreme and pivotal right—the right to
herself; to the care and bestowal of her own person ; and the free
control of all her conditions and relations.

And in dignity, purity, and beauty of position and character, the
world has seen no women who excel those of Ezperanza ; nor has
human society ever before offered, except in rare and individual
instances, conditions for the development of these noble qualities.
In talent, education, accomplishment, beauty, and elegance, they
would grace any court ; while in loveliness and purity they seem
to me angelic.

With an earnest spirit, I have sought to know the truth respecting those relations on which the harmony and happiness of life so
much depends.   I have searched into the depths of my own heart
and taken counsel also of the wisest here.   I have also well observed the passional phenomena around me.   And I come to these
conclusions.

There are three kinds or phases of passional or heart-love of
which individuals of both sexes are susceptible.   There is the love
of reverence, aspiring and adoring ; the love of peerage, or equal-
ity, in which like seeks to like ; the love of condescension, benevolence and protection.   With the first, we climb upward ;
with the second, we stand firm ; by the third, we raise others to
our own elevation.   There seem to me to be varieties of each of
these phases ; nor can I observe that one ever interferes with the
other.

I said last night to Melodia, when we were talking soft and low
of these sacred things, for such they are here esteemed, "Is it
true, dear Melodia, that you, and all here, are absolutely free, in
this matter of love ?"

"Assuredly!" she said, with a gentle look of surprise. "Free? What then is there to force or restrain us?"

"I do not see, and yet love has its laws."

"As all life has; and the laws of love, like all the laws of life, are very despotic or absolute, and not to be disobeyed with impunity. I am free to love, just as I am free to eat; but health, and even life requires that I do not eat what is not congenial to me. Every where, and in all things, freedom has this limitation. It is the right to do right—never can there be a right to do wrong.

" Love may be defined as the sense of congeniality or unity of being in two individuals of different sexes. It is an attraction like gravitation; and like all attractions, it must be free. But like other attractions, also, it has its laws; and these laws must be obeyed.

"The best thing for you, my friend, is to believe in the divinity of your nature, and to trust in the truth and wisdom of those you love. Only in this trust can your heart find rest and peace. Our life has much for you of soul-riches, if you can peacefully accept what comes to you because it is rightfully yours; but if you cannot trust me and others, with an entire faith that we will do what is right, both as regards you and all others, you will greatly mar your own felicity. You must feel that I am to be trusted with the guardianship of my own heart, and that Clara, and all you love must be trusted in the same self-guardianship. If I, or she, or any of us make mistakes, which we are not likely to do here, they will bring their own punishment and correction. Hard as it might be for you to see Clara forming a relation not all sacredly true to her, and to you, it would be a greater grief to her; and she will guard her heart much better than you can, by any selfish and jealous claim over her. Learn then to trust. How can you trust a woman's love for you, when you cannot trust in the truth of her sentiment for another?"

"But do errors never occur?" I asked; "Is the heart infallible?"

"In the transition, while mixed with the old life, we have all been liable to errors and mistakes. Our instincts have been perverted; but still we could only try them with the greater care.

21

The consequences of our faults were the only correctives. Each had only to live to his highest sense of right; and what better or what else was possible? you must still trust your feet though you stumble at times—you must go by your senses, if they have deceived you. So must you trust the heart. And be sure, my friend, that every woman, who lives our life, wishes, of all things, to be right, in what is most sacred to her."

It has been hard for me, dear Clara, and doubtless will be in the future, to rest as peacefully as I should, in this holy faith; but I know, in my deepest consciousness, that it is right; and that you are as worthy of my whole trust, as you are of my love. And I know that I can leave you in freedom. Do you remember what Pericles writes to Aspasia, in that beautiful book of our noble Landor? "Do what thy heart tells thee"—he says—"do all thy heart tells thee; and oh! may the beautiful feet of my Aspasia stand firm." It was the trust of the hero, and the prayer of the lover. And so, my blessed Clara, with the same deep trust, and the same fond prayer, will I ever say to thee, do all thy heart tells thee.

———

In my conversation with Vincent to-day, I took occasion to ask him what influences were used in this state of social freedom, to protect the young from the effects of passional excesses.

"There is no lack of such protection," said he. "Our young people live upon a pure and simple diet, and their senses are not unduly and prematurely stimulated by unhealty and exciting food. They are generally free from the hereditary taint of amative disease. Love comes to the pure mind of youth, as an ideal sentiment, and, in one of a natural life, and unstimulated passions, it does not soon take the form of a sensual desire.

"It is also a matter of observation and experience with us, that the first loves of the young, are the loves of aspiration and reverence. When the youth of fifteen loves, with a timid and worshipful reverence, a woman of twenty-five or thirty years, the very reverence and idolatry of this love protects him from the hope or wish of any sensuous expression. So the young maiden, in the flush of her womanly life, looks up to some heroic ideal, some man who embodies all that she can conceive of manhood. And those of us who are fitted to inspire, and worthy to receive, these fragrant aromas of the budding soul, are too wise, and too good ever to bring upon them the blight of premature indulgence of a sensual passion.

"Our youth of both sexes live in a sacred vestalate, until their lives are expanded and matured, and they are ready to perform the parental functions. This chastity gives vigor to body and mind. The power that would else be wasted, expands itself in the perfection of the whole organization, so that our young men are full of the strength of an unexhausted manhood, and our young women have all the power and beauty of perfect womanhood.

Compared with the world, all our lives are chaste and pure, and they are proportionally progressive, aspiring, and happy. The spiritual element triumphs over the material. As our lives improve, the children born to us will have superior organizations, and so on, we hope, through progressive generations, with increase of health, physical and mental power, longevity and happiness."

"And still on?"

Vincent turned his eyes on me as if to read the full meaning of my question.

"Yes, still on! Who shall limit the power of a progressive being? What grandeur and glory may not humanity be capable of in the now dawning future, when life and immortality shall be brought to light.

Life and Immortality," he said, with a slow emphatic utterance; "but this is a mystery, which the future must unfold to us."

You have a fine talent for music, my Clara, and for the arts of design. You have the capability to make an excellent player and singer, and also a good painter. But if we were to marry and live the routine life of civilization, these beautiful talents could never be developed. Have we not seen this in many cases? The mother of a family cannot be a great artist—the great artist must neglect her family. Whatever the talent of a young lady for music or art may be, soon after her marriage, the piano-forte is closed, the harp stands tuneless, the easel goes to the lumber-room. There are too many cares and duties.

I cannot endure that it should be so with you. I cannot be the means of hindering your progress in the development of all your faculties. But in the waste and monotonous toils of civilization development goes not onward. Even the round of fashionable dressing, visiting, and dissipation, is inconsistent with intellectual and artistic improvement. Our whole life is such a waste, dear Clara, a dreary, hopeless waste. Men toil for the means which women spend in a toil as unsatisfactory.

But here—here in this home of freedom, and beauty, and love, here every talent finds its culture and use. Here, my Clara, you can become a glorious singer and musician. Melodia will teach you with great joy. Here you will have many friends to appreciate and admire you. Here you can become a lovely painter with Eva-line, and your works will find their true place. You will have society, the best, the pleasantest, the most improving, without the necessi-ties of making formal morning calls, or giving expensive and tire-some evening parties. Here you can dress from morning to night with neatness and elegance, with a costume appropriate to every avocation.

I have never seen in any society so much attention paid to dress as here. It takes rank as a fine art. It is as if each person was a statue or picture, or a character in a drama, and took special care to dress the part correctly and with absolute taste. There is an abundance of clothing, both common and individual—always a three years' supply at least. The groups of construction who make the costumes of both sexes, and those for all uses, are ar-tists, who work with enthusiasm, and, guided by the purest taste, combine in every thing the useful and the agreeable. The fabrics are strong, soft, rich; the colors pleasing and harmonious; the forms elegant and superb. In ornaments there is a variety and beauty rivalling that of the nature around us. I have not seen one instance of slatternlyness or tawdryness. There is always neatness and good taste, and often great elegance. Not to offend the eyes of others, and to give them all proper delight, seems to be one of the social duties.

In New York I would not wish you to sing or play at a public concert or the opera. There is something repulsive in the idea of your being the town-talk; and having your name in newspapers, bar-rooms, and worse places; but here, I should be delighted to see you on the stage, in drama or opera, or in the concert-room; for it is only a larger family, and more select than any fashionable party ever was or ever can be in the world of civilization.

Oh! how often have I seen at our parties, men bending over sweet young girls at the piano-forte, or embracing them in the waltz or polka, from whom they would have shrunk with disgust, had they known them as I did. But here, dear Clara, there is not one, with whom I could not be as content to see you, as if he were your own brother. Not that you would be intimate with all, or find all equally attractive, but that you would have for all a kindness and respect.

And though your life here would demand an orderly and careful industry, yet you would have abundance of time for study, and artistic improvement. The burthen of work and care is so divided, and so well apportioned, that no one feels the weight; and no one would throw it off. Men and women perform all duties here, with as much alacrity as the muscles and organs of your body perform their functions; almost as unconsciously.

Doubtless it was more difficult at first, as it was to move your fingers rightly when you first began to play on the piano-forte; but you know how soon those movements, hard at first, became easy, habitual, pleasant, and almost involuntary. So is it here, in the beautiful order and harmony of this life.

And you shall come here, my Clara, and be taught by those who will so love and prize you, and those whom you also will prize and love. I know it, Clara, you cannot fail to love them; and though I may feel some of the old selfishness, which would seek to monopolize you, and deprive you and others of their rights, I know that I shall conquer it, and that we shall be a thousand times happier here than we could ever be in the isolation of which we have dreamed; or in the worldly society, of which we have seen enough to satisfy us of its hollowness and shams.

I have considered well of our dream of the little vine-covered cottage and pretty garden in Minnesota, or Iowa; where we could be all the world to each other. It is better that we have here all we can desire of each other, and as much more as we require. And then, Clara, should any thing happen to me, should I be taken from you, I feel how desolate the world would be to you; but here, I should leave you with those to whom I could entrust your happiness most joyfully — to those who would be parents, brothers, sisters, friends and lovers to you. I should leave you assured of every comfort and happiness. Do not be troubled at this, for it is needful that I think of it. Prudent men of small incomes insure their lives, that they may not leave their families destitute; but they cannot provide against spiritual destitution. Here you will be every way insured. It is a home to live in, and to die in.

The day that I see you here, dear Clara; the day I see your springy step upon this lawn, when your soft eyes shall shed a new radience over this landscape, when Harmonia shall fold you to her heart, and Melodia shall open her arms to you; when Vincent shall give you his earnest welcome, and Manlius smile his happy, approving smile; when I shall see you enshrined in a group of loving spirits, and all our loves forming an accord of rich and beautiful harmony, then shall I be completely happy — then shall we realize on earth the happiness that we have thought that heaven alone had in store for us. Then shall we know the meaning of the prayer, "Thy will be done on earth as it is in heaven."

———

The good Father Gautier, has a national fondness for the two arts of music and the dance, and he had desired that we should have this evening, first, a pretty opera and ballet, and afterwards a concert and ball in which all could join. So all had been prepared to meet his wishes. Oh! could you have seen the dear old man, with a group of his rosy little ones around him, sitting cushioned up in his arm-chair, in the center of the music saloon, listening to every note of the music, beating time with the dances, and enjoying the innocent delight with the zest of a child!

"The music is good," he said to me, when, at his invitation I drew near him. "My children sing, play, and dance very sweetly ; but I fancy I shall soon do better. I think our friends on the other side have better instuments, larger bands, and much finer music. Then, in dancing, there can be no comparison. When I get these poor old legs off, I shall dance again, as I sometimes dream of dancing."

When the opera was over, and the favorite singers and dancers had received their ovations ; the floor was cleared and levelled for the concert and ball. The arm chair of the good Father was wheeled to one side, and elevated upon a little platform. He slept a little while in the interval. He was sleeping, watched over with a hushed tenderness, until waked by the overture of the full band. He awoke, smiling happily, and opened his eyes as if upon the heaven of his dreams.

Then pealed forth a magnificent chorus of a hundred well attuned and well trained voices. It was the old man's favorite chorus. The tears ran down his pale and furrowed cheeks ; tears of extacy ; not, I am sure, of sadness.

Then came the dance ; a brief dance of an hour, in which old and young all joined, and in which symetrical figures, charming music, and a magnetic life circulation, produced a harmony, which must be felt. A few times in our lives, dear Clara, in our best moments, and in the most genial groups we could gather around us, we have felt something of this life ; but compared to this, it was as a rill to a river ; and I can conceive, that in the fullness of this life, when Esperanza has found its full growth and development, all its harmonies will be proportionally increased.

After the dance came more music. Melodia sang the Marseillaise. Gautier's brows contracted ; his muscles became tense, his chest expanded ; his eyes flashed out their youthful fires. But he soon smiled and shook his head ; and said, " Not that, dear one ;

that is of the old world and its struggles and contests; sing of the new Life and its harmonies and joys."

And Melodia sang a magnificent ode of Freedom achieved, of Harmonies established, of Peace, and Love, and Happiness. And the grand chorus, swelled by all voices, and filling all hearts, was the fitting termination of the evening's festival.

The plaudits of the assembly demanded that Melodia should be crowned with the votive wreath.

She bent her beautiful head, with the true humility of a great soul, while Vincent placed upon it the wreath; then stood a moment smiling her thanks; then walked to where the good Father sat, enjoying the triumph of his child, and mid the plaudits and vivas, took the flower wreath from her head and placed it upon his brows. As she dropped upon her knees before him,—all were hushed into a reverent silence. The old man could not speak. He laid his hands upon her glossy hair, and raised his eyes to heaven.

She rose and kissed his hand, and they bore him, exhausted, but full of happiness, to his repose.

XVII.

MY OWN DEAR CLARA:—The longing to see you, or, at least, to hear from you, comes over me, even here, with deep yearnings. How it would be in any of the dull places of our common world, I will not venture to surmise. Even here, this famishing heart-ache comes, teaching me that the heart demands all its attractions, and that there are no compensations for our spiritual wants.

If you could but write to me—but that is cut off, as if I were on the ocean ; and I think of the thousands of men who go to India or California, doubling capes in long sea voyages, and banished from all heart-ties. I have your likeness, and it rests night and day upon my heart. I look so long and lovingly into your sweet eyes, which seem to look at me with a tender reproachfulness. Do not think I do not know that you also feel this absence. But I hope my long and frequent letters may give you some happiness. I am very happy in writing them ; and should miss you far more, if I were not, some hours of every day, in this *rapport* with you.

Fancy me now. It is morning—the hour after breakfast. I sit in the beautiful little room assigned me, in the suite of Melodia, in my dressing gown and slippers, writing at a carved table. The floor is matted with a clean and fragrant matting, woven here from the flags of the lake-shore. The walls have been painted in lovely pictures by Melodia and her artist friends. You would never tire looking at them. In each scroll or medallion is a picture, harmonizing with the general design, but marked with the sign-manual of the artist. There is a personal interest in every line.

Professor Buchanan has given the name of psychometry, or soul-measuring, to the faculty which some persons possess, of being impressed by a writing, or other relic of an absent person. I have not much of this impressibility; but there are some here who are wonderfully gifted in this way. A letter of any person, held in the hand of Harmonia, is to her a revelation of character, appearance, relations, of all that appertains to them. I do not understand this faculty—but the fact of its existence is unquestionable. Why should not this room, then, have its own sphere? and every work of art which embellishes it, make its clear impression of the character and motives of the artist? It must be so; for I feel all around me the subtle, soothing, ennobling influence of Melodia, and with her's, other harmonious spheres, making life musical.

One day when we were talking of this impressibility. I took a letter of yours, sealed in a blank envelope, and which I always carry near my heart, and gave it to Harmonia. She held it a moment in her hand, then pressed it to her forehead—then to her heart. There came over her face a sweet, happy smile, so like yours, my Clara! and she said:

"There comes to me the image of a fair, pure, loving girl, with broad, white forehead, rosy cheeks and loving lips; a delicate, keen intellect, and many gifts. She seems peaceful in her life, and happy in her love. A pure, harmonic spirit, who ought to be with us; she would find our life in harmony with all her aspirations. Gentle, loving, beautiful spirit—she is one of ours." She handed the letter back to me, saying: "Names are not often revealed to me, but this must be your Clara, and I give you joy of the love of such a lovely spirit. She will come to us, and be very happy in our love."

I accept the prediction; for its fulfilment is the condition of our happiness.

Now I must tell you of yesterday.

First of all, in the interest of our life, our good Father Gautier fails visibly. Vincent thinks he can not stay with us above forty-eight hours. The noble, generous, devoted old man! I went to see him in his room yesterday, with Melodia. I wish you could see how nobly it fits him, like a well-made garment. Every thing, down to the smallest ornament, is in character and keeping. There is a book-case, with nice editions of his favorite French authors; and especially, all of Fourier, whose bust, modelled by Melodia, from an engraved portrait, under his inspection, and seeming to me very spirited and life-like, adorns its top.

The old man was sitting in an easy chair, near a window that looks out upon the lawn and over the lake. A prince could not be better cared for; and no money could purchase these loving attentions. I lose not only all fear, but all awe of death, when I see this beloved and revered old man, so calmly preparing to take leave of the earth-life — speaking of the coming change as of a pleasant journey; and with a faith in immortality so fixed, and a trust so firm, and yet so humble, in the destiny which awaits him.

"Ah! Melodia, darling," said he, with a voice weaker and more tremulous than the day previous, "I shall be the first — your first ambassador. This is quite an honor. First delegate from Esperanza. Well, it is time we were represented in our parent-society; and you may count on my influence."

There was no levity in this; but a genuine earnestness.

As we walked out of his room, leaving him with Manlius, who came to talk of some business connected with the domain, Melodia was silent, but not sad. After a while she said:

"I have looked forward to this too long to be troubled by it now. It must come, and as well to-morrow as a year hence. This life, especially when truly lived, is richly worth the living. I would neither shorten it, nor prolong it, beyond its true appointment. We can spare him, and almost any one now—any one, likely to leave us."

There was a little tremor of her voice; a thickening of the utterance, which told me that she thought of one whom she could not spare.

"I am a little wrong" she said, softly, "in saying we can spare any one. Doubtless the life would go on. That seems abundantly assured. I doubt not that all will be right; I believe that none will leave us, whose post of duty is here. There are those we cannot lose yet."

"What would be the result," I said, "were Vincent to die?"

I was very sorry that I asked this question. She stopped still in her walk ; her face became pale as marble, and like a marble statue in its cold stern beauty. There was a deep inspiration, and a little quivering of the muscles at the corners of the mouth ; but the color came back to her cheeks and lips, in a flood ; and the light flashed from her eyes as she said :

" Vincent will not die ! "

" Then she smiled sweetly, again, and spoke as calmly as ever of his fine, pure health ; his constitution, which shows no sign of age or decay ; and of her assurance of his living many years.

" Nothing can take him from us, but some violence ; and our good friends are too watchful to allow of that."

" Do you also feel sure of Harmonia ? " I asked, not without apprehension, so feeble seems her organization.

" She lives upon the life of the strong ones who love her ; and the inflowing life of the heavens also sustains her. Year by year she grows stronger, as if her spirit, aided by these genial conditions, was building up for itself, a new body. At times, disease has seemed to threaten her, but she has been carried through every crisis, and each has seemed to remove some obstruction, and to make her health better."

" This is wonderful," I said ; " and death has not yet visited you."

" No ;—why should he ?—if you must personify this transition. We live in the conditions of health, and not of disease. Our children are born to a full heritage of life ; and not, as in the world, to an inheritance of disease and dissolution. Ordering all our lives in harmony with natural law, what should make any one sick, or bring to us the pain of premature death ?

" There is no man or woman here who would become the parent of a child, unless assured that he or she could give it its right to health.

" Our vestalate consists of the young who are not yet perfeeted enough in their own beings to give a true birth to others ; and of those who are conscious of their inability ever to do so. The selfishness that for a momentary pleasure would perpetuate disease, and bring pain upon the individual and the social life, can have no place with us."

"Then disease and premature mortality must die out of the earth."

"Yes; it is our work to conquer these foes of humanity. It is our work to repeople the earth with healthy men and women, and replace the miserable, short-lived generations now scattered over its surface. So humanity will rise, redeemed from all its degradations. The earth will become the magnificent domain of a noble and happy race. The tree is planted, my friend, here; and its seed shall fill the earth; for it has in it the life of the heavens."

I went to meet Vincent, with my enthusiasm fully awakened. He looked at me. and then sat silent, instead of speaking as usual; as if he knew I had something to tell him.

And I had. "It appears to me," I said, "that you, who are enjoying the happiness of this life, and not doing your duty to the world you have left. There are thousands who would gladly embrace it, if they only knew of it. That knowledge you studiously conceal. Is it not your duty to go forth and tell the world that a true life may be lived; and that their false one, with all its evils and miseries, is not, as they think it, a terrible necessity."

He was not hasty to answer, but smiled one of those quiet smiles, which, but for his kindness, would be a sneer.

"The missionary spirit seems strong upon you," he said; "I have had it, myself, formerly. It is a good spirit; but tends to zeal rather than prudence."

"But it is this zeal that must reform the world," I said.

"Yes, after its own fashion. The zeal of the catholic missionaries, three hundred years ago, led to the conquest and desolation of the West Indies, Mexico, and Peru. It planted the cross in China, soon to be expelled; and in Japan, to be trampled upon ever since. But, in this missionary spirit, what do you propose to do?"

"If I had your approval, and that of our friends here, I would go out into the world, and tell them of your life and its happiness, and compare it with their own poor and discordant conditions. I feel assured that 1 could find hundreds and thousands, who would accept it with enthusiasm. I would lecture in all the cities and large towns in the country."

A smile played over Vincent's face for a moment, and then a shadow followed it.

"It is a hard thing," said he, "to repress the enthusiasm of youth, especially when excited in behalf of a cause so dear to me; but I have lived much longer in the world than you; and have had a more varied experience. The movement you propose is subject, like all others, to the law of requirement—the law of supply and demand. It is equally unwise to carry coals to New Castle, and warming pans to the West Indies; though Lord Timothy Dexter is said to have made a good speculation in that way; selling his mad venture for sugar ladles and strainers. If you bring people what they do not want, or are not conscious of needing, or are not prepared to receive, no success can await you. People are struggling to better their present conditions—not to change them. Go and tell them where they can find gold, and they will rush off by tens of thousands, across sandy deserts and stormy seas, braving all perils, fatigues, starvation and death. But go and tell them how they can live lives of purity, and health, and happiness, and few will hear, and fewer heed you. You doubt? Try it, if you will. In New York, with liberal advertising, out of seven hundred thousand you will gather a hundred idle or curious people; of whom, possibly, two or three may be interested enough to come again and hear you. It will be the same elsewhere; only, in the smaller places, there will be more curiosity, but not a much greater success. Do the work you have to do; but be prepared for the result I know must follow.

"The few who will hear you gladly, and be anxious to enter upon the life you picture, will be those who are hopeless of success in the world as it is, and who, in most cases, have no power to achieve it any where."

I felt a glow of indignation. It seemed to me that this man misjudged mankind. I could not believe them so blinded to their own happiness. It seemed to me that I could write an advertise-

ment, which would crowd any lecture room ; and that I could prepare a discourse on the falseness and evils of the existing social
order, and the beauty and practicability of the harmonic life, which
would carry conviction to every mind, and stir every heart to an
enthusiasm as great as my own.   I did not say this; but he doubtless knew what was passing in my mind, for he said :

" Well ; we will suppose that I am in error.   Attracted by the
novelty of the subject, crowds come to hear you.   Charmed by
your eloquence and convinced by your demonstrations, joined to
their own experience, they are ready to embrace a better social
state.   What next ?

" Now comes the work of separation from the Old and the preparation for the New life.   The ambitious man must abandon his
career.   The selfish man his selfishness.   The sensualist his sensuality.   The woman of fashion and society must give up her
favorite pursuits and projects.   The whole life must be changed.
All evil habits must be abandoned ; all false and selfish feelings
must give place to the true and good.

"Are there many who will give up, even their dietetic habits, for
all the hopes you can offer them—the morning coffee, the evening
tea, the noon-day dram ; the gorging on exciting flesh, and the
sensuality to which it excites nervous and dyspeptic organizations.

" When you have gathered an audience of a thousand persons,
how many will you find, who are ready to comply with the most
external requirements of our life.   How many live in a state of
decent cleanliness by performing daily ablutions ? How many can
you induce, for any consideration, to give up the poisoning and diseasing luxuries of the table, for the purity of our repasts?   How
many will conform to that law of chastity which lies at the center
of our life, and is the absolute condition, as it is the powerful
mainspring, of development ? How many will give up an erratic
and egoistic individualism, or intense and utter selfishness, and
come into the order of a true obedience, which is the necessary
condition of a harmonic life ? How many, even, will have the
strength to achieve that personal freedom, which is the first step
toward a life of truth.   Will your eloquence make them free when

there is opposed to you all the bonds of habit, custom, opinion, and law ; the obligations of children to parents ; the contracts and vows which hold men and women fast in the marriage slavery ; the selfish struggles for property, position, and station ; the whole power of this life, which so prisons, cripples, and starves all human souls ?

" These are the obstacles to your success. You cannot save the world, until it is ready to be saved. I gave many years of my life to this work, and my most earnest efforts brought me little but obloquy and persecution. My name was a bye-word. My good was evil spoken of."

"And here," I exclaimed, looking round upon this scene of industry and beauty, " here is your reward."

" Yes—it is well. But I thought to redeem the world *en masse* ; not to gather out of it a little scattered band of true souls, who were found worthy. Great multitudes followed Jesus, were healed of their diseases, fed on loaves and fishes, and shouted hozanah ; but there were very few ready to forsake all and follow him. It is of our gospel, of Him ; he that loveth father, or mother, or wife, or children, or houses, or lands, more than me, is not worthy of me. He that would save his own life, shall lose it. These are but the utterances of universal law ; they are found in all scriptures, and are applicable to all true movements. If they were true of the first coming, and the gathering of the typical church ; they are much more so of this second coming, in the glory of a purified humanity, and the social redemption of our race.

" Nevertheless, if you are called to do a work, you must do it, and be justified in your own conscience. Go preach our gospel if you have the internal monition, and all powerful *must*. I have told you the truth. Few will hear, and fewer heed you. But if you labor for a year, and save but one soul, you will have your reward."

" It is enough," I said, very humbly ; for I felt how little I could hope to do, when others so much advanced in progress and wisdom, had wrought for years, with so little of what the world calls success.

We have seen the world's triumphs. A regiment returning in

rags and sickness from Mexico, is received with a city's enthusiastic welcome. It was well—for courage and devotion should be honored, even when exerted in a doubtful cause. We saw the miles of Broadway and the Bowery thronged to welcome Kossuth ; a noble impulse of hero-worship, whether well or ill-bestowed. We have seen the popular ovations to art, in the persons of Fanny Ellsler and Jenny Lind. But if it were announced that Pythagoras, or Socrates, or Jesus, or Fourier would land on the Battery some morning, I am afraid there would be but a slim cortege to welcome them.

The hero of the future cannot find worship in the present. But may not the present be awakened to the dawning future? If I could do but this! How often do we hear people pray God to hasten the good coming time. And if we can do any thing to hasten the day that must surely come, it must be God working in us, to will and to do. So let me humbly do my appointed work, only making sure of the appointment.

Besides the regular requirements of industry ; the seasonable work of a great plantation, large gardens, orchards, and vineyards ; and the manufactures, artist-work, and household labors, there come at short intervals special works, which excite a new interest and enthusiasm, and in which our hardy, athlectic friends love to show their prowess.

In the order for this morning's work, for example, there was the preparation of a new garden-spot, upon a principle which Vincent, after a careful experiment, has developed into a wonderful prefection.

I had often noticed a portion of the garden, arranged in beds of fifty feet in length, by five in breadth, with alleys running between them, and remarked their exceeding richness and fertility. I have never seen any thing to compare with the rapidity and perfection of growth attained in these beds. But there has been so much to see and learn here, that I had never inquired into the mystery.

But, to-day I had a chance to see the process of preparing to
22

extend them over a new portion of ground, from which the season's crop had just been gathered. Many hands made light work. A space of ground fifty feet by two hundred was marked out,— deeply ploughed, and the soil hauled off to the depth of eighteen inches. It was then made smooth, with a slight descent, and now came a group of masons, and covered the whole with a floor of cement. On this bed was laid drains, in this case three feet apart, and fifty feet long; a certain number being connected by branch drains at each end, opening into a funnel at the upper or more elevated end, and into a reservoir at the lower, where a wall is carried along, with openings connecting with the drains.

Eugenia, whose passion for the garden extends to all its products, explained the whole process to me; and showed me its working in the beds now in operation. After the drains are laid the soil is restored to its place, and the garden is ready for planting. If the earth is not of a sufficiently light and porous character, it is made so by suitable additions.

The seed is planted, or the roots set in rows, directly over each drain; the drains are then filled with liquid manures, such as are most favorable to their growth, and the amount of these, and the degree of moisture can be very exactly regulated. At intervals, the liquids are drawn off, or absorbed, so that the air can circulate freely through the drains, and supply the rootlets with oxygen. The result is an increase of from three to five times the ordinary fertility; that is, an acre treated in this way, produces as much as from three to five acres, under even a pretty high cultivation; while in quality of production, there is a greater difference; so that the potatoes, peas, melons, etc., grown in these beds are kept for seed; and there is a continual improvement.

But the manner in which this work was done; its order, rapidity, and enthusiasm, excited my special admiration. There was no noise or confusion. Each group, working under its chief, went gaily into the contest of a friendly trial of skill and power. There was no lagging, and no soldiering; no idle overseers, and eye-serving laborers, anxious only to get, not to earn, the day's wages. Every one worked,—nay, far better, I doubt not, than if the garden had been for his own exclusive benefit. It was bold, hearty, springing work, which it would have done you good to see.

Eugenia and her little assistants were gathering the seeds of some annual flowering plants; and I joined her, and helped the work as much, perhaps, as I hindered it by conversation. I would have you know the sweetness of her spirit. It rests me, like looking at calm deep water. Look for nothing impetuous in Eugenia, nothing imposing; but expect a calm, beautiful soul, in a body as calmly beautiful. My feeling toward her is not an attraction which draws me to her, but a frank and quiet acceptance of all her life can give to mine of its fragrance and rest. Her face is not strikingly beautiful; but very calm and sweet; and her whole form, as I have told you, is of the most harmonious beauty. Evaline tells me that beauty in women tends to the portions of the body commonly displayed; and that nature is apt to slight what our art constantly conceals. I recognize the principle, where there are not the conditions of integral development. The finest forms in the world are found among people where nudity is the fashion—the worst figures are among the most carefully draperied civilizees. Why should nature waste her perfections? Those who are knowing in these matters tell me that you may see twenty pretty faces in Broadway, to one beautiful form; and that very handsome arms may be accompanied by other limbs of remarkable ugliness.

But it was not on any such subject that I conversed with the beautiful Eugenia, as I culled the seed bags of her favorite flowers. I questioned her on a subject of unceasing interest—the life of Esperanza; which I would examine on every side and through every available medium.

"But my dear Eugenia," I said, "after all, you must admit that that is a despotism."

"It would be one, to whose strongest will was not in harmony with the pervading will; and whose highest sense of right was not in accordance with our common sense."

"Nevertheless, it is a Procrustean bed; and the tall must be shortened, and the short drawn out, to suit its measurements."

"The humble shall be exalted, and haughty brought low."

"I have no doubt that you will find scripture for it; every body can defend himself with a text. But is it not true that there is a great sacrifice of individuality here; and an amount of order required, that is altogether unnecessary?" I would have ruffled her placidity if I could. She did not even smile as she answered.

"Order, harmony, beauty, truth, are terms, which, to me, are synonimous. I do not find or fear too much of either. Were I to allow my life to fall into disorder, and become inharmonic to those around me, all its beauty would be marred; it would become false and evil to me, and all the deep happiness I now enjoy would be at an end. In this order I find rest and peace. My life is useful and loveful. I am able to give happiness to others, and I enjoy all that I am capable of enjoying. What more?"

How could I answer to this what more? But I said—"Have you no ambition to triumph; no envy of those who are more dazling, more talented, more successful than you—of Evaline, whose picture was crowned the other night; of Serafa, whose poem was applauded yesterday; of Melodia, who never sings, but they crown her with garlands? Is there no pang in all this?"

She paused, and looked in my eyes with a sad inquiring look, to see if I were in earnest. It was very hard, but I kept on my face of cold inquiry; and the tears came into her eyes as she said:

"Are they not my sisters? Do I not love them? Their triumphs are mine. When I see Evaline's pictures I feel as if I had helped to paint them. My love is in the life that warms Serafa's muse; and when Melodia sings, every note goes to my heart, and I applaud her as deeply, if not as loudly, as any of all her admirers; for all here admire her; and envy has no place with us. Oh! what an egotist do you take me for! I have all of love and appreciation that belongs to me. Would I have more, or deprive any other of her rights? If these questions are serious, Mr. Frank, the falseness of the old society has poisoned you more deeply than I thought possible."

Still I would not explain.

"You are too good," I said. "Such entire unselfishness is unnatural. You have not even a lover you can call your own. Some other woman has an equal or superior claim upon whomsoever you love. Your love life feeds on sufferance, and dares not assert its rights."

" The rights of love, Mr. Frank," she answered with miraculous calmness—with a smile of tenderness, even due, perhaps, to some happy memory, " are not to be asserted. They assert themselves in the very power of the attraction, which affinity of being produces. You have to learn, perhaps, that it is not the most brilliant or beautiful who are most beloved. But what if it were so ? Where all attractions act in freedom, can there be any injustice ? In love, as in all of life, the true spirit asks only its own. I would no more interpose to hinder any love from going to another, than I would stop the sunshine or the breeze. There is but one love, in all manifestations. If my life is pure, and my heart is right, I do not fear that I shall not have all that is truly mine—and more than this would be a death to me. It would be like the surplus manna —or surplus food ; or any false and stolen thing, which we have no right to and cannot enjoy."

" Pardon me, dear Eugenia ;" I said, "I am not so bad, perhaps, as these questions make me seem. But I wish to know how your spirit accepts the spirit of the life around us."

" You might have been frank with me, then, and questioned me. I would have answered truly. To the disorderly spirit, all order seems despotism. To the excentric comet, the rounded orbits and regular movements of the planets may seem dreadfully despotic. Is there any orderly and beautiful thing in the world, that is not in this sense despotic. The musician must play his notes—the dancer must keep time and figure ; the painter must be governed by the rules of his art ; the architect cannot wander off into extravagances, much less the builder ; the farmer must plant and gather his crops in the seasons ; your heart must beat, and your spirits-heart must love in this sacred and universal order which you call despotism.

In the evening we had a pleasure quite new to me, and which it is strange that no one has hit upon ; for it has wonderfully popular capabilities. Mr. Paul, besides his genius as a painter, has a rare faculty of telling, and also of writing, stories. Last night he read a new tale to a full audience. It sparkled with wit and merriment ; with turns of pathos that asked for tears. The plot was of exciting interest, and the reading so good, so adapted to all the characters and incidents, and so accurate in bringing out all peculiarites, that the effect was scarcely less, and in some respects greater, than that of a well-performed play. It was an artistic and beautiful performance. I shall recommend to some of our lecturers, who have the talent for it, to try this with our Lyceum. It only requires to be well done to be very effective—but it may not be easy to find the requisite talent for such a performance.

Father Gautier was not able to leave his room yesterday. I did not see Harmonia or Melodia last evening, nor have I seen them but for a moment to-day. Melodia looked pale, but serene ; Harmonia worn with fatigue. Still, every thing goes on cheerily as usual ; and I cannot but hope, that spite of all appearances, I may see the good old man enjoying again the sunshine and flowers, and the music and dance, and the love of his dear children.

As I close my letter, Melodia has brought me a white rose. "Send it to your Clara," she said ; "tell her that our good Father pressed it to his lips, and that, when it reaches her, it will be the relic of a saint in heaven. She can thank him there. Father Gautier sends with it his welcome and his blessing.

XVIII.

THE TRANSITION OF DEATH.

My Clara :—The good old man, whose rose-kiss and blessing I have sent to you, has gone from the earthly form, and entered upon the glorious life of the spirit.

It was four o'clock in the afternoon, when the bell tolled out its signal—the nine strokes that floated like solemn music over the domain of Esperanza—to call his children to take their last look at the living form of their revered and beloved father.

Very soon all had assembled in the lecture saloon. There was an earnest solemnity; and some tears. But all took their places, as if for a pre-arranged ceremony. They were dressed as for a festival. The musicians had their instruments; the children bouquets of flowers. They stood in silence, or conversed in low murmurs, until a door opened, and a group entered, bearing the arm-chair in which Father Gautier reclined, supported by pillows. He was carried by Vincent, Manlius, Alfred, and Angelo; while Harmonia and Melodia, on either side, held his hands and his head. The chair was set upon a small platform, where all could see and hear him. It was the old man's wish to see his great, loving family around him, and to have them near him when he should take his departure, which he felt to be close at hand.

He was very pale—so pale, that for a moment I thought he was expiring. It was not so—but no one could mistake the signet of death set upon his noble features. After a few moment's rest, in a profound silence, broken only by deep respirations and suppressed sobbings, while Vincent held his pulse, and Melodia bathed his temples, he revived, opened his eyes as from a pleasant dream, and looked around with most tender, loving regards upon his assembled

children.   A little girl, scarce six years old, on whom his eyes
rested, sprang forward, kissed his hand, and gave him flowers. A
smile of more than mortal sweetness came into his face, as he
whispered her a benediction.

The odor of the flowers seemed to revive him; or was it the
united magnetism of so many loving hearts that brought back
brightness to his eye, and even a faint flush of color to his cheeks?

"Music, dear friends," he murmured, "once more music. Music, flowers, and love!" and he turned his eyes on Melodia, while
the band, at a signal given by Vincent, played one of the old
man's favorite airs. Visibly he gained in strength each moment.
His form dilated; his eyes grew more brilliant; it seemed as if he
might rise from his chair. I could not realize that this was death.

He said a few low words to Melodia. She stepped from his side,
and began to sing. But her voice trembled and choked with her
emotion. I heard his clear voice then saying " Courage, courage!
ma fille!" With a strong effort, she subdued her feelings, and
then sung with a power and pathos unequalled, a song of Esperanza, supported by the band in a subdued harmony, and a chorus of indescribable effect, from the voices of the children who
joined in it.

Through my falling tears I looked sometimes at Melodia, who,
in her white robes, seemed an angel, singing a song of welcome,
rather than a mortal, giving this musical farewell to a parting soul;
and then at the calm, happy face of the dying father. When the
music ended he sank back in an entranced repose; but revived
after a few moments, and took the hand of Melodia, who was at
his side again, and pressed it to his lips, with murmured thanks.

"Now, the dear children!" he said to Harmonia; "let me see
them all once more, and say good-bye to them. They gathered
around him, with their sad, tearful little eyes.

"O, my darlings!" he said to them in tones full of tenderness,
"your old father is about to leave this decaying form, and become
young again. He will be lost to your bodily sight, but he will
still be with you, and love you, and watch over you all. Do not
forget that I shall be with you, and love and bless you. I thank

you, my darlings, for all your love to me. You have made these last years of my life very happy. Heaven bless you all. Come, my little ones, and take the old man's parting blessing."

They gathered around the chair ; they knelt at his feet ; they kissed his hand and the garments that enveloped him; but they could not speak, for their sobbings and tears. The old man laid his pale hands upon their heads and blessed them. Harmonia led them softly away.

Even the sobbings were stilled in silence, as with a new energy the old man now beckoned all present to draw near. They closed around him in the perfect order that characterizes every movement here. Each one seemed to know the place that belonged to him, and which no other ever claimed.

I fear to attempt to give you even a faint idea of the dying utterance of the dear old man. I know not whether it was his voice, sounding from the confines of eternity ; his countenance, lighted up by the hopes of his near felicity ; or what of place or circumstance, made his words seem of more than mortal eloquence.

"Brothers, sisters, dear friends and children ! my time has come when I have the privilege of laying off this mortal envelopment, and putting on immortality. I, who have been the happy instrument of securing this earthly paradise to harmony, have now the honor to be the first called from it to join in the higher harmonies of our parent society in the heavens. 'Lord, now lettest thou thy servant depart in peace, for mine eyes have seen thy salvation.'

"O, friends ! I have loved you all. How can I thank you for your affection ? You have made my last days very happy. My life is bound up in your's, and my spirit will never leave you. Think of me always with happiness and peace.

"My children ! I thank and bless you, that your orderly obedience to the revealed will of heaven has planted this germ of harmony upon the earth, and enabled me to see the fruition of my hopes. O, spirits, who have watched over this infant harmony in the earth-life, I come to give you joy of our success. Henceforth, O, friends, think of me as a humble member of that heavenly

23

society, whose instrument I have been, and to whose glorious assemblages I shall soon welcome all my children.

"My earthly pilgrimage is ended. My life work is done. All toils, all sufferings, all disappointments, have found sweet compensations here. Your love, your fidelity, your earnest labors to be right and do right, have a thousand times repaid me for all. Do not grieve for me one moment; but give me your rejoicing sympathies, for I am now the happiest man on earth. All my hopes in this life are accomplished here, and all the glories of heaven are just before me.

"Rejoice with me, then, my children; and continue faithful to the principles of a true life, that you also may cheerfully welcome the summons to the Life of the Heavens. You have one feeble old man the less to care for here; but you will soon have one loving spirit the more to watch over your welfare and happiness.

"I would gladly embrace you all, but my strength is not sufficient."

He faltered, and paused a moment. In the hushed silence, I feared he had gone; but he rallied again, and said, as he took the hand of Harmonia, who knelt beside him.

"I bless the center of your life and love; and through this dear one, I will continue to bless you.

"And thou, O daughter of my heart," he said to Melodia, as she also bowed her head upon his knees, "in blessing and thanking thee, I bless the life of beauty and art, which makes this home a paradise, and helps to train all here for the higher beauty and more glorious art of our life of the future."

She rose, calm and radiant, and kissed the old man's brow. He gave his hand to Vincent, saying, "Well done, good and faithful servant. Henceforth, the old man shall be far more a help to thee, than he has been here. Forget not that there is much work yet to be accomplished. The whole earth—the whole race of man is to be redeemed. Be sure that we shall not be idle. Do the work that demands the doing. Friend of my soul, I shall not forget you!"

In simple words, but with a feeling that melted us all, the old man gave his hand and said a few words to each of those nearest to him. As I stood near this central group, his eye sought me, and he held out his hand to me. I sprang and took it in mine. The grasp was full of life and energy. It went with a thrill to the centre of my being. It was as if a spirit hand had grasped me. The light of his eye seemed to beam from the portals of the inner life. I bowed myself humbly to receive his parting word.

"And you, my dear young friend," he said; "you join me to the world to be redeemed. Go forth and do the work to which you are called. Work in truth, in fidelity, in obedience, and the work will be blessed. Never lose faith in the goodness of God or the destiny of man. Devote all to this work, and all shall be yours. Providence has brought you here.—Go forth, and be the instrument of its beneficient purposes. A poor, old, dying man, yet rich and happy beyond expression, blesses you, and those to whom you are sent, with the blessings of rest and peace.

"God bless you all—farewell.

"Once more, your voices, dear friends; let me once more hear the music that I love."

They sung—voices breaking through sobs; voices trembling with emotion; voices choking with love and grief. Still the beautiful harmonies struggled and triumphed; and as the chorus rose full and clear, the reverend head sank back; the eyes closed; a radiant smile of unspeakable happiness illumined his features; and when the last notes had died away, the spirit had left its tenement of clay; borne on the waves of that harmony, it had entered the haven of eternal rest.

Vincent listened for his breath;—it was gone. He felt for his pulse; the last flutter had died away. He pressed down the eyelids of the corpse, and said:

"Dear Friends:—Our beloved and revered father has breathed his last. May we all be as faithful in our lives, and die as happily Let us hail the entrance of his freed spirit into the triumphant harmonies of the heavens."

The band struck instantly into a triumphal march, so full, so grand in feeling, that, instead of shedding tears of grief, all were joyful in the spirit's triumph.

Then they softly bore the body away.

I wish, in this letter, to tell you all that relates to this first experience of Death in Esperanza. As I went out upon the lawn, I saw a pure white flag, flying at half-mast from the central tower. Groups were scattered in the walks and groves, in serious conversation. Angela came and held out her hand to me. The traces of tears were on her eyelids.

"You are very sorrowful," I said.

"Oh! the dear good father!" she exclaimed, the tears bursting out afresh. "I am a fool, but I can't help it. He has gone to the beautiful world, and I am glad for him. It is best for him and all; but I shall miss the dear old man so much. You don't know what a gallant lover he has been to me. He has taught and told me so many things; and such a dear, young, loving heart, that never grew old. He was as young in his feelings as I. We all loved him, dearly. And now we will give him such a pretty place; his body I mean. I suppose it is of very little consequence to him; but we must revere all that was ever partaker of his life."

At the sunset parade, a noble dirge was followed by a triumphal hymn, representing the sorrows and toils of earth contrasted with the glories of heaven. And through it all the bell tolled out its mournful cadences, minute guns boomed over the waters, fired from the little fort, and the steamer Fairy. All these mannifestations seemed the fitting and needful expressions of the feelings of this bereaved, saddened, but yet most happy family.

The usual amusements of the evening were suspended. There were no public meetings, nor songs, nor dances; not that they were felt to be improper, but that all were absorbed in reflections upon the event, or in preparations for the funeral. A group of joiners was employed upon a coffin; I went with another, by torch light, to a beautiful knoll, covered with trees, and flowering shrubs, kept as a future burying place, and where the first grave was now to be opened on the very centre of its summit; a spot which Father Gautier had long looked upon as his body's final resting place. While this grave was preparing, a little group was arranging the order of the funeral.

When all had been accomplished, Melodia invited me to join them in the beautiful room of Harmonia, which I have described to you. Can you conceive this cheerful, yet solemn meeting.— There was not one sob of anguish, nor one sigh of regret; and not one of these loving friends would have recalled, had they the power, the spirit of their beloved father. Their feeling was more like a deep and chastened joy, than a subdued sorrow.

After conversing a while upon the life and character of their departed friend, in which his merits and deficiencies were brought out with singular impartality; all joined hands, and sat in silence. After a few moments, Harmonia placed a black scarf over her eyes, and fell into that condition of spiritual clairvoyance, in which the scenes of the inner world are revealed to those in whom this faculty is developed.

After a few moments, she said. " I see a group of our friends, but Father Gautier is not with them. Ah, now he comes. A very lovely woman is leading him forward. He is dressed in a white robe, with a blue girdle, and in his hand is a bouquet a flowers. It is he ; I know him perfectly ; and yet, how changed he looks! He has lost all marks of age. If you can fancy him at forty, but more beautiful than he ever could have been—the ideal of himself —that is the way he looks. As he comes forward, Fourier opens his arms to embrace him. " Welcome, my brother," he says, "Welcome from the germinal harmony of earth, to the developed and still increasing harmonies of heaven!" The angelic being who accompanied him, and who so often came to him here, seems more beautiful than ever, and inexpressibly happy. Our friend comes near and looks smilingly upon us ; he kisses me upon the head—Melodia on the cheek. He wishes to speak to us. He says: " You see that I was right, friends. You were very good to me, and I was very happy : but this is better. I can here help the unfolding of your future. You have but begun. Not for an hour must you be satisfied with present achievement. Progress is the law of being ; continual development, continual unfolding.— I am drawn to you strongly, and feel that I shall be able to influence you more than those who have not been in so close a relation to you in your present life. This is my chosen and appointed work."

"Will our father say whether he is satisfied with our arrangements for his funeral ?" asked Vincent.

"He puts on such a droll look," said Harmonia. "He says, 'You need not take much trouble with that old body of mine, or any of my old clothes. Do what satisfies yourselves in the doing. Lay the old case quietly away, and think of me, henceforth, not as I was, but as I am. Let me come to you often ; for I can do you good in many ways.' "

The seeress took the bandage from her eyes, and in a moment resumed her usual appearance. Many, even at this day, would think all this a deception or an illusion. No one here questions its entire reality, or doubts that the good Father still lives—still loves his children, and has this power of manifesting himself to and through those who are fitted to be the mediums of such manifestations.

In the morning we were waked, not as usual, by the music of the band, but by the steam organ of the Fairy ; whose powerful tones filled the whole air with melody. The cannon again fired, and the bell rung, tolling no longer, when we assembled, after the morning ablutions. I saw that all wore the dress of ceremony.— The great festal banner floated mast head high, its golden stars glittering in the beams of the rising sun. The fountains were all at play, flashing rainbows. The emulous birds poured out their melodies, and sweet perfumes filled the air. The Fairy was decked in all her streamers, steaming in proud circles round the lake, and sending over all the scene her grand harmonies.

And there, upon the lawn, stood the funeral pall ; not gloomed in black, but covered with a pure white drapery, with white plumes, and garlands of flowers. These were no weeds of woe—but all tokens of the honors of victory. Our friend has fought the battle of life, and has come off a conqueror. Why mourn? We did not. It was a festival of solemn joy.

After the morning hymn, the Order of the Day was read by Vincent, as follows :

" We will now deposit the remains of our good and glorified Father Gautier in the place appointed.

"After the morning repast, all will resort to their usual industry for the appointed hours.

" The dinner will be a festival of commemoration.

" The afternoon will be observed by a cessation of industry, and thoughtful communion on the progress and perfection of our life.

" Supper in groups at pleasure--a festival of friendship.

" In the evening, commemorative music and discourses.

" Henceforth, the birth-day of Father Gautier is to be celebrated, with honors second only to those awarded to Fourier."

The procession formed as if by enchantment. Without a word of command or a perceptible signal, all fell into a fitting order of march. The music went before the coffin ; the children, all dressed in white and blue, with bouquets of flowers, walked on each side ; our little group followed, and then all the groups in a beautiful order. The bell rung, the cannon pealed, the Fairy poured forth her grand harmonies ; then our band struck up a triumphal march, whose words were sung by group after group, in chorus, as we moved along a flower bordered walk, through fields and groves, to the mound of burial.

Here the coffin was opened, and all passed around it and took a last look at the placid features, so calm and noble, of this man, who had had the great good fortune to devote himself and all he had to the realization of his idea of a true life ; and who, in this work, and this success, has achieved more glory than a hundred conquerors.

The coffin was lowered into the grave. Vincent stood at its head, and pronounced a few eloquent sentences, such as the occasion demanded—befitting the obsequies of a true philanthropist. All were gathered around the open grave ; and though it thus far had been a festive triumph rather than a funeral,—there were here some sobs and tears. The childen came forward, many of them weeping, and threw their flowers upon the old man's coffin. Then the earth was filled in, the mound raised above it, and on it planted with taste and care, roses, lilies, and other fragrant flowers, that the wasting body might pass in lovely forms, and sweet odors, back to its native elements from the realm of death.

All this was in the fresh morning hour ; and as our work was accomplished, the bell rung out its last peal ; the cannon roared among the echoing woods ; the Fairy filled the heavens with music. All returned, without special order, and conversing cheerfully, to breakfast ; then the festal costume was laid aside, and the morning's industry begun.

While others labored, in their varied, changing, and ever attractive industry—in work which is enobled by its uses—I have written these pages to you, O Clara mine ; trying to give you some faint impression of the scene around me. I had barely finished when the first signal for dinner was given ; and I remembered that it was to be a festival of more than ordinary solemnity, so I dressed with care ; and when I entered the saloon I found it draped and decked with surprizing elegance. The tables were ornamented more profusely than usual, with vases of flowers.

When all had eaten, Vincent, sitting at the right hand of Harmonia, at the table of her group, arose and gave the first toast :

" Honor and gratitude to the memory of our good Father Gautier ! "

This sentiment was repeated aloud, at the table of every group, and was drank with appropriate music.

No more toasts were given ; and all went out upon the lawn, and made up the groups or parties for the afternoon.

In the evening all assembled in the theatre. Many tasteful hands had been at work in its decoration for this occasion. No work is slighted here. It is a spontaneous expression of life—an energy that always seeks employment. And while the artistic groups had spoken to the eye, our musical friends had prepared a repast for the ear, so worthy of the occasion as to satisfy us all.

The favorite airs of Father Gautier, and those associated with his life here, were woven in a harmonic wreath to deck his memory.

I shall not give you a report of the speeches. They also were fully up to the requirements of the occasion. Vincent's was historical. Many contributed anecdotes of the good man; or gave expression to the gratitude all felt to him. Harmonia paid a delicate tribute to his affectionateness and love of children ; but it was left to Melodia to speak the crowning and the parting words. They were words which melted the whole assembly in tears; and all went forth filled with new strength, new hope, and new resolutions, to move onward to the achievement of the highest of human possibilities, in the truest life that can be enjoyed on earth, as the foretaste and preparation for the life of eternal progress and happiness in the Heavens.

XIX

DEAR CLARA: The solemnization of death; the near view of eternity; the passing away of that noble, loving spirit, full of courage, full of hope, and an unshaken faith in its immortal destiny, could not fail to turn my thoughts to our relations with the unseen world. I wished to know more of the religious faith of those dear friends, whose earthly life seems to me a heaven begun, and which has only to continue, under improved or progressing conditions.

I sought then an interview with one I thought best capable of giving me light: I sought Harmonia.

"I come to be instructed," I said, seating myself on the cushion she laid for me beside her feet, and kissing the little white hand she extended to me.

"You should go to men for knowledges," she answered, smiling. "It is their speciality. Women feel and love; they seldom reason, or know much. They have wisdom, perhaps; but not much science, usually. I reason very little — what I know, comes to me by other channels than those of logical deduction."

"What I wish to inquire about, belongs more to faith than reason, it is commonly thought," I said. "I wish to be informed more definitely of your religious views."

In all my intercourse here, thus far, no effort has been made to convert me to any dogma. There was no anxiety that I should believe as they do, or that I should even know what they believe. But now that I had come with my *demand*, the *supply* was cheerfully accorded.

"The history of our race," said Harmonia, "shows the existence and development of the Religious Sentiment. A higher, purer, better life, present and future, is the universal aspiration. Whatever form it may take, this is religion; and however varied in its manifestation, or erroneous in its dogmas, it is the same sentiment in all. It is the spirit of man seeking its unity with the Infinite Life and Love. Ideas of God and Immortality are, therefore, universal; and even when hidden under gross and sensual forms and creeds, have yet their own truth and life.

"We understand by God, the Life, Spirit and Infinite Unity of Universal Existence;—the universal synthesis;—the soul that lives in, and not apart from, all nature. It is 'God working in us, both to will and to do, of his own good pleasure.' God in the flower. God in the stars. Life, soul and being of all things. The sum of all intelligences and all loves. The heart and brain life—the love and wisdom of all. In this God, 'we live, and move, and have our being.' It is not a God, outside and apart from us, but the God is in us and we in him. 'I and my Father are one.'

"Prayer is the aspiration, striving, and effort for completeness of unity with this Infinite Heart and God of all Harmony. It may be uttered in words, or manifested in deeds, or enter, as with us, into the whole life.

"And this life, so far as it is a true one, is worship. Every true act, which is in harmony with the Divine Spirit, is an act of faith. Thus, we 'glorify God in our bodies and our spirits, *which are his.*' Thus, 'whether we eat or drink, or whatsoever we do, we do all to the glory of God.' We endeavor to live in His life, in its holiness or wholeness. Thus are we godly or God-like just so far as we live in the harmony of a true life.

"There is an axiom in mathematics—one of those simple, self-evident statements, so simple that they seem at first needless to be said, but which yet contain universes of truth. It is this: 'Things which are equal to the same thing, are equal to each other.' You smile—but we have found that just in proportion as we bring ourselves to the order, equilibrium and harmony of the Divine Life, just in that proportion do we find ourselves in unity with each other.

"As our God is in all the universe of things—the life and love of all beings, we find our truest worship, prayer and praise, in bringing ourselves into that harmony of being and life which unites us with the material and spiritual world; which is, truly, the God in us—God manifest in the flesh.

"We accept, you will perceive, the internal significance, and even the outward expressions, of the popular forms of religious doctrine. God is to us the sum and substance of all being—the universal unity of thought and life. Christ is God manifest in the flesh—God in humanity. And this God, in his human form, is he not poor, despised, buffetted, spit upon, and in all times crucified? And shall he not rise to a true life, and govern the earth in the spirit of Love? We truly believe in the regeneration of this new birth, and in the redemption of our race by the constant operations of this Holy Spirit.

"Our religion is not an intellectual speculation. It lives in our life. It is, so we esteem it, the religion which God everywhere teaches in the heart of man, and which can be found under all forms of expression, myth, creed and ceremony. All sacred scriptures, all symbols, all prophecies contain it. The human soul aspires, struggles, agonizes for its unity with the Divine or Universal Life. It seeks to be, and to express that being, in the unity of Nature, and the unity of the Spirit, which is the bond of peace.

"We believe in—rather, we enter into the very reality of—immortality. We are as certain of the continued existence of our spirit friends, as of our own present life. Material forms are forever changing; but through these, the spiritual identity is never lost, but goes on, forming ever new and higher, and more comprehensive unities, in the great God-Life, of which every spirit forms a part—the center of centers, and the soul of souls.

"I could give you our faith in the form of almost every creed. Thus we can say: 'I believe in the Holy Catholic Church, the Communion of Saints, and Life everlasting.' The Holy Catholic Church is the unity of all human souls, who aspire for a life of truth, and holiness—wherever they may be, or by whatever name they are called. The Communion of Saints is this partaking of a common life; this holy communion of all the good, in earth and in the heavens. And Life everlasting is in our consciousness, as surely as the God that worketh in us can never die.

"We seek to embody this Life and Spirit of God in all forms of use, and beauty, and harmony. In our persons; in our food; in our dress; in all our thoughts and feelings; in our industry; in our art; in poetry; in music; in the measured movement of the dance; and in the holiest acts of love in which we give new forms to the Divine Humanity, ever seeking its incarnation, ever flowing into higher and still higher forms of life.

"Religion, then, which literally means, that which binds again; religion, as an expression of the sentiment of aspiration to unity with the Universal, the Infinite, the Divine; is that which binds us in our harmony, and which animates all our life and work. It is no external theory; no cold form; no fearful doing of duties. It is our life's life. We began our preparation for this work with the motto given by St. Ignatius to the Company of Jesus: *Ad Majorem Dei Gloriam*—To the Greater Glory of God. That greater glory we have sought, in the development of all our faculties, and their harmonization with the Infinite Life; and just so far as this work was achieved in us individually, just so far did we find ourselves in a beautiful and loving harmony with each other; until it brought us to be 'all of one accord in one place'—all attuned to the same harmony.

"Religion, therefore, as we understand it, and as it finds being and expression in our lives, is the harmonizing influence—the toning power. It is the sacred bond that unites men to each other. Whatever unity has been attained in human societies, has come from the influence of the religious sentiment. There has been no organization, or approach to organization among men, of which some manifestation of the religious nature of man has not been the center and soul. All else is selfish, isolate, discordant, tending every hour to dissolution. Boodhism, Brahmism, Judaism, Islamism, Catholicism—all human unities or fragments of unities, are bound together by this common bond, in the life of humanity. Religion gave its life to Chivalry; it was the soul of

Free Masonry in the palmy days of that institution; it gives whatever vitality they possess, to all our benevolent societies, and all existing institutions. Strange as it may seem to you, the real bond and vitality of the institution of Slavery, is in the religious sentiment. It is not the fetter and whip, it is not greed of power and gain, that holds millions in bondage. It is a religious feeling of responsibility and duty, in master and slave. The Russian marches on death, at the command of the Czar, because this Czar is to him the representative of God. In the name of God and his Prophet, the Mussulman flashes his cimeter on the foe. The simple faith of the Mormon is the strong bond of his rude Theocracy. Everywhere, men submit to 'the powers that be,' only so far as they believe them to be 'ordained of God.'

"As there is in all this universe but one Life, in all its myriad forms; one God, in the aspiration of all faiths; one Love, in the yearnings of all hearts for their appointed unities: so there is but one Religion, and one Church. All colors and shades of colors blend in one pure element of light. All tones blend in one pure unison of sound.

"You ask our faith. It is the theory of our life. You have seen our life; it is the practice of our faith. Wherever faith and works—the theory of life and its practice—are in harmony, there is a life of order, peace, love and unity. In all the discordant societies of civilization, people preach and profess one thing, and teach and practise the reverse. The religion comes not into the life. Faith without works is dead. Works without faith are soulless corpses. The true life and the true religion for every man, is to live up to his highest idea of right—to have all being and all doing in harmony with those heaven-born, God-inspired aspirations and strivings of the spirit for the highest and truest life of the earth and the heavens.

"The records—the scriptures of this One Religion—the canons of this Holy Catholic Church, are scattered everywhere. In Prophecy and Psalm; in Oratory and Poetry; in Music and Art; in whatever breathes the spirit of *excelsior*, from the rudest to the most refined, every expression of human love and aspiration is the word of God. It lives in the Bible, and in all religious writings; in Jeremy Taylor and Thomas a Kempis; in Jesuit, Puritan, and Infidel; in Shakspeare and Milton, Shelley and Byron, Tasso and Goethe; as well as in all the Fathers of all Churches. So we find the brethren of our faith in all communions. We are, hence, tolerant of all, finding the good in all, and rejoicing in the progress of all. This is our all-comprehending faith.

"But what a sermon I have preached you! I feel the interest and importance of the subject. It is very important that you be clear in this central matter, and know what you must do to be saved. We were educated in various creeds. Some were Roman Catholics, like our good Father, who has just left the form; some were protestants against that church; and some against all churches. Now we have all come to the same unity of faith, and the same harmony of works."

" There is that in my spirit," I said, " which lovingly accepts of all you have told me. 'Thy people shall be my people, and thy God my God.' But there are still dogmas of the church, or the sects, of which you have not explained the significance."

" Well, you shall question me. Perhaps I may be able to explain them."

" For example, the doctrine of Hell? "

" Is it not another name for disorder, with which the lower side of humanity is cursed, and into which all are cast, who do not come into the regeneration of a true life? "

" And Purgatory? "

" Is it not a period of transition, purification, and preparation for a life of harmony? "

" And the Devil? "

" What but a bold personification of discord and evil? As all spiritual harmonies and unities find synthesis in the grand unity of an Infinite God, so may all evils center in a Spirit of Discord, Strife, and Hate."

" Will you explain my old stumbling block of predestination? "

" As the magnet separates the atoms of iron from the sand, so does the divine Truth seek out and draw to its embrace all who are fitted to receive it."

"And he that believeth not shall be damned?"

"Yes; is, and shall be. He that believeth not in the Divine Humanity, shall remain in error, discord and misery."

"And do you accept the Sacraments?"

"Verily; in all the richness of their spiritual significance."

"Baptism?"

"With water the holy man affiliates a soul to heavenly unities. Have we not moreover our daily baptism to purity of life?"

"And the Eucharist?"

"We who eat purely, discern the Lord's Body. And the bread, blessed by the ministration of our guardian angels, may it not become ordered into the Divine Life? You know that a glass of water magnetized by or through a healing circle, may become potent to cure disease. May not the bread and wine of this sacrament, blessed in a true order, become so divinized? These are for those who need them. Deny them not."

"And the sacrament of marriage?"

"None of all so desecrated and profaned! The union of man and woman in the life-giving act, should be the most sacred and divine of all unities. It is in this that men and women, in a truly consecrated union, enter most into the life and work of God. Such marriage is a sacrament. Working through ignorance, error, discord, and with 'a wicked and adulterous generation,' the church has done the best she could to preserve its purity. She has taken her priesthood and holy orders into a vestal life, and placed bounds to sensualities, by such marriage as the masses were fitted to receive. Let us not blame the church. 'She hath done what she could.'"

"But yet," I said, after all these beautiful explanations, you do not, that I see, adhere to these forms and ordinances of the church."

"Are they now needful to us? Need we make formal prayers, whose life is one prayer? Need we now special sacraments of the eucharist, who live in the life of the Lord? Shall we, whose lives are so ordered and harmonized as you have seen, still do those things which were useful in bringing us out of disorder? We know that we have only to live in the true order of life, and all the blessings will flow in upon us, that we have capacity to receive. Shall we now say to one another, 'know the Lord; when we all know him, from the least unto the greatest?' Religous ordinances were instituted as helps to the divine life. They are for those who need them. They would be for us—confession, penance, and redeeming grace—should any of us fall into disorder and sin."

I have given as faithful a report as I am capable of giving of this conversation. It seems to me, at once stragely mystical, and not less strangely real. I find an acceptance in my spirit which surprizes me. You know how little I have thought, for years, of all these things. It is true that I have recognized the existence and the manifestations of the religious sentiment; but I have never looked into the dogmas, or sacraments of the church for interior meanings. Our Swedenborgian friends find a spiritual significance in what seem to me very meaningless scriptures. I have never been able to comprehend their correspondences. But what shall I say of these expositions of Harmonia, made with great earnestness and solemnity? I can say nothing. Even while they seem to appeal to reason, they transcend reason. What I do see is, that this life is all purity, all beauty, all harmony. The disuse of religious forms may seem a kind of Phariseeism; but I know that there is a most earnest aspiration here, for a higher, and still higher life; and wherever there is aspiration, there must be humility. The religious element still works upward, but it is a triumphal progress, not a dark struggle with disease and sin. If this may be called a church it is not the church militant, but the church triumphant.

I see that the faith of uncounted millions of men, through hundreds of generations, must have in it great elements of truth and good. I apply this saying, not to one faith, but to all faiths and forms of faith, and I see that they differ mostly in names. I see that there is but one religion. When will narrow sectarians embrace the great catholic doctrine announced by the apostle Peter? "Of a truth, I perceive that God is no respecter of persons; but in every nation, he that feareth him, and worketh righteousness, is

24

accepted with him." Here is an end to all bigotries of creeds and nationalities. Here all meet, on this common platform of humanity—and this is the basis of the true "Holy Catholic Church."

"Your religion is sublime," I said, "in its doctrines, and beautiful in its manifestations. Has this faith, also, its recorded scriptures?"

She laid her hand on two beautiful volumes on her center table. One was a Greek Testament, the other a Latin copy of the Imitation of Christ of Thomas a Kempis. She took a flower from a vase and gave it me, and touched the spring of her music box, which played a jubilant melody. I was answered. We sat in silence until the sweet music was done, when she said:—

"Our scriptures are recorded in all the universe. We also have our written word. Here," she said, taking a small manuscript volume from her table, "is the record of some of the Lessons which have been given to us, from our friends in the world of spirits. Read them as you will."

"Can I copy them also?" I asked, wishing you should partake of all the good that came to me.

"Assuredly: these are but transcripts, put in our poor human words, of what the Divine Spirit hath gloriously written every where, in all the manifestations of His infinite life."

I copy for you, dear Clara, a few of these scriptures.

"Each ultimate atom has its corresponding soul-life, and consequent intelligence. Aggregations of atoms have a discordant soul-life,—associations of atoms have a harmonic associated soul-life."

"The great heart of Humanity has ever truth in its instincts."

"Only as each is true to himself or herself, can they be of use to another. Heed this, for it is the central principle of the new gospel.

"The circulation in a body is the condition of life to that body.

"The life is more or less perfect, according to the mode or form.

"The law of unimpeded circulation is the law of life, in all forms, and modes, of whatever degree of perfection.

"The hand of the weak man must obey his will—the hand of the strong man can do no more.

"The strength of the heart, and the wisdom of the head can only be demonstrated by perfect obedience.

" It is not by erratic action that the one gets power and the other light.

" The heart and head of a man and of a society must be corrected by consequences wrought out in obedience, and not by disordered acts and efforts.

" Fragmentary action, be it ever so wise in itself, is not for a body. Obedience is for a body, and a society ; and consequences are the only correctives. If there cannot be a perfect and orderly obedience, then there is not unity ; and the part that is extraneous or parasitic is to be cut off."

" The Divine Humanity is the sphere of Creative Unities.

"The sun is a correspondential expression from this

"Humanity corresponds to the sun—being a simultaneous expression.

" Out of both these expressions comes the form human.

" As the spirit is to the soul, so is the Divine Humanity to the Humanity. As the soul to the body, so is the individual man to the Humanity.

" In the ascending scale, forms become one with the Humanity ; and the humanity is absorbed again into the Divine. The oned or united forms graduate to the sun. The last is the absorption into the divine, whence there is no direct communication with the earth life."

" Humanity is one ; and contempt is for the young, the partial, and immature. "

I send to you these few passages, my Clara, that you may see something of the form of these revelations. Many of them, given during the period of germination or preparation, were instructions for that period. These seem to me, wise with a most heavenly wisdom. They carry in themselves, to me, the best proof of their supernal origin. And here is the proof, also, in the work accomplished.

Is Esperanza of heaven, or of man ?

I accedt it as an out-birth of the Life of the heavens.

XX.

THE ORDER AND THE WORK.

My Blessed Clara :—In a few days more, all the power of mighty steam will be bringing me to you. I shall glide down the Mississippi to New Orleans ; then home by gulf and ocean, taking one look at beautiful Cuba. I have never been at sea, and I want this experience. We shall just dip into the tropics. I will find you some fruit at Havana. We will sail along the gulf stream. Then, some bright morning, or soft evening perhaps, we shall steam up the Narrows, and I shall see the green glories of the Battery—pride of every New Yorker, and after a brisk walk up Broadway, hold you to my heart once more, after this long, long absence.

I wrote you yesterday of the Religion of Esperanza. There are no temples here, consecrated to divine worship; but the whole place seems a temple for a sincere and beautiful manifestation of a deeply religious life. Or, I may say, that all places here are so consecrated. The theatre is a school of virtue. There is no dissipation in the ball room. Life is so ballanced in use, and beauty, and enjoyment, that every part is good. No man here cheats his neighbors and plunders the poor, or wastes his life and riches, six days in the week, and then goes through forms of devotion on the seventh. So far as I can see or judge there is an entire unity of faith, feeling, and work throughout this little Republic.

And this word Republic, brings me to the subject of its Government, or the exterior bond of orderly relation which its members have with each other. How shall I define it? It is not a Democratic Republic, in our understanding of the term ; and yet the

288

will of the people is the only law ; perhaps I should rather say, that the will of each individual is in harmony with the spirit or law of the movement. The whole society seems like a body performing its functions, and controlled by its central life or motive power. There is no goverment of majorities, for there is no minority. All move as one, in a perfect unanimity. There is little or no discussion—none, in the sense of contentious debate ; there are no elections ; each one performing his function or office by the common consent. You might call it a Theocracy, but no orders are given with the authoritive sanction of " Thus saith the Lord." The society has grown from its germinal group, by the gradual addition of members, or groups of members ; and the central group, all harmonious in itself, has been the harmonizing power to all other groups or members. And there has never been, that I can learn, any question of leadership or authority. The principles and laws of the life, and its true order, are recognized by all. All conform to this order from the least to the greatest. Thus all are equal before the law. This law of order, which belongs to the life of the movement, requires leadership of those who are g fted with the requisite qualities. It demands co-operation, and obedience of all. The law of obedience, stated in one of the scriptures, copied in my last letter, demands that all be true to the life and its order.

In the beginning, and while they were passing through the novitiate, and the period of education and discipline, it was convenient that this order of life should be, to some extent, expressed in written rules ; since there were so many habits of disorder to be reformed, and so many temptations to irregularity and evil. The record of these rules remains for future use ; but in the smooth, perfected working of the society at present, they are like the instruction books and finger exercises of the beginner in music, to the perfected musician.

You will understand it by this analogy. Time, effort, pains, were required to learn to play ; but when the mind learned to read the written music, and the will had learned to give it expression, and the muscles all obeyed the will, how easy and beautiful to produce those harmonies of sound.   It is just so with this life.   It is not merely easy for these dear friends to be good, unselfish, industrious, orderly, loving, and beautiful in all things; but it is the free, spontaneous, habitual expression of all their life and thought. There is no more motive or temptation for them to do any disorderly act, than there is for you to make discordance instead of music, when you sit down to the piano-forte; or, which may be a still better comparison, than a player in an orchestra has to mar the harmonies of the music that he loves.

The central life takes hold of and receives love and wisdom from the life of the heavens, and all are recipients of this loving life, both individually, and through the established order.   If you believe that the Divine flows through the spirit spheres into the heart life of this society, then you may consider its government Theocratic. To an external observer, who should see its beautiful and perfect order, it would seem a despotism.   The law of this life is as despotic as the controlling forces of the planatary systems—as despotic as the life that forms the petals of a flower.   All harmonic movement is orderly, and, in the idea of many, order is despotism.

This life is orderly—it is harmonic; but where is the despot? It is not Vincent.   He humbly does his appointed work.   It is not Harmonia.   She is but the humble medium of the spirit spheres. Is the despotism in the heavens?   The suggestions of their guardian spirits fall as gently as the dews.   The growing plant might as well complain of the despotism of sunshine and shower.

On the spiritual plane of life, there is no longer need of outward force or harsh and arbitrary rule.   When every one says in his deep heart, "the will of God be done," how is there any longer need of law?   The old forms have vanished.   The society lives, from its own spontaneous, ordered life.   It is no longer a machine, operated by an external force.   It is not a mechanical automaton, but a living body, animated by a living soul.

But if there is any power which guides and governs, restrains and punishes, it is the power of a pervading love, which binds all here into the unity of one body.   I have said that religion was the bond of this, as, in some form, it must be that of all vital societies.

But I can see—can almost feel, the threads of a nervous system, which finds its center in the heart-life, and binds all hearts in a net work so sensitive, that every jar must be felt by every member.

The sentiment of love, developed in all the freedom of this life, must reach every heart, and be with every one a powerful motive. You can imagine the influence this must give to a woman like Melodia—who is so admired, adored and loved, perhaps I might say, by all. Such a love is a sacred bond to purity and order of life. And those who love her are also beloved by others, and so on. There is no point, where any individual, man or woman, could do any wrong, without the violation of this sentiment. It holds every one to duty, honor, and an orderly obedience, not to an isolate, despotic will, but to the principles of the ordered life.

This government then is the self-government of each individual, who, by his conformity to a central principle or life-law, is in harmony with every other. As each one seeks, finds, and happily performs the function for which he or she is fitted, there is order without force, and subordination without oppression. As far as I can see, every person here occupies precisely the place he should, in his own fitness, and in his relations to others.

And if, from want of numbers, or variety of capacity, or lack of development in any, there were danger that any function would be unfulfilled, then comes in the principle of devotion to the welfare of others and the general good. This heroic principle is always active, always seeking expression. There is no work so great, or so difficult, that it would not attempt and accomplish. There is no one here, however hard and selfish he may have been, or might now be, in the scramble and contest of civilization, who would not sacrifice everything, and perform everything, for the life. As there is no one here who would not face danger and death for the common defence, so there is no one who would not cheerfully do any thing required of him, in the spirit of the life.

Were it deemed duty for Esperanza to send out missionaries, there is no one who would not leave all the love and beauty of this Home, and encounter all the hardships of the world, to spread the truths of this Gospel of Harmony. Even the mormons can send out a hundred missionaries at a time, without purse or scrip, to go to the four corners of the earth with their new dispensation. You will not expect less devotion here. The missionaries of the Society of Jesus for three hundred years have marched bravely through torrid heats and polar frosts to martyrdom. Surely the missionaries of social redemption would not be less heroic.

We had last night an example of the spirit of order and enthusiasm which is here, not in momentary awakenings, as we have seen it, but as a perpetual spring of action. An hour after midnight, when all but the watch were in profound repose, the large bell of the tower rung out an alarum. In an instant, while I sprang to the window to see what was the cause, but where I met only darkness, I heard the rush of many feet ; then came a burst of light from twenty torches, held by as many boys, which lighted up the whole scene. I hurried on my clothes and went out upon the lawn. It was an alarm of fire ; but there was not one cry of fear or symtom of confusion. Every one was in his place. Some were on the roofs ; some at windows ; some were ready with ladders. Hose was attached to the hydrants leading from the large reservoir ready to deluge any portion of the buildings. All stood ready for the signal, every man in his place—every woman also in hers ; the children all provided for. But soon the bell sounded a few strokes again ; when the hose and ladders were removed, the torches extinguished, and all retired to their rooms again, and Esperanza reposed in peace.

It was an alarm of discipline—a test of order. I was rich in the feeling of security which this spectacle gave me. It was an organized earthly providence. How many hundreds of precious lives might have been saved, within our remembrance, lost on burning ships and steamboats, by such a discipline. Had the signal been one of outward danger, as that of the attack of an armed foe, or a mob, the whole military force of the home would have mustered with the same silent celerity, and in the same orderly energy. It is a community of peace, never attacking any, even by words ; but ready, to the last heart throb, to defend itself from all aggression. It is a community, I venture to say, that no mob would ever think of attacking ; and an organized force would not do it without first counting the cost, and having a powerful motive. Of all this there is little fear ; yet a watchful foresight guards against all contingencies.

I said there were no elections. When there is any thing to be decided, involving no principle, and which does not call for the exercise of wisdom, it is left to chance or destiny. If two persons, equally qualified, aspire to the same function in which but one can serve, it is decided by lot. For example, some arduous or hazardous work is to be performed, requiring but one, and half a dozen, equally capable volunteer to do it. He or she who has the over-sight, or who gives the order of the day, either selects the one to perform the work, as an honor for some special merit, or they draw lots. This is the end. Those who draw blanks congratulate the one who has the prize, and aid him in every way in their power.

There are other privileges, decided in the same manner. There is a certain number of horses ready for harness or saddle ; and if, at any time, more wish to ride than there are horses for this use, they draw for them. Then it often occurs that some of those who draw make presents of their rights to others. Generosity is con-stantly seeking for its exercise and satisfaction. Benevolence is the rule ; and selfishness, in its hard, isolate, grasping spirit, does not exist, or is not developed in any outward manifestation

My most manly friend, Alfred, whose reliability you would feel, like that of a block of granite ; whom you would trust utterly, every where and in all circumstances, exercises, I doubt not, as much power as any one here ; but it is a power that is never seen. Melodia leans upon him ; and though she may be his guide in many things, his judgment, in all practical matters, must have great weight, because it ought. Manlius holds the balance of justice, and is the universal referree, wherever there is any doubt of right—but I am assured that he is oftener appealed to by those who believe they have more than equity, than by any who fancy they have less. Vincent silently, modestly, and with unceasing industry works out the common welfare, by common consent.

Where all are right. there must be unanimity. Where all are

25

agreed in regard to the principles and laws of a movement, and all are devoted to a single object, there must be harmony. Where the interest of each individual is the interest of all, and the welfare of all is consistant with the highest happiness of each, there can be no clashing discordance or clamor of strife. Darling, it is here !

" Was it always so ? " I asked of Vincent, at the conversation of to-day ; for he gives me this hour, every day, with an unvarying punctuality.

" No—not always. A few years ago, we were civilizees, living in all the errors and discordances of civilization. We cheated and robbed, or were cheated and robbed, like the rest. We were social Ishmaels, our hands against every man, and every man's against us. We bought cheap and sold dear, without regarding equity. We were excited about politics, and mingled, more or less, in all its clamor and strife. We disputed matters of philosophy, religion, economy and morals. Out of all this discord we were obliged to graduate, and old habits of thought and feeling are not easily laid aside. But when the principles and methods of the harmonic life were presented to us, we rose above the plane of strife. We had henceforth but one combined interest, and one harmoneous work. We left the Old to fight its own battles."

"And did all come readily into the idea and practice of this new life ? "

" By no means. Many were with us for a time, and even very earnest and enthusiastic, and then fell away. Selfish appetites, selfish loves, selfish graspings of gain, took away some who seemed to run well for a season. With others, enthusiasm tended to various insanities. It was putting new wine into old bottles. But no one was ever thus severed from us without good reason. In the earliest and hardest struggle, when our numbers were fewest, and the persecuting clamors of the world around us the most malignant, not one fell away unless by some fault of character, that would have made him unfit for our life. We did not have one trial too many ; nor was one taken from us whom we could have retained without injury.

" In a great work, many tools are broken and thrown aside, or tried and found worthless, and yet the work goes on. Many seeds are germless or destroyed ; yet the great forests are planted. Those only were lost to us whom the work could spare ; and every instance of falling away from our life, we saw, after a time, if not at first, was a special providence. Each gave us some needed lesson, or help for a time, and was no doubt repaid in some good to himself. There were wintry sea-ons and days of darkness, but nothing was lost, and I knew every hour that the end was sure.''

'' Was the trial and discipline severe ? ''

'' You may not think it so—but it was sufficient. Purity and devotion were required of all. The chastity of an entire continence and the acceptance of the law which limits the amative expression to its most integral use, were not easily conformed to by people sunk in habits of sensuality. By this requirement we were severed from all self seeking sensualists, who demanded freedom, only for the satisfaction of their morbid lusts. Our simple diet repelled those who were dominated by a coarse and excited alimentiveness. Our devotion of all we were and had to this object found no sympathy with either the self-indulgent or the miserly. You wonder how we found so many as we have. You know that it was said that God has always a remnant. There were seven thousand who had never bowed the knee to Baal ; and though ten men could not be found to save Sodom, that was an exceptional case. Truths are in or under these old forms. Amid all the selfishness, disease, folly, and perversity of mankind, there are always those who are noble, pure, wise, and full of the aspiration of a true holiness. We found our own—they passed sweetly through the trials of the transition period, and here we are, and here is our Home.''

'' Beautiful home ! '' I exclaimed, as we paused in our ride on the brow of a little hill which overlooked all the fair prospect of fields and orchards, groves and vineyards, happy groups of industrious workers, lovely forms of architecture glancing among the trees, and the silver mirror of this sylvan lake ; ''all beautiful ! Oh ! that men could know what this life might be ! Is there no way to teach them.''

"The millions who have no power to live this life, and who would never make the sacrifices of their miserable and debasing pleasures to attain it, cannot be saved. They must die in their sins. If you have a mission to present our life to the world, you may find some who will accept it, and be ready to pass through the needed preparation. It is only thus that they can come. We can say, in solemn earnestness, 'strait is the gate and narrow is the way that leadeth unto life, and few there be that find it.' Those who are dominated by a morbid benevolence will exclaim against us, for not opening wide our doors, and inviting all this poor, maimed, halt and blind humanity to enter. It is a social suicide we can in no wise commit. Discord cannot come into our harmony. Whoso cannot accept our life, our life rejects. We can have no fellowship with the unfruitful works of darkness. Those who come here must be the tried and trusty; and these are few. Nevertheless, go seek them if you will, and in your own way. It has been our experience in the past, that many were called, but few were chosen. I use these phrases, because they were learned in my earliest years, and because they express my meanings. I also think them mystically prophetic of our life."

"I owe you many thanks, and I feel a deep gratitude," I said from my heart, "for all your instructions. In a few days, I must leave you, and all I love here, to go back into the world, and prepare to come to the home you offer me. Should my representations of this life induce others to wish to join me, will you tell me what is required of qualification and preparation?"

"Yes, it is proper that you have these requirements well defined. The demands of our life are not unreasonable, I think, but they are imperative.

"Youth is to be preferred to age, and health to disease; long formed habits are often hard to break, and diseases, not only difficult of cure, but always a burthen, and sometimes worse. As all must begin as children or pupils, in a novitiate, there must be in them the essential qualities of humility and obedience. It was understood as far back as Solomon, that there is more hope of a fool, than of a man wise in his own conceit. There must also

be a willing and cheerful surrender of the isolate and individual
selfishness, or there can be no attainment of the larger goods of
the associate and harmonic life. He who grasps his hand tightly
on a dime, cannot receive the dollar that is offered him. There
must be a giving up of the selfish life, in regard to both material
and spiritual riches,—and an entire devotion of all one is and has
to the life. This is to be shown in little things as in great ones.
All other loves must be subordinate to the central and harmonic
love, which includes all others.

" You are to be clear and stringent as to all habits of life, and
rules of discipline. There must be purity of person, food, and life.
He or she who cannot pass through the novitiate of a pure vestalate, is not for our life. Men and women, who held each other by
the bonds of law and custom, cannot come to us. They must be
as the angels. There can be no filth of tobacco, and all habitual
stimulants must be abandoned. There must be the capacity for a
steady industry. The idle, lazy, voluptuous and self-indulgent
are not for us. There must be, in every novitiate, a constant, earnest, and orderly effort for the development of all faculties. When
chastity has stopped the waste of life ; when energy comes from
these pure and invigorating habits, it is needful that this new life
be used to the last atom, in the work of development.

" You have seen our life, and know something of its requirements. We can trust you to judge who is qualified to live it here.
But a time of trial and preparation is needed for all. You
have the impulse to gather a group or groups, who are worthy to
come to us and enjoy our life. Well—the trial is before you. All
good angels aid you in your work."

Yes, my Clara, I must make the effort. Surely, we know some
who may be redeemed out of this sad discordance of the world
we know, and its hollow shams. What have we ever found in
what is called society, but pretension, stupidity, egotism, and selfish intrigues. We have seen the best—and how poor it is ! A
few kernels of wheat in bushels of chaff—some grains of gold,
lost amid heaps of tinsel and brass. How many, in all the circle
of our acquaintance, should we be sorry never to see again ! And

the terror of it is, that the purest are so soon corrupted into sel-fishness. The tender loving girl who "comes out," all beauty and sweetness, how a few seasons change her into a cold, heart-less, selfish coquette ; a husband-hunter. Pride or indolence, or ambition, or disappointment, destroy all that is beautiful in her spirit, and she is ready to sell herself like the rest.

Are there not some, whom we can rescue from such a wretched fate ? We will at least make the trial.

And, darling one, even the best side of this life of civilization—how poor it is. Suppose one of these lovely girls to be more for-tunate than most ; to give her hand with her heart, to the man of her supreme choice ; cannot you see, with a glance around you, what comes then ? Waste of health and life in a licensed and sanctified sensuality. Children beyond the powers of her vitality, and with a consequent weak hold on life, and great, exhausting sorrows in their sickness and death. A life of domestic cares and isolation, with little opportunity for development and enjoyment ; or a dull, tiresome round of fashionable dissipation ; or a wasting, wearying indolence. What has become of the promise of that blooming belle-hood ? Oh ! Clara, cannot we save some at least from this poor, false life of sham pleasures and too real miseries ? Let us try.

I know that the conditions of this life of industry, art, develop-ment, and true happiness will be hard to attain. I know that a very earnest effort will be required to conquer disorder in and around us ; to overcome idleness, and wastefulness of time ; to waken up our dormant faculties ; to work under the inspirations of devotion. But it is for us. Others have done it, and we can do it. It is not harder than the discipline of our military school at West Point. It is not harder than the seventeen years of Jesuit noviti-ate. It is far less revolting than the discipline of many religious orders. It is not mortification and martyrdom, but life and hap-piness. It is simply obeying the sacred injunction: "Cease to do evil—learn to do well." We can do this work—we will do it ; and we will invite those friends, for whom we have any real sym-pathy, to join us in our work.

I am so in earnest respecting what I have written you, that I paused in my writing to find Melodia, and ask her counsel in our proceedings. I found her giving the little Vincent his music lesson, for while he spends most of his time in the groups of children, he comes to her at certain hours every day. All grown persons here, have their beautiful relations with the young. The little ones learn many lessons from their chosen and beloved teachers.

When the lesson was finished, I told her of what I had been writing, and what I wished to do. She entered into my desires with a quick and tender sympathy, and gave me what seems wise counsel. It is that when I return, we look over our list of acquaintances, and invite those we feel free and happy in inviting to a little party. That I then tell them something of the story of what I have seen of this life, and invite those who are interested to ask their friends another evening to discuss the matter more fully. That I then explain very frankly, the nature and conditions of this life, and ascertain if there are any who are ready to seek it in the way prescribed. "If any can be found," she said, "three or four, perhaps, who are ready to give up all the old, and to devote themselves body and spirit, all they have and are, with a religious zeal, to this work; then read to them the pledges of consecration; appoint stated times to meet with them, for conversation and instruction; watch the unfoldings of their minds, and their progress in the orders of harmony, test their humility and obedience, and their subjection to the rules for the discipline of novitiates. If they take the pledges of consecration; if they live to all their requirements through the prescribed period, then are they truly novitiates of our life.

"Our life, with all its goods, material and spiritual, is open to them. When there is harmony in your little group, it will be fitted to join our larger harmony. But do not forget that we must reject all discordance. There must be no pity. The disorderly must be expelled, and the parasitic must be cut off. No law is more imperative."

I shall enter, with fear and trembling, and yet with a deep joy, upon this work. It may seem hard to you that I say it; but it is true that this prospect of usefulness increases my desire to come to you. I feel like one who puts out in a little boat upon the stormy seas, to try and save the lives of shipwrecked, drowning voyagers, Help me, darling, help me in this work. Look around you, and see if you cannot find some against my return.

I look anxiously, but I find so few. One, whose beautiful gifts of talent and beauty would be an added charm, even to Esperanza, is fast bound to a selfish and worldly man. She can never break her chain. I know that all her aspirations are for a pure and loving life of beauty and culture; but the big tears will come in her eyes, and despair into her heart. She will fold her hands in submission to her earthly fate and look for happiness to heaven.

I know another, a glorious woman, whose whole soul is filled with ideas of beauty, harmony, and a true life—but she, too, is bound; and in her prison she can only dream, dream, dream her life away. How strong are these bonds, that the word binds upon its victims. Our young men, who are free from such ties, have they not all yielded themselves to slaveries as hopeless and more debasing. Their lager beer and brandy; their oyster suppers, and luxurious fare; their sensual amours and entanglements; their selfish ambitions for fame or fortune. What can emancipate them from these? "Who is sufficient for these things?" And yet we must not distrust. Are there not others as good, as self-sacricing, as devoted as we? I count on you, my Clara, with an absolute faith. Are there not all over the world, those who devote themselves to what they recognize as the highest good—the religious orders of the church; zealous philanthropists; devotees of science, and art, and literature; volunteers on all forlorn hopes, moral and military.

O Darling! if the age of chivalry be past, does not its spirit still live in the heart of humanity? The heroic element is not lost. God lives, and man aspires to the Divine Life. Let us then trust and hope.

XXI.

The Children, and the Art Life.

Dear Clara:—I have tried to make all I see, hear, and feel, live for you ; but I feel, every day, how poorly I have succeeded. Even to me, when I shut my eyes, or ride off into the woods alone, all seems a dream, from which I must soon awaken. But when I turn my horse's head, and give him rein to gallop home, and this scene of beauty opens to me, like some enchanted land, I wake to the glad reality. I see the fast ripening corn ; the purpling grapes ; the golden pears ; the ruddy velvet of the peach ; the teeming acres of melons and tomatoes ; all the bountiful productions of a rich soil under a high cultivation, and I see what is so much better than all this. I see men, women, and children, better cared for, better cultivated, than all their surroundings.

Lovely as Esperanza is, in scenery, in architecture, in art, and culture ; what she excels in chiefly, is in her people. The earth has many fair and fertile regions, and many luxurious and princely homes. But the most beautiful plantations and gardens are cultivated by ignorant peasants, serfs, or slaves ; or by men whose only care is gain, and whose uncultured souls are deformed by sensual vices. But here — ah ! the happy contrast ! — here the soul is more beautiful than all scenery, architecture, or art, and it is the inner life of feeling and thought, that find expression and enjoyment in all these outward beauties.

When I dream now, it is oftenest of you. Then I am in our old walks, and rides, and haunts ; or I sit by you in the cosy little parlor of your dear home. I dreamed you sang me a new song, and the words, air, and even the accompaniment were so vividly present with me, that I thought, when I first woke, I could write them all, — but they would not stay. They went like all such dreams. I have dreamed an entire romance, chapter by chapter, descriptions, conversations,—the entire story; but I could never remember it an hour. Will these dreams ever come back to us?

And, sometimes, when I am dreaming of you, and our old life, this new life of Esperanza seems a dream, that I dream I am dreaming. It was so yesterday morning; but I woke to a burst of glorious music, and what seemed real was the dream, and what seemed a dream opened into the divine reality.

Oh! this music! Our bands give us old, hackneyed tunes; or negro airs, whistled into tatters; or, at the best, portions of the newer operas. But here, the music every day is the fresh expression of the life; and so charming that no words can express it. Melodia has promised to copy a few airs, with her own arrangement for the piano-forte, for you. We have old music, too; and the best of the old, sacred and secular; for the world of civilization is not forgotten. But the best music here, as the best art of every kind, is the outbirth of the life, and embodies its truth, freedom, purity and happiness.

An African traveler brought a negro, whom he had attached to himself as a servant, to Sierra Leone. The town, fortress, shipping, all the triumphs of civilization, first excited, and then crazed him; until he jumped overboard from a steamer in the harbor and was drowned. So I think it might be with this life, acting on weak and sensitive organizations; and even on this account, I see the wisdom of a period of thorough preparation.

The music which woke me from my dream and my dream's dream, was sublime enough to wake a world. Those who dread the toils of the day, its cares, its annoyances, or merely its ennui, may well hug the pillow. But here,—before one strain of that music was played, I was on my feet, breathing full breaths of pleasure; my pulse beating with its glorious life; ready for every thing of work or enjoyment. O ruddy sky of morning! O beautiful Aurora! How much happiness has my sluggishness lost me, in all the past years! Do you not remember, with an ever fresh delight, all the mornings we have been together? That great morning on the Cattskills, when we saw the horizon so far away, and watched the flying shadows over the vast valley of the Hudson. That was a morning in the grandeur of nature; but our mornings here are even more grand and beautiful, in their soul harmonies.

At first, I looked on every thing here as a critic; I listened with interest and pleasure, indeed,—but as a spectator listens. It is no more thus. My heart and soul join in their orisons of harmony. They stir my being to its profoundest depths. Tears flow from my eyes; and I feel a solemn rapture, such as no other religious service has ever inspired. Is not music the language of religion—of all love; even of the Infinite? I experience now, also, a universal, full hearted recognition. The children give me beautiful tokens of loving confidence. When the morning hymn was sung, a little girl of five years ran to me with a freshly gathered bouquet; and, as she gave it to me, held up her rosy cheek to be kissed for payment. Her mother smiled and held out her hand with a frank good morning; nor was there any one to chide, when I kissed the hand, as I had kissed the cheek. There is a little interval after the music, for these morning greetings; and amid the perfect order of every movement here, there is also an unconstrained freedom, that is its brightest charm. I can only compare it to a tree, firm and symetrical, yet covered all over with tender waving foliage and beautiful flowers.

As the time of my departure draws nigh, I find many persons and things to see,—and many inquiries to make; for I wish to be able to answer every question. Thus, in the Studio, this morning, I said to Angelo, who presides over the development of the Esthetic Life in Art, more perhaps than any other: "Do you never regret not living in some great city?"

"New York, for example," he answered, with a dry, droll smile; "with its magnificent galleries and noble patronage of art."

"Not New York, perhaps," said I, a little piqued in my patriotism; "but Paris, or Florence, or Rome."

"They contain great collections; and are very interesting, and in certain respects instructive to the artist; but they are not of the first necessity ; and the danger of imitation goes far to counterbalance the knowledge to be acquired. We have painters here, whom I should feel sorry to see at Rome or Florence, until they are more mature in their own growth. The life of art suffers from the bonds of custom, fashion and requirement, as much as the social life. Both must be in correspondence. Low life, low art. A high, pure, spiritual life, makes its art expressions in harmony with itself. The art of every age and people is the expression of its life, so far as it finds such expression. Now, as our life here differs somewhat notably from that of the world's great capitals, they can give us little aid in its true expression. We need not go for study, in the sense of imitation,—it would lower our standard : not for models,—we have far better of our own, than any hired models can be ; nor for patronage,—for we are above any such necessity."

As we talked, Evaline and Eugenia approached us. their arms entwined about each other in sisterly enfoldments. They joined in the conversation.

"That is all very well, Mr. Angelo,," said Evaline, "but I cannot so easily give up my old dream of going to Italy. You have been there, and saw the folly of it ; but none the less do I wish to see the folly, too."

"Well !" he answered cheerfully, "what hinders? You have money enough—*that* used to be the difficulty with us poor artists, you know. Why not go ? Here is Mr. Frank will be very happy to attend you as far as New York ; and for the rest, you are a brave girl ; and there are artists enough, going, on there, to afford you all the protection you will need. Why not go ?"

The gentle Evaline looked round this noble room, filled with mementos of her happy life and associations. She felt the pressure of the loving arms that were twined around her. She looked a moment into the calm deep eyes of Angelo, to see how much he was in earnest. Then a happy smile broke over her face.

"You are not very anxious to have me go, I think," said she. "After all, I don't believe much in Italy. If a body could go without a heart, it might do ; but I will wait for the party we were talking of the other day."

This party ; what do you think it was ?   Only this,   To charter
a fine, fast sailing clipper, and make a voyage up the Mediterranean,
to Italy, Greece, Egypt. This would be better than any other mode, for
they could lay in their own provisions and carry with them the life
of Esperanza. Beyond the simple charter of the vessel, there would
be but little expense ; and the trip might be made delightful,—if a
family so united, could be so long divided.   But all this, if not now,
will be in the future, when Esperanza has grown to her full dimen-
sions, and still more, when such homes shall be scattered over the
earth, making its beautiful places more beautiful.

Vincent had been busy all the morning.   I had scarcely seen
either him or Melodia.   There were other signs of preparation for .
some event of importance ; and I was left more alone than usual,
to prosecute my researches.   So I walked over the gardens and
orchards ;   I inspected again the machinery and operations of the
factories ; I lounged a little while in the library, which took me
back into the world of civilization ; then I went to make one more
visit to the nursery, to see the blossoming of the future.

If the world could but know the worth of its babies ! If men
and women could be as wise for infant humanity as they are for so
many other things !   Care, pains, expense, science, skill, are expended in perfecting all productions but just the most important ;
and these are left to ignorance and chance.   It is not so here ; and
here, therefore, there are only healthy, strong, noble, and beautiful
children.

In this sweet nursery, which is a real infant's paradise, I met
Harmonia.   With a passionate love of infancy, and much knowledge in its proper care and education, she spends many of her
happiest and most useful hours with these babes and their mothers
and nurses.   The little rosy darlings laughed and crowed, when
they saw her coming, and put out their little dimpled hands to be
taken to her bosom.

I stood watching this scene, which I have already described to
you ; and thought of the thousands of miserable, sickly babies,
growing up in poverty, filth, and every kind of wretchedness, or
swelling that horrible account of infant mortality.   And I thought,

if Esperanza had done but this, it would be so good a work, that all the world might well follow her example.

"I am glad to see this lesson so well learned," said Harmonia, divining my thoughts. "My heart has bled so often for the poor children of civilization! Here, at last, a human spirit may find some prospect of an existence well begun, and worth enjoying. We may find some worthy recruits in the world we have left, but our best hope of the future is here."

She went with me to the theater. In it was a busy work of preparation. Vincent and Melodia were on the stage, engaged in a rehearsal.

"You do not know what is going forward," said Harmonia." "They are very discreet, but I am not. To-morrow is my birthday. How many I have had, has been kindly forgotten by all my dear friends,—but they never forget when one comes; and to-morrow you will see how they celebrate it."

We stayed but a few moments; just long enough to give me a curiosity for the morrow's festival; and then I continued my survey, in the dear company so kindly bestowed upon me. My own mother could not be more tenderly kind to me; and she will be a mother to you also, dear Clara; a very wise, good mother; and if I am ever wrong to you in any way, she will see that the wrong is righted.

As we passed through the gardens, we saw busy groups of children, gathering and arranging flowers; but they did not gather round Harmonia as usual, but worked on, with a few shy glances, as if their business was a great secret, and of the most importance. "The beautiful children!" I said, aloud, "living together like brothers and sisters of one family; I wonder if they take account of their actual relationships."

"You might have the apprehension, that some of our children are no wiser in this respect, than many of the children of civilization. The thought is natural; but it is not justified by the fact. In the world, there is every motive for a woman to conceal paternity, unsanctioned by law; yet I have known, even in this moral country of ours, numerous cases, in which the reputed father was not the actual one. These children must always remain in ignorance, with the liabilities you may have feared for ours. Here such a thing can never happen; for there is no motive for concealment; and every father can proudly own his children, and every child can know its father. Birth is too sacred a thing with us, and the welfare of the immortal souls, who take their bodily forms from us, too important, for any hazard of evil or guilty secresy. As every child is born of a most sacred love, guided by the best wisdom of its parents, it has the best guarantees we can give it of a pure birth, a healthy and beautiful organization, the tenderest care, the most integral education, and the best development of all its faculties.

"And there is another thing, of which, perhaps, you have not thought. These children grow up to the heritage and possession of a home. Each one is an heir to a princely inheritance. In the world we have left, thousands of parents have no homes of their own; and of course none for their children. They pay high rents for poor shelter; and their children grow up, in ignorance and privation, to a like fate. When better off, the little homestead will not hold the growing family, and brothers and sisters are torn asunder and scattered over the earth. No sooner is a little group formed, with something of harmonious life, than it is rudely destroyed; and so on forever, amid sighs and tears. Aged parents pining in loneliness,—young hearts always bleeding. This is the life of civilization.

"But here, there are no such sorrows in store for us. The hive grows as the swarm increases. When the time comes that we can form a new home from the increase of the old, there will be no solitary scattering over the earth, but those who go will be well provided for, as well as those who remain. We shall all have two homes then. Over the whole earth, how many have any real home?"

"So few! so few!" I said, "are there any who have truly a home?"

"The desire for the home exists everywhere. It is a human instinct which forever seeks to embody its ideal; and little groups are formed by the family, but weak and soon broken. Larger societies have gathered, religious and others; but crude and imperfect in their organization. Aggregations of discordance do not make harmonies; nor is silence harmony. Many elements are necessary to a social harmony. One or two are not enough. The societies of the religious, in the Catholic Church, have depended chiefly on the religious element. Other societies have made industry more prominent. The Shakers unite these two; but these are not enough."

"Will you tell me what you think the most important elements of a society?"

"Yes; religion, love, industry, art; these four elements in orderly development and exercise, comprise the necessities of life. Religion gives us unity with the Infinite, and aspiration to the higher and more perfect life. Love is the sum of all attractions to, and harmonies with, each other. Industry is the basis of the physical life, and the natural outflow of its energies. Art is the cultivation and expression of the beautiful. Order is the perfect adaptation and harmony of these four elements.

"Every human being has some consciousness of wants, corresponding to these social elements. A true society must satisfy these wants. A group of faculties belongs to each, and that social condition fails of its purpose which does not give exercise to every human faculty, and satisfy, in some good degree, every human desire. You can see how far our life does this,—and how far others either do it, or fail of their true purpose. The true life of man includes all the goods of 'the life that now is,' as well as ' the life to come.' "

We were walking beside a thick hedge of current bushes; for the hedges here are all of flowering or fruitful shrubs; when on the other side we heard a group of children busily at work, and singing in full chorus:

> " Flowers, beautiful flowers, to crown thy natal day;
> Fruits, fruits delicious, accept from us, we pray;
> Sweet as the garlands, we bring thy hair to twine,
> As sweet and fragrant, be each love of thine.
>   Heaven grant our wish sincere!
>   Bless thee, our mother dear!
> All brightest blessings round thee ever shine!"

" Ah !" softly exclaimed Harmonia, " we have stumbled on
another rehearsal, it seems. Come ; we must go away. One can 't
eat one's cake and have it, too ; and sufficient unto the morrow
will be the goods thereof."

So we walked softly out of hearing of the dear little minstrels,
who were preparing so busily for the *fete* of the morrow.

Melodia sent me, by the bright Angela, an invitation to take my
supper in her lovely saloon, with Vincent and Serafa. Harmonia had
accepted an invitation to spend the evening with Evaline, and some
of her artist friends. On account of the festival of the morrow, there
was no general gathering of any kind in the evening, but many little
groups of congenial spirits ; while others were working away, with
a loving interest, to complete the preparations for the morrow.

I prepared myself with care for the evening. Never have I been
so careful in my dress as here, because I have never been in any
society where the arts of dress and personal adornment were so
highly cultivated. We have seen much greater expense, but never
such artistic taste, and such lovely effects of costume and ornament as here, where dress is one of the fine arts. There is beauty
of form, and harmony of colors, and adaptations. Nothing is done
by chance, but every shade has its purpose.

When I entered the room where the three were seated on a
lounge, I could not but admire the picture they made. And as I
came nearer, other senses were as pleasantly affected. Each had
selected some delicate perfume, and the three blended into a harmony of odors. When they spoke to me, their speech was musical,
and their voices delicately attuned to each other. Oh ! the coarse,
brawling, mumbling, lisping, spluttering, uncouth speech of our
" best society," where not one person in a hundred has any refinement of education ;—I can never endure it again. With these,
the simplest phrase is music. The Emperor Charles V., a very
accomplished man, but not very scrupulous, used to say that we
should speak Spanish with the gods, Italian with our lovers, French
with our friends, German with soldiers, English with geese,
Hungarian with horses, and Bohemian with the devil. You may

26

have spoken English with geese very often ; but here, you will find it musical enough for any purpose.

I went to sit by the side of Serafa, with the feeling, rather than thought of leaving Melodia more to Vincent; but she arranged it otherwise, motioning with her fan of sandal wood, that scattered its soft, oriental odor at every movement, that I should take an ottoman nearest her. It was a queenly act; slight as it might seem to one who did not know its purport. It gave to Serafa just so much of Vincent as I could balance on the other side. It was but little,—but the act was no less generous to her and also to me. So much for the wave of a lady's fan. Why not? Do not human destinies,—the destinies of nations even, hang on nods, or smiles, or a yes or no?

We had conversation, running like a quiet stream, now glittering over bright pebbles, now pausing in serene depths, now eddying backward to the past, now shooting forward to a widening future. We, or they, I should rather say, and I do it in no affected humility, talked of literature, art, science, poetry, philosophy, and especially of the philosophy of life. Serafa had brought a little ode she had written for the morrow. When she read it, Melodia took it, saying :

" Why, my darling, this ought to be sung, do you know ?"

" Doubtless, music would make it more worthful," said the modest poet ; "they say that very silly verses seem good, when they are set to music !"

" Naughty child !" said Melodia, opening the piano-forte, " your verses are so musical that no reading can properly express them,— let's see now if we can find some music for them." She read a few lines over hummingly ; then struck a prelude, that seemed the very voice of the verse, and then sang them gloriously, divinely. Vincent looked at her with a look of proud admiration, and Serafa was in tears. She went gently to Melodia, still seated at the piano-forte, and kneeling at her feet, said :

" Thank you, O beautiful One. Will you take my poor verses, and sing them to-morrow evening."

" Yes, darling ;" she answered, with her radiant smile of strength and happiness, a smile born out of the consciousness of power, " it shall be as you wish." Then she kissed her tenderly, and raised her up; then opening her desk, set me to copy the poem.

After that we had our supper, delicate enough for the food of fairies. Then she took a volume of the poems of Tennison, and improvised music for a dozen or more of his daintiest songs. Then she sang some duets with Vincent; I did my best to make out a trio sometimes; and so spend our time until the moon rose, and threw her pale light over the landscape. We walked out then, and down to the lake, which was rippled all over with silver in the cool evening breeze. We entered a boat; Vincent shook out the sail with a ready hand, and taking the helm we were soon gliding off, like a white ghost in the moon-beams.

When we had sailed a mile or more from the landing, so that the lighted edifice of Esperanza looked like a fairy palace, Vincent took his bugle from its case, which had been sent to the boat beforehand, and blew first a few long signal notes, whose echoes came floating back from every side over the still waters. He waited a moment for some answering signal. Melodia pointed me to a star of lights in a window of the central tower. It showed that Harmonia was in her balcony; that she had heard our signal, and that she was probably looking at our white sail in the moonbeams.

Then this lover-husband played old airs of years long gone,—airs of Moore's Melodies; airs of favorite songs; airs from Opera's; every thing that Harmonia had ever loved of music from her infancy up, and through all the days of the sweet unity of their loving life. He played them with a feeling that affected us all. Melodia sang the words in a low, sweet, melodious cadence, as he played the airs; weaving them into a musical garland. Then, we glided away into the shadows of the woods,—swept along the shores, and after one of the most beautiful little voyages of my life, we were back again at the landing, where Harmonia and Evaline met us, and with them we walked up the lawn, and said our good night adieus under the tree, where I had first seen the good father, playing with his children.

Vincent went with Harmonia, Serafa with Evaline, and I was left with Melodia.

As I looked at her queenly beauty in the moonlight, the thought of the oncoming hour of parting swept over me. I think she saw it in the expression of my features, the tremor of my voice, and the pressure of my hand; for she said, with a quiet solemnity:

"My friend, be calm and brave. You go to do your work, and you will return, if 'you do it all worthily. No change will come to those you love, and those who love you. All the riches of our life is for you, if you remain as now. Peace, hope, love; all joys, all happiness, are yours, if you are faithful to the life and its requirements. I pledge you all, and I give you, here, in the silvery moonlight, on this sacred spot, and under the eye of the pure heavens, I give you this token of acceptance.

She kissed my forehead,—I sank upon my knee,—I kissed her hand,—I wet it with my tears. She drew it silently away; and when I rose, the angel had vanished.

XXII.

My Darling :—I sank quickly into a sweet, dreamless slumber, my last thoughts of you, my last prayer for your happiness. I had slept some hours when my senses woke gradually to the loveliest of all midnight seranades, in which a full band welcomed the first moments of the birthday of Harmonia. From my window I saw her come into her balcony, in flowing white robes, with a gauzy scarf thrown over her head, and kiss her hand in the moonlight, to thank the dear friends who had so charmingly awaked her.

I sank again to sleep and heard no more until roused by a tender yet triumphant strain from Vincent's bugle, followed by the morning call of the full band ; then the morning hymn, after which came a fairy-like procession of all the children, with baskets of fruits and flowers, chanting the chorus we had overheard the day before. Harmonia kissed and thanked them, and after the usual morning lecture we went to a festal breakfast. The room had been decorated for the occasion, so that when she, whose birthday all so love and so delight to honor, went in leaning upon Vincent's arm, with one of the prettiest of flower-wreaths on her head, and looked round at the walls and tables, she burst into tears of happiness.

The work of the morning was accomplished, and dinner renewed these sweet testimonials of love and gratitude. Her health was drank in a fashion entirely new to me. At each table some one rose, men, women and children, with a toast. At one table it was Melodia : filling a glass of the pure nectar wine of Esperanza, she rose and said :

"Dear friends :—Let us thank the good God for the return of this happy festival ; drink to Harmonia, the interpreter of heavenly wisdom !"

"To Harmonia," said a young man, rising at a table near, "guide and counsellor of the young!"

"To Harmonia," said next a beautiful woman, "the loving mother of our little babes!"

"To Harmonia, sweet mother of us all!" said one of the dear little girls who had been foremost in the floral offering. And so the toasts went round.

Brief addresses were made by several of the younger portion of the society. One or two of them, in direct reference to the active part which had been taken by Harmonia in teaching the laws, and unfolding the science of harmony in life.

When it became evident, by a longer pause of silence than usual between speeches, that all had spoken who wished to do so, Harmonia rose and said, "I thank you all, dear friends, for the kindness and the love manifested toward me, not only upon the present occasion, but for all that has come to me through all the days since our gathering into the unity of this happy and tranquil life.

"It is quite natural that young persons of ardent temperament should treasure in the memory, and cherish with an interest approaching to devotion the names of their own dear mothers, and of all indeed by whom they have been blessed with care, kindness and love, during their infancy. Emotions of gratitude have their foundation in a law of our nature, and are in themselves right. It is well, however, that we all bear in mind the fact, that there is a line of balance beyond which excess of good may become an evil. Our own people, the full members of our society, understand each other, and were it not that we have a few friends from a distance, visitng us to-day, I might not have mentioned the subject.

"It is true, that the remembrance of the fact, that such a society has been gathered from the discords of the old world; and this beautiful home, built up within so short a time, may well be a vital joy to us all. It is true, that for our triumph over many obstacles, and the achievement in so short a time of this great success, we are indebted much to the wisdom and the experience imparted to us from the Spirit world.

"It is also true, that my friends, those who know most of my past life, can bear me witness, that I speak truly, when I say, that there is not much room left me to lay claim to personal merit, or for my friends to try their skill in setting up the claim for me, even were I vain enough to attempt, or desire it. I have, like other skeptical persons, disputed inch by inch, every new philosophy that has been brought to me ; I was not friendly to the faith ; I even went so far as to forbid my friends speaking of it in my presence. Thus it was, while I was neither asking or seeking light, that by the efforts of my angel friends, in the land of Spirit life, that the influence and the power flowed in upon me, and I became supremely blest, not in credence or in belief, but in faith and knowledge.

"My spiritual senses were opened, I saw, and conversed with spirits as though they were in the body ; they controlled my hand, and wrote whatever they wished, and gave convincing tests to many of my friends, who, like myself, had been up to that time unbelieving.

"These things were no less a surprise to me than to others. A few of us were designated by the spirits who offered us their counsel, and we were told, that if we would give attention to the rules which they were willing to offer for our consideration and our acceptance, if we chose, they would give us the benefit of their own experience, and teach us, what they believed would enable us to ultimate this society, and this blessed home in which we live and enjoy. Thus, you will perceive that I deserve no praise, and I claim no merit, but might say with the Apostle, ' by the grace of God, I am what I am.'

"Should what I am saying, appear not well timed, or not appropriate to the present occasion, I know you will excuse me.

"I feel that a spirit of watchfulness, humility and prayer, is needful for us all. We may thank the kind angels, honor the Spirit of Wisdom, and the law of "Salvation by Christ." We may sing praises to the Divine Author of Harmony and Celestial Love, yet we should be sparing of praises bestowed upon fellow mortals.

"I would not mar the present harmony by improper criticism, but I can not forget that we are the children of a race prone to idolatry, the enthusiasm of a joyous company may lead to extremes, there is danger of ascribing to the instrument, honor and praises, which are due to the wisdom of the angels, or the Divine influences which have controled, or spoken through those instruments.

"How was it even with the good St. John,—did he not manifest this same human weakness, when an angel had brought him glad tidings from the spiritual world, and explained to him some of the many wonders connected with angel life?

"His own testimony touching the circumstance, as we find it on record in the last chapter of Revelations, is given in the following words, (opening a gilt edged copy of the New Testament which she drew from her pocket, she read:) "And I, John, saw these things, and heard them, and when I had heard and seen, I fell down to worship before the feet of the angel which showed me these things.

"Then saith he unto me, see thou do it not; for I am thy fellow-servant, and of thy brethren the prophets, and of them which keep the sayings of this book; worship God.'"

As Harmonia closed and resumed her seat, Vincent rose and said: "Perhaps it is time for us now to adjourn till the evening; and yet I had thought of offering to sing something which has just now been freshly revived in my memory."

All faces at once beamed with a look of renewed interest and anticipated pleasure. Vincent felt his welcome, and calling Melodia to his aid, the two stood up together, and sang

"THE FOUR LEAVED SHAMROCK."

I 'll seek a four leaved shamrock,
  In all the fairy dells;
And if I find its charmed leaves,
  Oh! how I 'll weave my spells.
I would not waste my magic might
  On diamond, pearl, or gold;
For treasure tires the wearied sense—
  Such triumph is but cold:
But I would play the Enchantress part,
  And scatter bliss around
That not a tear, nor aching heart,
  Should in the world be found.

To worth, I would give honor,
 I'd dry the mourner's tears ;
And to the pallid lip recall,
 The smile of happier years.
And hearts that had been long estranged,
 And friends that had grown cold,
Should meet again like parted streams,
 And mingle as of old,
Oh! thus I'd play the Enchantress part,
 And scatter bliss around,
That not a tear, nor aching heart,
 Should in the world be found.

The heart that had been mourning,
 O'er vanished dreams of love ;
Should see them all returning,
 Like Noah's faithful dove :
And hope should launch her blessed bark,
 On sorrow's darkening sea,
And miseries' sons should find an ark,
 And saved from sinking be.
Oh! thus I'd play the Enchantress part,
 And scatter bliss around,
That not a tear, nor aching heart
 Should in the world be found.

I will not pretend to describe the beauty of the tune, or the enchanting manner in which this song was sung. I could not describe it,—Vincent and Melodia are both of them excellent singers, yet on this occasion both appeared to be inspired, and to excel all that I had ever before heard from them in music. Before this beautiful song was half completed, all was hushed into the deepest silence, not a sound to be heard, save the beauteous mingling of the two singing voices. When they finished the last line, there was not one person present, that I could see, whose eyes were not freshly moistened with tears. My own dearest Clara, many times since I have been here, I have wished that you were with me, to share in some beauty or some rare enjoyment; but never did I miss you from my side so much as during the singing of this beautiful song. Hope whispers to me that we may yet hear it together. Melodia thanked the audience for their quiet and atten-

27

tive appreciation of the song, and announced that the festive enjoyments would be resumed again at evening.

The evening came, which was to be the crowning festival in honor of Harmonia's birthday. Her tastes and wishes had been consulted; and as she does not dance, but is passionately fond of music, we had her favorite opera, and a musical concert. It began early. The band gave the overture to Massaniello with delightful spirit. You heard it with Salvi as the hero. Ours was not a thorough artist like him, but still very spirited. There could scarcely be a better Fenella than our Melodia. The opera went off with salvos of applause.

Then a cheering little social intermission. There was a jubilant interchange of happy greetings all over the house. The performers on the stage came among the audience to receive their praises. In a few moments after the curtain fell, a little troop of waiters scattered over the house bearing delicate refreshments. Then came more music; and at last the beautiful ode of Serafa was sung by Melodia and encored with enthusiasm,—then came a grand chorus. I thought this might be the end, but it was not. Vincent came forward with a little scroll of paper in his hand, and said:

"Dear Friends:—Years ago, when our home was yet an unrealized ideal, she whose birthday you are so kind as to celebrate, was surrounded by a little group of loving hearts; and then, as now, they wished to make her birthday a little festival. For one of these occasions she wrote a simple, heartful song. I found some music for it, and sang it to our assembled friends. Let me offer you this little souvenir of our germinal efforts."

The proposal was, of course, welcomed with enthusiasm, and he seated himself at the piano-forte, and sang:

All sweetly, humbly, joyfully,
　Rings music through my heart,
And sings itself triumphally,
　As if of heaven a part;
All solemnly and thankfully
　I feel its blissening power
As ringing out victoriously,
　It celebrates the hour - -

When angels meet us faithfully
  To found a home on earth,
Where lovefully and truthfully,
  Their heaven shall find a birth.
The song leaps up rejoicingly,
  The ringing music comes
Through all the heart's sweet lovingness,
  From the celestial homes.

The burden of its blessedness
  Is brooding o'er the soul ;
In purity, fidelity,
  The heavenly currents roll.
All sweetly, humbly, joyfully,
  It ringeth through the heart,
And sings itself triumphally,
  For 'tis of heaven a part.

There was no applause, only a profound silence, in the midst of which Harmonia, dressed in pure white, came forward without waiting to be called. Her face was lighted with an expression of deep joy.

There was no sound to interrupt her; you might have heard heart beats. She said :

"Beloved :—I have but this word to call you. My heart is full of gratitude to God, and the angels, and you. I feel a renewed thankfulness springing up in my heart toward the good angels who first came to me, or I would say, to us, and enabled us to become humble instruments of this work. To-day, I feel a renewed evidence, that there are greater goods in store for us.

"I feel an assurance that the way is soon to be opened, whereby our brethren and sisters in humanity can be more generally made partakers of the blessings which we enjoy. This assurance makes this the happiest of all birthdays to me.

"Rest, dear friends, in this hope. The future is all radiant and glowing with promise, and the fulfillment is hastening on ; my heart's gratitude and dear love flows out to you all ; may we all be enabled to so live, that both our example and our precept may be useful, and greatly help all with whom we associate, upward and onward, to new conditions of unfolding, and higher degrees of light, knowledge and wisdom.''

As she finished, flowers were thrown to her, a shower of beauty, and of delicious odors. In the midst Melodia came forward and placed a wreath of white lilies on her head, and kissed her, as if for us all, and the whole house rose, and in a moment all broke into one of those grand choral hymns, whose thrilling effect so sung can never be described. ⁄

After the singing of the beautiful hymn, the company all mingled as they chose to, in little groups, or in single pairs. I mingled for a short time with the many, after which I talked half an hour with Melodia, then retired alone to my room that I might think of you, and write these lines to you, my own beloved one, before I retire to rest on my pillow. I have not written it before, and it brings a strange, indescribable sort of thrilling sensation over me to write it now, to say to you, dearest Clara, that this is my last evening at Esperanza.

To-morrow I leave this lovely, this enchanting home. To-morrow I start on my journey to come again to you. It seems to me like a dream, when I think of the many weeks which have passed since I pressed your hand, kissed your lips, and saw those beautiful eyes fill with tears, when with trembling voice you said ''good by.'' I have loved you devotedly for years, but it seems to-night that I never loved you so well as now. It feels to me like I had gained greatly in my capacity,—my power to love since I saw you. Oh, I pray for your health and your happiness, and that I may have a safe and speedy journey to you. I trust that I shall not pain you, darling, when I confess that a sore trial awaits me in bidding farewell to this beautiful place, and the many beautiful and loving friends I have found here. It appears to me as though I should not be very well able to endure it, were it not that I hope to return again and bring you with me, to partake of, and share the life and the love that is here in waiting for all the pure in heart.

I have talked it all over to-night with Melodia, and she bid me go.

Never did this dear and beautiful one appear more loving, or more tenderly precious in my eyes than she did this evening, when she said, "go and bring dear Clara to us; both you and she are worthy of this life, and of all our united love; and perchance both of you may find all of us worthy of yourselves, and all the knowledge, industry, friendship and love you may bring to us." She assured me that her thoughts and her prayers would go with me on my journey, and that she would "pray without ceasing" for my safe and my speedy journey, and for my finding you with love unchanged, and willing to bear me company to this peaceful home.

To-morrow, the beautiful Fairy which brought me here, and a loving company will attend me, and see me safely on board some steamer bound for New Orleans.

I will, I think, write you one more letter before I reach you. I may find time to write you a note to-morrow; at any rate, I hope I shall find time and opportunity to write you again, so as to mail the letter before I sail from New Orleans.

I must close this now, and retire to my bed. Good night, dearest one. Good night.

XXIII.

DEAREST CLARA :—I begin this letter the last I hope, that I may ever have to write you on the turbid waters of the Mississippi. Will finish, and mail it at New Orleans, before embarking on my first voyage at sea.

At the dawn of day, on Monday morning, I rose to take one more walk over the beautiful grounds of Esperanza. I walked through the gardens and orchards; as I passed down toward the lake, I met Mr. S——, (a friend from the East, who is here on a visit, and who I think will be likely to join the society,) and we finished our morning walk together.

"How beautiful this is," said Mr. S——, as we stood upon a hill, and looked over the broad fields, orchards, gardens and edifices. "How very beautiful. These people have been aided by the wisdom of angels, man alone could never have accomplished this ; he is unequal to the task, so it seems to me."

Finding that I had been spending some time at the place, he asked many questions, and wished to have my opinion of the faith, and the life.

To both of us, it seemed a wonderful change from life in civilization. These people, now so united in the bonds of friendship and harmony, were but a few years ago most of them strangers to each other, and scattered far apart ; many of them were church members. Some were Catholics, and some Methodists,—some were Baptists, others Presbyterians,—some Unitarians, some Swedenborgians, Universalists, Shakers, Quakers, etc., etc. I believe nearly every Christian denomination has furnished a share, and the Israelites also, have been quite as liberal in supplying members for the harmonic life, as any of their Christian neighbors. These people were

318

first broken off, and liberated from the fetters in which their various creeds and confessions of faith had bound them, and like new land cleared of its first growth, were all prepared for the reception and culture of such seeds or plants as yield more healthy and valuable fruits.

Mr. S—— and I stood on a rising ground by the shore of the lake, and listened to the band of music, which every morning awakens the members from their repose. We heard the echoes of the morning gun, and the soft cadence of the morning hymn, and then walked slowly home to breakfast.

I was met and greeted with a sad tenderness by all the dear friends from whom I was about to part. Within an hour after we had finished our breakfast, the Fairy was at her wharf, and gave her musical signal that all was ready. I bid farewell to all, except the little party who were to go with me on the boat. Melodia wished to bear me company in leaving, as she had done in my coming. The dear, bright Angela, also, volunteered to go, as did likewise Eveline, Serafa, Paul, Alfred, and Oliver, who has been absent most of the time since I came. Oliver's mission appears two-fold, he transacts commercial business, and is also a messenger of glad tidings to those who are scattered and isolated, and who have been prepared, through suffering, for a more chaste and orderly life, yet have not known that this beautiful home, and loving friends, were ready and waiting to receive them. He accompanied us at the request of Angelia. As I walked toward the boat, all that I had beheld of beauty, all that I had heard of instruction, and music, or felt of love, came pressing into memory. I felt myself trembling between hope and fear, the fear came, that I might never return to this home of love again. The voice of hope whispered in mine ear, "Fear not, thou shalt return."

We went on board, and as the boat cast off and got under way, the band on shore gave us a musical adieu. Our boat gave back its answer of beauteous melody. Then the waving of handkerchiefs, sprigs of evergreen, boquets of flowers, or of whatever each one happened at the moment to have in their hand. We passed

swiftly around the point of a hill ; and thus I had my last view, for
the present, at least, of that ever peaceful and beautiful home. The
distance which the Fairy would take me was uncertain ; we might
find a boat bound for New Orleans any time at some landing, or
with our more rapid speed, we might overtake one. The day was
fine, the scenery along the river banks very beautiful. We walked
the deck, talked of the present and the future, of the friends near
us, and those far away. Melodia comforts me about you—says she
has a deep faith that you will not reject me because of the faith I
have in the righteousness of this pure and loving life. The fore-
noon passed quickly away : at noon, we sat down to our farewell
dinner—good bread, delicious fruits and sparkling wine. Most of
us sat and conversed around the table, after we had dined, for perhaps an hour-and-half. Melodia sung a "song of parting," I think
it was composed expressly for the occasion. I intended to get, a
copy of it and send you, but had not time.

When we arose from the table and went on deck, the smoke
of a steamer was visible down the river. Our engineer plied his
furnaces, and we rapidly neared her ; soon we came alongside.
She proved to be the "Belle, of Natchez." We took leave, shed
our parting tears, and I sprang on board. The Fairy turned
with a graceful circling sweep, and was soon hull down in the
distance, and the dear, kind faces of her passengers were lost to
the vision of my tearful eyes. Then came the loud, clear, ringing
notes of music from the little steamer, playing as she did when
first I met her. The tune was one which I had often heard Melodia
sing in her most playful and cheerful moods. I went to my state
room, shut myself up alone, and wept.

And now, through an ever-increasing distance, I look back upon
life in ESPERANZA. It was beautiful in the beginning ; it was beautiful every day ; and now, as I leave it, it appears more beautiful
than ever. God's blessing on thee, and all that are thine, oh Esperanza, my heart's earthly home.

The scenery along the banks of the Mississipi is a sort of grand,
gloomy monotony, the foliage gradually changing to a more tropical
character, and the melancholy cypress, with its festoons of funeral

mosses, fill the swamps on either side. But when I rose in the morning, the day that we reached New Orleans, the scene had changed ; the banks of the river were lined with sugar plantations ; the large fields of cane resembled our fields of Indian corn.

The white villas of the planters, often surrounded by pretty gardens, the villages of negro cabins, many of them neatly whitewashed, presented a scene in pleasing contrast with the desolation of wild, savage nature through which we had been passing the last four hundred miles. Looking off in the distance, I beheld the spires and domes of New Orleans, glittering and sparkling in the rays of the morning sun. I saw the gothic spires and the cross of the Cathedral, and the white dome of the St. Charles Hotel, rising above the flat crescent of the city. When our boat landed, I went to the St. Charles, established myself in my room, then walked out to view the city. It is now evening : I have taken a long walk this afternoon. I must write a few more lines to you before I sleep, and mail them in the morning, and be ready by ten o'clock to leave New Orleans on my rapid journey home to you. I have engaged passage on board a new, beautiful steamer, said to be a swift sailing and safe vessel. The captain is a pleasant New England man.

To-morrow I shall be far out on the Gulf of Mexico, and every hour coming nearer to you. I come to you with a great happiness, for I come with a great trust. I have written a few lines to the loved friends at Esperanza, and now I turn my thoughts, my hopes, my prayers, to you, my blessed, my beloved, my chosen one. When you read this, I shall be approaching you.

Our captain can not tell the number of days we shall be at sea, or when we may expect to be landed at New York : the winds and the weather will have a voice in deciding these things ; and beside this, the delays where we may stop to take in lading at other ports, can not all be determined upon now.

I pray for you daily, my dearest love ; I pray for your health, but most of all, that you, with me, may accept the faith, and live the life of Spiritual harmony and perpetual progress.

It is late, I feel the need of rest and sleep. I think I will have time to add a page or two in the morning before the steamer leaves the wharf. I wish I could know just now, dearest Clara, that you were well, and cheerful and happy. I wish I could know whether you were this moment sleeping, or whether you were awake and thinking of me, as I am of you. I think of you every hour. Good night, dear Clara; may you and I always enjoy good nights, and good mornings, good days, and good lives.

Morning.—My beloved, my own. The morning is here. I am awake, I am well, I have arisen, I am writing, and almost impatient for the coming hour, when I can know that the many miles now between us have began to fall rapidly, one by one, behind the flying vessel. I wish I could be with you to-day, I have so much to tell, and it is a tedious task when one has to write every word, compared with the pleasure of verbal conversation. Can you believe me, dearest Clara, I have seen a spirit or angel, I have felt the touch and heard the voice of a guardian angel.

After I had written you last night, I retired to my bed and lay for a time, thinking of you, and of the kind friends who brought me on my journey a part of the way to this city on their own boat. I had blown out my lamp and had let the window screens down to shut out the light of the gas lamp that was before my window on the street. I went to sleep. How long I had been sleeping, or at what hour of the night it was, I do not know, when I was awakened by the touch of a soft hand passing gently across my forehead and over my face. I opened my eyes, and saw an angel standing beside the bed. The room was filled with light, soft and delicate, resembling the brightest moonlight, with a rose color mingled with the silver. The spirit form was a female. I have not language to describe her appearance; no being of earth ever presented such symmetry and beauty.

I knew that I was visited by an angel; I felt no alarm, but a thrilling sensation, a mingling together of joyful emotions, with a feeling of humility. She was clothed in a robe of white, and wore a scarf of pale blue; around its edges was a border of golden stars, her hair was brown, slightly curling, and fell in ringlets upon the shoulders ; her eyes were blue, glowing with animation and intellectual love ; a crown of golden light was around her head.

She took me by the hand and, smiling, said :

"Child of the earth, I rejoice to find thee so quiet and tranquil ; I have many things to say unto thee. Once I lived on the earth, in the external or mortal body : more than a century of years have passed since I experienced the change in life which men call death. Neither the distance, or the difference, between our life and the life on earth is so great as many believe.

"I have not lost my humanity ; I retain my sympathetic connection with the human race. Though I am a spirit, and live in the angel world, I feel a sister's love, a sister's interest, and a sister's care toward thee and over thee. Though living in the external form, thou art nevertheless a spirit. I am one of thy appointed guardians, and have come this night to instruct and to bless with encouraging counsels.

"I have been near thee, and often with thee during all thy life, from childhood to the present time. I have saved thee from many dangers, guarded thy life from much evil. This night for the first time I reveal myself to thine external senses. Henceforward thou shalt often see me, and we will converse together face to face, as now.

"I was present when the marriage vow was made between thyself and Clara. That sacred pledge was sanctioned by your guardian angels ; you had not only our consent, but our aid in making it. Such pure, chaste love as you feel toward each other, rises like the fragrance of sweet incense to the heavens, and gives to angels joy. Other, and higher degrees of happiness are in store for you. I come to thee here and now to aid in thy higher unfolding.

"Thou hast little known how much of direct agency thy spiritual guardians have had in directing and controlling the journey from which thou art returning.

"We hope for results of great good, both to thyself and Clara, also to the society at that beautiful home of love, where thou hast been spending happy weeks, and learning many new and useful lessons.

"The Society of Harmonists at Esperanza have done well; they have done much for themselves individually, much for each other, and much for the erring and suffering race; they have a clear knowledge of the harmonial philosophy, on many subjects; a few things they need yet to learn.

"They live faithful to the highest light they have attained, and are succeeding quite as well as we anticipated. It was by our aid, advice, and guardian counsel, that this life of happiness and example was established on the earth. In connection with the most vital principle of their faith, they retain one serious error of opinion: from this error we wish to redeem them; for this end, we sent thee unto them. I now have allusion to the liberty permitted and practiced, of sexual intimacy with more than one of the opposite sex. *One love*, and one only, is the Divine law.

"Well dost thou remember the painful suffering which was thy own, in experience even greater than was confessed in those letters to Clara, when the theory of division, and distribution of sexual love was first presented to thee, and so earnestly, honestly, and ingeniously advocated.

"I saw it all; I was near thee during all that time. I heard the arguments, I read thy thoughts, and witnessed thy perplexity. I visited Clara when those letters reached her. I heard every sigh which she drew, as in sorrow and deep mental anguish, looking through tears, she traced the lines thy pen had made. It was a deep trial to you both; you bore it bravely, and the lesson will not be lost.

"Be content with the past, and all it has brought thee." Experience is the safe guide to wisdom. Clara is *thine*, thine *alone*; thou art *hers*, and *hers* only. Your union is the true 'conjugal love.' You will never separate on the earth or in the heavens.

"You will to go to Esperanza, and be a true example of Divine matehood, each to the other, and for the other will fill entirely all inmost askings of the heart for sexual affection and love.

" With this home of sweetest rest and peace, each in the heart of the other, you will radiate, and impart so much of the universal, fraternal, brotherly love to all others, that your example will be all that is requisite to establish the truth, and demonstrate the beauty and safety of sexual duality to the minds of all the members.

" I perceive in thy mind a query arising, why it was that this error was not corrected in the beginning, or first formation of the society; or why it was that the angel guardians did not select mediums free from error on every subject, for the central group of the gathering order.

" Be calm and patient; I will explain all. We find it very difficult, indeed it has hitherto been impossible for us to find mediums whom we could impress to speak or write our communications, without their being colored and modified by the opinions and faith which the mediums themselves entertained.

" This has been the case in regard to our mediums, and the communications we gave through them in forming the society now under consideration. They nevertheless done the best they could, and angels can do no more. They received our teachings, and imparted them to others in accordance with their own understandings and convictions, not knowing or believing that their own preconceived opinions had given color to some sentiments not in accordance with our wishes. We have been patient, and wish all to be patient with each other. Our object is not yet fully completed; we shall succeed in all that we have undertaken; we were aware of those difficulties in the beginning, and made allowance for them.

" Throughout the entire civilized world, the customs and laws in regard to marriage, are, in many instances, little better than granting and selling indulgences for lustful gratification and sexual abuse. There can not be health or happiness to the race until there is acquired sufficient wisdom and love, to secure to children an origin entirely free from blind and sensual lust. We intend the society at Esperanza to be exemplary in this, as well as in other needful changes and reforms which the world of mankind greatly need. Many of the active workers in the first gathering of the members, were persons who had suffered for a time in the bonds of marriage without love; the reaction in their minds after freeing themselves from the old bonds, would naturally lead them into the opposite extreme for a time ; this, though a matter of regret, must be patiently borne with ; the human mind, when greatly agitated or disturbed, requires time to settle on the line of truth between extremes.

" In our selection of mediums and persons, we made choice of those who had suffered much in life ; they were not only more easily influenced to engage in the work of reform, but they had also acquired a strength to endure the opposition and the persecution which friends and relatives in the world deal out to reformers. Those who have been fortunate in their marriage, and in all affairs of life successful, having reputations unsullied in the eyes of the world, could not be influenced, or induced to bear the scoffings and the ridicule which the mistaken and thoughtless multitudes deal out to all those who deviate from the popular pathway.

"There is an unfailing law of recompense, by and through which all who suffer will be rewarded; those who endure anguish and pain, acquire an increase of capacity for pleasure and enjoyment, and when the day of compensation comes, those who have mourned in solitude, and wept in secret places, will rejoice and be exceeding glad that they were accounted worthy to suffer for truth's sake.

"Dark and shadowy as human affairs now appear amongst all nations, there has been steady and gradual improvement from age to age, since the first morning after the creation of man. Creative Wisdom has made no failure—no mistake. The march of human progress is onward, toward the millenial day. There is no conflict between Reason and Revelation, neither is there between God and Nature.

"The knowledge of the truth of spiritual intercourse is fast spreading, and becoming established among the Nations. Kings and Queens, Emperors, Noblemen, Members of Parliament, Members of Congress and of the various legislative bodies, are receiving messages of truth and love from those who have proved the realities of life beyond the grave.

"We can, if we choose to do so, know and reveal the hidden thoughts and the most secret actions of men ; a knowledge of these facts, and of the great interest which all good spirits and angels have in human affairs on the earth will do a great work in restraining those who have hitherto been 'doers of evil.' We have begun the good work of human elevation in earnest ; we shall not cease from the heavenly mission until the knowledge of God covers the earth as the waters cover the sea. We are choosing from the multitudes, and sending abroad many messengers of spiritual truth ; we find many men, and a large number of women, whom we can impress to stand before the assembled multitudes and speak to the people, 'as never man spake.'

"The wisest men, those possessed of the greatest intellectual powers, and having the most liberal collegiate education, are not so capable of interesting and instructing a public audience as are many female speakers, when these latter are under our control. Old opinions, traditions, and superstitions are passing away ; for a time there will be great tumult and confusion. 'Cities of refuge' must be prepared ; in these all chaste and honest minds may retire and enjoy peace and rest.

"'It must needs be that offenses will come, but wo unto those by whom they come.'

"Those who attempt to stand alone in the midst of an excited multitude, will be stoned, and abused in exact proportion to their hight above that multitude, because their life is a reproof to all wrong doers if they are faithful to our teachings, to the example of Christ, and to the spirit of Christ in themselves. 'Examine yourselves, prove yourselves ; know ye not your own selves, that Jesus Christ is in you, except ye be reprobates.' The immediate disciples of Christ were socialists, not selfish, individual property holders.

"Go then, thyself and Clara, to Esperanza, and to those already gathered to that beautiful home, be ye a living example of divine matehood, a manifestation of the heavenly marriage upon earth, a representation of true sexual duality, an imitation of the angel life of 'conjugal love.'   The members of that home will at once discover, that by accepting your example, they will abandon only evils, whilst they will receive infinite gains ; they will give up no principle worth possessing, but will receive immeasurable riches.   I entreat you both to go ; all things are now ready.   The Sun of righteousness will soon arise with 'healing in his wings.'

"The time draws nigh, when

> " 'A gentle hand shall wipe the tears
> From every weeping eye,
> And sighs, and groans, and grief, and fears,
> And death itself shall die.'

" Your most intimate friends will discourage your going.   They will not believe success in a harmonic life possible.   Be patient, kind, and firm; look to the 'light within.'   Remember, in the 'work of righteousness shall be peace, and the reward of righteousness, quietness and assurance forever.'   Be hopeful and trustful; I will visit thee again during the voyage.   I go now, to visit the object of thy love, and whisper words of comfort in her ear.   I will tell her of thy safety, and of thy coming.

" In the early morning, whilst they remain fresh in memory, write the words I have spoken, the record may prove useful in the future.   'Believe not every spirit, but try the spirits whether they be of God.'   Every suggestion, whether presented from within the mind, or from the mind of another, in or out of the external form, bring to the test of reason ; when the external judgment is satisfied, and the witness in the soul sanctions, go forward; if otherwise, wait."

With a like radiant smile, with which she came, she bade me adieu.   Gradually the light faded from the room, and I was alone. I have more to relate when we meet.

In the bonds of true affection, I remain your own

FRANK.

CONTENTS.

CHAPTER VI.

CHAPTER VII.

CHAPTER VIII.

CHAPTER IX.

CHAPTER X.

CHAPTER XI.

CHAPTER XII.

CHAPTER XIII.

CHAPTER XXI.

CHAPTER XXII.

CHAPTER XXIII.

THE

ILLUSTRATED MANNERS BOOK,

A Volume of Five Hundred Pages,

ILLUSTRATED WITH TWO HUNDRED ENGRAVINGS.

———•◆•———

This book has twenty-six chapters, containing the principles of Politeness and Refinement, with the most minute and careful directions respecting the person, dress, conduct, observances, decorums, customs, conversation, courtesies, fashions, delicacies and requirements for all occasions and relations in life.

The chapters on speech and conversation, writing, and correspondence, pronunciation of foreign languages; on chorographic exercises, and on fashion and the toilet, are of exceeding interest and value. This book is beautifully adapted to the important uses for which it was expressly written, and will be found worth many times its cost to every thoughtful reader. It should not only be read, but carefully studied, chapter by chapter.—Price one dollar.

Sample copies forwarded by mail (postage paid,) to any part of the United States, on receipt of the price.

Orders to the trade supplied on liberal terms.

Address   VALENTINE NICHOLSON,

CINCINNATI, OHIO.